# SHOT THROUGH THE HEART

## NICOLE HELM

# COLTON 911: GUARDIAN IN THE STORM

## CARLA CASSIDY

# MILLS & BOON

First Published in Great Britain 2021
by Mills & Boon, an imprint of HarperCollins*Publishers* Ltd
1 London Bridge Street, London, SE1 9GF

www.harpercollins.co.uk

HarperCollins*Publishers*
1st Floor, Watermarque Building,
Ringsend Road, Dublin 4, Ireland

*Shot Through the Heart* © 2021 Nicole Helm
*Colton 911: Guardian in the Storm* © 2021 Harlequin Books S.A.

Special thanks and acknowledgement are given to Carla Cassidy for her contribution to the *Colton 911: Chicago* series.

ISBN: 978-0-263-28338-9

0521

**MIX**
Paper from
responsible sources
**FSC˚ C007454**

This book is produced from independently certified FSC™ paper to ensure responsible forest management.

For more information visit: www.harpercollins.co.uk/green

Printed and bound in Spain
by CPI, Barcelona

# SHOT THROUGH
# THE HEART

**NICOLE HELM**

For the members of the Hermitage
who always love a good farm animal.

# Chapter One

Holden Parker didn't need a mission to make him feel alive, but boy, it sure did help. Six weeks of investigating and not one minute of fieldwork had left him antsy and ready for action. *Real* action.

He hadn't joined the secretive North Star Group five years ago to wait around. He'd joined to do some good in the world.

For four years, he'd been able to stay in the field, constantly working to help bring down the Sons of the Badlands, a powerful gang that had run roughshod over the poorer communities in South Dakota.

In the past year, assignments had slowly dried up as the Sons had withered down to a noncriminal element. Holden knew he wasn't the only one who'd been afraid that was the end of North Star.

But the head of the group had come through with a new assignment a few weeks ago, and even though Holden had only been backup on that mission, it had been good to be in the field again. He was ready for more.

After six long weeks, Shay had *finally* called a leader meeting for this morning. Which meant assignments were going to be doled out—real, in-the-field assignments. Holden practically skipped to the meeting room.

He met Sabrina Killian in the hallway and grinned, because next to a mission and a nice, cold beer, there were few things he enjoyed more than irritating Sabrina.

"You know it'll be me next. Shay's not sending you out on a mission when you're still banged up," Holden said, nodding at her arm, which had spent six weeks in a cast up until yesterday.

Holden himself felt much better with it gone. Then he didn't have to feel guilty for not letting her finish off the guys who'd ambushed her on their last mission. He knew she could have taken them, but he'd also known her arm was seriously injured, so he'd stepped in.

Sabrina had *not* thanked him.

She scowled at him now, and he knew she hadn't forgiven him for it. Sabrina wasn't the forgiving sort. He supposed, perversely, that's what he liked about her. In a little-sister sort of way.

He saw too much of himself in Sabrina, which was why he'd convinced the old head of North Star to give her a job after she'd tried to beat him up in a seedy South Dakota bar years ago. He'd seen too clearly a person bent on destruction, just like he'd once been.

"We'll see," she muttered at him, walking shoulder to shoulder down the narrow hallway.

"Hey, remember when I saved your butt a few weeks ago?" He slung his arm around her shoulder. She shrugged off the gesture before giving him a saccharine-sweet fake smile.

"Hey, remember when I kicked your butt a few years ago? Besides, if you'd given me a little more time, I could have taken those guys on my own. Fractured arm and all."

"Must be losing your touch. Want to try me now?" Holden offered, spreading his arms as if to offer her a free punch.

She tossed her long, dark ponytail over her shoulder.

"When you've hung up your warped moral code about hitting women who were *this* close to being Navy SEALs, I'll fight you."

Before he could respond to that, someone cleared their throat.

Holden turned to see Shay standing in the entrance of the conference room, arms crossed, boss glare on her face. She'd been with North Star longer than any of them and had been tapped by their old leader to take over when he'd retired after a major injury almost two years ago.

Holden wouldn't say he liked her better than Granger McMillan, as he didn't really *like* having a boss, but what he did like about both his former boss and his current one was a shared desire to take down the bad guys. And a willingness to get the job done.

"Children," Shay said blandly. "If you'd enter so we could get this started?"

Sabrina sent Holden a haughty look, then sailed into the room in front of him. She took her usual chair, so Holden took his. He glanced at the empty one next to him. Reece wouldn't be coming to this meeting. Or any following meetings.

Reece Montgomery had quit. Left North Star for domestic bliss. Holden tried not to think about it, because the whole thing gave him the creeps. That a contained and hard man like Reece Montgomery could be undone by some innkeeper and her son was a bit *terrifying*.

Holden had no desire to be taken down in such a way. Ever.

Elsie Rogers sat at her computer in the corner tapping away, and at least some things would stay the same. As head of IT, Elsie barely ever left the digital light of her computer screen, and Holden doubted she ever would.

But Shay was going to have to promote one of the lower

field operatives to replace Reece. It had been six weeks
and she hadn't done it. And no one had pressured her to.
Holden knew he should. He was now the senior field operative, after all. But he kept his mouth shut instead. They'd
had enough change the past few years.

"What we have in the wake of the whole situation from
a few weeks ago is two highly dangerous weapons in the
hands of two highly dangerous individuals," Shay began,
standing next to Elsie as she spoke to him and Sabrina.

"So, let's go," Holden said.

"As if anything is that simple. From what our friends at
the FBI can figure, we've just tangled with a highly spe-
cialized, complicated death machine."

"I thought it was a weapons dealer," Sabrina said with
a frown.

They'd taken down a group selling black-market weapons to the wrong kind of people six weeks ago. The group
had been thoroughly dismantled as far as Holden knew.

"Turns out, the weapons being supplied were only a
small cog in a much bigger machine. Which means they'll
just replace their weapons dealer. The FBI is putting a
team on finding out more about this machine, but our job
is much more urgent. While the FBI is trying to smoke out
the head of the big group, we've got to stop two different
hit men. Before we fully took down the weapons-dealer
group, they shipped off two untraceable, highly powerful guns—and distributed them to two ghosts. And I do
mean ghosts."

"Sounds like a challenge," Holden said, kicking back in
his chair and balancing it on two legs. Man, he was ready
for a challenge after all this downtime and *thinking*.

"Two hit men. Two guns that can make a joke out of
Kevlar. We don't know who the hit men are. We don't
know who the targets are. We don't even know how much

time we have before they act. We know nothing. Except the guns themselves. The first lead we've gotten, thanks to Elsie's tireless work, is the delivery of ammunition for our weapon to two different PO boxes. Each equally untraceable, as the owners don't exist and security footage gives next to nothing away."

"So there's video of the ammunition being picked up?" Sabrina asked.

"Elsie's hacked what she can, and I'll show you that in a moment. Either way, you're going to split up and scout each address out. Our first target is Wilson, Wyoming. This is the only video we have of our suspect retrieving the package from the PO box."

A grainy security feed showed up on the big screen on the wall in front of them. A man dressed head to toe for winter weather walked over to one of the boxes. He kept his head completely turned away from the camera, blocking a row of boxes from view. He was wearing too many clothes to make out any sort of defining characteristic.

"A bit overdressed, isn't he?" Holden murmured.

"It's still cold enough at the upper elevations, but you're right. Seems odd. Especially since we know what's in the package. And what makes it more shady…" Shay nodded to Elsie, and another grainy video clicked on.

This video was similarly set up to the first, but definitely a different post office. "Evening, Nebraska."

Another person, dressed a bit heavily for a summer afternoon, came in in much the same way the man from the earlier video had. Too many clothes to make out defining characteristics, face kept pointed away from the camera, blocking the box as they opened it.

"That gives us two targets. I want you both on it. You can take a team if you want, but the first stages might be best done alone until you actually find the target. Though

I'd want a team close by for backup. A full team completely in place before you take action."

"Define full team," Holden replied with a wide grin. He knew it would irritate Shay, and that was ever his goal. Because when she was irritated, she didn't get that far-off look in her eye that reminded him a bit too much of Granger before he'd been injured and quit North Star wholesale.

Holden didn't want to lose another boss. He didn't want to lose North Star and the missions that kept him employed and satisfied.

"We've got two people, at least, about to be killed, for reasons unknown to us. And that might only be the tip of the iceberg. Either way, we have very little to go on. It's important. But it's not more important than your own lives," Shay said sternly. Too serious these days. The weight of running North Star Group had definitely changed her.

Holden wasn't sure it was for the better.

"Don't you think that depends?" Sabrina asked.

Shay fixed her with a hard look. "This is a dangerous mission. You're risking your life by taking it on, but that doesn't mean you have to play hero."

"How would we live with ourselves if we didn't?" Holden asked, with none of his usual humor or joking. He'd joined the secretive North Star Group as a way out of the gang he'd gotten himself mixed up with. He'd joined to take down the people who'd lied to him and hurt him when he'd been at his weakest, angriest and most vulnerable. He'd joined to be the good guy instead of the bad guy. Mostly thanks to Granger McMillan.

Now, the Sons of the Badlands had been eradicated. As much as Holden was proud to have been a part of it, it didn't mean his need to erase all the bad he'd done had disappeared. Or ever would.

Shay got that *look* on her face that Holden didn't want to parse or think on. It was too much emotion, too much *change*. They didn't need it. They needed to act.

Holden turned to Sabrina as the same time she turned to him. In unison, they said the exact same thing to each other. "You take Nebraska."

"Not a snowball's chance in flat prairie hell," Holden replied.

Sabrina dug a coin out of her pocket. "Flip for it?"

"Who carries change around?"

"I found it yesterday in the gym. Thought it'd be good luck. Come on. Call it in the air. You win, you choose where you want to go."

Holden shrugged and grinned. "Sure. You should know luck always falls on my side."

She flipped the coin, and Holden called heads. When it landed tails, he muttered an oath.

Sabrina widened her eyes and laid on the fake regret. "Oh dear. It looks like I get to pick, doesn't it?"

Before Holden could argue with her, Shay interrupted. "All right. Sabrina, you're headed to the Tetons. Holden, that means Nebraska for you."

Sabrina reached over and slapped him on the back. "Don't worry. I'll send you pictures of the mountains."

"Great," Holden muttered.

No, he didn't want to go to Nebraska, but hey, a mission was a mission. He'd be glad for it. Flat prairie and all.

NEBRASKA WASN'T QUITE the hell Holden had imagined, but it wasn't exactly a dream either. It wasn't all flat. In fact, there were some interesting rock formations that reminded him of South Dakota, where he'd grown up.

Which brought up feelings of nostalgia, regret and a determination to complete his mission and get back to Wyoming headquarters. Ideally before Sabrina did, so he could be deployed to the Tetons and irritate her in the process.

Sabrina's constant text messages of the picturesque Teton range was a constant reminder there were a lot prettier places in the world than Evening, Nebraska. This place was *all* small town. Lots of farms. Lots of flat, even with the occasional rock formation.

The town of Evening was minuscule. Made up mostly of a brief Main Street with a handful of businesses clearly kept alive only by a farming population that didn't have anywhere else to go for mail, banking or necessities.

The post office was a stone square of a historic building. Outside, there was a plaque that said it was on the National Historical Register and that it had been built in 1875. Inside, the lobby would *maybe* fit five people.

He'd been watching for a few days now. Inside, there was a small wall of PO boxes, and a counter where a friendly enough woman worked every day from nine in the morning until she closed down the entire building to take her lunch break from noon to one. She'd be back at one on the dot and stay open until four.

It was clear from moment one she did not trust strangers or appreciate any of Holden's charm. Still, she answered his questions. Though it had only been to say she had no recollection of a stranger renting or using PO box 10. In fact, she acted as if that particular PO box hadn't been rented in years.

Holden didn't think she was lying, but that meant someone had gone through a lot of trouble to know which PO boxes were empty, and how to break into a PO box. Quickly, too. The security video Elsie had hacked into had showed the man in and out in under three minutes.

A ghost, as Shay had said. The slim positive side to a ghost was he likely thought he had ample time to take out his target. Which meant Holden had more time to find him first.

Holden hoped. Because otherwise this was a *very* dead end.

On his third day in Evening, Holden watched the post office from across the street, pretending to smoke a cigarette outside the small general store. He deleted yet another smug text from Sabrina and her picturesque assignment, then asked her if she'd gotten any closer to her target.

He smiled when she didn't respond. She was no closer than him. He wasn't *glad* they had zero luck, but he'd enjoy the chance to still beat her to solving his assignment first.

He scanned Main Street again. The chance of his target coming back was probably slim, but the chance of seeing him walking around, shopping at the general store or driving down the street? Well, it was possible.

Even in the middle of the day, things were pretty quiet in this small town. Every once in a while someone would walk by, go in and out of the businesses. Sometimes people drove by. Some stopped. Some didn't.

Holden would watch them all without them knowing. A skill he'd developed once, many years ago, picking pockets.

A rusty old truck rumbled to a stop in front of the post office, blocking his view. Holden frowned and tossed the cigarette in the trash can. Pretending to take a casual stroll, he moved across the street and then down the sidewalk as the driver got out of the truck and walked to the post office door. She wore an oversize coat, jeans streaked with dirt and a ratty-looking stocking cap over messy braided pigtails.

For half a second, he thought she might be a child, but she'd been driving. Besides, she was too tall and her face wasn't really childlike. Youngish. Early twenties, probably. She stepped inside, and Holden angled himself so he could watch her through the windowed door. She didn't stop and chat with the woman behind the counter like the rest of the patrons had done since he'd been watching.

He inched closer, keeping her in view, but he stopped short when he saw what she was doing.

She was pulling a few envelopes out of the exact mailbox he'd been watching. Number 10. He counted once, twice, then three times to make sure it was in fact the mailbox that supposedly nobody owned. The mailbox someone had ordered high-powered, black-market ammo to be delivered to.

Holden eyed the woman. Could she have been the overdressed person who'd gotten the ammo earlier in the week? He'd assumed it was a man, but...

Before she closed the door to the box, she looked back over her shoulder and locked eyes with him, as if she'd felt him watching.

*Damn.*

Holden smiled lazily. Looking away would bring more suspicion than being a creep. He hoped.

The woman looked back at her mailbox. Her coat collar and pigtails obscured her face, but he figured his best course of action was to stay here and then hit on her. She might remember his face, she might be weirded out, but hopefully she wouldn't think much of it beyond that.

Especially if *she* was his target.

After a few more moments, she walked out of the post office. She kept her eyes straight ahead on her truck and didn't give him a second glance.

"Hi there," he offered.

She didn't respond. Didn't look at him. She just walked by, going straight for her truck.

*Hmm.*

"I thought small-town folks were supposed to be friendly," he called after her.

She gave him one cold look, then slid into the driver's seat of her truck. When she drove away, Holden noted her license plate number, the direction she was going and the size of her tires, then backtracked to go find his car.

# Chapter Two

Willa Zimmerman didn't like the creeping sensation that she was being followed. She didn't *see* anyone on the old, cracking county highway behind her, but she'd been taught to never, *ever* ignore her instincts.

The man was following her.

She glanced at the pile of envelopes in her passenger seat. Messages from her parents were rarely a *good* thing. But she wouldn't be able to determine how bad things were until she was in the safety of her own home.

"You'd think they could just leave me out of it, Stanley," Willa muttered at the snoozing sheepdog in the back seat. He didn't even lift his head to pretend to humor her. "Goats are better listeners," she muttered, turning onto the long, winding gravel road that would lead her home.

She checked her rearview mirror again. Still no sign of the man, but she knew he was there.

She also knew he wouldn't get past a certain point. At least not in one piece. Which was a slim comfort when all she wanted was to be left alone to see to her farm.

She glanced at the letters again. No doubt there'd be a warning included. What Willa didn't know yet was the urgency or level of the warning. Part of her wanted to ignore the letters, ignore the man, ignore who and what her parents were and just…live this perfect life she'd built.

But no life was perfect without a little imperfect payment.

She bumped along the gravel road as her house came into view. Even with a threat in the ether, the sight of her house and barns and menagerie of animals made her smile. Maybe she couldn't have a normal life, but the abnormal one she'd built for herself was her idea of paradise.

Mostly.

She parked the truck at the end of the gravel lane and hopped out. Since she hadn't seen her follower, she likely had about five to ten minutes before he got a little surprise she'd have to tend to.

She opened the back door of the truck and urged Stanley out. He sighed heavily and took his sweet time jumping out and onto the ground below. Then he huffed out a breath as if offended he'd had to move.

"You're the one who wanted to go with," she told him as he lazily made his way for the house, where he'd no doubt find a place on the porch to sit and sleep some more.

The noises of goats, pigs, sheep and chickens filled the air as she shoved the letters into the oversize pocket of her ancient coat. The letter would be written in code, because her parents were nothing if not dramatic.

She really didn't want to face it. Maybe that wasn't fair, but as she moved toward the house, three more dogs coming to greet her with happy yips and jumps, she considered, not for the first time, ignoring her parents completely.

If she cut them off, couldn't she prevent their drama from touching *her* life?

Like always, a wave of guilt followed that thought. Then a pang of longing. Even though her parents weren't the farming type, when they weren't off on "vacation," she usually saw them once a week for dinner.

It was her only true human interaction. As much as she loved her animals, and her farm, a woman could only hold so many one-sided conversations with a goat before she started missing *human* companionship.

Willa shook her head. This was her life, and there was no use wishing it could be different. She took a seat on the porch stairs, and two cats immediately slunk out from under the porch to wind around her legs.

She opened the envelope then absently scratched Angela's soft head.

Dearest Willa,
    We're enjoying our trip and hope things are safe and sound at home. Give Yellow a big hug for us.
Love,
Mom and Dad

Yellow. Well, it was better than Red, Willa supposed. What would she do with all her animals if her parents ever gave her a code red? She had doubts she'd even be able to follow through.

Her parents would *not* like that.

The alarm sounded, and Willa sighed, squinting off into the distance. It would have to be taken care of, and quickly.

What she wouldn't give for a normal life.

HOLDEN STUDIED THE area around him as he drove. Farm, farm, farm. Flat waving grain or green fields dotted with cattle. It was a nice day, with puffy white clouds wafting in the bright blue sky. He had his windows rolled down and couldn't deny that it was...nice. Relaxing. A pretty drive on a pretty day.

He slowed at every turnoff. Mostly they were gravel roads, no names, but a mailbox and gate at the end of each. Some gates were closed, some open. Sometimes he saw farm machinery out in a field, or a house far off from the road, but sometimes the fields seemed completely devoid of humans' presence.

He couldn't decide if it was delightful or downright creepy. He'd grown up in South Dakota but had always lived in Sioux Falls—not exactly a bustling metropolis. But a city. Sure, the occasional trip to the Badlands and its eerie, isolated landscape had given him a taste for wide-open spaces. But it felt right there to look out and see something that appeared untouched by human hands.

Here it felt… Well, Holden couldn't quite put his finger on the words for what it felt like.

As he drove slowly, he studied each gravel lane for signs of a vehicle being driven down it recently—puffs of dust or fresh tracks in the little strip of grayish mud between road and gravel.

The first time he found both, he turned down the gravel without hesitation. He hadn't seen another soul on the drive out of Evening, or to Evening. Or *anywhere*.

The gravel road wound around, curving this way and that, following a creek, avoiding a large, seemingly out-of-place rock cropping. Holden kept his speed slow, pretending he was enjoying a leisurely country drive on a pretty day.

He kept his windows rolled down, listening for anything, eyes sharp and assessing the situation even as he let a fake, easy smile play on his face.

A prickle of unease went across the back of his neck, and Holden slowed to a complete stop. Something was off. And weird. The road didn't seem to lead anywhere.

He turned off the engine and scanned the area. He listened. There was a slight breeze and the smell of clover and cow pies in the air. It should have been off-putting, but something about it was so bucolic he found himself smiling.

It was the most silence that hadn't bothered him in... ever.

Then he heard a rooster crow. Followed by the echoing *baa* of sheep? A few seconds later, a moo followed.

What kind of living hell had he fallen into?

He shook himself out of the odd mood, the odd reverie of *peace*, and turned the ignition so the engine of the car purred to life. He'd follow the road the rest of the way. He wasn't ignoring that gut feeling that something was off. He was just considering the possibility his gut feeling was born of being weirded out by picturesque American heartland.

The gravel road wound around another thicket of trees, and Holden could see the hint of a house or a barn between the trees. He slowed his car to an absolute crawl, keeping his eyes on the building through the trees.

The woman could have led him into a trap. Alternatively, she could be a complete and utter innocent bystander. But there was something about *all* this that had his instincts humming.

As he came around the corner, before he could fully get an idea if the building was a house or a barn, his car made a shuddering noise and the entire vehicle jerked, which caused him to yank the wheel, since he was gripping it hard and hadn't put his seat belt back on.

Somehow that small yank had the whole car tipping toward the slight hill to the left. If he tipped any farther, the whole car would flip, and then...

Holden had a split second of inner swearing before the whole world went dark.

He had no idea how much time passed before he found himself blinking his eyes open. His vision was blurry, but the world around him was definitely dark. And…enclosed. He wasn't on the ground. Or in his car. He was lying on something…not soft, exactly, but not hard.

He blinked a few more times then tried to sit up, but as he tried to move his arm to leverage himself into a sitting position, he couldn't. At least not far.

Something clanged next to him, like a chain rattling against metal. He turned his head through the pounding pain in his temple to look at his arm. Around his wrist was a handcuff, connected to a long chain that was attached to the other handcuff, which was fasted around the metal frame of a rusty old bed.

Terror spurted through him for one debilitating second, but he forced himself to breathe. Think. He'd been in a few tough spots before. He'd gotten out of those. He wasn't dead, so he could get out of this one.

If he could figure out what on earth had happened.

He looked around him. He appeared to be in some kind of…barn. Very old, if the cracks between boards that made up the roof were anything to go by. The sides appeared to be made up of stones with more aging, warped boards stacked on top.

There seemed to be *some* light outside, but it was dim. It allowed him to make out his surroundings in shadow, making him think he must have been unconscious for a few hours at best.

And somehow he'd been moved into some horror-movie barn and chained to a rusty old bed with an uncomfortable mattress. He looked down at his feet. They were chained to the bed frame as well. And in between his legs were two glowing eyes.

Holden tried to scramble out of the way, but of course he was *chained* by every limb to this creaky bed frame.

A door squeaked open, the screech of metal on metal

making Holden wince. The animal between his legs began to paw at his knee.

"Oh, you're awake," the woman said. "I suppose that's a good thing." It was the woman from the post office. She looked perfectly calm, as if this was normal. She was still wearing the same outfit she'd worn at the post office, and she studied him with serious green eyes.

"I'm chained to a bed," he said, just in case she'd somehow stumbled upon him and didn't understand the situation.

"Mm." She tilted her head to the side, studying the bed below him. "Such as it is anyway."

"You chained me to a bed."

"Yes," she agreed, as if that wasn't *insanity*. "Seemed the safest option. Oh, Kelly. Don't be a pain." She walked over and picked up the creature between his legs. A cat. A very large, very fat cat.

She gently put the cat on the floor of the barn then turned to him. "So. Who are you?"

He glanced from the woman to the cat, who was sitting next to the woman's feet, creepy cat eyes squarely on him. "Who am *I*? You chained me to a bed in some dilapidated barn in the middle of nowhere."

She looked around the barn as if seeing it for the first time. "I admit it's a bit rough around the edges, but dilapidated is harsh, don't you think?"

"I…" Holden was left utterly speechless, a sensation he couldn't remember *ever* having.

He studied this woman. It was hard to believe she was some kind of ghost assassin, what with the farmer overalls and the fresh-faced beauty. Holden knew looks could be deceiving but still, her gaze was frank, wary, but not… cruel.

But regardless of who or what she was, she was obviously unbalanced. What with him being chained to a bed and all.

He closed his eyes for a moment. He had to get his wits about him. This jumbled, speechless feeling was a side effect of being knocked out, surely. Once he could get his mind in working order, he'd find a way to escape this.

She hadn't killed him, after all. He opened his eyes and frowned at her. As far as he knew, she hadn't even hurt him. She'd just…what exactly? Dragged him into a creaky old barn and chained him up?

"You probably need something to drink," the woman observed. She walked over to a little cabinet and grabbed what appeared to be a tin cup, like people used when camping. He couldn't move enough to see her as she walked farther into the barn, but he heard the groan and then whoosh of water running through a pipe.

When she returned to his field of vision, she had the cup in her hand and was studying the chains on his hands. She made a considering noise, then did something that allowed the chain to move more liberally against the metal frame. He was still chained to it, but he could lift his arm.

She handed him the cup. "You should probably drink all this. I don't know that it'll help the whole head-wound thing, but you don't want to get dehydrated."

His brain clearly still wasn't working because all he could do was stare at her. Baffled. Utterly and completely baffled. "You dragged me into your creepy horror-show barn and chained me to a bed."

"You seem to be having a really hard time with that, but yes. That is what happened. Are you having, like… short-term memory loss?"

"Are you having a break with reality?"

She blinked and managed to somehow look offended. "No. But when some man follows me home from town and then tries to drive onto my property, I think I have a right to defend myself."

"I didn't do anything to you."

"You followed me. Like a stalker."

"So call the police."

Her expression changed. He couldn't read the change or what it meant, but it was almost like she'd clicked some new armor into place. "This'll do. Now. Drink the water."

She shoved the cup into his hand. He probably could have grabbed her arm. With the extra movement of the chains, he could probably debilitate her.

But all he could seem to do was curl his fingers around the cup she handed him.

# *Chapter Three*

The man took the cup, but then he just lay there as if he wasn't quite sure what to do with it. Willa had bandaged up his head wound and the other cuts and scratches on him from his car accident while he'd been unconscious, but clearly he wasn't quite one hundred percent.

"You probably need to sit up to drink," she decided when he simply held on to the cup.

"How?"

She knew it was silly to feel sorry for someone clearly here to do her some harm, but she couldn't help it. He was injured and confused, and she *had* chained him to a bed in an old barn she mostly used for storage.

"I'll help you." She went around to the back of his head and grabbed his shoulders, pushing him up. She perched herself on the edge of the bed, letting his back lean against hers in an upright position so he could drink his water.

His back was warm, and she could feel the movements of his muscles as he lifted the cup to his mouth. It was such a stark reminder of how isolated her life was. How devoid of any real human contact when her parents weren't home. Because she felt some odd relief inside herself to be touching another human being.

*Get it together, Willa.*

"Do you feel dizzy?" she asked, staring hard at the stone foundation of the barn's walls.

There was a pause. "No."

She found she didn't believe him. He was a big guy. Clearly very strong. The fact he hadn't tried to fight his way out of the chains showed he was either still out of sorts or smart enough to think his situation through first.

Willa still hadn't been able to think through her situation. After the security measures had been deployed when the man had crossed over onto her legal property, she'd gone out. He'd driven a small compact sedan, which had flipped at the impact of the device meant to pop a car's tires and maybe damage its undercarriage but not actually flip it.

She'd had to drag him out of the car and then back to the barn. After she'd searched the bag he'd had in the back seat. He had tactical gear, but only one gun. Not a particularly fancy one. None of it pointed at hired killer.

Her best guess was this man was here to kidnap her. She shouldn't be giving him water or asking after his head injury. She should be taking care of things.

Her parents would scold her for her soft heart, and then they'd worry over her more than they already did. It was half of why she hadn't sent a message their way. She wanted to handle this on her own. To prove to them she could be left alone to have this life she wanted.

She might be an adult, but she was connected to her parents no matter what any of them did. Their work left Willa a vulnerable target, and it had taken years to convince them she didn't have to bounce from place to place with them. She could build her own home on her own two feet and stay safe.

She'd sacrificed friends and relationships with pretty much anyone to have that freedom and independence. She wouldn't give it up just because this man didn't *seem* like a cold-blooded killer. Especially since she knew he very well could be.

"I don't suppose you're going to tell me what on earth is going on?" he said after a while. His voice was deep. Calm. Sure, he sounded a little baffled, but not too out of it for a man who'd been unconscious for a few hours.

"I don't suppose you'll tell *me* what on earth is going on?" she returned. Because, truth be told, she wanted to tell him everything. She liked truth and honesty and clearcut answers. She didn't want to play her parents' games.

But if this connected to them, she had to.

He sighed and didn't answer before taking another sip of his water.

"What's your name?" she asked.

This time his answer was a derisive snort.

She didn't mind that so much. "You can call me Willa."

"Willa what?"

This time it was her turn to snort derisively. "I could tell you, but then I'd have to kill you."

"Is that not the plan?"

"You're here and alive, aren't you?"

"Here," he repeated. "Chained to a bed in a horror film set come to life."

"It's not *that* bad," Willa returned. "It's just rustic. My other barn is much nicer. Well, it has to be, because that's where the animals live. The ones who don't live in the house with me, that is. Or, you know, are outside animals. Kelly here prefers this barn," she said, pointing at the cat, though she supposed from his angle behind her, he couldn't see her point.

He said nothing for a few more minutes. "Does it hurt?" she asked after a while.

"What? The lump on my head I can only assume is the size of another head?"

She shouldn't smile. She shouldn't be *enjoying* a conversation with a man who was here to hurt, threaten, kidnap or possibly even kill her. But it was just so nice to talk to someone who wouldn't only make animal noises in return.

Which, speak of the devil, was followed by the sounds of a goat bleating incessantly. Then said goat showed up in the barn opening.

"Dwight, why do you have to be so ornery?"

The goat bleated again, and Willa sighed. She had to carefully scoot away from the bed so the man wouldn't fall back down on the old, hard mattress. She tried to be gentle as she held his shoulders until he was back to a laying position.

She walked over to the doorway where Dwight stood. She turned back to the man. "I'll be back in a bit with dinner. And some new bandages."

He stared at her with steady blue eyes. She couldn't read his expression. She knew she should feel *some* fear, but she didn't really.

"So, you're just going to leave me locked up like this?" He frowned at her and the goat. "With whatever the hell that is roaming around?"

She studied the large man chained to the bed in her barn. "I suppose I am." What other choice did she have? "And this is a goat. His name is Dwight."

"I'm dreaming," he muttered to himself. "I'm in a hospital somewhere and this is some drug-induced coma dream."

"Hate to break it to you, but you're stone-cold awake. Don't worry. I'll be back in a bit, and Kelly will keep you company while I'm gone."

As if on cue, the cat jumped back on him—this time

on his stomach instead of in between his legs. He let out an *oof*, as Kelly was not a small cat.

"You've got to be kidding me," the man muttered as Willa grabbed Dwight's collar and began dragging him back to his pen.

With a very out-of-place smile on her face.

HOLDEN STILL HELD out hope this was a really realistic dream, but that hope aside, he'd gotten his brain in gear enough to start fiddling with the chains. It wouldn't take much to break his way out of these.

If the cat stopped trying to sit directly on his face, like some kind of demon bent on his death by suffocation.

He jerked his head to the right, trying to get the cat dislodged, but that only sent a throbbing, stabbing ache through his temple. He groaned in pain, which finally dislodged the cat.

She jumped off him gracefully, then glared up at him as if he'd inconvenienced *her*. "Ease up on the attitude, princess. I could skin you alive if I wanted to."

The cat clearly didn't fear his threats, as she lifted one paw to her mouth and delicately began to clean it.

Holden blew out a breath. He had some ideas on how to break out, but he'd wait. The woman had said she'd come back with dinner. So, he'd hold tight until after, when she left and closed the door for the night.

She wasn't going to kill him…he thought. So he could bide his time.

The woman—Willa, if that was her real name—had left the barn door open. So he'd been able to watch night fall. Birds flew in and out. He saw a trio of dogs run by at one point. He'd heard chickens and sheep.

And he hadn't seen one hint that any other *human* being lived anywhere near here.

"I'm in an insane asylum. I'm in hell. Maybe this is purgatory," he said aloud, if only to hear himself speak and try to convince himself it wasn't some weird dream.

As if on cue, Willa appeared in the doorway, carrying a little tray and a lantern. She was too pretty for it to be purgatory. Which was not a productive thought—at all.

"I brought you some dinner," she announced, her voice friendly and warm, as if this was *normal*.

Holden didn't bother to move. "Am I going to be unchained to eat, warden?"

"No, I don't think so."

"Then what? You're going to feed me?"

She made an odd noise—like she'd been trying to snort derisively but a squeak came out instead. "Um, *no*." She came to stand next to the bed, still holding the tray and staring down at him as if she was considering *how* he was going to eat.

"So, what are you going to do?" he asked, trying not to sound as irritable as he felt. Maybe her cheeriness was an act, but maybe it was something he could use to get what he wanted. If he kept his charm in place. A tall order right now.

She sighed. "It's quite a conundrum, isn't it? It'd help if you told me who you are and what you're doing."

"Would you believe me if I did?"

She considered that. "I guess it depends. What's your name?"

She had an odd, open conversational manner about her. It kept him on uneven footing. Or maybe that was just the head injury that had his real name slipping out. "Holden."

"Holden," she repeated. "Well, that doesn't sound made up."

"Gee. Thanks."

Her mouth curved. It made no sense she was smiling.

It made even less sense he wanted to smile back. This woman had *chained him to a bed*. While he had a *head injury*. From some sort of…setup. She had to have had something to do with his car flipping.

Somehow.

She bent down and put the tray on the floor. He could see a plate with a sandwich, an apple, a baggie full of Goldfish crackers and a water bottle.

"Who *are* you?"

She smiled up at him, the stray tendrils that had fallen out of her pigtails creating a reddish curtain over her face. "I told you my name is Willa."

"That hardly explains why a seemingly perfectly nice woman booby-trapped my car, dragged me into a godforsaken shed and chained me to a bed from the 1800s."

"The bed is more likely 1950s. Barn, yeah, 1800s. Probably 1875, if I had to guess. Kind of amazing, isn't it? Imagine the history this place has seen. I wish whoever owned it before me had kept it in better shape. I'd fix it up, but it seems such a travesty to mess with what's always been here. I always think I'll do some research and see who owned the place before I did, but I never seem to get around to it."

"Am I on drugs?" Maybe she was poisoning him. Because surely he wasn't chained to a bed while a pretty woman talked about the history of the building he was being held prisoner in.

"You're probably hungry," she said. She clicked something on his chain that gave him more range of motion again. Then she handed him a sandwich. "You could probably leverage up on your elbow and eat this with the other hand. Right or left?"

He took the sandwich with his right hand and leaned his weight on his left elbow so that his head was raised up enough that he could chew and swallow. He glared at the woman. "Explain to me what this is."

She stared right back. "You first."

Holden didn't say anything. He ate the sandwich. When she handed him the apple, he ate that in silence too.

He could make up a story about just happening to be in the neighborhood. Reece had used being a wildlife photographer as his cover on his last assignment. Holden could do the same, but he didn't have a camera to back up that claim.

"What do you think this is?" he asked, handing her the apple core.

She took it then handed him the bag of crackers. "What do *you* think it is?"

He wasn't going to get anywhere with her. Still, he couldn't seem to make himself create an elaborate story. His brain was still too fuzzy. Or maybe he just didn't understand enough about her to make up a good story that she'd fall for. He didn't know, but his usual quick thinking was not working for him.

He'd break out tonight, get out of here and then…

*And then what? Fail your mission?* No. Failure wasn't an option. Still, he wasn't convinced this woman was the hit man. But that didn't mean she didn't know something about who the hit man was. He hadn't seen anyone else, but that didn't mean she wasn't working for someone. Or maybe the daughter of a man who killed people for a living.

It was possible. A lot was possible.

She switched out the empty plastic bag for the bottle of water in more silence. She petted the dog that had followed her in while she waited for him to finish. Sometimes she looked out the door and into the night.

She seemed…wistful. Quiet. *Sad*, a little voice inside him whispered, as if there was any reason to feel empathy for this woman he didn't know, who might just be sad because it was her job to kill him.

When he finished the water, he handed her the empty bottle. "You know, you're going to have to let me have a bathroom break at some point."

She seemed to consider this. "I suppose you're right." She eyed the chains and the bed. "Well, no time like the present."

She popped her head under the bottom of the bed, and something clanked. She did the same at the top.

"Go on, then."

He sat up, surprised it had been that easy. Then he realized that though his feet were no longer chained to the bed, they were still chained together. With only enough give to do a slow, clumsy shuffle step toward the door.

His hands were still handcuffed, but the chain between cuffs was long enough he had decent reach. He couldn't make a run for it, but he could grab her. Threaten her. There were a lot of things he could do.

She led him outside, the pace slow and wobbly. She made a hand-waving gesture in the dark. "The animals all go out here. Don't know why you can't."

"A little privacy?"

She made a harrumphing sound. "Fine. But I'm just a few steps away in the barn. You try to run for it, you'll be sorry."

"Fine," he muttered, waiting until he heard her footsteps retreat to take care of business.

Once done, he took a few steps back toward the door, but he looked around as he moved. It was pitch-black. Country dark. Insects buzzed and animals rustled about, but it was mostly quiet. He turned in a slow circle, testing the bonds of the chains on his feet, trying to get an idea of his surroundings.

Behind him, there was a building. It was little more than a dark shadow, but one of the windows had a light on that glowed. Not a barn, but a house. It looked downright homey and cozy.

*And you're chained at the wrists and ankles in this homey, cozy loony bin.*

She marched out of the barn, carrying the lantern. "All right. You've had your time. Come on now. Dawn comes early."

He stood where he was. She rolled her eyes in the flickering light of the lantern. She marched over to him, and he assumed she was going to grab his chain and lead him back into the barn.

He didn't let her. He managed to grab her wrist, holding her in place. "Tell me who you are and what this is," he demanded. If she was a man, he would have bent back her hand or done something to bring her to her knees.

But she was a woman, and he'd made a promise to himself a long time ago never to hurt a woman. Even if it ended badly for him in the process.

"Don't test me, Holden. It won't end well for you." She jerked her wrist out of his grasp.

He could have held on tighter, but it was the cold look in her eye, like she'd had back at the post office, that had him letting her go.

He shouldn't be fooled by her sweet demeanor. There was something under the surface with this woman.

With no warning, she pushed him over, and he couldn't maintain his balance because of the tight cuffs around his ankles. He fell awkwardly and hard on the ground, and it jarred the pain in his head so badly he groaned.

A few clanking sounds later, he realized she'd chained him to the door handle of the barn. Outside in the dark.

Then she sailed away, toward the lighted window, a dog following her like a wagging shadow in the lantern light.

Holden stared after her. His hands were chained at an awkward angle, but she hadn't chained his ankles to anything, which would make this slightly easier to get out of than the bed had been.

Maybe.

She'd told him not to test her, but of course he was going to test her. He just now realized he was going to have to be very careful not to underestimate her.

# Chapter Four

Willa paced her room. She was angry. He'd grabbed her. He'd tried to intimidate her. Wearing chains! That she'd put there! It made her darn near vibrate with rage. He'd tricked her and then tried to...

*What? Free himself?*

She let out an annoyed huff. Jim gave her a side-eyed look from where he was curled up on his dog bed.

Worse than being angry, she felt guilty. Not just for chaining him up and taking care of the intruder the only way she knew how, but because she'd let her temper take over. Her parents had always told her that's when you made mistakes. When you let your emotions get the better of you.

That was why she hadn't followed in their footsteps. She rather liked being able to have an emotional response to things. She *wanted* to be angry, or afraid, or guilty and not have to think through every possible outcome of every possible decision she made by shoving those feelings away.

She *wanted* to be angry and not worry anger had led her into a mistake. She wanted to feel guilty, darn it. It wasn't normal to treat people like this. It wasn't normal she had to be alone. None of this was *normal*, and that wasn't her fault. It was the curse her parents had put on her simply by bringing her into this world.

She flopped onto her bed. Pam let out an aggrieved

meow and moved farther up on the bed. It wasn't fair to blame them. They'd tried to get out. They'd only wanted a normal life too. She was their normal life.

But it hadn't worked.

Now there was a man chained to her barn door. She didn't know what he was after. Or why. She only knew it had to connect to her parents. She'd certainly never done anything remarkable enough to get herself a stalker.

It was summer, so she could certainly leave Holden outside overnight and he wouldn't freeze to death. He'd be fine. Even with the head injury.

Which shouldn't matter. He was here to hurt her. No matter what feelings she entertained, she had to remember that.

Holden. Was that his real name? He was probably a fluid liar. Assassins and kidnappers usually were. But usually they chose names like Bob or Pete. Not *Holden.*

Willa shook her head and got back to her feet. She would deal with him in the morning. She'd deal with everything in the morning. Hopefully her parents would get her email by then and have a plan in place.

She got ready for bed. She would sleep. She would sleep *soundly*, because she had nothing to feel guilty about. Her doors were locked. Her prisoner was locked up. There was nothing to be afraid of.

She knew she should go get the gun she kept in the kitchen cabinet. Mom and Dad always insisted she keep more than one gun, and to always have it within reach, but she hated having a deadly weapon in her room. It felt so grim.

She crawled into bed, determined to live her life on her terms. Let her parents handle their own problems. She'd gotten a message to them. Or at least tried. They didn't always get the coded emails in a timely manner.

She blew out a breath and resolutely closed her eyes. She was going to go to sleep. She was going to live her life and let her parents deal with the effects of theirs. End. Of. Story.

She lay there, repeating that to herself, as her body refused to relax and sleep. Because no matter what she told herself, reality didn't have to follow reason. Or what *she* wanted.

She wasn't sure how long she lay there, nerves taut and unable to sleep. But she wouldn't give up. Eventually exhaustion would win. *Please.*

Jim let out a low growl and got to his feet from where he'd been sleeping. His body quivered in concentration, that low growl continuing as he began to pad toward the door.

Fear shuddered through Willa. Even though Jim occasionally barked at some wild animal outside, this was different. No wild rush to go downstairs and outside. A careful, menacing growl.

What with everything that was going on, she couldn't ignore it probably *was* different.

She didn't curse her parents, or her lot in life. There was no point. She got back out of bed.

"Stay," she ordered the dog. She grabbed the first weapon she could find, the fire poker that hung by the fireplace in her room—both that acted more as decoration than were actually used functionally.

Jim whined as she walked past him. Willa gave him a sharp look. "Stay," she repeated. She wouldn't have any of her animals getting caught in the crossfire of this mess. No. She would handle it.

She wanted the independent life. She had to handle it when the danger of her parents' life spilled over into hers.

That was just…it. She didn't have a choice in that. She only had a choice in how she responded.

She crept down the hall and paused at the top of the stairs. She listened intently. She could still hear Jim growling from her room. She heard the normal creaks and groans of the old house settling.

Then another creak that sounded much more like a footstep on a loose board than the others. Faint but unmistakable.

Willa took a deep breath. Her options were to go lock herself in her room and hope for the best. Call the police— something her parents would be *really* mad about. Or try to handle the intruder herself.

*With a fire poker?* Well, she could try to get to her gun. The stairs led her down to the living room. She'd have to creep around through the TV room, the bathroom hallway and then to the kitchen to get there. All without accidentally running into the intruder or giving herself away.

Still, it was the best option in her mind. So she crept down the stairs. The house was dark, and though her eyes adjusted, there was no way to tell if the shadows were human beings, animals or simply her eyes playing tricks on her.

She made it to the bottom of the stairs, where she paused and listened. Nothing. Not a hint of someone moving or even breathing.

She crept forward, moving by memory and feel through the living room and TV room toward the kitchen. After making it through each room, she paused. Listened. Then moved forward again.

She finally made it to the kitchen, but even without pausing, she knew the intruder was in here. There wasn't the noise of breathing, or the sounds of footsteps, it was just a…feeling. Of not being alone.

She wouldn't be able to get her gun. Not by creeping around. She'd likely bump into the intruder, and that wouldn't be any good. She'd rather fight for her life face-to-face, in the light. So, she'd have to use the element of surprise and hope for the best. She squared her shoulders and felt around on the wall until she found the switch.

On an inner count of three, she flipped the switch on, fire poker at the ready.

Holden was standing in her kitchen, much closer to her than she'd imagined the intruder would be. How could he be within reach and she hadn't heard him?

He didn't even wince at the sudden light, though he did pull a face. "Good God," he said, pointing a gun at the bunny-shaped door stopper on the ground next to the back door. "What *is* that?"

Willa didn't bother to answer him. She swung the fire poker at him. She knew she should aim for his face or his crotch, but she couldn't quite bring herself to. So she hit the arm with the gun instead, hoping she could get him to drop it.

He barely flinched, so she raised the poker again and whacked his shoulder as hard as she could.

"Hey! Would you stop that?"

"No! You have a gun," she said, bringing the poker back so she could swing it again.

"Yeah, well, I'm not going to shoot you," he said, lowering his arm with the gun, and holding his other hand out as if it would stop another swing of the poker. "At least I won't if you stop whacking me with a… What even is that? A fire poker?"

"Yes."

"Let me guess. From 1875," he said dryly.

She looked at the slim metal object in her hand. "Well,

I don't really know. It came with the house. 1875 seems unlike— Why are we discussing fire pokers?" she demanded, pointing it at him as if she could use it like a sword.

But Holden shook his head as he looked around the kitchen. He frowned at the ceramic bear family lined up on the windowsill. "Why is this place some sort of animal menagerie of horrors?"

"Why do you have a gun?" she demanded, still waving the poker in his direction.

He looked back at her and the poker. "Why don't you?"

"Why do you ask so many questions?"

"Why do *you*?"

Willa huffed out a breath. "How did you get out of the chains?"

He grinned at her, and she knew her parents would find a million faults with how she was handling this, but chief among them would be that she was mesmerized by that grin for a second.

"Magic," he offered.

She was charmed, and that was all wrong. He had a *gun*. He was creeping around her house in the middle of the night. He'd escaped the chains she'd put on him, and not by *magic*.

"What are you doing sneaking around my house with a gun if you're not going to shoot me?"

"Trying to figure out who you are."

She frowned. If he didn't know who she was, why was he here? What was he doing? Or was he just looking for confirmation for what he already suspected? Maybe her parents not being here had thrown him off. Maybe he was looking for them, not her.

Either way, he was a threat. So she should absolutely

not set down the poker. She shouldn't trust him not to shoot her.

She sighed heavily and did both. "Do you want some tea?"

*TEA.* SHE SET DOWN the weapon and offered him…tea.

"No. No, thank you." Holden shook his head at himself. Why was he being *polite?*

She shrugged. "I'm going to make some tea." She crossed over to a cabinet. She was in her pajamas. A cozy sweatshirt and shapeless sweatpants with thick socks on her feet. No wonder—it was colder in here than it was out in the dark night air. Her hair was still in the pigtail braids, and her face was as fresh as it had been before.

She didn't seem…fazed by any of this. When she opened the cabinet, he immediately saw the gun sitting there.

He adjusted his grip on his own, but she didn't grab it. She shoved it aside and pulled a tea bag out of the cabinet.

This was no cold-blooded assassin. It just didn't make any sense. He knew he could be fooled. A man would end up dead if he believed he could never be fooled.

But there was also something to be said for gut feelings. Maybe he didn't know what or who she *was*, but it wasn't a killer.

She moved around the kitchen. She pulled out a mug in the shape of an elephant, the trunk acting as the handle. It matched the teapot, which had what appeared to be a scene from *The Jungle Book* painted on it. Seriously, what alternate dimension had he fallen into?

"Where'd you get the gun?" she asked conversationally as she made the tea.

"I went back to my car." Once he'd gotten himself out of the chains, he'd made quick work of figuring out how to get back to his car. He'd seen her truck parked, then followed the gravel road behind it. A few dogs had happily trailed after him, not a one of them barking in alarm. He'd found his car, gotten his gun and his phone, but left the rest. He'd been able tell someone had gone through his stuff. He could only assume it was Willa.

She hadn't taken his gun, or his phone, or anything that was of use to him. He shook his head. He should have taken off. He should have called in to North Star instead of sending the quick message that he was okay and would have a more detailed report tomorrow.

He should accept she wasn't the person he was after and get back to the task at hand, but something about this woman…

"Why were you at that PO box this afternoon?" He had no doubt she'd answer his question with another question, but he couldn't seem to stop himself from asking them. Couldn't seem to stop himself from giving away parts of what he was doing.

She paused in her tea preparations. "It's my PO box," she said. Unconvincingly.

"No, it's not. I asked about it. Specifically. Who rented out number ten. The answer was no one."

"They aren't allowed to give you names," she said, her back still to him as she poured hot water over her tea bag. Her movements were precise, and if he hadn't been looking for it, he might have missed the slight tremor in her fingers as she put the pot back on the stove.

"No, but they can tell me if a box is rented or not. Number ten is not rented. But I get the funny feeling you're not the person who picked up the package of illegal ammunition."

She turned to face him, eyebrows drawn together in

confusion. "Illegal ammunition. What would I do with il-legal ammunition?"

"That is the question."

"I…" She chewed on her lip. "I didn't get any ammu-nition from the box. Ever. I do sometimes use it, without it being rented to me. But I can't tell you why or for what. No, I suppose that isn't true. I *won't* tell you that."

"I could help you if you would."

She stared at him for a moment. An earnest look in those haunting green eyes. Damn it, he did not have time to be haunted.

"I don't need any help," she said at length. "Unless it means getting you out of my hair, of course."

"You're the one who chained me to a bed in your barn."

"You're the one who followed me home."

She was infuriating. Holden scrubbed a hand over his face. If she was of no danger to him, he supposed it wouldn't hurt to give her a little information. But it galled that she wasn't giving him any first. Usually he could charm, demand or threaten anything he wanted out of people.

Willa just looked at him blandly and boiled the water for her tea, answering any question he had with one of her own.

But she could have killed him. She could have fought him. She could have done a lot of things, and aside from trying to beat him with an ineffectual fire poker and chain-ing him to the bed and then the door, she'd bandaged his wounds, fed him and offered him tea.

*Tea.*

"I'm not here by accident," Holden said, gritting his teeth against the frustration he felt. "I'm here because of that PO box. It's connected to something. Something dangerous. Now, maybe you're not, but you using it is a heck of a coincidence for me to ignore."

She stood there, leaning back against the counter, and though her eyes were on his, he could tell she was somewhere else. Thinking things through. Trying to decide what to tell him.

Pressuring her wouldn't get what he wanted. He wasn't sure patience would, either, but he thought it was the better option at the moment.

"Tell me who you are, what you know and what you're after, and maybe I'll consider supplying some necessary information based on that," she said. As if the demand was reasonable when he was the one in her kitchen with a gun.

"I can't do that."

She raised an eyebrow. No matter how friendly or familiar she acted, she was not a pushover in any way, shape or form. "Can't or won't?"

Holden shrugged. "A little bit of both."

They stared at each other, at an impasse. Her green eyes were sharp and direct, and she held the ridiculous elephant cup in small hands. Freckles dotted her nose, and the pigtails and slouchy sweats gave her a childish air. But she was no child. Her look wasn't cold like it had been at the post office or outside when he'd grabbed her arm, but it was intelligent.

Whoever she was, whatever she was, it was far more complicated than Holden wanted to give her credit for.

He felt something…shift inside him. Something snapping into place he couldn't have understood if he tried.

And he most certainly didn't want to try.

"Look…"

She frowned at his forehead. "You have…" Then she lunged at him, and because it had been so unexpected and so...bizarre, he couldn't brace himself in time. He tumbled to the ground, her on top of him.

But he quickly forgot the lunge when something exploded and splintered above them. He rolled them over so he was on top of her, protecting her from what else might come.

She looked up at him, eyes wide. "Who's after you?" she asked.

It dawned on him them. Pieces clicking together. Maybe he still didn't understand who she was, or why anyone would be after a pretty woman on some isolated farm, but it was clear.

"They're not after me, Willa. They're after you."

## Chapter Five

Willa pushed Holden off her—or tried. He didn't budge. Even when Jim skittered into the kitchen, whining and barking at turn. She pushed Jim away from her face, where he was enthusiastically licking her, then tried to push Holden off her again. "That's ridiculous. No one is after me."

Which, of course, wasn't necessarily true. Someone could be after her. To be honest, she'd always expected kidnapping over murder. After all, she was more use to anyone who wanted to get something out of her parents if she was alive.

Unless someone wanted to punish her parents. A possibility, but that meant someone had to know who her parents were, then trace them to her.

Her parents had given her a yellow warning, though. It wasn't a red, but it was a warning nonetheless. To be careful. To be watchful.

Someone had shot at them. But the red dot had been on Holden, not her. "The red dot sight was on your forehead, not mine."

"That you saw," he returned. He was looking around the kitchen, studying doors and windows. Jim had a similarly alert air about him, but the strangest thing occurred to Willa.

Jim hadn't so much as growled at Holden. He'd rushed into the room, licked her face, and now sat in quivering alertness as if awaiting orders.

"We have to get out of here," Holden said. He moved off her but immediately grabbed her arm. "Keep low as possible." He started to drag her toward the TV room. She tried to shake his grip off her arm.

"You're going the wrong way."

"We're not going out the front door," he said, flicking a glance at the bunny door stopper.

"Of course not. That's the back door."

"That doesn't change my answer."

"Fine. You stay here in this drafty old house, and I'll go to my lockable-from-the-inside storm shelter."

He muttered something she couldn't quite make out. "What kind of lock?"

"One even you couldn't get out of, I promise you that. Just follow me." She led him to the back door. Jim whined behind her. "It's all right," she said soothingly to the dog. She kept low and reached up to turn the knob, but it was Holden who eased the door open.

He was different now. Sharper. *Deadly.* She had no doubt he would take down anything in his way. It gave her a cold chill, but as he eased the storm door open and held out his hand for her to take, she took it. She couldn't seem to help herself from believing he was the good guy.

They slid into the dark night. She inched forward, still crouched low. They didn't speak. They just moved, Willa leading him down the porch stairs then across the yard. Jim followed behind without making a sound.

Willa had learned the hard way her dogs couldn't wear tags like normal dogs. Because nothing in her life was *normal*, and tags clanked together when a dog walked.

She entered the barn—the one where many of her ani-

mals lived, not the one where she'd chained up Holden—
Holden and Jim behind her. She moved through the soft
hay and tried not to think too much about who was out
there and shooting at them.

One step at a time. First they had to get to safety.

She went to the very last stall. "Hi, Creed," she murmured as the sleepy goat clopped over to her. She gave his
head a pat but moved to the back of his stall, grabbing the
broom. As quietly as she could, she swept the hay out of
the way of the door. There was no way to see it in the dark,
but she knew where it was, knew where to feel around on
the ground for the latch.

She pulled on the latch, and the heavy door groaned and
creaked open. "Hurry," she whispered to Holden. She went
into the opening first, dangling her legs until she could get
her feet on the rungs of the rope ladder that would take her
down into the dark space.

Once they were in with the door closed, even in daylight, anyone would be hard-pressed to find the hidden
door. Creed would kick around the hay, obscuring any
hints of where they'd gone.

She hoped.

"What the hell," Holden muttered from above, but he
followed her down the ladder into the space below.

Willa felt a pang that there was no way to get Jim down
here with them, but he'd eventually go off and find a bed
with the other dogs. She had more dog houses than dogs
scattered about the property, and even though Jim was
mainly a house dog, he knew how to hang with the outside dogs.

She reached solid ground and hopped off the rope. A
few seconds later, Holden followed suit.

"I closed the door behind me but couldn't feel a lock."

Willa shook her head. "It locks from down here." She

called it a cellar, but it was more of a safe house. There were provisions and tunnels out, if they needed out. Her parents had *insisted* on this when she'd informed them she wanted a place of her own. Willa had let them build in whatever security measures they'd wanted. She'd felt like she was humoring them.

Apparently not.

She brought the generator to life, flipped on the lights, then booted up the computer that would allow her to lock the door—and any other door on the property she wanted.

"What…is this?" Holden said, sounding somewhere between bewildered and awed.

Willa looked around the spacious room. It had most of the comforts of home, including actual walls over the metal casing. There was a little kitchenette on one side. Cots that weren't too uncomfortable on the other. A door that led to a bathroom with all the necessary indoor plumbing. She could live down here for a year and never have to go aboveground.

A depressing thought.

"Where do these doors go?"

"Different places," Willa said, suddenly feeling tired. Not with being shot at. She'd lived with her parents too long to be surprised or overly upset by that. She was tired of having to endure her parents' lifestyle on her own.

Except… She studied Holden. She supposed she wasn't alone, but this stranger wasn't exactly the biggest comfort. Still, better than alone, she supposed.

With the computer humming, she armed the lock and engaged the video feed. Once her parents got her message, they'd be able to see the feed, too, and determine if they needed to come help. Or send help.

Oh, she really hoped they didn't send help.

"Who *are* you?" Holden asked, that baffled tone back

in his voice, but with none of the irritated exasperation he'd had over her ceramic bears.

"How many times are you going to ask me that?" she wondered, tapping a few more security measures to life.

"How many times are you going to answer that with a question of your own?"

She shrugged negligently. When she turned to face him, his expression was…new. Hard. Furious. He hadn't had that look on his face even when she'd offered him a chained dinner earlier. Even when he'd tried to threaten her.

This look was devoid of all confusion. All kindness. It sent a cold shudder of fear down her spine, but she fought to keep her expression neutral, even if on the inside she was scared.

*Never show an enemy your weakness, sweetheart. Always be on guard.*

Her father's voice smothered some of the fear. Because it just made her feel sad. It made her think of the things she hadn't shouted at her father that she'd wanted to. *I don't want enemies! I don't want to be on guard! I just want to be normal.*

"You have to tell me," Holden said, his voice like ice as he adjusted the grip of his gun in his hand. "I have to know what's going on."

The fear subsided more. It was hard to be scared when you were just exhausted. "Or what? You're going to shoot me?"

HOLDEN LOOKED DOWN at the gun in his hand that she'd nodded to. It was pointed at the floor, but he didn't blame her for the question. He was pissed and gripping the weapon a little too tightly.

He purposefully loosened his grasp, rolled his shoulders and tried to get a leash on his temper. It wasn't her fault this had spiraled out of his control. He'd made some clear missteps here. From letting himself get injured to not leaving when he'd had the chance.

Taking out his frustration over that on her wouldn't get them anywhere. The problem was he didn't know what would. He'd never been in a situation like this—where the person he was trying to help had so many secrets he didn't know how to even begin to untangle them.

And worse, she didn't seem like the type of woman who had secrets. He kept forgetting himself because she seemed…

She'd hit him with a fire poker. She surrounded herself with animals—real and fake—at every turn. She lived in a crumbling old farmhouse and wore slouchy sweats and looked pretty as a picture.

Now they were in some high-tech cellar hiding out from the shooter. "How does a solitary farm girl who defends herself with a fire poker have all this hidden underground?"

"I'm not a girl," she muttered. "I'm a grown woman. And none of that matters."

"How exactly does it not matter when someone is trying to kill you?"

"*You* were the target," she returned.

"I'm not the target. It's impossible." He'd been sent here to save her. He'd been sent here to take the hit man out.

She gave him a haughty look and crossed her arms over her chest. "The red sight light was on you."

He opened his mouth to argue, but that was just reflex habit. Because she was right. He hadn't seen the light. She had.

And she'd tackled him to the ground. The horrifying realization that she had saved his life slammed into him all at once. He'd been so focused on her, on the house, he hadn't thought there might be someone outside. Someone targeting them. This odd little farm girl with a full-powered underground safe house had saved *his* life.

He felt oddly…weightless. Like he'd lost all tether to the ground. "You saved me."

She blinked once, then twice, as if she hadn't realized that either. "I…suppose I did."

He didn't believe he was the target, per se. He was here to stop a hit man, which meant he was likely now a target as well as the actual target. But how could *she* be one?

Yet she'd chained him to a bed. Then a door. She'd also fed him and bandaged him. When he'd broken into her house, she'd hit him with a fire poker. Then saved him from a gunshot wound.

She made no sense. *This* made no sense. But she'd saved his life. His *life*.

Maybe he had to be the one to give first. He raked a hand through his hair. Hell, he hated giving in to anything, but he'd be little more than brain-matter splatter if not for her.

Quite unfortunately, he owed her some answers. He blew out a breath, once more taking in the scene around him. He wasn't even sure North Star had anything like this in all their various hideouts scattered around Wyoming, South Dakota and Montana.

Her computer tech wasn't as fancy as Elsie's, but it had a security camera, among other things. And apparently some kind of internet connection even underground.

Holden studied the split screen. There was a feed of the interior of the barn they'd sneaked into, and what he thought might be the exterior. On the dark exterior screen, Holden couldn't make out anything, but she must have had infrared on the interior camera, because when a man crept into the barn, Holden could see him.

"Do you know him?" he asked. The resolution wasn't very good, so his face wasn't clear, but the general appearance would be something to go on if you knew someone well enough.

She squinted at the grainy man on the camera. "It's hard to tell. I don't think so."

He couldn't ignore the fact that she gave him answers on occasion. Probably more than he'd given her. *And she saved your life.*

"I work for a group."

She turned away from the computer to study him. "A group?"

"A secret group. I can't tell you everything, but I can tell you I was sent to Evening to track a hit man."

"So, he is after you."

"No," he replied, tamping down his frustration. Why was she so reluctant to believe she was the target when she had all this? "He doesn't know I'm after him. He's looking to kill someone."

There was a flicker of something in her expression, and she looked away from him. "Why?" she asked, but her voice had changed. Guarded.

"I don't know the whys. Or the whos. Or the hows. All I was given was the fact ammunition for the gun we know was sent to him was shipped here. It was my job to unearth whatever clues I could. That led me to you. You used the same PO box."

"It was a coincidence."

"I might have believed that if I weren't standing in the middle of all this." He swept out an arm to encompass the entire room. "This isn't the kind of thing people have if there isn't the potential they'll be threatened at some point."

"Do I really seem like the kind of person who'd be threatened?" she asked, lifting her chin.

"No, you don't. But the circumstances undermine everything you *seem*, Willa."

She didn't say anything to that. She watched the man on the screen. There was no recognition in her gaze, and the line between her eyebrows pointed to a woman who was utterly baffled.

But she had all this. What could it mean? She seemed alone here, but that didn't mean she *was* alone. There were times at North Star headquarters when only Betty and Elsie were around, two young women who had impressive skills but weren't trained operatives. Could he have stumbled upon a similar group, with a woman who just wasn't a field operative?

Or a woman who was connected to someone like him. A woman who could be a threat because of what she'd mean to someone else. "It's not you. It's someone you're connected to."

She whipped her head around to look at him, which was how he knew he hit the mark.

"What? Husband? Boyfriend?" He ignored the odd tight feeling in his chest at trying to imagine what kind of man would leave her here and unprotected.

She snorted. "Honestly."

"A family member, then? Someone who could be gotten to through you. Or someone who pissed off the wrong guys. But why would anyone leave you behind, on your own?"

Her spine had stiffened, and her gaze was intent on the screen. But Holden didn't think she really saw anything. She was just trying to keep her gaze off him and her feelings under wraps.

But he'd hit a sore spot, or she wouldn't be ramrod straight and silent. Not Willa.

"I'd certainly have some resentment if I was left helpless on my own."

"I'm not helpless, and I was hardly left alone. You have no idea how hard I had to work to be independent. To convince them I could…" She trailed off and closed her eyes in disgust.

She'd given away a lot more than she'd planned, that much was clear. "Them. Parents. Who are your parents, Willa?"

"Who's your *group*, Holden?" she shot back.

He might have been frustrated to have questions answered with questions again, but she stood, anger sparking off her, and it left him speechless.

Her eyes flashed, she advanced on him, and if it hadn't been for his excessive training, he might have actually retreated out of sheer surprise.

"I'm not the only one who can guess things. Who can use what you've said and haven't said against you." She poked him in the chest.

He raised a warning eyebrow, but her anger was clearly impeding her judgment completely. "This group of yours," she said, disgust dripping off every word. "You set off to do good things, but under some kind of mask so you don't have to follow laws." She poked him again.

This time he grabbed her wrist. "Watch it."

She wrenched her hand out of his grasp. "Oh, I'll watch it." She flung her arms in the air. "You're so derisive of them leaving me alone, but you must not have anyone in your life. That's it, isn't it? You had no one in your life so you joined some vigilante group to feel fulfilled. Ignore laws, ignore rules and pretend to be Superman. Prance around feeling important because you risk your life you clearly don't care all that much about. Well, you must not have anyone you love. Your parents must be dead and you must not have any siblings or grandparents or anyone you care about. Or maybe more important, no one who cares about you."

It shouldn't have hurt. Why should the truth, more or less, hurt? But he found himself wanting to rub his heart—not where she'd poked, but where it beat despite the ache inside. "Well, Willa, direct hit."

## *Chapter Six*

Holden betrayed no emotion on his face, and yet it felt like the entire space around them was filled with an aching, painful throb of hurt.

It was all her fault. She'd only been so angry he'd seen right through her. Angry that she'd betrayed her parents in a way. No one was ever supposed to know, and yet…

There was no way to hide it from Holden. Not when they were being shot at. She believed his story. Clearly there was a hit man. What didn't add up to her way of thinking was why he'd shot at Holden first.

If the hit man was meant to kill her, it was punishment for her parents. A message or something. *Yes, we know who your daughter is. Yes, we'll kill anyone you've ever loved.*

She fought off the shudder of fear. She was inside and safe. He was out there.

She had a strange man to deal with in here. One who wasn't going to kill her. More than likely anyway.

"I mean, you got a few key things wrong," Holden said flippantly, with a careless shrug.

He was a very good actor, and yet she found she didn't believe the flippant or careless remarks. Maybe she couldn't see evidence of it, but she could *feel* his hurt.

"The parents are dead, sure. By the time I was sixteen. I had quite a few brothers and sisters, though, but the funny thing about being an orphan is you don't often get to keep them. When you're sixteen, there's not a whole lot you can do about it. Whether you care or not."

The story broke her heart. She didn't think he meant it to. She didn't think he meant her to feel anything. But she couldn't help it. "I'm sorry."

He fixed her with a glare. "I don't know why you'd be sorry."

"Because I don't know what it's like to have brothers or sisters, but I can't imagine how hard it would be to lose them *and* parents. To be left alone."

"Oh, I wasn't alone. I was ripe pickings for the gang in the neighborhood. Vigilante group? Lady, that 'vigilante' group saved my life. And you have no idea the good we've done in the world."

He whirled away from her, shoving his hand through his hair. She could tell he didn't know why he was telling her this. He was irritated with himself.

It was foolish to sit here and think *poor boy* when he was a man with a gun, with a mission. When, if she really was the target, his job was to save her.

*You saved me*, he'd said. Awed and, if she wasn't totally mistaken, not quite comfortable with it.

She couldn't say she was comfortable with it either. She hadn't meant to. She'd just…acted.

"This is all irrelevant," he said, turning back around to face her, and there was a blank coldness in his expression that said loud and clear *this* conversation was over and he was in charge now.

Willa had no desire to be *in charge*. Her plan was to wait for her parents to get her message and take care of their own mess.

But she couldn't tell Holden that. He'd figured out way

more on his own than her parents would be comfortable with. Then she'd lashed out like a petulant child.

*And hit the mark.*

He frowned at the security feed. The man was still poking around the barn. "Can you get a picture of him?" he demanded.

"Yes, but it's not going to be enough to go on."

"We'll decide if it's enough. Take the picture." He pulled his phone out of his pocket and dialed.

"Oh, you won't be able to get service down..." She trailed off as he raised an eyebrow. Apparently he had some tech of his own. He turned away from her and spoke into the phone. "Els? I'm sending you a picture of someone I want you to try to get an ID on."

Willa watched him talk to *Els*, on a phone that shouldn't have worked underground. He was still tense, focused on the mission, but there was a comfort, an understanding there. He had people he could call and work side by side with.

She had nothing.

She looked back at the computer. It was silly to feel sad, to check her email quickly, hoping for some response from her parents.

*Nothing.*

There was a man who wanted her dead. She should be far more worried about that than her lack of human companionship. Especially since her parents hadn't gotten her message. What if they were dealing with their own problems and her SOS never reached them?

Holden came to stand next to her, but not because he was going to talk to her or involve her. He tugged the keyboard away from her and began to tap away, listening to the woman on the phone.

She watched as he took the picture she'd taken and

converted it into a file and sent it off to some unknown email address.

He made noises into the receiver, giving assent every so often. "Got it," he said into the phone as he pushed the keyboard back to her. "Keep me updated." He shoved the phone back into his pocket, then took a moment to study her.

Willa frowned at him, studying him right back. He stood awfully close, since he'd needed access to the computer she was sitting in front of. She could see the bandage she'd originally put on his head had bled through and needed changing. Still, even with the bloody head, the hours of unconsciousness earlier today, he seemed... completely strong and capable.

His blue eyes were guarded and alert. He still held the gun as if it was a part of his arm. He was tall and broad and *strong*, and it was odd that she wasn't really...afraid of him. He could be anyone. He could do anything to her.

But he hadn't. They'd saved each other instead. Because he hadn't disappeared when they'd been shot at. He'd said *we*.

When he finally spoke, his voice was devoid of any emotion or strain. It was straight detached authority.

"I've got a team coming to sweep the area."

"They might not find the guy," she pointed out.

He nodded. "If he can't find us, I imagine he'll disappear for a bit until he comes up with a new plan. Or report to a boss. Too many options, really, but we've got a slight visual. If my team doesn't get him, we'll see if we can't identify him and go from there." He nodded toward one of the cots in the opposite corner of the room. "You should get some sleep."

She glanced at the cot, then back at him. "What are you going to do?"

"Wait."

"Then I'll wait, too."

He shook his head and took a few steps away from her, though that steady blue gaze never left her. "You're just an innocent bystander in all this, Willa. Let the professionals handle it."

She'd been told that all her life. No, she hadn't wanted anything to do with her parents' lifestyle, but everyone acted like that meant she was helpless. A pawn to be moved around and protected, but not trusted. Not involved.

She'd saved *his* life, and he was dismissing her. It didn't sit right. At all. Maybe she didn't have a normal life, but that didn't mean she wouldn't fight for the right to *have* a life.

"No, I don't think I'm going to do that anymore."

HOLDEN FROWNED AT WILLA. He wouldn't say she looked fragile, exactly, but shadows were beginning to appear under her eyes. She was all she appeared. An innocent woman stuck in a bad situation through no fault of her own.

So, why wouldn't she let him handle it? "Look—"

"No. You look. I don't care who my parents are. I don't care who this hit man is. I don't care who you are." With each *I don't care*, the fury in her voice rose another octave. "It's my house. These are my animals and my responsibility. It's *my* life. I won't just go to sleep and let everyone else handle it. That's over now."

Holden wanted to sigh and rub his temples, but that would give the illusion of weakness, and he couldn't allow any of those. He was in charge here, and she had to understand that.

"Look, I don't know what your deal with your parents is, and you won't tell me, so I have to take this over and handle it. That's my assignment. Keep the target from ending up dead and take down the hit man."

"I'm not dead. Could I have been? Seems that way. But he decided to shoot you first. When I had my back to the window, he could have taken me out without you being the wiser. Until it was too late. So, explain to me why you think I'm the target?"

She made a few too many good points. "I'm not the target."

She shrugged. "As I've said more than once—you were the one with the sight on your head."

It grated that she was right. He still didn't think he was the target. That was instinct. But her point that she wasn't the target, either... Well, it wasn't completely off base. "Tell me about your parents, Willa," he said earnestly.

"I can't do that, Holden." Her response was just as earnest, and it almost seemed as if there was some apology in her gaze. He was deluding himself.

"Then you're of no help to me. Go to bed."

Her expression went mutinous. Furious. And there was something particularly warped inside him that he found that attractive. That he found her attractive under all these insane circumstances.

She stood in front of him, chin raised and eyes flashing. "Do you want to make a bet?"

"Huh?" He understood next to nothing about this woman, and he found that...a little too fascinating.

"A bet. Let's make a bet."

"What kind of bet?"

"If I can knock you down before you can knock me down, I help. If you knock me down first, I'll go sit in a corner like a child."

The cold chill of memory shuddered through him. "I don't fight women," he said flatly.

Her hands curled into fists, and she cocked her head to the side. "Then I guess I'll win."

She struck out, a decent jab. Holden dodged it.

She didn't just have good instincts—she'd been trained to fight. Each strike was precise, strong, and got her closer to landing the blow. He dodged, enough that most of the punches or elbows missed. Sometimes she'd land a glancing hit, but they didn't hurt.

Still, she didn't tire herself. She just kept moving forward, and Holden stayed on the defensive. Once he grabbed her fist to keep it from landing, but she only pivoted and swept a leg out.

He hissed out a breath when that kick landed. Hard. "Stop this."

"No," she said. Her voice was a little breathless, but she didn't stop. She kept advancing, striking out, missing, but never giving up. She made a glancing blow across his chin, which had him stepping back. But she'd maneuvered him on purpose—because he stepped on something and had to overcorrect to stop himself from tripping. Which gave her the chance to sweep out her leg and land a kick at just the right place on his knee to have his leg buckling.

He didn't *fall* to the ground but momentarily went down to his knee which, even if he'd be able to jump right back up if this was a *real* fight, was clearly a loss for him in her book.

She stood above him. Grinning. She was sweating a little and breathing hard, but her green eyes danced with mischief. "I win."

He scowled up at her. "I didn't fight back."

She shrugged. "That sounds like your problem." She held out a hand as if she was going to help him up.

A few scenarios ran through his mind at that moment. Pulling her down and pinning her to the ground. Telling her *No, I think I won* chief among them. But his body had an odd, electrical response to that little fantasy, which meant he couldn't indulge it.

Still, he took her hand and let her help him up, even though he didn't need it. Her hand was slim and small, but callused and work-roughened. She was strong. A lithe kind of strength. Her fighting style wasn't graceful. It was principled, determined and effective.

She let go of his hand, but he found his own grip on her arm tightening. She raised an eyebrow at him. She wasn't exactly who she pretended to be. Or maybe she was. Maybe she was all the little facets of herself she'd shown. Friendly farm girl. Cold, icy operative. Strong, determined fighter. He wasn't sure he would believe all three facets in anyone else, but in Willa they somehow made sense.

"I'm not a child," she began reasonably. She tried to tug her hand out of his grasp once, but when he didn't loosen his grip she simply relaxed her hand in his. "I'm not even a liability. Just because I'm not part of this whole world doesn't mean I wasn't trained to fend for myself. My parents didn't leave me unprotected. They finally let me have my own life because I proved, over and over again, I could handle whatever threat came. And I did. *I* wasn't the one he shot at. You were. And, if I have to remind you, I saved your life."

Her discomfort with that had clearly disappeared, while his only grew. He said nothing, just stood there. Still holding her hand in his. Why? He didn't have a clue.

"If we work together, Holden, we might be able to figure this out," she said, so earnest as she stepped toward him. So that there was maybe a foot between them at most. "But we'd have to tell each other everything, and I know we both think we can't. But I'd be willing to bend a little, if you were." Her green eyes were darker down here, or maybe she was just more serious. More…something. So many different people wrapped up into one.

*And don't you recognize that deep in your soul?*

He'd rather forget his soul had ever existed for the moment. So, he focused on reason and sense and the assignment. She was right, on too many counts. He didn't agree that meant he was the actual target, just that something more than just taking her out was going on.

There were things he *could* tell her, especially with North Star sending out a team he would no doubt need to rendezvous with. And if she would unbend a little to tell him what her parents were involved in, he could handle this. Really handle it.

"All right," he said after a while. "We can try it your way."

She grinned up at him, and there was a jolt that had him thinking about Reece again. Giving up everything he was all because some pretty woman had wrapped him up in her. Holden wouldn't follow that same path.

He wouldn't.

But he finally understood how easy it would be.

# *Chapter Seven*

Willa's heart was hammering in her chest, but she didn't tug away her hand like she wanted to. Holden was playing some kind of power game, and she wouldn't let him see that it affected her—in any of the ways it affected her.

She wanted to clear her throat, but that would give her away, too. She kept the easy smile in place and tried to swallow surreptitiously. "Well, since I saved you and all, I think you should go first."

He stared at her for a very, *very* long time. She managed to keep her expression bland, her outward demeanor cool. Inside she was a riot of nerves and some other fluttery feeling she didn't want to give name to.

His eyes were *very* blue.

"I've told you most of it. My group is tasked with stopping a hit man. I can't be the target because the hit man doesn't know who I am or that I'm after him."

"How do you know?"

"Because I know."

She shook her head. "That's hardheaded. They could have found out."

"Okay, they found out I'm after them. That doesn't negate that they had a different target to begin with. One they're supposed to take out. Regardless of me."

She hated to admit it, but that was true. She could argue

coincidence—after all, she hadn't gotten the ammunition in her PO box. She didn't know who these men were or whom they were after. Maybe they'd unwittingly involved her in something that had nothing to do with her?

But her parents had sent the warning message. Yellow meant to be on the lookout.

"It would help if we knew who your parents are," he said carefully. He was trying not to press. Not to demand. She'd give him credit for that. "And who they're involved with."

She blinked, realizing in a way she hadn't before that he…suspected her parents. Of being the bad guy in this scenario. "You think they're…" She trailed off. She wasn't supposed to out her parents. Ever. No matter the circumstances.

She had wanted to tell a great many people in her life who her parents were, or at the very least what they did. So they'd understand her. She'd always kept her mouth shut. Always swallowed down the truth. Because she was supposed to. For her safety, and for her parents' safety.

"You want to protect them," Holden said softly. "I understand. We always want to protect our parents, but have they protected you?"

"Yes. Always. You don't understand. You couldn't. They tried…" Willa moved away, and Holden finally let her hand go. She had to move. She had to think. She had… Oh, what she wouldn't give to have one of her animals down here to cuddle into for a minute or two.

But there was only Holden. Which meant she had to rein herself in. Figure things out. Decide what was worth telling and what wasn't. She had to use her brain. Just because she hadn't followed in her parents' footsteps didn't mean she didn't know how to figure out a difficult situation.

The facts were facts. And if she arranged them without emotion, she could put together the puzzle enough to make the next step. "My parents could be the targets. They could be the ones this hit man is supposed to kill."

"They've done things worth killing over?" he asked. Blandly enough, but the question had her temper simmering again.

She aimed a haughty look over her shoulder. "Haven't you?" she returned.

His expression didn't change much, though she could have sworn the air between them got colder. "This isn't about me."

"No, but you're in the same boat, aren't you?"

"Am I?"

Temper straining, she started pacing again. "Oh, you're more obstinate than a goat."

"I don't know what to say to that, but you're not exactly amenable yourself."

She let out a huffy breath. Of course she wasn't. Of *course* she wasn't. She didn't owe him amenability.

But she didn't see a way out of this, a way to help her parents, if she didn't offer him a glimpse into who they were. They hadn't responded to her SOS. They could be fighting off their own thing. They could be out of range. They could be oblivious.

She couldn't reach them. Not if they didn't want to be reached.

Holden had told her…next to nothing. But he'd wanted to tell her nothing, so she supposed *next to* was something. It wasn't just *his* secret he'd told her. He'd mentioned a group, talked to a woman named Els on the phone. A team was coming to look for their shooter.

"What's your last name?" she asked.

He paused, considering. Considering if he was going to tell her? Coming up with a fake name? So many things that pause could mean.

"My name is Holden Parker. I can't tell you the name of the group I work for, but we're an independent group who only takes on jobs that will help people. Yes, I've done things people would want to kill me over. Maybe it's rationalization, but I like to think that as long as I've been with this group, every thing I've done wrong has been in the name of right and protecting innocent people."

He said it all so seriously. So intently, his eyes on hers. He could have been lying, but there was such *conviction* in his voice, in his gaze.

"What about before you were with this group?" she asked, not sure why her voice came out so hushed.

"My before doesn't really matter here, Willa."

Sadly, he was right on that score. She'd wanted to know for herself, and that wasn't fair. "My parents aren't all that different. I can't tell you the group they work for, because I don't know. Before I was born, they were with the CIA. They tried to quit. They didn't want to be spies anymore. They wanted a normal life. With me. But it never worked out that way, and after years of jumping around trying to escape the demands of who and what they were, they gave up. They took jobs to do good in the world." She swallowed. "I didn't want to be a part of it, so once I was an adult and could convince them to leave me on my own, I did. They take the jobs they want, that they think will do some good. And I have nothing to do with it. Except to be their liability. Because they love me. Because I'm theirs."

Holden looked around the room they were in. "That's why you have all this?"

She nodded. "And no friends. It's why I don't talk to the post office lady. I have to be alone. Separate. So that no one can use me to get to them."

She'd always thought it would feel freeing to tell someone the truth. The real truth, but she just wanted to cry.

To take it all back. Because now it was up to Holden not to use that information against her.

And once again, she didn't have any say in the matter.

SPIES.

But it wasn't that revelation that left Holden speechless. It was the sheen of tears in Willa's eyes. It hadn't been easy for her to tell him all that. She'd probably promised to always keep it a secret. Especially if her parents were government spies.

But she'd told him.

He shouldn't feel awed or humbled by that. She'd had no choice. There was a hit man out there. If she hoped to survive, she had to trust someone.

*And she really trusted you?*

"If you've kept this separation, how would anyone know you're connected to them?" he asked, instead of addressing any of the emotion in the room. Because emotions didn't matter, couldn't matter, when lives were at stake.

"There are always ways to find things out, no matter how deep you bury them. This has always been possible."

"What was the consensus? You'd just be killed for their job?" He didn't know why anger spurted through him. Why he held such blame and contempt for two people he didn't know. Who were probably a lot more like him than he'd want to admit.

"It's easy to blame them, Holden. Believe me. I know. I've done it. But what were they supposed to do? See into the future and know they'd never be able to escape one job they took because they wanted to do good in the world?"

Holden didn't know what to say to that. He *wanted* to argue, but this wasn't the topic of importance right now. He had to figure out what they were going to do if the North

Star team swept the area and didn't find the hit man. If Elsie couldn't get an ID.

Willa would still be in danger if they didn't take this man down. Holden's assignment was to take the man down—just as much as it was to keep the target from being killed.

"Something isn't right," Willa muttered to herself.

"Gee, you think?"

"No. More than just…someone being after me. Or you. Or…whatever is going on. Something doesn't add up. I got a message to them." Her frown deepened, and she twisted her fingers together. "I sent them an SOS, but they haven't responded. I just can't stop thinking about the fact that he could have killed me, and he didn't. Which means he wants me…not dead. Not yet. So, why?"

"Kidnapping."

"Yes. I've always been aware that could happen. Kill you. Take me. But then what? My parents warned me to be on alert, more so than usual. That's what I was getting from the PO box. A message from them. A warning. They knew something was off, but they didn't tell me to hide. They just told me to be careful."

"They thought they could take care of it?"

"Maybe. Or maybe it was only a feeling—no fact. You'd understand that, wouldn't you? Sometimes they just *feel* like something is off and they don't know why, they just know it is." She looked at him with heartbreaking eyes.

He had to stay strong against those eyes. "Yeah, I understand that."

"It feels like something is off. I know I'm no spy, or… whatever you call yourself. But it doesn't add up. Not cleanly. And it should."

Holden tried to look at things from her perspective. Someone who'd probably known from an early age she could be a target like this. It made sense to trust her judgment on the matter.

"We've got tech on our end—bigger than what you have here. We could try to get a message to them."

She shook her head. "It's too dangerous. For them." She sucked in a breath. "They'd do anything to protect me. And have. I don't know the details, but I know they've sacrificed to keep me safe. I have to do the same for them. I just have to."

Holden didn't say what he wanted to. *But I don't have to.*

"I've done the one thing I'm allowed to do if there's an emergency."

"Do you hear yourself? *Allowed* to do." He tried to tamp down his anger over the position her parents had put her in. He knew what it was like to be naive and young and unprotected. How easy it was for so many bad things to happen. "You're a grown woman. Act like it. Make your own choices."

Her expression hardened. "Believe me. I do."

He wanted to argue some more. Or maybe just order her around so that he could do his job and stop dealing with all these conflicting emotions that had more to do with who he'd been before North Star, before the Sons. A person from a very long time ago who didn't exist anymore.

He'd left all that behind. But she'd somehow brought it all back to life inside him.

*Enough.*

His phone chimed, and he pulled it out to look at the message. Clean. Meet?

They'd sent Gabriel. By Holden's opinion, Gabriel would make a good replacement for Reece. He was still a little young, and Holden would give him a few more challenging missions before he actually put him in a lead position, but it was good Shay had chosen him to lead the sweep.

"I'm going up," he told Willa. "You'll stay here."

"No, I'm coming with you."

"You're staying here."

"I need to take care of my animals. I can set things up so they're okay for a few days on their own if I have to, but you have to let me do that first."

He knew he shouldn't be weak, shouldn't give in, but he also understood fully that she had all those animals and animal figurines because she couldn't have people in her life. She'd filled the void with things that couldn't be used against her or her parents.

"We can't take chances. You have to stick with me until we have a better idea of what's going on. Regardless of your animals."

"You're not my boss, Holden. I didn't ask for you or your group. This is my life you've crashed into. I don't owe you diddly squat."

Holden didn't know why that hurt. She was right. She hadn't asked for this, and technically she had very little to do with what he was here for. He was here to stop a killer—not protect Willa, but to stop the person trying to hurt her. There was a gray area there in how to do it, but his job wasn't *her*.

"Whether you asked for it or not, my assignment isn't fulfilled if you're dead. So, I'm going to ask you to do as I say. I'm going to ask you to trust me to keep you safe while we stop the man who's after you—however he's after you."

She seemed to consider that, watching him with green eyes he knew with a glaring clarity that would haunt him no matter the outcome of this mission. She closed the computer and flicked a switch that had the lights dimming and the sound of the generator going silent.

"I could trust you, Holden, but trust is a two-way street." She turned to one of the doors and flipped a combination on the lock. It creaked open, and she pulled it the rest of the way open. "If we go through here, we can get in through the house and not disturb Creed. Have your man meet us at the front door. East side of the house."

She didn't wait for him to agree. She simply slid into the dark tunnel. Holden blew out a frustrated breath and texted Gabriel. Then he followed her into the dark.

## Chapter Eight

Willa half wished she could stay in the dark tunnel that would lead her into the basement of her house. Here in the dark, her life was not in danger. There was no team. Her parents were off somewhere safe.

And she didn't already trust a man who distrusted her. A man she barely knew. A man she *shouldn't* trust, because this could all be an elaborate lie.

But she couldn't work herself up to that kind of suspicion. So, she'd just have to trust him and hope for the best. Hope to hear from her parents soon.

"This is some movie-level stuff," Holden said from behind her in the tunnel. She'd unlocked the door to the basement before she'd shut down the computer in the main room so when she reached it, she only had to pull it open.

She didn't bother to respond to Holden. Maybe it was movie-level stuff. But it was also her life. The only life she'd ever known. Whatever attempt her parents had made at normal had been mostly before she'd been old enough to remember.

So, she'd grown up with security measures and over-the-top tech, all in the name of keeping her safe.

Everyone always trying to keep her safe.

She shoved away the bitterness. It didn't do her any good. She waited for Holden to follow her through the door before she closed it back up. She set the lock from the outside, then pulled the false wall in front of it.

The basement was dark, but Holden had pulled up the flashlight on his phone. He pointed it at the wall, where you could no longer tell there was a door.

"Serious movie-level stuff," he muttered. "Gabriel is waiting on the porch."

Gabriel. "Do you use real names?" Her parents didn't. Code names, usually. Even with people they worked closely with on the same mission, she didn't think they ever used their real names. Even with her, they were simply Mom and Dad.

She thought about Holden saying his parents had died when he'd been a teenager. He'd had those years of normalcy, supposedly. And still tragedy had touched his life.

None of which mattered. All that mattered was figuring out who'd shot at them. She would be part of it. She would not be hidden away like her parents always forced her to be. Not as long as they didn't respond to her message.

She would not hide in case they were in trouble. She would not *cower* just because things didn't make sense. They'd trained her to fight. Taught her to be self-sufficient.

No one would push her away from the opportunity of helping them if they were in danger.

She moved through the basement. Holden used his light to follow her, but she knew the way in the dark. When he finally responded to her question about real names, his voice was clipped. Detached.

"Yes. Most of us. For the most part, whoever we are or were disappears once we join the group. So our names are safe. Not really tied to anyone."

They used their real names. But disappeared when they joined the group. She had to assume they weren't tied to anyone because his group collected people who didn't *have* anyone. People like him who'd lost his family.

They climbed the stairs in silence, and Holden gently pulled her back before she could open the door. He slid it open himself, inch by inch, leading with his gun. He held a hand out behind him—a silent order to stay where she was until he made sure it was safe.

She frowned a little but remained where she was. Being involved, making sure her parents were okay didn't mean she had to take risks or chances. Sometimes she'd have to rely on Holden's experience.

And sometimes he'd have to rely on hers. Whether he realized it now or not.

Eventually he motioned her forward, and in silence she followed him through the house and to the front door. He shined his light on the bunny doorstop that lay askew.

"Did you move that when you broke into my house?" she asked in a whisper.

"Yeah," he replied. "What the hell are those things?"

"Doorstops. The house is old. In the spring and summer if I want the doors open, I have to use the stops."

He shook his head. "Why *rabbits*?"

"What's wrong with rabbits?"

"They're rodents, Willa."

"What's wrong with rodents?"

Holden muttered something unintelligible and eased the heavy door open. The storm door opened from the other side, and a man slid in the opening.

"Parker," he greeted Holden.

"Gabe. What have you got?"

"No sign of the shooter. Based on our scan, he acted alone. There is a problem though."

"Yeah, what's that?"

"The shells we found? They don't go in the gun we're looking for."

It was strange. Appearance-wise Holden and this Gabriel were night and day—dark and light—and yet they *felt* the same standing there. It was in the posture, or the air of power, or *something*. You knew they were trained to handle whatever came their way.

*You were, too.*

But one thing she'd learned—not from her parents, but from experience—was it was best when she was under-estimated. So, she didn't tell them her theory. And when Gabriel and Holden went outside to "check the perimeter"—which she knew translated as "have a talk without the woman"—Willa got to a little work of her own.

"WHERE'D SHE COME FROM?" Gabriel wanted to know as they walked the perimeter of the house. Much as Holden trusted Gabriel and the other team members, there were some things he wanted to see for himself. Like where the shells had been. Like the shells themselves.

"What do you mean?" Holden asked, searching the dark for some sign of…something. Who shot at someone, missed and then just disappeared?

It didn't add up. Which Willa had pointed out very astutely.

"Nice-looking."

Holden straightened like a shot. Based on the way the other man's eyes widened, he assumed his face was arranged in a way that screamed *murder*. He tried to school it into something softer. The sharp disapproval of a teacher, rather than…wanting to strangle him with his bare hands.

"She's a victim in a situation we're trying to mitigate, Saunders."

"I didn't say we weren't," he returned, but the words were careful. Measured. "Just commentary."

"Commentary is best kept to yourself unless it's relevant to the assignment."

"Yes, sir."

There was some sarcasm in the *sir*, but that didn't bother Holden any. Made him feel a *little* old, when he wasn't. Well, maybe by North Star standards he was. Especially now that Reece was gone. Wasn't everyone but Shay and Betty younger than him?

Holden grimaced. He didn't want to be *old*, even if it was just in this small microcosm of people.

But he was the leader, and he had assignments to lead. "I want the shells back at headquarters for tests. You can send someone else. I want you to stay close as secondary."

Gabriel nodded. He stopped at a rock a few yards from the house. "This is where I found the shells."

Holden studied the area. He'd want to look again in the daylight instead of the two narrow beams of light from their phones. But this would be a good vantage point. Still, how had Holden not sensed something was wrong? Why hadn't any of her dogs?

Granted, they didn't really bark or growl at him. Wouldn't the point of having all those animals around be for them to act as some kind of protective element? Or at least an early alarm?

So many things that didn't fully add up. He looked back at the house. Willa had a light on and was in the kitchen. Probably cleaning up the shattered glass.

"We need the bullet too," he said, watching the shadow of her movements. She'd told him things, and yet he knew she'd kept things from him, too. Probably always would. His job was to protect her, but she'd protect her parents.

He wanted to blame her for that, but it was hard to find the frustration. If his parents were alive, he'd do everything in his power to protect them too.

"Something doesn't add up here," Gabriel said, his voice low and quiet in the dark of night.

"No, it doesn't." Holden crouched by the rock, tried to figure the angle of the shooter. Tried not to think about how he should have been more careful.

Eventually he stood. "Do another check. Not as wide, but even more thorough. I'll get the bullet and meet you back out here."

"Afraid to let me inside because I've got eyes in my head?"

Holden didn't give Gabriel a look. He would have said the same thing once upon a time. Hell, if Sabrina was leading this and he was on secondary, he would have said the same to her. The fact it *annoyed* him was neither here nor there.

So, he said nothing at all. He strode for the house and trusted Gabriel to do his job. He went in through the front door, studying the house with new eyes. When he'd first sneaked in, he'd been looking for signs of who Willa really was. Now he was looking for signs of weakness.

She had that whole safe house underground setup and she lived in this rickety old farm house like she didn't have a fear in the world. Where she tried to live a normal life, with only animals for companionship.

He could not let that affect him. Sympathy, empathy, they weren't the enemy, but they could make it harder to do what had to be done. Much as he felt his new mission was to protect Willa, he couldn't trust her one hundred percent. She still had secrets.

Soundlessly, he made his way to the kitchen. He stood in the shadows, just out of sight, watching her sweep up glass. She talked the entire time. To a dog and a cat who sat obediently away from the glass.

"Windows can be replaced," she was saying. "Any *thing*

can be replaced." She sighed, resting on her haunches—broom in one hand, dustpan in the other. She looked at her animals. "I don't know how I'm going to protect you guys though."

"We'll figure out something."

She jerked in surprise, but she didn't screech or fall over. She simply eyed him warily. "Will *we* now?"

"Much like you, they're innocent bystanders."

She sighed and got to her feet, dumping the dustpan's contents into a paper bag. The glass clinked together, and she looked up at the window that had exploded. She'd taped cardboard over the opening.

"Innocent bystander. I don't feel like that. I feel like a pawn."

Since that's essentially what she was, he chose to change the subject. "Do you have anything I could dig the bullet out of the wall with?"

She turned and studied the wall where there was a hole. It didn't bother Holden that it could have been his head that bullet had been lodged into. He'd been shot at too many times to count. He had a healthy grip on the idea of mortality.

But Willa had gone a little pale as she studied the wall. He wondered how deeply she'd considered her own. Likely more than the average woman, but that didn't mean some people ever got comfortable with it.

She turned away and opened a drawer. She pawed around in what appeared to be a collection of junk—rubber bands and random screws, cords and pieces of paper, then pulled out a pair of needle-nosed pliers.

She handed him the tool, and he worked to get the bullet out of the wall with minimal damage to the wall, but either age or damage made much of the drywall and plaster crumble away as he dug around for the bullet.

Much like the shells, the bullet didn't match the ammunition for the high-powered gun they knew about. Still a deadly bullet and weapon, but Holden had to wonder why a hit man who'd been sent a specific weapon would then use a different one.

The only reason he could think of was that Willa wasn't the target. Not specifically. He didn't want to worry her, but she had a connection to two people hooked up with government missions and danger.

"Willa…" He sighed. "Do you know where your parents are?"

Her expression didn't change. There was no shock or worry or surprise. Because clearly she'd already come to the same conclusion he had. "I don't know. They're not answering my messages." Willa looked back at the window and hugged her arms around herself. "You think they're the actual target."

There was no getting around it. "Yes."

When she looked back at him, her eyes were direct, no sign of tears. Her expression was grim, but not afraid. "I do too. Which means you have to help me find them."

## Chapter Nine

Holden's mouth moved into a frown. A disapproving one. She knew it would be difficult, but she had to convince him to let her be part of his assignment. She couldn't sit back while her parents were in specific danger.

She'd done it her whole life. Let them be in danger. Just…*hoped* they'd be okay and she wouldn't be left helpless and alone. But what if they needed her now? What if that's why they hadn't responded to her help message? What if they *couldn't*? Could she really just sit around and wait for news they were dead?

No, she couldn't.

This was different from anything that had come before because they weren't communicating with her. Because Willa herself had been shot at, not just threatened. Besides, in this moment she had… Well, Holden wouldn't see himself as her partner, but they *could* act as partners. For this. She just needed to be a part of it.

She wished her doubts about Holden were more pronounced. They *should* be. Intellectually she knew she'd already given too much, trusted too much. But when push came to shove, she couldn't seem to help it.

And he hadn't tried to hurt her, had he?

"My assignment is to stop the hit man, Willa. It's what

I'll do. If your parents are the target, I'll do everything in my power to protect them."

"You need my help."

He dropped the bullet into a bag. He'd send it back to his group and hope to get some information from the study of it, if she had to guess.

"You won't be left unprotected, Willa. Even if he shot at me, clearly you're a target in all this."

"I'm not worried about me. I'm worried about them. You have to let me help."

"Help what?"

"Help with your assignment. You don't know my parents. You don't know who they are or what they look like."

"I don't know the hit man either. I'll find both. It's my job to find both. Whether you want to believe it or not, I'm very good at my job."

Oh, she *wanted* to believe it, but that didn't make it possible for her to sit on the sidelines. Not this time. Not until she heard from her parents directly. "It'd be easier with my help."

"I don't see how."

"Do you want me to prove I can shoot a gun? That I can sneak around unheard? Do you want me to prove everything they taught me, because I can. I will."

"It's not that I doubt your...capabilities."

But he did. Of course he did. He looked at her and saw a weak, silly woman surrounded by animals. No matter how much she explained to him how she'd been trained to protect herself, he wouldn't believe it. She could probably *prove* it and he wouldn't believe it.

Because he didn't want to. Didn't have to.

"Fine." And it was fine. She wasn't tied to him. She didn't need him. She had her own two feet. Her own mind. Her own choices. "I'll go after them on my own."

"Not an option," he said, his voice cold and authoritative.

Which stirred the anger she was using to cover up her paralyzing fear. "So funny—I don't remember consenting to let you boss me around or tell me what I can't do."

He groaned out loud. "Willa. Just…hit pause, okay? It's the middle of the night. You're tired. You've been shot at. Let's just go to sleep. We'll talk about it in the morning."

"Oh, *we're* going to go to sleep?"

His expression was bland. "Sure."

"For some kind of spy, you're a terrible liar."

"I'm not a spy, and I'm not *lying*. I'm trying to do my job and you're getting in the way. How are you going to help me? I know what I'm doing. I'm *trained* in what I'm doing. You're a farmer."

"I know their habits. How they operate. I may not know where they are, but I can tell you things about their past missions that might give you an idea where to start. Yes, you have the whole whatever-you-are-that-isn't-a-spy thing down, but I know *them*. If we work together, we can save them faster. I'm sure of it."

The back door swung open. Willa jumped, though she stopped a surprised shriek from exiting her mouth. A woman stood there, and Holden immediately relaxed his hand on his weapon. Though he was clearly surprised by the woman's appearance.

"Shay."

Willa blinked at the woman. She was tall and, well, very pretty. Her hair was blond, her eyes were blue, and Willa figured if she wasn't dressed head to foot in tactical gear, you might even be convinced she looked elegant.

But she *was* in tactical gear, and she had that same aura of control and action that Holden and the other man from his team had.

"We need to talk." Shay's gaze flicked to Willa. "Alone."

Willa might have wilted at the authoritative look on a different day, but today... "This is my house. If you want alone, you can leave it."

Shay's eyebrows shot up. "It seems you left a few things out of your report, Parker."

Willa had the fascinating view of Holden tensing. She wouldn't say his expression was guilty or defensive, exactly, but it certainly wasn't controlled.

"I have a handle on the situation. I'm not sure why you're here."

Shay eyed Willa again. Willa kept her chin up and her gaze direct. She wasn't going to be afraid or nervous. If Holden wouldn't help her, it was always possible this woman would.

"Did she give you that bump on your head?"

This time Holden's gaze slid to Willa. "Not exactly," he muttered. "Willa. Give us a few."

Willa didn't even bother to respond with words. She crossed her arms over her chest and stayed resolutely where she was. She would not be maneuvered. She would not be...set aside. It felt too much like being a kid again. Set aside so Mom and Dad could handle whatever new job they had to take.

*Had* to. Couldn't escape their former lives. She'd always believed that. But for a brief, horrible moment, it occurred to her that maybe they just hadn't *wanted* to quit. Not enough.

She shook the thought away. Or tried. Because Shay nodded toward the door and Holden went outside. Shay followed.

Willa was left alone in her house. Out of the loop. Pushed to the side. While a bunch of people she didn't know decided things about her life, and her parents' lives.

She couldn't control them. No, she'd learned that from living with her parents. She couldn't control anyone.

But she could control herself, decide herself and act herself.

So, she would.

HOLDEN STOOD OUT in the pitch-black night feeling unaccountably…caught. Why? He didn't have a clue. He'd done everything he should have done. Followed protocol.

Maybe he'd left a few details out of the report. Maybe he'd been a little vague when it came to Willa. But that didn't mean he needed Shay to appear on the scene. Nor should he feel anything but competent and ready for the next step now that she was here.

Why was everything so backward? He didn't know, but it had to stop. "I've got it covered. I don't know why you're here."

"You didn't say you'd been hurt," Shay said gravely.

"That's not why you came. You couldn't be here all the way from headquarters this quickly if Gabe dimed me out."

"It's not diming you out to inform your superior of a serious injury. You need a new bandage. There's concussion protocol to follow."

"Hey, Mom? I'm fine."

She didn't laugh. She didn't so much as sigh. "This isn't a joke, Parker. You know the rules."

"Yeah, I know the rules. I also know I'm fine and I know what I'm doing."

"Last mission you stepped in when Sabrina was still fighting because she was injured and you knew it."

"It's a bump. There's also not someone currently attacking me. It's different than what happened with her. You have to know it's different. And we don't have time for this. I've got the bullet. Gabe's got the shells. We need to run tests. We need to move forward before the hit man closes in on the target."

"You don't think she's the target?" Shay said, inclining her head toward the old farmhouse.

Holden looked back at the house. Lights were still on. He knew he'd been fooling himself that Willa would go crawl in bed and sleep, but he'd held out some stupid hope she'd just…let him handle it. "I'm not sure. She's not the only target, if she is one. She thinks it's her parents. They've got connections to spy groups. Including the CIA. Which would have been in my next report, once I'd finished gathering evidence."

"Why do you sound unsure?"

"Something doesn't add up. I can't figure out what. It might be her." Holden thought about the pseudobunker belowground. "Can we get Elsie out here?"

"If necessary."

"If there's the potential this connects to the CIA, I don't want anyone but her poking around on the computer Willa's got."

"Willa. That her real name?"

Holden shrugged, trying to sound detached. Because he *was* detached. Even if Willa had saved his life. "Not sure. She might not be sure. Her parents are spies. After seeing the setup, I believe it. Or maybe I believe they're involved in something. She thinks it's good. But what if it's not? She wouldn't know. She's their daughter."

"Unless she's part of it."

Holden considered. Tried to really, dispassionately consider it. "It wouldn't fit. I just can't see how her playing me would fit."

"Women have ways to make men think they're weaker than they are."

"I work with you and Sabrina. Who do you take me for?"

Shay seemed to consider that. Then she jerked her chin toward him. "How'd you get the bump?"

He explained the car accident in more detail than he'd given North Star before. Left out the part about Willa chaining him to a bed. It wasn't hiding things. It was just not including information that was neither here nor there. He was out of the chains now.

"This spy thing…"

"She won't give me their names. I'd say you guys could investigate her, but we don't know what our hit man knows. We don't want to bring more suspicion on her. But she's got a fancy computer in that underground bunker of hers. If Elsie can hack into it, she might be able to find things Willa doesn't know or doesn't want to say."

"Will Willa let that happen?"

An idea formed. One he didn't particularly like, but it would get the job done. "If I let her come with me to track down her parents, she won't have to know."

"You can't take a civilian around with you on a dangerous mission."

"She wants to go. She claims her parents taught her some skills." He thought about the way she'd fought him in some attempt to prove she could knock him down first. No, he hadn't fought back, but she'd held her own. "She demonstrated some."

"Gross."

"Get your mind out of the gutter, Shay. I've known this woman less than twenty-four hours."

"Please, Holden. I've seen you work."

Torn between offense and amusement, Holden shook his head. "She tried to fight me. She's okay."

Shay made a considering noise. She studied the house, and Holden knew she'd consider his plan. Pros and cons. Even if she didn't agree, she'd take the time to consider it.

Shay shook her head, and Holden was sure he'd either have to disobey a direct order or find some new, better reasoning for Willa coming with him. Which was more likely: Willa letting them search her computer, or convincing Shay to let him take Willa with him?

He really didn't know.

"You know she's running, right?" Shay said conversationally, rocking back on her heels as she slipped her hands into her pockets.

"Running?"

"I'd lay my life savings that she's already climbing out a window on the other side of the house."

Holden stared at the house. She wouldn't. He didn't exactly expect her to crawl into bed and sleep, but she wouldn't run. She couldn't. "She wouldn't leave her animals."

"You so sure about that?"

He was. He *was*. But he found himself moving forward anyway. Creeping around the house until the back was in view. He saw no sign of her, but there was an open window, the screen missing. No, not missing. It had been carefully propped up against the house on the ground.

Holden swore. Shay chuckled and slapped him on the back. "She's got your number, Parker. Admit it."

"Like hell," he muttered disgustedly. "Get Elsie here. Get her in that underground computer, whatever it takes. I'll keep Willa busy trying to find her parents. Keep in touch. I want to know anything found the second it's found."

"Anything else?" Shay said blandly, a subtle reminder *she* was the boss, not him. Still, it was his assignment.

"That should do it."

## Chapter Ten

Willa moved through the dark with practiced ease. The moonlight helped, but she'd taken this path before.

Maybe Holden didn't believe in her capabilities, but she knew them. She felt a twinge of guilt about leaving her animals behind. She had a plan in place for that too—she was nothing if not prepared—but a neighboring farmer making sure they were fed and watered wasn't the same as being loved.

But it had to be done. Some things just had to be done. Like breaking into her parents' safe and escaping into the night, away from Holden and his *group* and whatever their priorities were.

*Her* priority was her parents.

She hadn't given them their insisted-upon thirty-six hours, but she thought the existence of a hit man, another secret group, and being shot at meant they'd have to forgive her for engaging in emergency measures early.

It'd take a while to make it to town. The sun would definitely rise before she'd get there. That was okay if she was careful. The RV storage facility where her parents stored their car was pretty isolated. Even in the light of day, it wouldn't be too difficult to sneak in and take it.

She'd have to slow down, though. If she kept running,

she'd wear herself out before she completed the long, long trek. But if Holden caught her...

Surely it would take him some time to figure her out. Some time to talk to the woman and make their plans. *Surely* he'd assume she went to bed and leave her to it.

"Don't be an idiot, Willa," she muttered to herself. He'd know. He'd find out. She had only minutes to make her escape count. Luckily, she knew the area and—

She heard the footsteps a second too late. In the next second she was tumbling to the ground, someone tumbling on top of her. She didn't scream. She fought. She would always, *always* fight.

Hands clamped around her wrists, so she used her legs to kick wildly.

"Damn it, Willa. It's me."

She huffed out a breath, as if *that* changed anything. "I know exactly who it is," she said, *almost* landing a knee where he'd definitely be knocked back by the blow. But he shifted at the last second.

They grappled, but all he did was try to grab. There was no attempt to hurt her or even immobilize her. It was like he was dodging blows, waiting for her to get tired or just accept that he'd found her.

"Would you stop?" he gritted out, barely dodging a fist to the nose.

She would have liked to have connected, but he maneuvered her onto her back on the cool, damp ground. He used his legs to clamp her legs together, so she only had her arms to try and escape. No matter how she tried to wiggle away, his legs kept her locked tight.

She could land a very, *very* painful punch in this position, but even as she balled her fist and considered it, he hopped off her.

He flicked on a flashlight, which had her wincing away

from the sudden brightness. She lay on the ground and blew out a breath. They'd grappled, and she'd accomplished nothing. But at least he'd accomplished *less* than nothing.

"How do you get by in your job never, ever hurting a woman?"

He didn't say anything to that. He got very quiet and very still, and she remembered what he'd said when she'd said he must not have anyone who loved him. *Direct hit.*

"I can't believe you'd leave your animals," he said, completely ignoring her comment.

She opened her mouth to lecture him about how much *care* she put into her animals, but that would give things away she was trying not to give away. Eventually she got to her feet, brushing off dirt she couldn't see but could feel.

"If you're going to drag me back… Well, you're going to have to fight me. Actually fight me. I won't go back until I've done what I have to do." She balled her fists, got into a fighting stance and readied herself.

He heaved out a sigh. "I'm not going to fight you, Willa."

"Then you have to let me go. I mean, there's no *letting*. I'm going." She started to move, but he only stood in her way. Arms crossed. He held the flashlight, illuminating the area around them enough for her to see his face was smudged with dirt, so hers probably was too.

"You aren't going anywhere. At least, not alone. You don't know where the man who shot at you is. He could be here."

"He could be. And he'd likely fight back."

"He'd shoot you dead."

"You don't know that."

Holden groaned. "You might be the most frustrating woman I've ever met. And maybe if you'd stuck around and actually cooperated—"

"Cooperated? You told me to go to bed! I won't be pushed aside while my parents are in danger. I won't."

"You might have been cordially invited to accompany me," he said dryly.

She opened her mouth to argue, then snapped her mouth shut. Had she been rash? Should she have waited? She narrowed her eyes at him. No. No, that wouldn't have gone the way she wanted, no matter what he claimed.

"You're going to come with me?"

"You're going to come with *me*."

She rolled her eyes. "Do you know where to begin?"

"Do you?"

She thought of the papers in her pocket. Codes again. Codes he wouldn't be able to crack. At least, not quickly. She chewed on her lip, and in the glow of the flashlight his eyes narrowed.

"Willa," he said, a warning tone to his voice. "What do you know?"

She opened her mouth to tell him. It was like second nature, somehow, to want to tell him everything. To be thrilled he was going to work with her on this. She needed to be more careful. More wary of him.

"Let's just consider you on a need-to-know basis. And you don't."

"That doesn't work for me," he said, and his voice had a hard edge to it. But he wouldn't fight her or hurt her. It was hard to be afraid of an edge that wouldn't cut. What must be in his past, she wondered.

"You're not going to threaten it out of me. Or torture it out of me. Why would I tell you anything?"

"So I help you, Willa," he said, sounding irritable.

"Maybe I don't need your help."

"Fine." He turned away from her and started walking back toward her house. He was calling her bluff. That was fine. She didn't need his help. She knew where she was going, and maybe she didn't know what she was doing or how exactly she was going to do it, but she had a target. A place to go. She...

She muttered a swear and then scrambled after him. "Wait. Okay, wait." She didn't *need* his help, but it might come in handy, and didn't her parents deserve as much help as she could offer? He hadn't brought his team along, but he still likely had more resources than she did.

"I'd like your help." When he didn't so much as move a muscle, she sighed. "Please."

"You have to tell me what you know."

"Couldn't you just...let me lead and trust that I know what I'm doing and I'll fill you in as needed?" She knew he wouldn't agree to it, but at least if she'd asked, she didn't feel quite like she'd utterly let down her parents.

"How about we start with the thing you're not telling me."

Willa wanted to pout. How did a man who didn't know her know she was keeping things from him? How had he caught up to her so quickly?

It was just an unfortunate reminder that even if she was capable of weathering threats, she was out of her league when it came to actually ending them.

"I wasn't lying to you before, exactly. I don't know who they work for, and I don't know where they are. But... I do have access to a few answers."

"How? Where?" he demanded.

She didn't need to tell him about the papers. She didn't *need* to tell him anything. She could lie. She *could* lie. Intellectually, she knew she was capable. But emotionally... Well, it just didn't seem possible. "Obviously they knew that their work was dangerous. That something might happen to them and I'd never get appropriate word. So, they always leave me some coded information about who I can contact if I have real cause to believe they're in danger."

She didn't include the other stipulations. She was supposed to wait thirty-six hours. She was supposed to research a few things before she went straight to the source. For their own safety, and hers.

But they'd never, ever given her reason to worry before. There had never been a legitimate reason to take their last resort. She was still struggling with believing she should. Maybe that's why she hadn't actually looked at the information yet. She'd just grabbed it and ran.

Because she'd let emotions win over sense. Over careful thought. She was afraid for her parents, irritated with Holden's high-handedness. Emotions had won, and she'd made mistakes.

She blew out a breath. "How do you do it?"

"Do what?"

"Make decisions without letting your emotions get in the way. Mom and Dad are forever scolding me about it, and I did it again. Felt then acted without thinking it through. I don't know how to turn it off. The feelings. The fear."

"You shouldn't have to do it. You're a civilian."

"I wish. I *wish* it were that simple, but it's not. I'm stuck between two worlds, and I don't fit into either. I don't know how to be comfortable in either. I can't sit around and hope they're okay. I know too much. Understand too much. But I can't shut off how scared I am for them. I can't shut off how much I love them. So, how can I? How can I lock it all away until it's convenient?"

She stood there waiting for an answer. A magic one that could give her the capability of doing what her parents did.

"I don't know your parents, Willa, but they left you with some elaborate underground compound. That doesn't strike me as something people who can shut off their emotions do. If they really shut emotion off, wouldn't they have given you up for adoption or something to keep you far away from them?"

Willa didn't know what to say to that. It kind of made her want to cry. She knew her parents loved her, but they left her so often. They'd put her in danger before and likely would again. Sometimes she wondered if they just…loved their life a little more than her.

But Holden, a man she barely knew, had a point. That point brought up *more* emotion. Tenderness toward her parents, and maybe even a little toward Holden.

Holden, who was going to help her. Or maybe he was going to use her, but if it got her to her parents, did it matter? "There's a car. At a storage facility for RVs and boats. Outside town. It's a trek, but I figure whoever was shooting at me wouldn't be able to track me to that vehicle. Not right away, anyway."

"And then what?"

"Then I'd follow their code. I'm not sure what it'll lead me to. Them? Their superiors? Something else entirely? I don't have a clue. I can only follow it and hope I'm wrong—and not so right I lead the bad guys right to their doorstep."

He inclined his head. "Solid plan. Lead the way."

She blinked. Once. He…was agreeing to her plan? *And* letting her lead? She opened her mouth to ask if he was sure, but then closed it. She didn't need him to be sure. *She* was sure.

So, she began to walk. She knew where she was going, though she considered taking a circular route in case this was some kind of trap. It felt like one. He'd agreed too easily. Especially after arguing with her about partnering up not that long ago.

"The woman…"

"Shay?"

"Yes, her. She's…okay with you working with me?"

"*Okay* isn't the word I'd use. She agreed. Reluctantly."

"Why?"

"You have information I don't."

He said it so matter-of-factly she had no choice but to believe him. He saw her less as a partner or leader and more as the means with which to get the information he needed. Which didn't bother her. She hadn't yet proved to him just how good of a partner she could be.

But she would.

They walked. Walked and walked. Sometimes she tried to engage Holden in conversation, but he almost always turned it into asking her more about her parents and what she knew about what they did.

They continued to walk, even as the dark of night began to slowly lighten into the glow of dawn. Willa took a deep breath of almost-morning air. She was often awake at this time, tending to her animals. She loved the otherworldliness of it. The stillness. The light that no other part of day could quite emulate.

"Must you hum?" Holden muttered grumpily.

"It's just such a beautiful morning."

"It'd be a hell of a lot more beautiful in bed. Asleep."

"Once we get to the car, you can take a nice little nap." She took in her surroundings, satisfied with the progress they were making. "We're getting close. I'll want you to stay out of sight while I get the car. I think I can sneak it out without anyone seeing me, but if I do get caught, it'll be a lot easier to talk my way out of it with Earl if I'm alone."

He eyed her disapprovingly. "You've proven you're a flight risk."

"Don't be silly."

"You've run away from me once. You won't run away from me again."

An odd shiver ran through her at the seriousness in his tone. Odd because it wasn't fear or worry. It wasn't even foreboding. It felt a bit like anticipation, and that didn't make *any* sense.

So she ignored it. "You'll be able to see me the whole time. Besides, if I run, I have no doubt you'll find a way to follow me and pretend like you're the big, bad wolf who's going to really punish me this time, while dodging punches and telling me to *quit it*."

Cheerful despite the lack of sleep, she went back to humming but only got about a half a step farther before Holden grabbed her by the arm. It was unexpected, and not gentle, but not a rough grab, either. He seemed to excel at touches that were powerful without being threatening.

"I want you to be very clear about one thing, Willa," he said, his voice cold and authoritative. "I don't hurt women. I won't. But I'd incapacitate you if it became necessary."

Despite the chill in his voice, his hand was big and warm and gentle. She smiled. She couldn't help it. "Of course you would," she said indulgently. She even patted his hand. He likely had to believe it. A man like him had to believe he was the strongest person in the room. And he was. No doubt he was stronger than her, but if he refused to do little more than roll around and hold on to a woman's arms or legs, he'd never actually *incapacitate* her or any other woman.

The world tilted, and suddenly she was on her back, but...gently. Nothing jarred. It wasn't like falling. Because no matter that Holden had knocked her off her feet, he'd also somehow cushioned the blow.

Which didn't really prove his point. She supposed the way one of his large hands cuffed hers together over her head was supposed to prove it for him, but that just meant he was leaning over her. Looking at her with an odd light of triumph in those dark blue eyes of his.

She didn't feel incapacitated. She felt…alive. Like every nerve ending sparked with energy. That triumph in his gaze faded into something else.

And his gaze dropped to her mouth.

HOLDEN WONDERED IF a head injury could cause a person to detach from their own body. To have a personality transplant. To be changed utterly and completely just because a woman he could damn well take down, but wouldn't, acted like he was *cute* for explaining the truth to her.

He was a man who enjoyed women, when time allowed, but a certain kind of woman. Not a guileless farm girl who somehow had secrets and spies in her family and looked up at him when he'd knocked and held her down as if he was holding her hand.

How could he be attracted to freckles, and a nose just a shade too close to sharp? Her hair was like gold in the pale light of dawn, and her eyes that deep, mesmerizing green. Her mouth…

Holden jumped to his feet so fast he nearly tripped over himself. But there was no way he could…

No way. It was just a trick of the pearly dawn and…his head injury. It had to be that.

Not just…her.

She leveraged up on her elbows, still lying sprawled on the ground where he'd taken her down. To prove a point.

Why could he never seem to prove a point with this woman? He was an accomplished field agent and had been for years. After all the mistakes of his early adulthood, he hadn't made any for years. He'd honed himself into a machine. Machines didn't make mistakes because women were...

Whatever she was.

"Why are you looking at me like I'm a snake?"

Snakes were a hell of a lot less dangerous than this woman. "How far are we from the car?"

She got to her feet, and though he had half a thought to help her up, he kept his hands deep in his pockets.

"You know, I'm not a total shut-in," she said, brushing the dirt from her pants.

"Huh?"

"I went to school. Off and on. I even had a boyfriend my junior year of high school. Terrible kisser, but, you know, he did actually kiss me." She pulled a face. "He was not *good* at it."

"Why are you—"

"And that was like seven years ago—my junior year, that is—so I'm not as young as I look."

"I didn't—"

"So, don't start treating me like I'm some kind of freak. Life's been weird, but I'm not some wolf child who doesn't know anything about life outside my menagerie of animals. I *like* animals, but that doesn't mean I'm completely..." She trailed off, clearly frustrated with her lack of having a word for whatever she wanted to say.

"I don't know what you're talking about," he replied.

And he didn't. More or less. Maybe he hadn't pegged her at twenty-four, but not too far off. And he'd never considered that she'd been totally sheltered. She seemed to know how to deal with him just fine.

"I know what I seem like. But I'm not...that. I'm not naive. I'm not incompetent. And most important, I'm not stupid. You'll need to understand that and believe it." She set her gaze to the east. "I'd say we have a mile left. Let's not waste daylight."

She started marching and Holden followed, not sure what else to do in the situation. If he tried to explain himself, it'd be overkill. And show too much of what he'd been thinking back there when his only thoughts could be the assignment at hand.

But the words were there. The explanations. The excuses. And the strangest urge to lay them all at her feet, when he was much more comfortable keeping complicated emotions to himself.

They walked the last mile in silence. As the storage place came into view—nothing more than a big field with a tall chain-link fence around it and a tiny office situated in front of the gate of the fence—Willa's pace got slower. Until she came to a complete stop.

"You'll need to stay out of sight. You see the road there? Keep walking down it. Pretend you're a hitchhiker." She gave him a once-over, her mouth curving. "You kind of look like one."

He gave her a doleful look that had her chuckling. He schooled away the smile he wanted to give in response. "I'm not letting you out of my sight, Willa."

"Just to get the car. You walk down that way, and I'll get the car and drive and pick you up. I can't guarantee no one's in the office, even if it is early, and I don't think it's wise to let anyone see you. Especially if someone out there is looking for me. I get the car, I meet you down the road a little ways. Stick your thumb out. Voilà."

Holden studied her. He didn't think she was lying. That was her plan, and she was right. It was best for their purposes, if someone was following her, if they thought she was alone. Vulnerable.

She wouldn't be. He'd be damned if he'd let her be. But

that didn't mean he felt comfortable walking away from her while she went to get a vehicle. It would be far too easy for her to take off, and then he'd lose more precious time trying to track her down.

Time that could lead to her parents or whoever else was the target ending up dead, and no matter that it'd be her fault, he'd feel like he had blood on his hands.

Hands she took in hers. A surprisingly firm gesture. Maybe a little desperate. "You're going to have to trust me," she said, squeezing his fists with her much smaller hands. "We're going to have to trust each other. We can't work knowing the other person is keeping secrets."

It should be of no consequence to him that she was a liar. That no matter how entreating her gaze was, or how oddly comforting her hand on his was, she lied. And it hurt. Which made the words that came out of his mouth next far too bitter for the situation. "But you are keeping secrets, Willa."

## *Chapter Eleven*

"Holden." She didn't know what else to say. Yes, she had a few secrets. She'd phrased that poorly. She'd only wanted his trust. His partnership.

Maybe she was letting her loneliness get in the way of good sense. More feelings when she was supposed to school them all away.

She dropped his hands, feeling vaguely slimy. Like she was the one in the wrong. "Then I'll trust you first," she said, squinting her eyes against the rising sun. She couldn't predict what he'd do. She could only control herself.

Herself. Someone who couldn't escape her emotions. No, she couldn't. Maybe it was time to stop fighting them. Maybe she had to *trust* them. "I trust you, Holden. I'm going to trust you to realize the best option is for you to start walking down the street and for me to meet you a ways down and pick you up. If you don't, well… Then I was wrong about you and I'll have to live with it."

She started walking away from him. She was desperate to look back, to see what he would do, but it would only undermine her point.

No matter who she wanted to be, or what world she felt more comfortable in, deep down she wasn't the image she gave off.

If he'd wanted to kiss her, and part of her desperately

wanted to believe that's what that moment had been, he wanted to kiss the damsel in distress. The weak, innocent, too-young-looking woman who loved animals more than people and wanted a simple life free of the fear and danger of her parents' lives.

She *wished* she could be that simple. She *wished* that's who she was.

But it wasn't.

She approached the gate to the storage area. She peered in the little office building, but the lights were off and the hours clearly stated. She glanced at the little security camera pointed at the gate. Likely there were more on the inside.

That didn't bother her so much. She knew the owners, and while she knew they wouldn't appreciate her breaking in, she was taking what belonged to her parents. She could probably sweet-talk them out of pressing charges.

Maybe.

She bit her lip. Charges didn't actually worry her in the overall sense. But if law enforcement put some kind of flag on the car, she'd have the kind of police interest she didn't need when she was trying to sneak somewhere to help her parents.

"Taken care of."

Willa whirled around at Holden's voice. He was shoving his phone into his pocket and going straight for the lock on the gate. "Security cameras are down. It'll be explained to the owners as maintenance from the security system. We'll get a replacement car in here within the hour to make it look like your parents' car wasn't taken."

He picked the lock in under ten seconds and was shoving open the gate.

"How—"

"Oh, and there are two operatives who are going to stay

at your farm and take care of your animals, so you don't have to worry about whoever you were going to call to help on that score."

He was walking into the storage area, and she was rooted to the same spot. "How did you…"

"Come on now. No time to dawdle. We have to be out of here in five minutes or the cameras will come back on."

She looked up at the security camera. She supposed there'd be plenty of time to ask him how he'd done any of it.

She had to remember she was dealing with a man like her parents. He had contacts and access to all sorts of things she'd never understand. She might be able to hold her own, but he could flip the game. She wouldn't be able to beat him, but she could keep up. If she kept herself ready to take whatever change, whatever surprise came her way.

So, she led him to her parents' car. Before she could open the driver's side door, he did. She scowled at him. "I'm driving. You don't know where you're going."

"Do you?" he countered, holding his hand out, presumably for the keys.

She wanted to drive. She wanted to stay in control. She wanted to run this and have him follow her around and step in only when necessary.

Of course it wouldn't happen like that. She was the tagalong, help-only-when-necessary part of this partnership. It grated, but for now, she'd just have to swallow her pride a little bit.

It was for her parents. She would do anything to make sure they were safe. Even hand him the keys and then walk around to slide into the passenger seat.

He started the engine immediately and was driving through the rows of RVs and boats to the gate.

She didn't need to be told to get out and lock it back up

behind them when he paused outside the facility. Ideally, no one would ever know they'd been here.

*Ideally.*

"Are you sure you can get a replacement in? We want to be as under the radar as we can possibly be. If the car is flagged as stolen…"

"I'm sure," Holden said simply. "Now, which way?"

"Head east for right now. Just stay on this road."

"We're going to need to stop and get some gas."

"There's a station about ten miles along this road. Just get going."

He did so, and Willa had to decide if she'd pull out the papers here in the car, or in the bathroom at the gas station.

She'd asked him to trust her. She'd said they had to trust each other. Even while she'd been keeping secrets. Secrets he'd seen through.

She studied his profile as he drove. He was classically handsome. All square jaw and high cheekbones. The stubble that had grown in overnight gave him a rough edge, even with the slight cleft in his chin, but his eyes were so blue he somehow still looked…very close to regal. She could picture him in a suit, or something equally elegant. As easily as she could picture him in jeans and a T-shirt enjoying a drink in a bar.

He was a man who could slide into surroundings and have pretty much anyone eating out of the palm of his hand.

*Including you.*

She didn't like that feeling, even being sure just about anyone would fall for it. But she was hardly *anyone*. She was the daughter of spies.

Spies who needed her help.

She was torn between what they'd want her to do and what *she* wanted to do. But hadn't she learned a long time ago she wasn't them? Couldn't be them. So, she had to be herself. Trust herself. And against her will, she trusted Holden Parker of some secretive group.

She'd saved his life. He'd attempted to save hers. They had to do this hand in hand, and she couldn't expect his hand if she didn't put hers in his.

She dug the papers out of her pocket and spread them over her lap.

"It's in code."

She hadn't even noticed him glance her way, but she was used to that kind of unnoticed split focus. "Of course it's in code."

"Do you know how to break it?"

Now she spared him a killing glance. She could stand him underestimating her, but honestly.

"Okay, okay, you can break it," he muttered, eyes back on the road. "How long?"

"Ten, fifteen minutes. Just keep driving. Stop at the gas station when we get to it. We'll go from there."

HOLDEN DROVE, ONE eye on the road, the other on Willa. She focused on the paper in front of her, and whatever decoding she did was in her head. She was wilting, though, exhaustion beginning to stamp itself across her face.

She'd need a nap once she could tell him where they were going. He opened his mouth to ask her how close she was, then closed it. He had a feeling she'd get that flinty, offended look again, and he…

Well, he wasn't sure why that affected him, but it did. He didn't like it. Irritated he was changing the way he did things, demanded things, because of her *feelings*, he focused fully on the road in front of him. Everything around them was flat, and he could see the gas station sign in the distance.

Summer sunlight shimmered across the concrete and the fields on either side. It was pretty country, he had to admit. Prettier still if you were looking for a kind of peace. *He* wasn't, of course, but he understood why Willa would be searching for some.

"Why Nebraska?" he found himself asking, when he should be quiet and let her work.

She lifted her head from the paper, squinted into the sunny morning. "Well, my choices were limited to an extent. It had to be somewhere small, out of the way. A place people wouldn't happen upon."

"I'm not saying Nebraska doesn't make sense for that, but so do a lot of states."

She slid a glance his way, as if considering to tell him something important. "I know you said your parents are… passed, but you knew them. You knew who you were and where you came from?"

He wanted to evade that question, but it wasn't fair when he'd asked a personal one of his own. "My parents weren't close to theirs."

"But you know who they were. You knew if your ancestors were immigrants or Revolutionary War heroes or what have you."

Holden didn't. Not because he hadn't been able to, just because it hadn't been a topic they'd discussed. Holden's parents had moved away from their own parents, and the contact had been limited and tense. He'd never wondered about *history*. He'd only been concerned with his mother living.

Then she hadn't.

"I wasn't allowed to know," Willa was saying. "I'm not supposed to know. The names my parents use aren't the names they were given by theirs."

Holden's eyebrows raised. "That sounds like you know."

"I figured it out. When I still thought I might follow in their footsteps and be a spy. I was about twelve, and we'd settled in a place in Indiana where I went to middle school for seventh and eighth grade. My classmates were doing projects about their grandparents. I had nothing. So I set out to find something."

"Without your parents knowing?"

Willa nodded. "Sometimes I have to wonder, because of what they do and who they are, if they let me find out what I wanted to know. If it was…a cookie crumb of sorts. Regardless, I found it. I traced my ancestors as best I could. Civil War heroes and revolutionaries. You name it, they did it, and then for some reason, in the 1870s, they moved from Maine to Nebraska. Became farmers and lived quiet lives. My grandfather didn't even fight in World War II. I could never find out why they moved, why they changed. Maybe even if my father hadn't cut ties with his family for whatever reasons he did, I'd know. Or maybe I wouldn't. But I found a place not too far from where they settled and started to farm."

Holden tried to absorb all that and file it away as information about her, and her parents. No feeling. Just facts.

But it painted such a…picture. A young woman who wanted roots.

He'd lost all contact with his sisters and brothers. First because of the state, and then because he'd been labeled *bad* because of his connections to the Sons. He'd lost due to fate, and then he'd lost due to his own dumb decisions.

He thought about Sabrina, and a few other people he'd stumbled upon and brought into the North Star fold. Because they'd reminded him of himself.

Because they'd felt like a way to make up for his past mistakes.

Willa wasn't trying to do that, but it had a similar impe-

tus behind it. Reaching out for connection. For some tie…
since they couldn't have ties of their own.

Willa rubbed her eyes. "This code is particularly difficult. I guess it makes sense. It'd have to be a real emergency for me to want to pound my head against this." She
yawned and looked out at the upcoming gas station. "Coffee. I definitely need some coffee. But we'll keep heading
east until I can figure this out."

"You're tired."

"I'll muddle through." She shrugged as they pulled into
the gas station. "Gotta figure this out before we rest."

He stopped in front of a gas pump. She studied him
and frowned. "You need a hat to cover up that bandage.
People will remember that. Some people might even ask
questions. You want to blend in."

She was right about that. He had a lot of things in his
pack, but he didn't think he had a hat.

She reached into the back seat and picked up a hat with
a mesh back that read *Haines Feed Store*.

She plopped it on his head, gently pulling it down and
over the bandage. She studied him with serious green eyes.
"There." Her mouth curved. "You almost fit in."

"Almost?"

"I'm not sure you could ever look like a farmer, Holden.
But the hat helps you look less…lethal." She patted his
shoulder and moved to get out of the car, but she was holding on to that piece of paper with the code.

He narrowed his eyes, grabbing her arm before she
could slide out. When she looked back at him, frowning,
he refused to let himself feel guilty about being suspicious.

"You can't run," he said sternly.

She met his gaze, all open innocence. "I'm not going
to run." She dropped the piece of paper in the console between them as if it hadn't been her plan to take it with her

in the first place. Then she got out of the car and walked into the convenience store.

He believed her, though he probably shouldn't.

But that didn't mean he trusted her yet.

## Chapter Twelve

Willa couldn't stop yawning. There was a sign on the door about not using the bathroom without buying something, so she stared at the cooler full of caffeinated drinks. She wanted coffee, but the gas station fare left a lot to be desired, so she'd have to settle for a soft drink.

If she could engage her mind enough to pick one.

She had to stay awake long enough to crack the code. She was usually really adept at it, but this one was tough. Or she was that tired.

Or she was that afraid, knowing her parents had purposefully made it a challenge because they didn't want her coming after them half-cocked. Maybe they'd made it impossible. Maybe it was a lie.

She wanted to lean her forehead against the cool glass and have a good cry. And then sleep for twelve hours straight. At least. Then she wanted to wake up and have this all be a dream.

The door she'd been all but leaning against opened, and she had to step back. Holden pulled out a variety of soft drink bottles. "There. That should do it. Come on. You're dead on your feet."

She wanted to argue with him, but of course he was right. "How come you aren't?"

"Practice," he returned simply.

She wanted to grumble and pout, but they got up to the checkout counter and she forced a polite smile at the cashier.

"I need to use the bathroom."

The woman eyed her then pulled out a big pipe from underneath the counter. A tiny key dangled off it. "Round back," she said with a smoker's rasp as she began to ring up Holden's purchases.

Willa took the ridiculous "key fob" and walked out of the gas station. It was mostly empty. There was an old man in overalls—no shirt—walking his dog down the scraggly sidewalk in front of the gas station, but that was it. No cars drove by.

Willa let out a breath and tried to roll away some of the tension in her shoulders. No one was following them. She just had to figure out the code and they could get to her parents. If they didn't stop anymore, surely she could get to them before they were hurt.

This wasn't about killing. Whoever had shot at them hadn't killed her, and if they *wanted* her it was to threaten her parents. To get something out of them.

She rounded the corner of the station to the back. There were two cars parked here. She'd only seen one worker in the gas station, but that didn't mean someone hadn't been in the back. Both cars were unremarkable, aging sedans that fit the means of the workers.

Willa studied the two doors on the back side of the building—rusting and sun worn—the signs between men and women so faded she could barely make them out. Still, she'd spent enough time on the road to know that she wanted the women's bathroom—they were cleaner. Always.

Of course, *cleaner* didn't mean clean. Willa wrinkled her nose as she stepped inside the dark, dank bathroom.

There was one lone lightbulb to flick on—no windows to let in the sunlight.

The floor was sticky, the sink rusted, the soap dispenser empty. On a sigh, she did what she had to do and then attempted to wash her hands the best she could. She hoped she could get a shower soon. Maybe scrub herself with bleach.

On another yawn, she grabbed the pipe and opened the door back into the bright day. She squinted against the sun before stepping forward.

The blast of pain was so sudden, so fierce she stumbled back. Which gave her a second to gather her wits before the man stepped in the doorway of the bathroom. She hadn't dropped the pipe, so she used it.

She didn't know what he'd done to her head. Punched her or hit her with something, but she knew if he got her in here and closed the door, she would be in some serious trouble. She was having trouble seeing with it being so bright outside and so dark in the small bathroom, so she could only swing the pipe wildly and try to use it as the worst weapon she could muster as she pressed forward.

She would not be pushed back into this bathroom. She would not go down that easily. She could fight. She wouldn't panic. The circumstances weren't comfortable, but self-protecting wasn't supposed to be. If she could just get him out into the sunlight, her eyes could adjust and she'd stop feeling like she was fighting blind.

She pushed. She whacked the pipe against the man. He grunted but got one meaty, sweaty hand wrapped around her arm and jerked her backward. She slid a bit, but immediately charged. No, no, she would not be stuck in this gross room to die.

She pushed. She hit. At one point, she bit. That had the man howling out in shocked pain, and it gave her the chance to push past him and out into the bright light of day. She knew he'd followed, was on her heels. But she was at least free from the horrible-smelling room.

Now she could *really* fight.

*Finally.*

"Now you're going to regret it." Something hot and sticky dripped into her eye, but she blinked it away and held her fists up. She realized then he had a gun strapped to his hip. But he wasn't using it.

He wanted her alive. It was both relief and irritation. Oh, he was sure as hell not getting her alive.

She advanced. Her first kick wasn't meant to hurt, but to knock the gun off the holster on his side. It didn't work, but it had him thinking about the gun. He grappled for it, and as he did she slammed a fist into his face as hard as she could.

The gun toppled to the ground as he brought his hands up to his face. Clearly, he didn't think she could fight. He hadn't anticipated *this*. They never did.

So, she didn't let up. She punched, she kicked, she shoved, until he was back in the bathroom and she was outside. She slammed the door shut as he tried to reach out and stop her. The scream of pain echoed across the quiet morning, though it was muffled almost immediately as she managed this time to get the door completely shut. She shoved the pipe into the handle of the door so that he wouldn't be able to push out. "You messed with the wrong spy's daughter," she muttered, leaning against the door as she tried to catch her breath and fight off the dizziness stealing over her.

She flipped around and leaned her back against the door. She needed to get away from here, but her energy seemed to drain from her body all at once.

Holden skidded around the corner, gun drawn and murder in his gaze. She might have been afraid if her head didn't hurt so much. "About time," she muttered.

Something flickered in his gaze, but then it was gone. "You're bleeding," he said flatly.

"Yeah, you should see the other guy." She wasn't sure how much longer she'd last on her own two feet, so she didn't reach up and touch the spot on her head that hurt like hell. That would likely send her into a full-fledged faint, and she wasn't going to do that in front of Holden.

"He's in the bathroom," she managed, breathing through the weird haze around her vision.

"Move aside," he said in that same cold, flat tone of voice.

She moved out of his way, didn't even think about questioning him. She was too busy trying to remain upright.

THERE WAS RAGE. There was guilt. So many familiar feelings piling up in his chest, but at the center was something worse.

Fear.

There was a trickle of blood down Willa's face, and she was pale. If he had to guess, she was barely managing not to pass out.

She'd fought off someone and locked him in a bathroom, and Holden didn't want to tear whoever it was limb from damn limb until there was nothing left. Not in the moment.

He wanted to scoop her up and get her away from here. He wanted to deposit her back at her farm and keep her safe and sound. He wanted to erase the wounds on her face and comfort her. *Heal* her. Apologize, prostrate, for ever having let her out of his sight.

He wanted, so desperately, to make it okay.

But that wasn't his job.

He jerked the pipe out of the door handle and opened the door, leading with his gun barrel.

The man sat on his butt in the middle of the bathroom. His face was bleeding, his hand hung at an odd angle. He looked up at Holden with venom in his gaze. "I don't care if I die."

It was a bluff. Holden could read the terror in the man's gaze. Maybe surprise that Willa wasn't such an easy target. He was trying to put on a brave face, but he was *terrified* of dying.

Which meant he didn't think he'd die by failing this mission. Odd. Still, Holden would play the game. "Then it's good I'm not going to kill you," Holden replied, though he held the gun pointed at the man. Not at his chest or head as the man might have expected. "Just shoot off an important piece of anatomy."

The man covered his hands over his crotch, eyes widening. "Hey."

"Three seconds to tell me what you know." All the ocean of feelings inside him had been cordoned off. His voice was mostly flat. If there was any inflection, it was pure violence.

"The cops'll come. That cashier knows you're the only one who's—"

"Three."

"—been here. You'll be wanted for murder."

"Two."

"You don't know what you're getting yourself into here, son. Just let me go and—"

"One," Holden said with a shrug, flicking the safety off the gun.

"All right! Don't…" The man huddled in the corner of the stinky, scummy bathroom and held up his hands. "You can have her. I know they put an open call out and all, but a couple grand isn't enough to kill another guy over. Come on, man. We're all just trying to make a buck."

Holden's brain scrambled to put that information together. Open call. So, he wasn't the only one after Willa. He glanced at her quickly. She still stood right there, looking like death.

*Your fault, Parker.*

He looked back at the man. Open call. A couple grand. "Funny, I met another guy who said the same thing. He made the mistake of getting in my way."

"I won't. Promise. I've got other jobs. You take the girl." He held up his clearly broken hand. "Too much trouble. I don't want her. I'd take a percentage…" The main trailed off as Holden's finger curled around the trigger.

"Okay, okay. No percentage. You take her and drop her off. You take the money. Just let me go and I'll disappear."

Drop-off. "Where'd they tell *you* to drop her off? Because the last guy either had a different point, or he was lying to me." Holden shrugged. "I don't like it when people lie to me."

"Different…" The man didn't even try to hide his confusion. "You mean they're giving us different ones?"

Holden shrugged. "Seems like. Which one they give you?"

His expression went cagey. "Which one they give you?"

"Who's got the gun, smart guy? I…incapacitated the last guy who didn't answer me. I'll do the same to you. No skin off my nose."

"For a couple grand? Surely you aren't that desperate," the man said, a wheedling note to his voice.

"Think again, friend."

"Fine. Whatever. I'm out of this one. Killdare Wildlife Refuge. Lake three."

Holden nodded. "Guess the last guy was lying to me.

You'll live." But Holden slammed the door and shoved the pipe back in the handle. It immediately began to rattle.

"Hey! Hey, let me out of here." The man banged on the door, but Holden slid his arm around Willa's waist and pulled her forward. "We got to get out of here and quick. Can you jog or do you want me to carry you?"

"I can…"

But Holden didn't bother. She wasn't steady on her feet, so he swept her up into his arms.

"Hey," she protested—weakly at best.

He carried her to the car, hoping they could get out of here before the cashier wondered where her bathroom key had gone. He carried Willa all the way to the car and deposited her in the passenger seat.

He resisted every urge to check her wounds, to buckle her up. They had to get out of here before the police got involved.

He skirted the hood and got in the driver's side. The cashier was coming out the front door of the station, yelling at them to stop.

Holden didn't stop. He got in the car and drove. Fast.

He had to get away from here, and any police interference. Then he'd figure out where to go from there.

"Hey. Eyes open," he said sharply when hers started to droop. "Where's this nature area?"

"I don't know," she mumbled.

"Yes, you do. You need to tell me how to get there."

She blinked, straightening in her seat. "I'm not familiar with it. It can't be around here."

Holden swore under his breath. "Grab my phone and search for it, Willa."

She slumped again. "My head hurts."

"I know. I know it does." He bit back an endearment and had to fight the desperate need to stop the car and take care of her wounds. But they had to get somewhere safe. "But you don't want to pass out, do you?"

"No." She blinked a few times, squinted. She lifted her hand.

"Don't do that," he said sharply, and she dropped her hand before touching the gash on her forehead. "Grab the phone. Look up Killdare Wildlife Refuge."

She blew out a breath and grabbed his phone. He watched her out of the corner of one eye, keeping his attention on the road as much as he could.

Her fingers were clumsy, but she tapped something into his phone. She squinted at the screen. "It's up in the corner."

"What corner?" Holden demanded. Every ounce of energy was centered on making himself keep going.

"You know. The corner." She made a vague hand motion. "South Dakota. Wyoming. That corner."

Holden frowned. Nebraska meeting South Dakota and Wyoming. There weren't any decent-size towns in that area, but he wasn't familiar with the wildlife refuge either. Worse, that was hours away.

But he did know of a North Star safe house in that general area. They could get there, duck out of police notice and patch her up. Regroup. Come up with a plan.

He glanced at her, still squinting at his phone. She was bloody and there were bruises already blooming on her face and neck. It made him want to tear something apart. Or maybe turn back around and go ahead and shoot the moron in the bathroom.

But they couldn't do that. Especially if the cashier had already called the police.

"You'll tell me if you feel sick," Holden ordered, increasing his speed as he put his full focus on the road in front of him. "If your vision doubles. Anything majorly off, you tell me. And for the love of God, don't try to touch it."

"You're so bossy," she said grumpily. "Do you think my parents are there? At this refuge?"

"No. He was supposed to drop you off. Doubtful they're there."

"He wasn't anybody, was he? Just some random...bad guy. Trying to get paid. He didn't know anything. He's not the real threat."

"He did enough of a number on you."

She shook her head, then winced. "I was paying attention. I looked at the cars. The people. He shouldn't have been there."

"But he was. That ambush could have killed you."

She made a scoffing sound. "I don't see how. I kicked his butt with no help from you."

Holden wasn't sure how he'd ever live with those minutes of buying drinks and snacks and taking his sweet time to check on her. When he knew they were in danger... He'd just been so sure they were too sneaky...

They *had* been. No one could have followed them. Something was off. So off.

Unless someone knew she'd go for that car in the storage facility. He slid her a look. She was deathly pale and bleeding. He could hardly float the idea her parents were giving the wrong people information about her when she was beaten up.

Because of him.

Worse than even that, there was the fact ammunition had been delivered to Evening, and that moron in the bathroom hadn't used it. Hadn't had it on him.

Was there someone else? Someone not so bad at their job. Someone who knew something. Someone who was tracking them, even now?

Holden checked his rearview mirror. No signs of a tail, but that didn't mean they were in the clear.

"You see a town up there called Vollmer? That's where we're headed. You navigate. Back roads as much as possible."

"I just want to go to sleep," she said, sounding so sad he thought his heart might crack in two.

But he didn't have time to have a heart right now. "You'll stay awake, Willa. One way or another. Now. Where should I turn next?"

# *Chapter Thirteen*

Willa's head was pounding. She felt sweaty and nauseous. Still, she stared at the map on Holden's phone and told him where to go. She didn't mention wanting to puke. Or how badly she wanted a drink of water or a bottle of pain relievers.

She just told him where to go. She understood how important it was for them to get out of range of the police. There was no doubt in her mind the cashier had called the police. No doubt in her mind she would have given a very good description of Holden and Willa to the police at that.

They'd been driving for hours, though. It felt like days. Still, no one had stopped them. And they hadn't stopped. Holden drove a bit like a bat out of hell, and every bump jarred her quickly stiffening body.

But she could tell they'd made some progress. There were trees now. Far more rock outcroppings than there were back in Evening.

"Hand me the phone," he ordered.

He'd been so stiff and authoritative the whole drive. She understood it was because there was a danger they didn't understand and couldn't predict. Because he had a lead, and now he needed to follow it.

And she suspected he was being so…uptight because she'd been hurt. She didn't know why that'd make him all robotic, but she couldn't ignore the fact he hadn't acted like this the whole time—even after she'd tried to beat him with a fire poker.

Still, she was too…drained and hurting and miserable to try and fight with him right now. She handed him the phone and didn't even complain when he kept driving like crazy with one eye on his phone.

He took a couple unexpected turns that had her entire body jostling as he went off-road.

"What on earth are you…" She trailed off as a small cabin, completely surrounded by trees, came into view. He didn't slow up, and the car stopped just inches away from the front door.

"Where are we?"

He didn't answer, just got out of the car. She moved to follow, pushing open the door, but he was there before she'd gotten it half-open. He had her up in his arms again before she could move.

She could walk and she opened her mouth to tell him so, but she wanted desperately to simply lay her head against his shoulder and go to sleep, knowing she'd be safe here— in his arms. The image was so appealing, and everything hurt, so she just…let herself. Rest her head on him, close her eyes and let him take her wherever. She didn't even open her eyes when he stepped into the cabin. She let herself drift until he was putting her down on a surprisingly soft mattress.

"Don't go to sleep," he said sharply. But her eyes were drifting closed again, and sleep seemed like a wonderful alternative to…everything.

She vaguely heard him banging around in another room. It kept her from fully falling to sleep, but she could still kind of float in a weird, gray, exhausted, pained space.

Until he took her by the shoulders. She'd lain down

and didn't quite remember it, but he pulled her into a sitting position. When she opened her eyes, he was scowling at her. But his face was close and his eyes were on hers.

So incredibly blue. She'd seen multiple oceans, seen the bright blue of a tropical island. She'd seen so many blues the world had to offer, and still his eyes reminded her of a Nebraska winter sky, on the days the wind was so cold it felt like knives, but also like the world was hers and hers alone.

Then he pushed something against the throbbing pain on her temple, and she yelped in surprise. Then groaned at the stinging burn of what she could only assume was some kind of antiseptic.

He did it again, and she tried to bat his hands away. "Stop that," she said to him, trying to squirm out of his reach.

"You stop that," he returned, holding her in place with one arm. "I've got to clean you up."

"Use water," she said, still trying to fight him off, though she didn't have much energy to put any strength behind it.

"Sit still," he ordered through gritted teeth. "You had a fight in a middle-of-nowhere gas station bathroom. You're lucky I'm not dropping you into a tub of bleach."

Willa grimaced, suddenly feeling ten times grimier than she had. "I need a shower."

"You need to sit still and let me make sure there aren't any serious injuries here." When she tried to wiggle away from him again, he blew out a breath. "Was I such a baby when you were bandaging me up?"

"You were unconscious."

"I can arrange it."

"Big talk," she muttered. Then sighed. "I guess we're going to have matching head wounds."

He grunted, still prodding at the pain in her head. It still stung, but not with the same force. He lifted her hair out of the way, this way and that. "I think you should be okay without stitches," he muttered before dropping her hair. He studied her face with narrowed eyes, and then his hand was on her cheek. "Does anything else hurt?" he demanded, holding her face gently and staring at her fiercely, practically nose to nose.

Her whole body hurt, and she wondered just what he'd do if she told him that. Would he touch her everywhere?

*Honestly, Willa, is now the time for silly fantasies?*

She didn't mind making time for them usually, even when in danger, but her heart was thudding dangerously against her chest, and she couldn't break the moment. If he didn't, she was liable to do something incredibly stupid. Like touch him back. "It was a fight, Holden. I won."

He muttered something truly filthy and then, in direct contrast to his swearing, gently laid his forehead against hers, his big, rough hand still cupping her cheek.

She was almost afraid to move, afraid to breathe. He was touching her with such gentle reverence, like she meant something to him, and she wanted...

Well, she wanted that. Even more when his mouth touched hers. It was light. Featherlight. The gentlest touch of lips.

Her eyes fluttered closed, and she sank into it. Hey, he started it. Why not apply a little pressure, fit her bottom lip at the seam of his lips. Reach out, slowly and gently so as not to break the moment, and rest her hands on his shoulders.

He was so tense there, and yet his mouth was still gentle on hers.

"I'm...sorry." The words were unexpected, but any sting she might have felt by them was completely undercut by the fact his lips were still touching hers…as if he couldn't quite bring himself to pull away.

"For what?" she asked, a little too breathlessly, making sure her lips didn't leave his until he did the pulling away.

He pushed off the bed and stood. "Everything." He stepped away, first running his hands through his hair then over his face. "This has been a mess from top to bottom, and the last thing I should have done was take advantage of you."

She wanted to think it was sweet, but the last part irritated her. If she was a different kind of woman, like the kind of women he seemed to work with, he wouldn't feel *guilty*. He just thought she was…fragile. "Well, don't be stupid," she snapped.

"It isn't stupid."

"It is. That kiss wouldn't take advantage of a pig."

"I'm sorry… What?"

"It was a nothing kiss, Holden. I mean, I'm not saying I didn't enjoy it, because I did. Immensely. But it wasn't an advantage when I could have backed away, pushed you off."

"You've been injured. You might have a concussion. I didn't even bandage you up, I just—"

"Oh, shut up. Congratulations. You ruined it. Now, is there a shower in this place? Never mind. I'll find it." And she set out to do just that, letting her anger lead the way.

HOLDEN HAD NO idea what had just happened. He had no idea what had come over him. Just that she was safe and beautiful, but hurt and… He'd just needed to…

It was ridiculous. He'd been out of line. The apology had been the appropriate response, even if it *had* been a nothing kiss.

It hadn't felt like nothing. It felt like being turned inside out. It felt like being absolved of every mistake he'd ever made, and there was no way he could ever be absolved.

He heard the pipes groan. She must have found the shower. Something he wouldn't allow himself to think about too deeply.

There wasn't time to think about anything, except… this assignment that didn't add up. Too many pieces, not enough information, and what little information he had didn't make much sense.

They wanted to take Willa. That was clear. If they had her parents, and were trying to get some kind of information out of them, bringing in Willa would be an incentive for them to spill the beans.

Surely if her parents really were adept spies, though, they'd know whatever information they gave would be the end of all three of their lives.

The sound of water running stopped. Holden braced himself. He had to focus. He had to keep his normal, un-biased, analytical, *intelligent* wits about him. He was going to have to bandage her up and keep his hands to himself. What they both really needed was sleep. They didn't have a ton of time, but a couple hours would put them both on better footing.

Willa waltzed back into the room, wearing nothing but a towel.

"What the hell are you doing?" he demanded. Horrified that he couldn't seem to make himself look away. Her legs were long and toned, a creamy white that must have rarely seen sun. Her arms were tanned and impressively muscled. Her hair was free, an even redder gold when wet with little drops of water trickling from the ends of it over down to the towel. Freckles littered her shoulders and he…

His tongue felt well and truly twisted and stuck in his dry throat.

"Well, I'm not going to put those gross bathroom-fight clothes back on now," she said dismissively. She smirked at him. "Do you have anything I could wear?"

He stalked to the closet and pawed around for something that might fit. He tossed a T-shirt and some sweatpants at her.

She began to drop the towel, and he whirled away. Oh no. No, no, no, she was not going to play this game with him. He wouldn't fall for it. "Do you really think now is the time for this?"

"No. I don't. But I get some enjoyment out of you being all huffy and uncomfortable and if you don't find a way to enjoy things even in the toughest circumstances, life can be a real pain."

He happened to agree with her. Or had before he'd taken this job. She'd seemed to take all the humor out of him. She made him feel stiff and uptight. She made him feel like Reece, and that was unacceptable.

He was loose. He was fun. He was *charming*. What kind of spell had she put on him?

Still, he didn't turn to face her. He kept his back to her, his eyes on the ceiling and his thoughts on the fact he had to somehow handle this when he'd never felt so tested in his life.

"Do you have a plan?" she asked. When he didn't answer, she huffed out a breath. "I'm dressed, you big prude."

He turned around slowly, cautiously. She was indeed dressed and back to sitting on the bed. He crossed over to her, reluctantly taking a bandage from the first aid kit.

He did have a plan. But he hated the plan. Worse, he knew she'd be all about it. Maybe if he talked it out, he could come up with an alternative. Something that didn't involve putting her in any more danger. "Did you hear what the guy was saying?"

"Not really. Something about it not being enough money to kill over?"

"He said it was an open call." With as much space between them as he could manage casually, Holden adhered the bandage to the cut on her temple. "Which is basically where someone sends out a job to the kind of people who do stupid things for money and says they'll pay whoever does the job."

"Like Craigslist for bad guys?"

"Something like that." He held up a finger so she'd sit and wait and went to the kitchen to grab an ice pack. When he returned, he handed it to her, and she put it on her temple without needing the directive to do so.

Her expression was thoughtful. "He had a gun and he didn't shoot me. So the job was, what? Kidnapping me?"

"Seems like." But it didn't add up to the ammunition being sent to Evening. Holden doubted very much if the guy from the bathroom had been the man who'd gotten the ammunition. Now that he'd had time to think it through, the man in the bathroom had been much shorter than the man in the post office video. Also not the brightest or meanest man he'd ever met, which meant he didn't fit for hit man. He was just some moron who liked to get paid for hurting and scaring people.

"What are you thinking?" Willa asked.

"I'm not sure yet. Something doesn't add up here." But he didn't need to tell her all the different ways. Why so cheap if the kidnapping was important? A few thousand bucks wasn't much for an offense with a pretty steep punishment.

"You know what we have to do, Holden. I know you do."

# *Chapter Fourteen*

Willa could see by his expression that he did. He didn't like the idea, obviously. She couldn't say she was too keen on it either, but what other option did they have? She'd checked to make sure her parents hadn't returned her message when she'd been on Holden's phone.

Nothing.

They wouldn't ignore her SOS. They were either continually busy or in serious trouble. There was only one way to get to them.

She watched Holden pace, clearly trying to find another way out of this. She gave him a few minutes to do so. After all, she'd like to do the one where the chances of her ending up dead weren't quite so high.

So, she watched him pace and think from her seat on the bed in the cute little cabin. Was it his? It didn't seem like it. Too utilitarian. It didn't suit him. It probably belonged to his secret group.

She sighed. She was clean, bandaged, wearing no underwear under clothes there were a little too big for her. Holden had kissed her, then acted like seeing her naked would be a personal assault. She refused to let the gravity of the situation undercut her enjoyment of *that*.

"You have to take me to the drop-off, Holden."

He scowled at her. "It's not the only option."

"It is. You have to pretend to be one of these guys who took the job, and succeeded. You could do that, right? Whoever these guys are wouldn't know you work for some group?"

"No, they wouldn't," he said bitterly. "It could be done, but—"

"No buts. That's the plan. You drop me off, like the guy said."

"Then what, Willa? What do you think happens then?"

"They probably take me to my parents and torture me in front of them until my parents tell them what they want to know." She shrugged. She didn't want to think too deeply about the specifics, even though she knew it was something of an inevitability. "But I'd have you."

He looked a little bit like she'd shot him. She was surprised he didn't crumple to the ground.

"I know it's risky, Holden. I understand enough of what my parents do to understand the dangers. But if we work on this together, maybe you could figure out where they are. Or who they are. You and your group could save us."

"Or you could end up dead," he said flatly.

"Yeah. And so could you and my parents and anyone." She knew he wanted her to take this more seriously, but she'd always known this very situation was possible. What and who her parents were had been a shadow over her entire life. Part of why she'd leaned so hard into independence and her own farm was that she'd known her life expectancy could very well be very short.

What she'd never thought possible was help. Someone by her side. Her parents would save her if they could, lay down their lives. She was sure. But Holden could actually *help* her accomplish something. He was her partner now. It gave her an optimism she could only be grateful for.

"You'll drop me off where the guy said," Willa said resolutely. "I don't think my parents will be there, do you?"

"No," he said, an acidic bitterness to the word.

"We'll have to play it by ear, of course. Maybe you let them take me. Maybe you don't. Maybe you follow them. Maybe you bring in your team. I'd trust you to make the right decision in the moment. It really depends on who's there and what the setup is."

He whirled away and began to pace, muttering to himself. There was emotion there. Waves of it. The kind her parents had always warned her about. The kind she'd never been able to fight.

And still, she trusted him to do the right thing. Maybe he'd made a few missteps to his way of thinking—her chaining him to a bed, her fighting off the kidnapper on her own—but he'd handled the kidnapper in a way that never would have occurred to her, getting information out of the guy. They were closer to getting somewhere than she would have been on her own.

"It's the plan you had in mind, isn't it?" she asked gently.

He stopped pacing, and she watched fascinated as he reined all that energy and anger and—she thought maybe—a little fear in. He was cold eyed and tense when he faced her, but not emotional. "Yes," he said through gritted teeth. "That doesn't mean it's the best one."

She smiled at him. "You know it is."

He stood there, still as a mountain. His gaze was blank, but his jaw was tense. He was waging an inner battle. "We need some sleep."

Irritated he wouldn't admit it, she started to get off the bed. "My parents' lives—"

He pushed her gently back onto the mattress. "Willa, you haven't slept for over twenty-four hours, and it's been longer than me. If we're going to face this down—and I'm not so sure we should—the least we need to do to prepare is sleep for a few hours. Not twelve. A few. Brains don't work without sleep."

She knew he was right. She *was* exhausted. But how did she sleep knowing her parents could need her immediate help? How was sleep supposed to solve anything?

She blew out a breath. "For how long?"

He pulled out his phone, tapped the screen. "We'll get four hours. I'm sending a message to my team. They'll scout the area and see what they can figure out before we get there."

She had to suppress a smile. He might *want* there to be another way, but clearly he knew they'd end up doing this. They had to.

"Go to sleep." He started to walk out of the room.

"Whoa, whoa, whoa. Where are you going?"

"To sleep on the couch."

"Yeah, right. You're going to go out there and work. Not gonna fly, buddy. Lie down in here." She patted the bed next to her.

He frowned at the spot but crossed over to it. "Maybe I don't want you taking advantage of me," he said, but he lowered himself onto the bed. With as much room between them on the mattress as possible.

"Of course you do."

He snorted, but he settled his hands over his chest and closed his eyes. She had the sense he went to sleep almost immediately. But as she stared at him, the dark blond lashes against his cheek, the strong jaw she was half tempted to run her fingers across, he turned away from her.

"Go to sleep, Willa," he ordered.

On a sigh, she set out to follow orders.

For now.

HOLDEN SLEPT FOR two hours. It was more than enough with the mixture of worry and adrenaline coursing through him. He eased out of the bed and let Willa continue to sleep.

He pored over the maps Elsie had emailed him, texted with his team as they arrived on-site and started a preliminary sweep of the area. When Shay phoned him, he considered ignoring the call.

He knew she was going to tell him things he didn't want to hear. Worse, he knew he wasn't as in control of himself as he needed to be. Shay would see it. Read into it. *Correctly* read into it.

But he had a job to do, and he wanted his boss on board. "Hey."

"We got ID on the guy at the gas station. Some penny-ante, low-rate thief. Can't imagine he's much of a threat."

Holden explained what the man had told him. He didn't outline his concerns about things not adding up. Shay would come to that conclusion on her own, and he didn't want Willa trying to eavesdrop if she woke up.

"What's Elsie got?"

"Not much," Shay said. "Computer is pretty encrypted, but she thinks she's making progress."

"Someone needs to be watching her. If there are multiple men trying to kidnap Willa, Elsie isn't safe at that farmhouse alone, even if she is in the bunker."

"She isn't alone."

"I thought you sent my whole team to the wildlife refuge."

"I did, but I called in a favor. You don't worry about Elsie. You worry about how you're going to get to these supposed spies."

"I'm going to have to let them take her, Shay." He had to say it out loud. He had to hope to God someone had a good reason for him not to do it.

But Shay wasn't that person. "Probably."

Holden bit back an oath. "How am I supposed to do that?"

"Would you do it if it was me? Or Sabrina? Or any of us, quite frankly?"

"She's not North Star."

"No, but she's not just any civilian either. Girl's got chops. Trust her to use them. Then do everything in your power to make sure it doesn't get her killed." Shay paused. Meaningfully. "I can send someone else in if you don't think you're emotionally detached enough to—"

"I'll handle it. Over and out," Holden muttered, hitting the end button with far too much force. If there was going to be blood on someone's hands, it was damn well going to be his own.

He got to his feet. The safe house had an array of weapons, and he picked what would be best for this mission. He picked out a few for Willa too. She could fight like the devil—no doubt her parents had trained her in how to shoot a gun as well.

Then he pushed away his guilt at pawing through her things and found the papers she'd been trying to make sense of before the gas station stop.

The code was complex, and he spent far too long trying to beat his head against it before his phone alarm went off, telling him to wake up Willa.

When he woke Willa up after her four hours of sleep, he foisted a sandwich on her. "Wake up. Eat. We leave in fifteen."

She blinked at him, sleep clouding her eyes. "Dream you was much nicer," she muttered.

He didn't let himself dwell on *that* comment. He left the sandwich on the nightstand and went back to getting ready. When she emerged from the room a few minutes later, she was pulling at the shirt she was wearing.

"I can't wear this."

The T-shirt was white and dangerously close to see-through. The sweatpants were baggy and loose. Holden wrenched his gaze away and went to the mudroom. He pulled her clothes out of the dryer then returned to the main room and handed them to her. "Washed and dried."

"Well, aren't you handy."

"Something like that."

She frowned at her own clothes, clean and warm from the dryer. "Did you sleep? You were supposed to sleep."

"I slept. Just not the full four hours. I had plans to make. Now, we need to go. We don't want to wait till dark. Get dressed, and eat that sandwich."

She grumbled but did as she was told. She still had shadows under her eyes, bruising that made his stomach clench into nasty knots. But she was awake and alert and...

Hell, he didn't know how he was going to do this. Only that he had to.

When she returned, they loaded up the car in silence. Holden didn't tell her the plan or where they were going. She didn't ask. She pored over her papers.

"Any luck?"

"Not really. Part of me wonders if it's...purposeful. Too hard for me to crack so I can't help them."

"I don't know anything about cracking codes, but I've got one of my men on it."

She frowned over at him. "Huh?"

"I sent a picture over. We don't have any code experts right now, but we have a few people with those kinds of brains."

"I didn't say you could do that."

"Are we on the same team or not, Willa?"

"We are, but these are codes my parents put together. This was for me. For me alone."

He couldn't say she sounded angry. Maybe closer to betrayed. Which he could hardly let bother him. "I have a job to do, Willa."

"Yes. I'm very well aware. I shouldn't have…" She shook her head and blew out a breath. There was *still* something she wasn't telling him.

It, along with his own ridiculous reactions, grated. The whole thing grated. He flicked a glance at her. She'd stopped looking at the code and stared very hard out the window. She twisted her fingers together, clearly lost in her own secretive thoughts.

"Sometimes I don't know if I'm doing the right thing," she said very quietly, and the sadness in her tone had that frustration twining into something closer to guilt.

"No one ever knows if they're doing the right thing, Willa. We just do our best guess."

She shook her head. "I just don't know if they would have wanted me to take that code. They gave me no clear SOS. It's just, I didn't think they ever would. Maybe I should have left it. Maybe I'm making things worse."

She was nervous. *He* was nervous. Which was fine. Nerves weren't something to conquer. They were something to control. He supposed any other emotions plaguing him at the moment were the same. He'd accept them.

He'd control them.

"We can't second-guess at this point, Willa. We have to move forward, armed with the information we have. I have a team in place, but they have to stay pretty far back to avoid detection. They won't intervene unless I give them the signal. Mostly, I want them there so if we do have to let these guys take you, I have more than just myself following the trail."

"But what if the guys suspect something?"

"One of two potential outcomes. One, they close up shop and head back to wherever they're headquartered. Not a bad option because we can follow them that way too."

"The other option is bloody shoot-out?"

Holden spared her a look. "They might try the offensive, but I have five guys on the area. From all my scouts, they've only got three."

"Three?"

"It's just a drop-off."

"A few thousand dollars. A few men. I can't say I feel all that important."

It was the part that grated. It was the part that didn't add up. Still, Holden kept his shrug nonchalant. "Maybe they don't expect you to put up much of a fight. Maybe you *aren't* that important." He wished he could believe it. "Maybe you're…an insurance policy. They have a different plan in place, but they'll use you if you have to."

She frowned at him. "Why do I get the sneaking suspicion you have a completely different and much more terrifying hypothesis?"

# Chapter Fifteen

His eyes stayed on the road, but she could have sworn his grip on the steering wheel tightened.

Fear drummed in Willa's throat, but she breathed through it carefully. It was all scary, but panic wouldn't solve anything.

"Holden."

"I don't have a more terrifying hypothesis. I don't have a hypothesis. But I don't like when things don't add up. You not being worth more attention doesn't fully add up." The car slowed. "But we don't have time to figure it out, because here we go."

She saw the sign for the wildlife refuge, and her heart thudded hard against her ribs, the beating seeming to echo in her ears. *Here we go.*

After they entered, Holden slowed to a stop next to a big sign that had a map of the area plastered on it.

"Lake three," he said, reaching through his rolled-down window and tapping the map. "This one right here. I want you to get a picture of this map in your head. If you have to run, you run north or south." He pointed to both directions on the map. "I've got men on either side there. One grabs you, he'll say, 'North Star.' That's the cue to let them take you wherever. They're safe. I've got east and west points, too, but they're farther out. So north or south. That's all you have to remember. I tell you to run—"

"I run north or south. I got it. Holden, what if this code tells us something important? Or to stay away? Or..."

"Do you want to backtrack? We can go wait in that cabin if you want, Willa. We'd be safe there. We can take the time to figure out the code."

She could tell he wanted her to agree. She knew she couldn't. In order for this to look like Holden really had her, he had to bring her today. Much more time and whoever had her parents would surely suspect this whole thing. She shook her head. "As long as they might be in danger..."

He gave a sharp nod, then started driving again.

"When we see the signal, I'm going to get out of the car slowly and carefully. I have weapons in the backpack I'll wear, but they'll search me probably. That's okay, I've got more in the car. The most important thing is to stay calm and let them do as much talking as possible."

Willa nodded. She tried not to look as terrified as she felt. She needed him to believe she was capable of this. That they were equal partners.

"I'm going to have to shake you around a bit, and when I do, that's when you start the waterworks, okay? Act like you're scared and I've roughed you up. We want them to think you're as weak as possible. The more they underestimate you, the better off we are."

Willa nodded. It centered her, oddly. She could act as scared as she felt, and it would only work in their favor.

"It is my last resort option to leave you with them. Understand that. If we have to go that route, you'll have six highly trained field operatives following you. I won't let anything happen to you."

It was probably foolish to think him saying *I* over *we*

meant something, but she could be foolish in her own mind. Especially now.

They pulled up to the sign for lake three. There was a lone fisherman standing at the lake. He held a pole but wasn't dressed for fishing. He was smoking a cigarette, and even though the jacket he wore concealed everything, even Willa could tell he was armed to the hilt.

"I'm going to get out. You stay in until I come get you. Remember, if you have to run, it's north or south. North Star is your safety net."

Willa nodded. She didn't trust her voice or, more, her expression now that the fisherman was watching them.

"Don't move."

Holden slid out of the car, and Willa could only sit in the passenger side seat, watching. Holden had his back to her, but she could see the fisherman as he turned to Holden.

Holden must have said something to go along with the wide hand gesture he made. The man flicked his cigarette into the lake. His eyes were dark and hard. He had a scar under one eye, a nose that listed to the left and a missing bottom tooth. He looked every part the bad guy.

Willa wished that could comfort her in some way. But so many things didn't add up, and she didn't know how to wait until they did.

She looked down at the code in her lap. She'd figured out one part, but it didn't make any sense on its own. Industries. That could be anything. It was a name. Something Industries. And she thought maybe the last word was *warehouse*.

A warehouse for something called… Maybe Ross Industries. She wished she could search in her phone, but she knew anyone could be watching her, and they'd think it irregular enough she was sitting here unrestrained.

Had Holden thought that through? Surely he knew better than to… He started stalking back toward the car. She couldn't read his expression, didn't know if it was real or a mask. He opened the car door and didn't waste time, didn't say anything.

He took her by the arm and pulled her out of the car. She pretended to try to shake off his grasp.

"You're sure lucky they wanted you in one piece, sweetheart," Holden said, pushing her forward with more theatrics than force. He took her to the fisherman, who'd since dropped his pole.

"What's your name?" the man demanded.

"None of your business," Willa retorted, but her voice shook, and she looked at the sun, rather than the man, which helped her eyes water effectively. "I don't know who you are or what you want, but you've made a mistake and you need to let me go."

"Or what?" Holden said with a nasty laugh.

She knew he was playing a part, but that didn't make it comfortable how well he fell into the role of sleazy bad guy.

"We need some proof you brought us the right package," the man said. He held up a hand, and a man materialized out of the woods surrounding the lake. Willa didn't have to feign fear. This man had his weapons strapped across his body like armor.

Like a very valid threat.

"Well, you don't need me for this part," Holden said, and he licked his lips and looked around nervously. He even loosened his grasp on her arm. "Just hand over the fee and I'll be out of your hair."

"Can't pay you until we have confirmation," the man replied, and his cold stare never left Willa. The other man came over to him, carrying something. He handed it over to the fisherman.

It was some kind of cloth. It looked a bit like the hand-kerchiefs her father liked to carry. The cold shudder of trepidation turned into an icy ball of fear as the man pulled a pair of glasses out of the handkerchief.

Willa let out a gasp, one she didn't have to feign. It could be coincidence, but clearly they wanted her to, at the very least, think they had her father. At the very worst, they knew enough about her father to replicate the things he would have carried on him. "Those are my father's. Where did you get that?"

He nodded at the second man. "Excuse us." Both men turned their backs on Willa and Holden. Willa wanted to run. Away, to save herself. At them, to get her father's belongings. But all she could do was stand next to this lake and breathe too hard, furiously fighting the tears that wanted to fall.

Someone *did* have her parents, and now they wanted her.

Suddenly Holden was close. Too close, his mouth prac-tically brushing her ear. "The minute the third guy comes out of the trees..." Holden muttered so quietly she almost couldn't hear him. "Fight for your life." Then he slid the handle of a knife into her hand.

HOLDEN HAD NO better grasp of what they were getting into, but he could see clearly based on how the men were po-sitioned, what weapons they had and what vehicles they didn't, that this wasn't supposed to end with either him or Willa making it out alive.

He'd made out two men in the woods straight off, though he knew he wasn't supposed to. He was *supposed* to be a penny-ante thief who wouldn't think to look for complications.

The hidden men were complications. Even when the one came out to "confirm" Willa's identification.

This was no kidnapping drop-off. Maybe they were only planning on killing him so he couldn't talk to anyone about the package he'd dropped off, but why make an open call then? That in and of itself left a trail.

It was possible, more than possible, that something had changed with Willa's parents. Either they already gave the information they were supposed to keep secret, or they'd already been eliminated—which made Willa the loose end that needed tying. It could even be they'd escaped, and Willa's head was going to be the payback. But the fact they had Willa's father's belongings had Holden, unfortunately, leaning toward them already being dead.

But still. Too many possibilities. Too many options. Holden wasn't about to let either of them be heads on a platter. Maybe she'd never forgive him if he prioritized her life over her parents' lives, but she was the life he had in his hands. Hers was the life he had to save.

He wanted to give her a gun, but it would take more time to get one out of the pack, so the knife he'd been able to conceal in his belt would have to do.

His team would come running once he shot his gun, but that had to be done at the right moment. When he and Willa weren't so close to the men here, who had much more powerful and lethal guns than he had access to at the moment.

There was also the possibility these three men had their own team waiting, though it would have to be much farther away than his if his team hadn't caught wind of them in their survey of the area.

The two men by the lake came back to them. "Come with us," the fisherman said, pointing toward the woods.

Holden gave it one last chance. "You don't need me anymore. Just hand over the cash and I disappear."

The man from the woods shook his head, but he didn't

speak. He grabbed Willa's arm and started pulling her toward the woods, the fisherman doing the same to Holden.

Holden didn't fight back yet. He let himself be dragged, though he put up a bit of a fight. Worked on looking scared instead of ready to fight for his life.

The third man stepped out of the woods and Holden watched, waited, calculated. Once they were within reach, he dug in his heels. "Now," Holden said firmly.

He landed an elbow into the taller man's nose with his free arm, then used his backpack as a weapon, flinging it off his back and at the new shooter. He didn't expect to hurt him, just wanted to knock the gun away for the extra seconds it would take for Holden to tackle him to the ground.

It felt a little bit too much like slow motion, because as the pack hit the gun, causing the gunman to jerk with the force, Holden had to trust Willa to fight off the third.

Until he could get to a gun and fire off a warning shot, his team would not advance.

Holden dived, knocking into the third shooter. It was easy then to land a few key punches and rip the high-powered weapon out of the man's hands.

He picked off the fisherman, who instead of going after him had turned his attentions to Willa. She'd clearly managed to knock both men off her, keeping them too busy dodging blows to shoot. If they were going to. Holden still wasn't completely convinced they were meant to kill Willa, but they certainly weren't afraid to hurt her.

Holden couldn't shoot the man she was currently grappling with because he could too easily hit her—no matter how good a shot he was, they were moving too much. So he had to throw himself into the fray.

He dived in and landed a punch, but got the wind knocked out of him by the man's elbow. Willa got a nasty shin kick in, but the man took her by the hair and threw her to the ground, raising his gun to point at Holden. Holden pushed him and grabbed him by the shirtfront, ready to use his own badly bruised head as a weapon, but out of the corner of his eye, Holden saw the man he'd knocked to the ground lift his arm. He ignored the one pointed at his heart and shot the guy on the ground who was still trying to shoot Willa.

Kill Willa.

For what? Why was she the target when she hadn't been a day ago?

Holden braced for the bullet that was no doubt coming for him. But when the shot rang out, just as he was attempting to jump out of the way, he felt nothing.

The man he'd been holding crumpled to the ground. It took Holden a second or two to let him go. To look up and see Gabriel, gun in hand, standing at the edge of the woods.

"Saved by the sniper," he muttered to himself, turning to find Willa. She was splattered with blood, but most of it wasn't hers. Thank God.

The North Star team began to tighten their circle around the nasty scene. One member to each immobilized or dead man. Gabriel came up to Holden, grim faced and serious. "We were moving in before your shot. We got an urgent message from Shay to move in."

"Why?"

Gabriel shrugged. "Wasn't given the details. Just told to get you guys out."

Holden frowned at that. It wasn't like Shay not to lay the whole picture on the line. She didn't like her operatives acting without knowing all the details, all the whys and all the possible outcomes. "You got your phone?" Holden had left his in the car, knowing he didn't want any of the men he'd originally been meeting to get a handle on North Star property.

Gabriel handed his over. Holden went through the complicated process of patching through to Shay.

"Saunders?"

"What's going on?" Holden demanded.

He heard Shay sigh. But when she spoke, it was all authoritative demand. "Report on the situation at hand, Holden."

"We fought them off, then my team saved my butt. What's going on that you sent them early and not on my signal?" Thank God she had, but that didn't ease the discomfort in his gut that something was very, very wrong.

"That code Willa's parents left her? It isn't just a location, or information about who they're working for or why. If our code breaker is right, they gave her evidence on an entire arm of the organization the feds are after. An organization that'll do anything to make sure it doesn't get into the feds' hands."

# Chapter Sixteen

Willa watched as Holden's expression went completely lax. His surprise terrified her more than fighting off men with guns. What could surprise Holden at this point?

"We've got to get out of here," Holden said, taking her arm. And giving her absolutely no comfort whatsoever. He tossed the phone back at his team member without a second glance.

"But—"

He shook his head, issuing orders to the members of his team. They'd take care of the mess, no doubt, but Holden was leading her to the car. Getting out of here. When none of this had gone to plan.

"Hold—"

"I'll explain everything when we're back at the safe house. I promise."

But he sounded gutted. A little horrified. "Is it my parents?" she asked, feeling light-headed. Some mix of adrenaline wearing off and utter terror that he'd gotten news her parents were dead and none of this mattered anymore.

"No. No word on your parents," he said, and his hold on her gentled as he opened the passenger side door.

She let out a relieved breath and all but melted into the seat. But there was a tension, a worry in him as he walked around the front of the car, and she couldn't help but feel both seep into her bones.

If they hadn't had word on her parents, what was so bad? That they'd been willing to kill her?

She'd had a decent amount of certainty the men had wanted her alive, until Holden had said *now* as they'd reached the third man. There'd been something about the look that man had given her, the way the gun was pointed at her, that made her believe they meant to kill her. Then and there.

Why would they want her alive in one breath, and dead in another?

Holden didn't drive fast this time. No, the pace was well within the speed limit, his gaze was steady on the road, and even when they turned off onto the unmarked path to the cabin, he kept his silence.

The silence felt oppressive, but Willa didn't know what to say to break it. She should demand answers, but she was terrified of them.

They'd come anyway. Whether she asked or not.

Holden stopped the car in front of the cabin they'd been in. Had it only been a few hours ago? It was full on dark now, and Willa wished she was home with her animals. But there was starlight and moonlight and...

She glanced over at Holden as she followed him to the door. Something was going on. Something he didn't know how to work out. She figured a man like Holden wanted to figure it out before he told her.

There was no time for that. If these men suddenly wanted her dead, then the chances of her parents living through this grew slimmer and slimmer with every minute.

They stepped inside, and Holden locked the door behind her. He set a security code, and though he didn't make a full tour of the cabin, she could tell his eyes swept everything, making sure no one had come in while they'd been gone.

"We should change our bandages," he said, and she had to assume he saw nothing suspicious. "Ice everything down. Get a meal in. Then sleep. We both need to sleep." He moved for the kitchen.

Willa didn't scoff or argue. She simply stood in the middle of the living room and stared at him. Waiting.

He grabbed an ice pack out of the freezer and turned to face her.

"You'll explain that phone call to me now," she said, sounding calm and measured. She wasn't sure how. She felt a lot like sinking to the floor and crying.

But there was no time.

Holden sighed and dropped the ice pack on the counter, then scrubbed his hands over his face. "It was Shay. About the codes your parents gave you. It isn't just whereabouts or even the name of who they're working for."

Willa shook her head. "I know there's a lot on the papers, but they include a lot of decoy information so that—"

"My team broke the code, Willa. We know what it says. It's evidence. Evidence against a very dangerous organization. They know you have it or have access to it. That's why they wanted you alive."

"But then they didn't."

"I know. Something happened. Something changed. They wanted you dead."

Willa absorbed that blow, but it didn't take long. Her wheels were already turning. Because something had changed and it wasn't her or Holden, but she didn't know a darn thing about Holden's group.

For a while there, whoever had her parents had only wanted to kidnap her. They could have killed her back at the farmhouse, but they'd tried to kill Holden. The job that had been set out for two-bit criminals had been to take her, alive, to the drop-off location.

Something changed. His group had the information her parents had left her for emergencies only. "This group didn't always know I had access to evidence. Neither of us knew we had evidence. Right here. With us."

Holden's eyebrows drew together. "What does that mean?"

"It means they didn't know I had a code, which includes even more important information than I thought, until you sent pictures to your team. Up until that meet up at the lake, they only wanted to take me. They didn't want me dead."

If he hadn't put that information together, he didn't show surprise, and yet something in him changed—she couldn't have said what. Only that it made her...uneasy. On top of scared and suspicious.

"My team isn't dirty, if that's what you're saying."

"I wouldn't know, Holden. I don't know anything about them. Why should I trust them? Why should I trust…" She didn't finish the sentence, because it was ridiculous to question trusting him at this point. She did, whether she'd wanted to or not, and they'd worked together to save each other's lives more than once at this point.

"Go ahead and say it," Holden said flatly.

Temper started to mount, mixing with fear. She knew irrational outbursts could only follow, but how much was a woman supposed to just *take*? "I wish I could say it! I wish I could mean it! But I trust you. With my life, turns out. So don't get all testy on me. Someone in your team had to have done *something* that allowed this bad group…" The group. If the code had a name or a whereabout, they had a lead on where her parents were. "The group—does the code say who they are?"

"You sure change channels fast," he muttered.

"My parents' lives are at stake. I don't have time to be angry or fight with you about whether your team is dirty or not. I *have* to get to them before they're killed. I have to."

Holden blew out a breath. "Let's call Shay."

IT ATE AT HIM. Even as Shay explained to both him and Willa on speakerphone that the group who likely had Willa's parents was called Ross Industries, which was obviously a front for something else. Elsie was working on that, but carefully. Elsie confirmed that there was no way her searching had led anyone to know they or Willa had evidence against them.

"I know you want to move on your parents, Willa," Shay was saying in her calm, authoritative tone. "Trust me, I know. But if we have any hope for avoiding loss of life, I need some time. We'll send an entire team in."

Willa sat on the couch. Hands clutched together on her lap. "Is there any way you can guarantee my parents are still alive?"

There was a pause. One far too long.

"I can't at the moment," Shay admitted. "But I will do everything in my power to get you some kind of answer in the next few hours. Okay?"

It was more than Holden had expected out of Shay, but he'd forgotten in the two years of Shay's leadership role that she'd once been a person who rarely went by the book—even North Star's.

"Thank you. Thank you. I…" Willa trailed off and looked up at him, some inner debate warring in her expression. "If you can use me as some kind of bait or trade or whatever, I want you to."

"Willa—"

"No, don't argue with me," Willa said, cutting off Shay's

protests. But her eyes remained on him as she spoke. "I want you to promise me, if I can help, you'll send me. I need you to. They're my parents. I have to do everything in my power to save them. I'd like to do it with your help, but if you can't promise me that, I walk."

"It's a little hard to walk when I've got an agent on you."

"I walk," Willa repeated firmly. To Shay. To him.

Holden could stop her from walking. He could stop her from doing a lot of things.

But he knew he wouldn't. He understood too well what a child would need to sacrifice to save their parents. He couldn't stop the car crash that had taken his father before he'd been born. He couldn't stop the cancer that had taken his mother far too young.

If he had the opportunity to give Willa the chance to save her parents, he would. He had to.

Somehow, she understood that. Or at least guessed at it. Or maybe she just underestimated his ability to keep her prisoner if he wanted to. But he had the sneaking suspicion she just…understood him.

A problem, that.

"Stay in the safe house for now. Let me get men on the ground at this warehouse, a good sweep and some intel. We'll update you in the morning, and the minute I get confirmation on your parents, I'll pass it along to Holden. But for tonight, I want you two staying put. It's part of our job to keep you safe as well, Willa. Not just your parents."

"I know it's silly, but—"

"Your animals are in good hands. We've got three people here at your house, and between the three of us and some internet searching, we've been taking pretty good care of all of them. We'll do our best to continue to."

"I appreciate it," Willa said, though Holden didn't think she sounded all that sincere.

He picked up the phone, clicked the speaker off. "We'll hold tight. You've got someone with Elsie, right? If they're looking for information, it's not unreasonable to think they might return to the farmhouse."

"I'm here. So is Granger."

Holden nearly bobbled his phone. "Granger?" Holden couldn't check his surprise at Shay involving their old boss.

"Came kicking and screaming, but I told him we were spread thin and he didn't want Elsie caught in the cross-fire, did he?"

"Fight dirty."

"When it suits. Keep your target there under control. Holden, if I find out her parents are dead, I'm not passing that along until this is over."

Holden closed his eyes. He wished Shay hadn't told him that. Still, he gave her a quiet affirmation before hanging up the phone.

Willa was still sitting on the couch, her hands folded together. She was deep in thought, and every once in a while she leaned forward and wrote something down on a scratch pad of paper. Then she'd sit back, link her fingers and think again.

Holden should do something. Eat. Sleep. Figure out what the hell was going on with this Ross Industries. But all he could seem to do was watch her.

"What are you writing down?"

"A list. A list of things we need to do. *I* need to do. I realize your group is on it, but I need to be doing something, too. I'm sorry, I don't trust your group. Not enough."

"Willa."

"No, I'm sorry. Shay said something to you after you were off speaker. You don't want to tell me, fine. But secrets are secrets, and I don't trust that. I won't." She stood, holding her piece of paper. "First, I want you to get the address to that warehouse."

"Willa. They didn't give it to me for a reason. It might not even be where your parents are."

She waved that away. "We don't need to use it, per se. I just want you to have it. In case we need it. I want you to have it as backup. Can you do that?"

"Can? Yeah. Will I?"

She kept speaking as if the answer to that question was an obvious yes. "We'll wait here tonight. I agree with that. We'll need the intel your group finds before we make any moves. If someone in your group is dirty—"

"North Star isn't dirty," he interrupted. But she'd planted a doubt earlier. It had happened, now and again, when they'd tried to take down the Sons. Someone would be compelled to step over that line. Hell, the explosion they'd had two years ago had been due to Granger trusting the wrong double agent.

She looked up at him, stern as a schoolteacher. "You're letting your emotions cloud reality, Holden."

"No, I'm letting facts and experience and my gut influence my decision making, as it should be. First of all, we don't know *what's* going on with this Ross Industries. The change from kidnapping to murder could have to do with *anything*." Including the death of her parents, but he wouldn't say that to her. He couldn't.

So, he continued on *his* point. "It's not Shay. I know that. Down to my soul, I know it's not Shay or Elsie. You'd have to meet Elsie and you'd see it too. She's…good. The bone-deep kind you don't see all that often. The five we had out with us this afternoon? Apart from trusting them with my life for years, it doesn't make sense. They came in and saved my butt. They could have let them take us. They didn't. I'm not saying there's not something…more here.

A computer hack? Someone saying the wrong thing to the wrong person. But I don't see a leak. Not a purposeful one. It can't be. I know these people. I trust these people."

She blinked up at him, her expression softening into something he didn't trust. Not for the life of him.

"They're like your family," she said softly.

He stepped back as if she'd struck him. Something worked through him, and he didn't know the emotion, so he tried to convince himself it was offense. "I can do my job impartially."

"No. No, that isn't what I mean." She moved over to him and reached her hand up to touch his face. "You don't have to *be* a job, Holden. When it's people you love, it isn't so easy to *be* the job anymore. You're family. You care. I don't mean you can't do your job, partially or impartially. I mean, you *care*."

He took her arm by the wrist and pulled her hand off his face. "I don't think you understand."

"I do. I grew up with my parents doing what you're doing. They loved each other. I may not have understood everything they did or went through, but I could watch and guess. You care about your team, so it's complicated. I care about my parents, so it's complicated." She blew out a breath, and it was only as she made a move to walk away from him that he realized he'd kept his grip on her wrist.

She seemed to realize it then, too. She looked first at his hand holding her, then up at him. There wasn't questioning in her gaze so much as consideration. She didn't pull away. If anything she drifted closer.

It was all her talk about care and complications, and the truth here. With her hand in his, with her green eyes on his. Not just his team, who *had* become his family. But her. Who'd somehow become…something. "I care, so it's complicated," he said. For himself. About her. Though he should have shut his idiotic mouth.

He should have left it at that. He should have walked away. Gotten to work, because even if they were staying put for the night, surely there was still work to do. But he didn't let go of her hand, and when she rose on her tiptoes, he didn't push away.

He let her kiss him, and he kissed her back.

## *Chapter Seventeen*

It wasn't like when Holden had kissed her earlier today.
Had that been today? Had it only been days since she'd
known him? Willa felt like she understood everything
about him. She felt like he was a part of her life. Inex-
tricably.

No doubt she'd feel differently once this burned out.
She might even regret it. But for now she wanted to feel
something other than lost. Something other than alone.

Because she wasn't alone. Maybe it was only for a short
while, but she had him, and his kiss lit her from the inside
out. It wasn't gentle or tentative. If he had regrets, he was
saving them for later.

She wrapped her arms around his neck and poured everything she was into the kiss. If she had to stay here and
let someone else take the reins to her and her parents'
lives, why not take something for herself? Mistakes felt a
lot less scary when life or death hung in the balance not
too far away.

Holden's arms were strong and tight around her. His
body hard, sturdy against hers. His mouth was an anchor
to something new. Something bright and wonderful and
*connected.* His teeth scraped against her bottom lip, and
she felt alive. Well and truly linked. Not just to some ran-

dom guy, or even the guy who'd helped her, fought side by side with her.

But the man who'd talked to her about his family, who'd bandaged her cuts gently because he cared that she'd been hurt. He'd spoke of one of his teammates as bone-deep good, and so was he.

She understood he thought himself as bad because he'd gotten mixed up in something bad once when he'd been a teenager and grieving, but he wasn't. He was good and noble, and his need to set things to rights made her care about him as much as this attraction did.

She knew she'd never be able to explain that to him in words, so she tried to explain it to him in feelings.

Everything gentled. Imperceptibly almost, but her knees felt weak as his hands cupped her face. Heat was intoxicating. It dulled thought and reason. Gentleness went deeper. It was the promise of something more than what they had. It gave her hope. One that wasn't particularly comfortable.

But she'd never been after comfort.

Holden tore his mouth from hers. "I can't do this," he said, his voice rough and low.

But he was breathing hard and still holding her tight. His words didn't match his actions. At *all*. "Why not?"

"It isn't right."

"Why not?"

He gave her one of those disapproving looks, and though he started trying to put distance between them, she wouldn't let him.

"Well, why not, Holden?"

"Stop saying why not," he ordered, trying to pull her arms off his neck. But she simply wouldn't let him.

"Then give me a good answer."

"We're in the middle of something dangerous. You're

worried about your parents. You've somehow planted worries in my head about my own team."

She heard excuses more than reasons. Because even if the reasons were true, they paled in comparison to this. "But you care. And I care."

"Willa…"

She would miss the way he said her name in exasperation. The loss of it would feel insurmountable if she wasn't also facing the loss of her parents, or even her own life. Maybe she'd die trying to save her parents. She would if she had to.

She didn't want to die without this moment. It would be a waste. "I know in a few hours it all changes. Trust me, I know. But I also know… You have to take what you can get. Even when it's not perfect. That's what my life taught me. Nothing's ever going to be perfect, so you reach for all you can."

"Maybe I don't want to reach because I know what it feels like to lose."

"Oh, Holden." It just about broke her heart in two. Maybe she should trust him. He'd suffered losses far more significant than she ever had. But she couldn't understand shutting herself down because of what *might* come. And much like she'd never wanted to be a spy like her parents because she wanted free rein over her emotions, she didn't want to control her emotions now. She wanted it all. "Feelings aren't win or lose. Not these."

She'd never convince him of that with words, so she kissed him again, hoping to find a way past all those protections. All those walls. He deserved more than the little prison he'd made for himself. He'd let his group become his family, though he hadn't admitted it to himself yet, but he was still so often separate from them.

She understood that, too, even if her loneliness was

somewhat self-imposed. Or necessary. Or *whatever*. For a few hours, she had license to be *with* someone. To give herself over to the opposite of loneliness, to connection and care.

He lifted her off her feet, and she laughed against his mouth. It felt good to laugh. To pause everything. There was nothing else to be done, so why not find solace in something that wasn't bleak at all?

He carried her into the bedroom, his mouth never leaving hers. She held on tight, wanting the moment to last, wanting to rush ahead. Wanting anything and everything from him. She tugged at his shirt and he deposited her on the bed, then pulled it off himself.

He was pure rangy muscle, and Willa's stomach and heart jumped in time—attraction, and something that felt a little deeper than the word *care* she kept using.

She reached out and smoothed her palm over the splotching of scars on his side. "What happened?"

He knelt on the bed next to her, then tugged at her shirt until she lifted her arms and let him take it off her. "Explosions."

"Plural?"

He shrugged. A careless yes.

But it wasn't careless. He'd been marred and marked by the work he'd chosen to do. To make something right. She kissed the white line on his shoulder. "And this one?"

"Knife. Got that one trying to escape the gang I'd gotten myself mixed up in."

Gotten himself. Hardly. To her way of thinking, anyone who'd gotten him involved in a gang had manipulated him and used his grief against him. But he wouldn't appreciate her theory, so she kept her mouth shut.

She pointed at the scar on his side, still pink as though the injury hadn't been all that long ago. "That one?"

He looked down as if he didn't even know his own scars. He shrugged again. "Shot."

He laid her back on the bed, his hands trailing down her sides. He unbuttoned her pants, slid them over her hips and off. She was in her underwear, with a *man*, and she didn't feel self-conscious. She felt... Well, the way he looked at her made her beautiful. Her skin practically *hummed*.

"Do you want to keep talking about my scars?" he asked, looking down at her with a smug smile.

"Maybe," she offered, making a motion that he should take his own pants off as she sat up.

He grinned and dropped them. There was a jagged line on his thigh. She simply raised an eyebrow.

He looked down at it, as if he didn't even remember it was there. "Oh. Sabrina and a broken bottle."

"Who's Sabrina?"

"Another agent."

"She hurt you with a broken bottle?" Willa asked, unable to keep the outrage out of her voice.

"It was before she was an agent. We got in a bar fight."

Willa didn't know *what* to make of that, but she found she didn't like the name Sabrina. Or the way Holden sounded almost proud she'd wounded him with a broken bottle, for heaven's sake. "Is she pretty?"

Holden laughed. "I guess so."

"What does *that* mean?"

"She's more like my little sister than anything else." He pressed a kiss to her neck, one that had heat shuddering through her like a storm. "Want to ask me any more questions?"

"Hmm. Oh." She slid her fingers through the hair at his temples, liking the slightly coarse texture, so much different than her hair. "Who patches you up when you're hurt in the line of duty?"

"Betty. She's our doctor." He nibbled down her shoulder, and she found she liked that as much as she liked him answering her questions without stiffening up.

"You really are a little family, aren't you?" she murmured, kissing his jaw.

He rolled her onto her back, pinning her to the mattress. It was meant to be playful, to change the subject. He was even smiling, but it faded. Slowly. She wasn't sure it was doubt causing him to sober, so much as…fear.

"I want you, Holden," she said, trying to match his smile, but there was such seriousness in him. "That's all that matters for a little bit. I want you."

HOLDEN COULDN'T REMEMBER the last time he'd been so relaxed. Though he had always worked hard to put off a careless air, there'd always been a center of…well, whatever made a man get involved with a gang, then leave it for a secretive group that worked tirelessly for years to take down that gang.

He tried to remind himself it was wrong. A man like him letting a woman like Willa curl up next to him, head on his shoulder, hand curled over his heart.

"You should have told me I was your first," he murmured, trying to work up some kind of moral outrage on her behalf. But he was having a hard time keeping his eyes open, and mostly he wanted to press his nose into her hair and fall asleep.

She yawned. "Why?"

"I…" He wasn't sure he could articulate why. She was too sweet, too responsive to do anything but take his time. Linger. It had been…beyond what he'd known this kind of thing could be.

It should have scared him, but he hadn't worked up to that yet.

She was beautiful. He wanted her. Not just in the moment. He wanted her in his life. The way she went toe to toe to him. The way she understood him in ways he wasn't altogether certain he understood himself. Or maybe she just put words to things he tried not to.

It wasn't done. It wasn't possible. Maybe Reece had gone down that particular road, but this was different. Holden wasn't Reece.

Besides, it was clear to Holden—or at least he was trying to make it clear to himself in the aftermath—she knew she was going into a dangerous situation, one she thought she might not come out of on the other side. So, she'd had some kind of last hurrah.

Well, that was fine and dandy, but she needed to be clear about one thing. "You're not going to die. That isn't going to happen."

She eased up onto her elbow, looking down at him. Her hair had mostly fallen out of its band and was a curling mass around her shoulders. She looked fresh faced, satisfied and so damn beautiful it *hurt*.

The expression of confusion melted slowly into one of understanding. Why did she always seem to understand him?

"I didn't have sex with you as some kind of virginal last hurrah before I plan on dying, Holden."

Since he felt scolded, he shrugged and tried to act nonchalant. "I didn't say you did."

"But you thought it." She gave him a quick peck on the mouth. "I'm starving." She slid out of bed, grabbed his T-shirt and slid it over her head. "Is there food in that kitchen?"

"Yeah." He got out of bed, too, pulling on his jeans. He didn't feel like pawing through the community clothes to find a shirt that would fit him, so he followed Willa into the kitchen.

She hummed to herself, and though she clearly didn't know where anything in the kitchen was, she poked through cabinets and drawers with the quiet confidence of someone who might have lived here.

"You're smug," he grumbled.

"I am. Quite smug." She grinned at him. Her hair hid most of her bandage, but Holden could see she'd bled through. "You need that bandage changed."

She glanced over at him. "Right back at you."

He muttered to himself as he collected the first aid supplies, and though he was trying to act grumpy or harsh, he didn't feel any of it. The whole thing felt so right, so comfortable, he couldn't seem to muster up the necessary self-loathing or situational irritation.

Must be the lack of sleep. And food. He'd think straight once they ate and slept.

She had a peanut butter sandwich made when he returned, laying all the supplies out on the counter. He motioned her to come closer, and she did.

She offered him the sandwich, but since his hands were full, he just leaned forward and took a bite. Then he went about changing out her bandage while she ate.

Then they switched, him finishing off the sandwich and her rebandaging his head.

"Matching head wounds," she said with a smile, smoothing the adhesive gently into place.

"Yeah, the difference is you gave me this one and then chained me to a bed."

She laughed, and the hand that had put on the bandage smoothed over his cheek, then rested there. There was something in her eyes. Something he intellectually knew he wasn't ready for, but his heart seemed to be galloping ahead without heeding any reality.

"Willa…" He couldn't say it. He couldn't *mean* it. Thank *God* his phone went off.

He grabbed it like a lifeline, moving away from her soft touch and softer eyes. Glancing at the phone screen he saw that it was Shay. "Parker," he greeted. He heard the distinct sound of gunfire and glass shattering. He didn't bother to ask what was going on. "I'm on my way."

"Bring her," Shay demanded. "We might need her. Approach with caution."

Then the line went dead. Holden held the phone for one second in shock, but then immediately pushed himself out of it.

"Get dressed," he ordered. "We have to get to your farmhouse."

"What's going on?" she asked, but she was already moving for the bedroom and their clothes.

"I'm not sure." But it was bad. Very bad.

## Chapter Eighteen

Willa's heart felt as though it was permanently lodged in her throat, beating too hard and making it difficult to breathe easily. She tried to portray a sense of calm as Holden drove at rapid speed, back toward Evening and her farm.

Her farm. Her animals. Would they be okay? She couldn't even think of it. She had to put them out of her mind. She just…had to.

Holden had explained to her the brief exchange he'd had with Shay on the phone, and it worried her. Why would anyone go there? Even if they knew she had the evidence—which she herself hadn't yet decoded even if Holden's group had—they had to know after the fight this afternoon that she wasn't home.

"Maybe I could try to call Shay on your phone and give her some info. There are places to hide. Security codes. I could give them information."

Holden didn't spare her a glance. "Elsie was already in your bunker."

Willa blinked, somewhat taken aback. "How?"

"We have skills, Willa. She needed to hack into your computer to see if she could find anything pertinent about your parents."

"She… Why would you guys *hack* into my computer?

I'm cooperating with you." She didn't know how offended to be. It wasn't really the time for it, but…he hadn't told her they were hacking her computer, either, and that didn't feel right.

This Elsie person had been combing through her files. Her *parents'* files. "Did it ever occur to you *that's* how they got information about me and that evidence?"

"Elsie knows more about computers than most of the people in the *world,*" Holden replied, his gaze never leaving the road as he raced against time. "She knows what she was doing. If she'd thought someone tracked what she was doing, what was being communicated, she would have either stopped it or let us know."

"I could have given you or her the passwords. I could have *given* you access, if you'd asked."

"You could have. She still would have hacked around or whatever it is computer people do to make sure you weren't only showing us part of the information."

"We're on the same team."

"We've got a dangerous criminal group. Two spies. Their daughter who can fight like the devil and has a whole underground bunker system. You tried to run and you kept some things from me along the way. Let's not play the game of trust and being on the same team."

It hurt, but it also reminded her of something more important than her childish hurt. "I have a way to get in where no one can see us."

"We don't know where their men are, Willa. We have to—"

"Trust me, Holden. I have a way." She ordered him to take a hard left, so he did. She directed him down gravel roads and dirt roads, then over the open field that would lead to the back of her property. To one of the escape hatches her parents had put in. "Here. Stop here," she said when they reached a swell of earth, covered in sod. She got out of the car, and Holden followed. His eyes were assessing, and his hands rested on either gun at his hip.

"I need a gun too," she said.

He hesitated, and that hurt. But she had to bury it in reality. In what they had to do. "You have to trust me. We have to be in this together."

He curled his hand around her neck. His grip was tight and fierce as he held her so they were almost nose to nose. "I let you fight off that guy at the lake all on your own. I didn't want to, but I knew you could and would take care of it. There isn't a bigger gesture of trust I've got than that."

She wanted to cry. She wanted to kiss him. But all she could do was take the gun he offered, then walk up the small swell of earth. She knelt on the ground, felt around until her fingers brushed metal. She pulled up the pole, then pushed, twisted and gave it a hard yank. It unlocked the door, hidden under the piles of sod. She lifted the hatch.

"This leads to the underground room we were in the other day. We can get to the house or the barn. Whichever you want."

"How... Willa, are you sure your parents don't use this as some kind of...home base?"

"Of course not," Willa replied, without thinking it through. They'd always said it was about her protection. And why would her parents take the trouble to go underground here and not tell her? She didn't use the underground area much at all herself, but still, wouldn't she know if they were under there? Wouldn't they...let her know?

With a sinking feeling in her chest, she realized they probably wouldn't. Especially if they were working.

She shook her head. "We'll figure that out later. Come

on." She climbed into the hole. It was narrow here at the opening. "You might have trouble fitting, but you need to pull that door closed behind you."

She heard his grumbling from behind her. The tunnel was dark and tight. She'd never used this portion. She wouldn't call herself claustrophobic, but this particular tunnel being so narrow had always bothered her.

She breathed slowly, deeply, as the light gradually faded and they were in complete darkness.

"Does it lock?"

"We can lock it from the command center," Willa said, her voice strained.

"You okay?"

"Yeah. Can't say I like this one. Just keep moving forward. I'll be able to tell when we're closer to the more reasonable tunnels." She crawled forward, knowing there was no backing out. She was stuck. She couldn't get out.

*Breathe in, one, two, three. Breathe out.*

The walls weren't closing in. It wasn't possible. Feeling like they were was only irrational fear.

"Willa, honey, you're panting."

It was strange. *Honey.* She liked it. That was silly, but if she thought about silly things like endearments, she wouldn't feel like she was being swallowed whole by the earth.

If she lived through this, and she rather planned to, she'd call him… Dear? Too old-fashioned. Babe? No, that felt all wrong. Maybe she'd just call him honey back. She liked it, and if she…

If *they* made it out alive. He had to survive, too.

She swallowed as a new fear took over. "Where should we go? The bunker?" She had to focus on the reality of the situation, not the dark, cramped tunnel. Not life and death. Just getting from point A to point B.

"House. I think that's where Shay would be. You wouldn't hear gunshots from inside the bunker, would you?"

"No."

"Then house. Definitely."

She crawled what felt like endless minutes until at last the tunnel ended in a bigger "room" that connected all the tunnels together. The tunnels that led to the bunker and house and other places on the property were all deep enough to walk through without crawling.

*Thank God.* She got to her feet and led him to the path to the TV room door. It was still dark since she hadn't been able to be in the main room and switch on the lights via the generator. So she had to feel her way, which kept her pace slower than she knew Holden wanted.

Finally, she reached the end of the tunnel. "Here we are. How do you want to do it?"

"I'm going to go first, okay? You'll wait until I give you the signal to follow. I don't know what we're walking into yet."

She didn't say anything. Her throat was tight. She couldn't see anything in the dark, but she could feel him there. She didn't want to lose that.

"Willa?"

She cleared her throat and reached forward, unlocking the clasp that kept the door in place. She pulled it open slowly and quietly. There was a panel still covering the opening, but light streamed in through the cracks and she could make him out in the dim light.

"Honey, don't cry," Holden said reaching out and touching her wet cheek.

She hadn't realized she was. She was too numb with fear to know tears were leaking out. She wiped them away with her sleeves. "No, I'm okay. Really." She sniffled. "It'll be fine. You just slide the panel to the left, slip out and let me know when I can come out."

His eyebrows drew together, as if trying to figure out her emotional outburst. But what was there to figure out? She was scared. A woman could be strong and scared at the same time. Heck, women usually *had* to be both.

She straightened her shoulders and nodded him toward the panel. "Go on."

"All right." He reached out for the panel, but she found herself incapable of holding all these emotions in. She couldn't fight like her parents, ignoring love when they had to. She couldn't. "I love you. So please don't die," she blurted.

The kiss was sudden, fierce, and she nearly fell over. If Holden hadn't been holding her so tightly, she might have. When he released her, she knew this was the only thing she could have hoped for in the moment.

A kiss that felt too much like a goodbye.

"Same goes, Willa. Same goes," he muttered, and then he was sliding the panel open.

*SAME GOES. You are an utter, bumbling moron.* Even as Holden searched the room, the *same goes* echoed in his head and threatened to split his focus.

But there could only be one focus.

The house was eerily silent, sometimes interrupted by a creak or groan that would make Holden still as he tried to figure out if it was old-house noise or people-moving-around noise.

When he was certain the room itself was safe, he motioned Willa out from the tunnel. They worked together in silence to close up the door and replace the wall paneling. Once that was done, he took her hand.

He didn't have to tell her to be quiet, to follow him carefully. She knew. She understood.

Holden didn't hear gunshots or breaking glass. He hoped to God that didn't mean he was too late.

Willa's grip tightened on his. It gave him center and focus, her gripping him so fiercely. He had to be strong for her.

He eased forward into the hall that would take him to the living room. He didn't have a clue as to where anyone would be, but he might be able to tell something from the living room, where you could see the kitchen, stairs and upper half of the upstairs.

As he poked his head into the room, he immediately saw Shay and Granger next to the big picture window. A couch had been moved out of the way, and shoved in front of the front door.

Shay was sitting in the floor, Granger crouched over her. Though the curtains were drawn, Holden saw the shattered glass littering the floor. Holden had to assume someone had shot through it.

It was a strange thing to see Granger McMillan standing there. He'd been the one to offer Holden a job in North Star, and like many of the other operatives, Holden had looked up to him like he'd been some kind of saint. Definitely a hero.

Then Granger had been shot in the explosion that had left scars on Holden's side. Granger's recovery had gone well enough, but he'd never returned to North Star.

Holden had to admit Granger didn't look the same. He sported a heavy beard. Holden might have expected him to look wan, or rangy, but he'd done the opposite, adding a bulk that appeared to be all muscle, as if he'd spent his off time purposefully building himself into a different man.

"What happened?" Holden asked, keeping his voice low.

"Bit of an ambush. Not sure who's out there, or how many, but suddenly they were shooting up the house. We held them off, but…" Shay trailed off, staring at them more closely. "How did you guys get in here?"

"Tunnels under the house, came in through the inside. Are they still out there?"

"I think so. We don't have enough to recon. I've got a backup team coming, but I told them to proceed with extreme caution since we've got nothing on what's going on out there."

Holden frowned at the way Shay was still sitting and had one hand clamped over her arm.

"What's wrong with you?" he demanded.

"Nothing. I'm fine."

"She's not."

"I *am*."

"She got shot."

"I got *clipped*. In the arm. Hell, for all we know it was a piece of glass. I'm fine."

"She won't let me field dress it."

Holden muttered an oath. "Don't be stupid. Get it dressed. Where's Elsie?"

"In that godforsaken bunker," Shay ground out, glaring daggers at Granger. "I want her to stay there."

"She's seeing what she can do to hack into the security measures, but it takes time," Granger offered, but his attention was on grappling with Shay to get her arm free so he could dress it. "She says it's quite the encrypted system. She can kick through it, but there's hoops to jump through and whatnot."

"I'll go. I'll go help," Willa said, her hand still in his. "I can get video and security measures all up in five minutes tops. It doesn't seal off the whole farm, but it'll make things more difficult for anyone trying to get within the property lines."

"Not sure security measures are going to help when they're already here," Holden said, though he knew that was emotion more than sense talking. Still, he had to say it. He had to…

Willa grabbed his arm, eyes wide and determined. "Let me go do this. I know the tunnels, how to get in and out fast and easy. You three hold the fort here. You just get a message to Elsie so she knows to look for me. It'll help. You know it will."

"We shouldn't separate," Holden said, but Willa was already moving away as if he'd agreed.

He swore under his breath. "Fine. Go. But get everything set up, then I want you and Elsie up here." They all needed to be together where he could be certain they were protected.

"Okay. I will." She dropped his hand and arm and scurried off, and Holden had to fight down all his instincts to stay where he was and not chase after her.

"Do me a favor and knock Shay out so I can get this wrapped around the wound," Granger grumbled.

He'd torn a piece of fabric from his own shirt, and if Willa wasn't off in those tunnels alone, Holden might have found some humor in the situation. "Best not to knock her out. We might need all hands on deck." He glanced at Shay. "Why are you being so difficult?"

"Because this moron disobeyed a direct order."

"I'm your superior," Granger muttered, taking the arm she reluctantly held out.

The gash was deep, but Holden had to admit it looked more like a cut from glass than a bullet. She'd need stitches, but it'd hold for now.

"No, you left," Shay said through gritted teeth as

Granger inspected the wound, then wrapped the strip of fabric around it. "*And* left me in charge. You're officially a subordinate."

"I didn't even want to get roped back into this—"

A gunshot rang out from outside, but wherever it hit the house wasn't close to them. It seemed to knock Granger and Shay out of their argument.

They all were on their feet, guns out and ready, in seconds flat.

"Shay, get that message to Elsie so she knows not to shoot Willa. Then go to the bunker. There's something about this place that gives me a bad feeling. Granger, take east. I'll take west."

"You're not in charg—"

But he had no reason to listen to Shay's orders when they didn't know who or what they were up against. Besides, Shay might be his boss, but this was *his* mission. He'd come to believe that bunker and the tunnels were more than just safeguarding Willa.

What? He didn't know. But he wanted Willa in and out ASAP.

Another gunshot exploded somewhere in the dark night. As far as Holden could tell by listening, that one hadn't hit the house.

Which raised the question…if someone out there wasn't shooting at the house, what were they shooting at?

# *Chapter Nineteen*

Willa had never been afraid of the dark that she could remember. When she'd been very young, her parents had trained her how to move in the dark. How to keep her calm in the dark. How to defend herself in the dark.

Willa felt as if all those lessons had deserted her. She had to force herself into the dark tunnels again. Though she gratefully didn't have to crawl through the narrow one, something about this oppressive dark made her feel like everything was all wrong.

But she had to get to the bunker. Video would help Holden's team figure out what they were up against. The security measures she could enact didn't have the potential to eradicate the threat, but they could definitely diminish it.

Holden needed her help. She blew out a breath as she felt through the tunnel, ducking as it got a little shorter as went from under the house to outside. It would get taller again when she was under the barn and nearing the bunker.

She hadn't had a chance to ask after her animals. There was too much danger to worry how the crew was holding up. She could only offer up a silent prayer that in the light of morning every person and every animal would be safe.

*Please God.*

She stepped forward, the ceiling a more walkable height yet again. She let out a soft whoosh of breath. There were a few hurdles left. First, Elsie had to have gotten the message that the woman who would walk into the bunker wasn't an enemy. Second, if Elsie had engaged any of the locks from the inside, she would have to *hear* Willa pounding or yelling at the door, and then want to open it.

Yelling would be a bad idea. As much as she doubted her voice would carry through subterranean tunnels, she didn't want to risk anything.

*Are you sure your parents don't use this as some kind of...home base?*

She didn't know why that question of Holden's bothered her, why it kept popping up in her head. So what if they did? It would be their right. Yes, her feelings might be hurt if they were underfoot and never told her, but they'd built the tunnels.

*To keep you safe.*

If they hadn't done it for that reason, it hardly mattered. Either way, they weren't the bad guys here, so even if they used them, it didn't matter.

Willa stumbled to a stop as a dim light spread out into the tunnel. It was the door opening. A tall figure stepping out into the swath of light.

Willa's breath caught, then she raced forward, tears springing to her eyes. "Dad. Dad. Oh my God." She practically fell into his arms. She furiously blinked back the tears, holding on to him tight. He was alive. He was okay. He was here. "Oh, thank God you're okay." A panicky laugh escaped her mouth. "Here. Oh, thank God."

"Wills." He sounded almost surprised, but his arms were strong and tight around her.

"Where's Mom? She's okay, isn't she?" She had to be. Had to be. Willa pulled back to look at her father's face.

"She's not far away," Dad said, an odd, sad smile on his

face. He brought up his hands to her cheeks, searching her face. He sighed. "What happened to you?"

Willa reached up and touched the bandage on her head. "It's been a strange few days." She was tempted to tell him *everything*, but now was not the time. "Where have you been?"

Dad glanced at the room behind them. Willa couldn't see Mom or Elsie, but surely they were in there. "It's a very long story." He sighed, then looked back at her. "But you're here. Which is good. Everything will be okay now that you're here." He smoothed down her hair, and Willa gave in to the luxury of hugging her father as tight as she could.

He expelled a breath that was something like a mix of pain and relief. "I am so, so sorry, Willa," he said into her ear.

"Sorry?" She wanted to laugh again, but she pulled away from him instead. "But you're here."

There was something about his eyes, about the odd slant of his mouth that had her backing up.

He frowned a little. "What are you doing? Mom's just inside." He swept a hand toward the entrance, and Willa found herself taking full steps back. Away from her father. A man she'd always loved unconditionally, without suspicion.

But something was wrong. Something was *all* wrong.

"Come in," he insisted. "We have a lot to talk about."

But a cold dread settled through her. She didn't want to go in.

She was being ridiculous. Of course she needed to go inside. Her parents would take care of everything, like they always did.

*Except the past few days.*

The past few days. Nothing had made sense. This certainly didn't. She was being…foolish to question it.

Except her parents had always told her to listen to dread. No emotional outbursts, but by God, a spy had to listen to their gut. She didn't want to go in there. She didn't want to understand why her father's expression was so…off. Sad. Resigned. And just a little lost.

None of those things had ever been her father.

"Dad. Tell me what's going on."

"On?"

Her dread intensified. "There are men shooting at my house. You've been ignoring my SOS messages, or, as I thought, had been taken or killed by someone so *couldn't* respond. But here you are, apologizing and then acting like something isn't going on?"

"Come inside, Wills. Your mother was always better at explaining things than I was."

"Then call her out here."

"Willa." He sounded hurt. She believed him for a second, but none of it made sense. *None* of it.

And then there was a gun. In her father's hand. Lifting toward her. No, it didn't make sense, and no, she didn't want to believe this of her father, but when a gun was pointed at a person, there were only a few options.

She chose to run. Back into the dark. Back to Holden. It was all wrong. *All* wrong, but Holden wasn't. He'd save her. *No, Willa, it's time to save yourself.*

She zigzagged as much as she could in the narrow tunnel. The gun didn't go off, and she had to be grateful he wasn't shooting blindly in the dark.

Maybe he hadn't meant to shoot at her at all. Maybe she was being paranoid and reading everything wrong.

Well, that was something she'd figure out, but she wasn't about to risk it. Even when it came to her own father.

She was running too hard, breathing too heavily to hear anything. Was he chasing her? Had he given up?

*Is any of this real?*

Someone slammed into her hard, and she fell to the ground. If it was her father and he had the gun still, he didn't use it. They wrestled on the cold, hard ground. Willa fought tooth and nail, but her opponent was stronger, better in the dark.

"We have to end it." Dad's voice, breathless and strained. He worked to get a hold of her arms and pin them down, so she fought wildly. Punching, kicking, wriggling away.

"They can torture me, I don't care," he continued. "But I won't give them you. I won't let them do that to you."

Willa didn't understand what was happening, what he meant, but she knew she couldn't give in to it. "Then let me go," she said, trying to push him off her.

"You'll never be free. We'll never be free. It has to end."

Willa didn't want to know what he meant by that, but she had the sinking suspicion she knew exactly what he wanted.

He wanted to die, and her to go with him.

THERE WAS THE occasional sound of gunfire, but nothing close. The lack of lights outside kept them from seeing who or what might be out there. The lack of full-frontal attack made Holden's nerves hum.

Three of the windows on the main level had been shattered by gunfire. Holden considered heading upstairs. It might give him a better vantage point, but the incessant dark of the country night wouldn't allow him to see anything.

Besides, he didn't want to be that far away from the tunnels and Willa.

Whoever was out there wasn't out there to attack. Or, if they were, they were supposed to wait, hold back, break a few windows. It was attention seeking at best.

Holden met up with Granger after their inside perimeter check. "Any word from Shay?" Holden asked.

"No."

"Should have heard something by now," Holden said with a frown. "This isn't anything. What's with the random gunfire? Surely they don't think there's an army in here. They're waiting for something."

"Elsie was getting somewhere with that computer, but she hadn't briefed us yet when the guns started. Do you think they could tell she'd gotten the information they want?"

"How?" That was the question that plagued Holden. *How?* "None of this adds up, Granger, and you know as well as I do that means we don't know what they're really after."

"So, we'll figure it out."

"They're just there to hold our attention, or maybe make sure we don't run. They're not attacking."

"They could be amassing more men or ammunition or something. They could be working to blow us up."

*Could,* Holden thought. But it didn't feel right. He thought of Willa in the tunnels, and Shay. They weren't back yet, and there was no attempt at contact. "Unless someone else is down there."

"You think that's possible?" Granger returned, his eyes staring out the gap between curtain and window where they stood in the TV room. "Elsie acted like there was no way in or out."

"If you didn't know where to look," Holden muttered. "Let's go down there."

"And leave the house unprotected?"

"Screw the house," Holden replied, already moving to the other room. Shay had left the panel off, and he couldn't blame her for that. The door was closed though.

Or was. It swung open as Holden reached for it, Shay stumbling quickly into the light. She squinted against it, panting.

"Someone's fighting down there. I need a light. We need someone at the other entrance. I don't know if they got in or what, but we've got to move."

The only people who could be fighting in the tunnel were Willa and someone else, unless two new people had entered the tunnel from who knew were.

"You two to the barn and the other opening. I'll take the light to the tunnel."

"Holden." Shay didn't say more, and Holden refused to parse what the expression on her face meant. He had a flashlight on him, and he was going to get to Willa.

He nudged Shay out of the way and moved into the tunnel. He pulled the door closed behind him, plunging the world around him into darkness.

He took one deep breath to get his eyes as accustomed to the dark as he was going to get, then he moved forward. He held his gun in one hand, flashlight in the other. He kept it off. Though Shay had claimed someone was fighting, Holden heard nothing.

Moving forward carefully and stealthily was a battle in restraint he was slowly losing. He wanted to run and race forward. He wanted to bellow Willa's name. But none of those things would get her out of this alive.

She had to be the one who'd been fighting. There was no other explanation. Maybe she'd won and gotten to Elsie in the bunker. She could do it. He had faith in her.

But still he moved forward, dread solid and heavy in his gut. When things didn't add up, what a man believed and had faith in didn't always add up either.

After what felt like eons, Holden saw what he thought might be…light. He moved forward until it became clear there was indeed the tiniest sliver of light. It was the door to the bunker, just barely ajar.

Holden moved toward it. Quietly, he moved until he was as close to the door as he could get without pushing it open.

He heard a voice, and it made his blood run cold. Because that was a man's voice, and as far as he knew, only women were down here.

# *Chapter Twenty*

Willa didn't know if she'd fully lost consciousness, but a blow to her already wounded temple had made her woozy enough to forget to fight. It made her forget what she was fighting for. She could feel her body, and she could *feel* herself being dragged into the bunker. She even watched as Dad tied her up.

Willa stared, uncomprehending, at the nylon rope pulled tight around her arms. She could move her legs, but she didn't know what to do with them. The ground was cold under her, but there was something warm and soft next to her. A light scent, faint, like a memory.

"Willa, baby."

Was that her mother's voice? Willa told herself to look toward it, but she couldn't seem to turn her head. She couldn't seem to make her body do any of the things it should.

Was she already dead? But she heard her mother's voice, and something that sounded like a sob. No, that wasn't right. Her mother didn't cry. She had to be dreaming.

*You need to wake up, then.*

But there was pain and confusion, and she kept shying away from taking a grip on full consciousness. This fog seemed better. Safer. She could make things make sense here. Nothing made sense outside the fog.

"Willa. Talk to me, sweetheart." Mom's voice was more like a whisper now. Was it really her mother? Maybe she was hallucinating. But there was a warm body next to her.

Willa had no idea how long it took her to find the strength to turn her head, toward the voice, toward the warmth. She tried to blink and focus as a face wavered in her vision. Close. So close.

Mom's green eyes. The nose so like Willa's own. Her mother. Not a figment of her imagination. Not some afterlife hallucination, because Willa could see her. Feel her pressed next to her.

"Mom," she managed to croak.

"It's going to be okay," Mom said fiercely. But there were tears in Mom's eyes, and Willa didn't know how things could be okay if her mother was crying. Her mother was a spy. A woman trained to withstand torture, to take down any threat in her way.

But big, fat tears rolled down Mom's cheeks.

Everything was so woozy, so off. Willa knew she had to find some strength, some concentration. Her head pounded, but something had to be done. Mom was crying. That wasn't right. Willa had to find the strength to make something right.

"This wasn't how it was supposed to go," Dad was muttering, pacing in front of them.

Dad. Who'd fought her, hurt her and then dragged her inside the bunker. The bunker. Willa squinted through the pain and the fog and tried to understand her surroundings.

She was sitting on the ground, shoulder to shoulder with Mom, who was shoulder to shoulder with another woman. That woman had to be Elsie. She was completely still, her head nodded forward. Willa would have thought she was dead, but she wasn't particularly pale, and there was a slight rise and fall of her chest.

"Alive, but drugged," Mom whispered, her gaze following Dad going back and forth in front of them.

He slapped the barrel of the gun against his palm as he moved. His eyes looked even wilder in the full light of the bunker. Willa could clearly see the fear in her own mother's eyes.

The gray fog threatened to take over again. Safer there. Easier there. But the cold trickle of fear cut through her ability to fully let go.

"It has to end. It has to end. We have to end it," Dad said. Over and over and over.

Willa knew she wasn't functioning at full capacity, but she still understood her father wasn't...sane. Panic crept through the gray cloud of pain and centered her in the here and now. Her temple throbbed violently. Both an outside burning feeling where she was sure she was bleeding, and an inside bone-deep pointed pain.

And still Dad paced. Willa didn't think he'd always been like this. God, she hoped the man she'd known and loved hadn't been an act with this underneath.

But whoever was pacing in front of them now was not the father she loved. Who'd taught her how to fight, who'd protected her. This was someone else.

He'd tied her up. He'd tied *Mom* up. And poor Elsie, who had nothing to do with her family's current problems except she was part of a group trying to stop a hit man.

How did it all connect? Holden and Shay and Mom and Dad and the men who'd shot at her house?

"I don't understand anything that is going on," Willa said, thought it felt a bit like someone else had said it. Like she was two different people—the body and the brain, severed.

Except she'd said the words and Mom was weeping quietly next to her.

"There's nothing to understand, Wills. Nothing," Dad said firmly. "Too many mistakes. The mistakes have to be corrected. I have to correct them."

Mom took a deep breath beside her, and when she spoke, whatever trace of upset and tears were gone. She was calm and forceful. "William, look at me."

But Dad only shook his head. "Have to be corrected," he mumbled, still tapping the gun. "They want us dead. There's no escape."

"We have always escaped before," Mom said, but her voice cracked at the last word. "William. Please."

Dad's head shaking grew more violent. "No, no, no. Too late. It's over. It has to be over. I have to end it." He stopped moving abruptly, looking straight at Willa. "She has to be first."

Willa tried not to react. Or cry. She tried to hold on to the gray fog, but it kept lifting, leaving her with more and more clarity that the chances of her making out of this alive were getting slimmer and slimmer.

"William! She is your daughter." Mom's voice was like an odd echo, followed by sobs that couldn't be coming from her mother. Her mother was too strong. Too brave.

"We should have done this a long time ago. All three of us. Until we're all dead, they can hurt us. But once we're dead, they can't."

He was going to kill her. Willa couldn't reconcile it. Even as the gun was pointed at her, and she knew her father would pull the trigger. Purposefully. With the intent to end her life.

Mom was screaming and sobbing now, fighting the bonds around them, trying to maneuver her body in front of Willa's. But Willa knew it wouldn't matter.

He wanted them both dead. To end it.

He held the gun steady. His eyes were cold, detached.

"They can torture me, but I won't let them torture you. We've been found out. Our cover is blown. We're surrounded. There's no escape this time. They can get what they need out of me. But not you. I won't let them hurt my girls."

Dad's voice broke. Mom was sobbing. Willa couldn't find it within her to cry or plead. She didn't know how to argue with his words when she hardly knew who was after them. What they were up against or what had caused him to break with reality.

Besides, he was too far gone. His mind had broken, cracked into something deranged.

All Willa could do was close her eyes and hope for some kind of miracle.

The weeping grew louder as Holden inched forward. He could hear the voices but still couldn't see anyone in the main room yet.

He forced himself to focus on the entryway to the main room. The brighter light. The angles. He couldn't think about the weeping. Whether it was Willa. If she was hurt. That would split his focus. It might make his hand shake when he had to be nothing but cold. Precise.

He had to do everything in his power to get Willa out of there unharmed.

He got close to the main room entrance then paused, straining to hear over the quiet crying.

"No, no, no. Too late," a man's voice was saying. "It's over. It has to be over. I have to end it. She has to be first."

A woman's voice rang out. It started tough and authoritative but gradually got desperately panicked. "William! She is your daughter."

*She.* The she had to be Willa. These were Willa's parents? That would explain how they'd known to get into the tunnels, but why would the dad be talking about ending it? What did Willa have to be first to do?

He thought about just walking in. If Willa was with her parents, surely they'd taken care of whoever she was fighting with. Surely things were okay.

But something—a gut feeling, a deeper understanding he didn't fully comprehend yet—kept him where he was. Listening. Waiting.

"We should have done this a long time ago," the man said. "All three of us. Until we're all dead, they can hurt us. But once we're dead, they can't."

Immediately Holden moved closer, until he could actually see into most of the room. Willa, the woman he assumed was her mother and a slumped-over Elsie were tied together in a corner. A tall, slender man holding a gun paced in front of them.

Holden raised his own weapon. He could take the shot to kill. In another situation, he wouldn't have thought twice. But this was Willa's father. He couldn't…do that in front of her. Not while she was watching.

But he could hardly let her die, and if the man was dead set on killing his own wife and daughter, a shot aimed only to injure might end up with him still getting off a shot on Willa or her mother or Elsie.

He could make a noise, try to lure Willa's father out toward him, but that could also force the man's hand and make him shoot quicker. Right now, with a pacing man, muttering nonsense, there was still a chance he didn't talk himself into shooting them.

As long as Holden didn't force his hand.

There was no good solution. Nothing he could do that didn't risk Willa. Holden held his gun steady, trained on the pacing man. As long as he wasn't acting, as long as the gun was tapping against his palm and not pointed at anyone, Holden had a chance to come up with a solution.

He racked his mind for any possible end result, but he was distracted by a tapping sound behind him. Soft, but distinct. A North Star code. He looked over his shoulder and saw Shay and Granger coming through the tunnel exit.

Holden held up a hand, a nonverbal silence sign. There was no time to express his relief, no way to ask them why they'd come this way and not through the outdoor bunker entrance, and he couldn't risk being heard to explain everything he needed to explain to them.

He had to rely on rudimentary battlefield hand signals and hope to God they understood. Both nodded as if they did, so Holden motioned them close.

They huddled together in the opening between back room and main room. Holden gave himself a moment to breathe, to center. To focus on the end result.

Willa and Elsie safe. Nothing else really mattered.

"On go," Holden said under his breath, knowing his voice would be muffled by the sound of crying coming from inside the room. "No loss of life," he added, because the last thing he wanted for Willa, even knowing her father was the bad guy in this situation, was for her to have to *watch* him die.

Holden would do whatever he could to spare her that. If it meant risking his own life. He wouldn't leave her with that image. What she was enduring now was bad enough.

He wouldn't let her die, and he wouldn't hurt her more than she'd already been hurt.

He breathed, watched, listened. The man began to speak again.

"They can torture me, but I won't let them torture you. We've been found out. Our cover is blown. We're surrounded. There's no escape this time. They can get what they need out of me. But not you. I won't let them hurt my girls."

He began to raise the gun to point at Willa. Directly at Willa.

"Go!"

As Holden had hoped, the sudden yell drew Willa's father's attention to him and not Willa. Holden, Shay and Granger moved into the bunker as one.

Willa's father swung the gun toward them, but his angle would hit Shay, so Holden shot at the man's arm. There was a howl of pain, and the gun he'd been holding clattered to the floor. He didn't fall to the ground, and another gunshot rang out.

Granger shooting to get the man off his feet.

Holden didn't have time to regret it as blood bloomed on Willa's father's shirt and he grabbed his side and stumbled backward.

Shay was already untying the three women, and the one Holden assumed was Willa's mother immediately scrambled forward to her husband. Granger was wrestling the man's arms into a submissive position, and Willa's mother wasn't impeding his progress at all. She was just crying and murmuring things to her thrashing husband. Granger had it under control, so Holden turned to Willa and Elsie.

Elsie was completely limp. Shay moved to her immediately, checking vital signs when Elsie didn't move even once the ropes were off.

"Mom said she was drugged. I don't know what or how, but she's not dead. She's breathing," Willa was saying, pushing the now-lax rope off her.

She didn't immediately stand up. Her wound from yesterday was bleeding again, and she was pale as death. "Did he hurt you?" Holden demanded.

"He…" She looked at where her father lay on the

ground. Then back up at Holden, green eyes heartbreakingly vulnerable. "Is he going to die?"

"I…don't know." He didn't know how to lie to her, but the expression that crossed her face—pain and a sense of loss that he had to assume was more than one kind of loss—made him wish he had.

He held out a hand and helped her to her feet. She wavered once upright, and Holden grabbed her before she fell over. Then he simply…held on. Somehow he was murmuring things, and he wasn't even sure what. Just that she was okay and it would somehow be okay. It was a jumble even to his own ears.

Willa sobbed quietly into his shoulders, her fingers digging into his back as he held on. Vaguely he heard Shay on the phone with Betty asking for any kind of medical backup they could get, but to be careful.

Careful, because there were still men out there. "They said they were surrounded. What does that mean?"

Willa sniffled and shook her head. Though she pulled her head off her shoulder, she didn't release him and he didn't release her. "I don't know. I don't understand anything that's going on. Mom…"

Willa's mother turned from her husband. He was lying still, but Granger was still holding pressure on the stomach wound. Shay was on the phone, cradling Elsie's head in her lap, giving instructions to Granger, likely relayed from Betty, on how to stop the bleeding.

It was a madhouse, and they still weren't safe.

"We were undercover, working for Ross Industries. Our assignment was to get the names of two possible hit men targets. We'd gotten them, but we were made before we could relay the information. William and I ran for it, coming here. We thought the bunker, but…" She looked back at her husband. "He…snapped. He told them where we were. He said we had to end it."

When she looked up at Holden, he saw Willa's green eyes, heartbreaking and devastated. "This isn't him. I don't know what happened. He just…cracked."

Holden looked at Shay and Granger. They were still hovering over the man like he had a chance to live.

But they had to get out of here first.

# *Chapter Twenty-One*

*He just cracked.*

Willa felt an odd relief. Her father wasn't evil. He'd been good. He'd been the man she'd thought. He'd just *cracked.* But that knowledge did nothing to help the situation.

She couldn't seem to stop clinging to Holden, but they were still in danger, and they had to get Dad to some kind of medical center. They *had* to.

"What about the hit man who got ammunition here?" Holden asked Mom.

Mom looked down at Dad once more, then slowly got to her feet. She took a deep breath and straightened her shoulders. "He was picking up the ammunition and one of the names. I met with him myself."

"And gave him the name?" Holden asked incredulously.

She shrugged. "It was the job, and the only way to get the name and get out in one piece. William and I were supposed to be out by now, reporting the name to our superiors."

"You haven't yet?" Willa asked breathlessly. She looked wildly around at Shay and the man who'd come in with her, then Holden. Panic rose. Someone was out there going about their life about to be killed? Willa couldn't stomach it. She couldn't *stand* it. "We have to. We have to get the names to whoever will stop them. No one should die."

"People die in this world, Willa," Mom said, looking down at Dad's still body.

Willa looked up at Holden, desperate to find someone who agreed. Who understood. But his mouth was grim, and his eyes were unreadable.

And still he held her.

"We need to think this through strategically. We have injured people who need medical attention. How many men are surrounding the house?"

Mom moved around Dad's too-still form and went for the computer. "I can bring up the generators and the computer. That'll get video on them. Willa?"

Willa knew Mom was asking her to help. Together they could get all the systems up and going faster. But she was loath to stop holding on to Holden. He felt like an anchor. Like a safe port in storm.

But her father was likely dying, after suffering a psychotic break, and she didn't want that to happen to anyone else here.

She released Holden and stepped over to her mother. "Why can't we go out the south field exit?"

Mom looked back at Dad. "He destroyed it."

Willa swallowed against the panic and moved to get the generator running.

"What about the names?" Holden asked. Everything about him flat and unreadable, but he was asking about the names. Willa found something unwind inside her.

They could do this. Good could fight and win.

"I can tell you one, but not the other. Only William knows the other."

Everyone in the room looked down at Dad. Pale. Blood dripping onto the floor no matter how much Granger held pressure on it.

"We thought it'd be safer that way. If one of us got

caught…" Mom trailed off. She shook her head and focused on the computer. "That's why we left Willa some evidence, too. Coded. We just wanted her to have some leverage. But William…told them." Mom swallowed. "When they found us out, he told them everything. That's why they wanted to kidnap her."

Willa closed her eyes against a wave of pain and fear and then turned to focus her attentions on the generator. She couldn't look at Dad. She'd break right along with him. She had to focus on the generator. On the danger.

She didn't know anything about the hit man's targets. Maybe they weren't that good of people anyway. Still, fear and guilt ate away at her insides like acid. It wasn't fair whoever the targets were might die simply because they were stuck here or that Dad might die.

*Might die.*

*Just cracked.*

After a few long, excruciating minutes Mom got the cameras up and began studying the images. Though the tracks of tears were evident on her face, and her eyes were red and puffy, she appeared calm and in control. An expert spy.

*He just cracked.*

Shay hung up the phone. "We've got ten on the ground. It's the most we can get before morning."

"How many men do you think your ten can take out?" Mom asked, her eyes sharp on the computer as she tapped at keys, bringing up the infrared censors that would be able to pick up video in the dark—a feature Willa hadn't even been aware of.

Willa thought of what Holden said about Mom and Dad using this when she didn't know it, and it had to be true. It had to be true. Willa shook it away. Didn't matter now. All that mattered was survival.

Mom studied the different video screens. She was pale and clearly shaken, but Willa could see in this moment she was a spy. She was doing her duty, no matter what mistakes Dad had made.

"Twenty to thirty, depending."

"It doesn't look like we've got more than fifteen. I don't know their backup situation, but I wouldn't think it'd be on-site since they should think there's only two of us here." She glanced at Holden, then Elsie on the ground. "I don't know if they knew about you."

Shay nodded. "We'll take the chance. We've got a medic team waiting to transport to the closest hospital."

"Both of them, or just yours?" Mom asked. There was no bitterness in her voice. Just a weary kind of acceptance.

"Both," Holden answered firmly, brooking no argument from Shay or Granger.

"I'll give my team the signal to move," Shay said, sitting with Elsie's head in her lap, and somehow looking every bit the fierce leader of her group. "I've got contact with my lead, and he'll relay orders to his team."

"Wait to have them move," Holden said. "Give me five. I'm going to go out."

"No," Willa felt herself say without fully thinking it through.

"It'll make it eleven men on the ground," Holden said firmly, but he wasn't looking at her. He was looking at Shay. "You two stay here with Elsie and…him. Betty told you how to take care of them in the meantime. Here, I'm superfluous. I might as well be out there helping the team."

This time Willa said her no with more force, with more intent. "You can't just go out there."

"Yes, I can."

Shay tossed him something, and he caught it easily, immediately hooking it to his ear. Some kind of earpiece.

"He'll keep in touch," Shay said, and Willa knew it was for her benefit. "It connects to my phone. You and your mom can relay what you see to him and the rest of the team."

Shay carefully moved Elsie's head off her lap, gently laying it on the floor. She stood and began to pull off the heavy black vest she was wearing.

"I'm not taking your vest," Holden said irritably. "You might need it here."

"That's only if they get through you first, which, if you have a vest, there's less chance of. Take it."

"Please," Willa added. "Please take it."

Holden scowled, but he walked over to Shay and took the vest. He loosened the straps then fitted it over his head. "There? Happy?"

She wasn't. Even a little. She moved from the generator to him. Too many fears. Too many possible outcomes. So much bad had already happened. She wasn't sure how much strength she had left. So she didn't reach out and touch him. She just looked at him and felt like her insides were being crushed by bricks. She could feel tears welling in her eyes, but she used all her strength not to shed them. "Just…be careful."

Holden leaned down and gave her a quick, hard kiss. "Don't leave this bunker until it's safe."

Then he was gone. In a blink. Willa stared after him. Gone into the dark. Where men with guns were waiting.

"Who is he?" Mom murmured.

Willa didn't know what to say or how to explain. All she had was one simple truth. "I love him."

"Well, I can tell *that*, but who *is* he?"

Willa turned back to Mom and the computers and the work they had to do to keep Holden and the rest of his group safe. "A very good man."

HOLDEN MOVED THROUGH the night. It was familiar, routine, habit. It was an assignment like any other. Except the odd, terrifying need to get back in one piece.

He'd never had anyone to get back *to*. At least not since he'd started down this path. North Star might have become his family, but he'd never fully thought of what they might feel if he was hurt or dead. So he'd never had this everpresent nagging worry that he had to avoid it.

The earpiece crackled. "Headed straight for a group of three. Reroute east a good bit and you might be able to sneak around behind them and meet some of your own men." It wasn't Shay's voice in his ear—it was a woman he didn't recognize. Which meant it had to be Willa's mother.

That felt a little weird, but he followed her instructions. As far as he could tell, she was on the up and up, unlike her husband.

He moved east, circled around back. He tapped a tree softly, using the North Star code to announce his presence. He listened for the reply, and once he heard it approached.

It was Gabe and an operative named Mallory. Gabe gestured toward the group of three they were watching, then laid out the plan of action in field signals.

Approach and, if undetected, subdue. If detected, shoot to debilitate.

Holden nodded, and then they moved through the dark and the trees.

The voice in his ear got loud. "You've got two on your back. Now."

Holden whirled as the first shot went off. He wasn't sure it hit anyone, but he immediately shot back. One stumbled but didn't lose his footing. "Gabe and Mal, stay up front. I'll take these two."

They spoke their assent, more gunfire echoing through

the night. It was hard to aim in the dark, though sound and the woman's voice in his ear helped.

"Ten o'clock and three o'clock," she said, giving him enough of an idea about where his attackers were to shoot in the general direction. He was pretty sure he got one, but an explosion hit his chest before he could fire another shot.

The bullet hitting his vest was hard enough to knock the breath out of him, and he stumbled backward and fell on his butt. He didn't lose his gun, but he landed awkwardly enough it was going to take precious seconds to get back into shooting position.

Precious seconds he didn't have. Holden was prepared to roll onto the ground and hope for the best when he heard the sounds of pounding…not feet. Too light to be feet. Then there was a growl, the sounds of snapping teeth. Followed by the high-pitched scream of someone Holden didn't think was on his team.

"Get it off me! Get it off me!" the voice he didn't recognize yelled.

A flashlight beam clicked on. Gabe's. He swung it around, counting out the three bodies they'd taken out on one side. On the other side, one body was crumpled on the ground. The other was writhing and screaming as a dog bit his arm. His gun arm.

"Jim."

The dog stopped, then trotted over to Holden as if nothing had happened. Mallory swept in, collecting all the guns. Gabe tied up the man who was still screaming about the wolf attack.

"It was a dog, dude," Gabe said. "Perfectly nice one," he added, gesturing to where Holden still sat on his butt.

Holden reached out and scratched Jim behind the ears. "You might have saved my life, bud."

The dog plopped down next to Holden and contentedly

let Holden pet him while Holden listened to the instructions in his earpiece.

"You've got all of them. Shay's sending in the medic team. Your orders are to follow, flanking them in case of more men."

"Got it," Holden muttered, loosening the straps on the damn vest. His chest hurt like hell and he couldn't quite get a full breath, but he was alive. Thank God for that.

Holden got up, Jim getting to his feet and following close by Holden wherever he walked. Gabriel relayed the orders to the rest of the team, and they waited for the medic team to emerge, then fanned out in a careful protective line. Jim never left Holden's side.

In the end, that was it. They waited and waited as the medical team entered the bunker, as they got Willa's father and Elsie out and into the transport vehicle. No one came. Aside from the FBI anyway.

Inside Willa's house was a hub of activity. Different groups appraising other groups, getting facts and information straight. Holden had to sit with one FBI agent for far too long, and when he was done, there was one person Holden didn't see in the crowd.

He tapped Shay's arm, drawing her away from the heated argument she was having with Granger.

"Where's Willa?"

Shay looked around, frowning. "I'm not sure. Maybe you should ask her mom? Vera's over there talking to some suit from the FBI."

But Holden didn't want to interrupt or worry Willa's mother when he didn't have to. When he looked down at Jim still next to him, Holden suddenly knew exactly where she'd be.

He walked back outside, Jim following, and to the barn. The sun was beginning to rise, but the world was mostly still dark. There was a dim light shining from inside. He stepped in to find her exactly where he'd thought, and yet so much more *her* than he'd realized.

Not just with her animals, but sitting on the floor of the barn surrounded by them. A cat on her lap, goats behind her. Dogs everywhere.

His chest hurt more, but it wasn't the nasty bruise he'd likely have from the impact of the bullet on the vest. It was just her.

He didn't know what to say. There were too many *feelings*. Because her part in this was over and she was safe and now...

What now?

"Hi," she offered. "Everyone's here and okay, but I can't seem to find..." She trailed off as Jim trotted in behind him.

"Pretty sure your dog saved my life," Holden managed. She looked so fragile there, sitting in hay surrounded by animals. Someone had rebandaged her head, and the gauze was a stark white against her ashen face and reddish hair.

Jim trotted over to Willa, and she simply buried her face in the dog's fur and gave him a tight squeeze. "Aren't you brave and clever," she murmured to the dog.

"I like to think so," Holden replied, hoping to make her smile.

She looked up at him. Her lips almost curved, but it was hardly a smile. She just stared at him for the longest time.

Uncomfortable with the silence, Holden fidgeted. "Did your mom catch you up?"

She shook her head, still holding on to the dog for dear life. "No, she was still talking to...whoever and filling them in."

"Do you want to know?"

She looked down at the cat in her lap. She didn't answer.

But he figured knowing might help her break through the shock she was surely feeling.

"Your father's in surgery. It'll be a while before we know how he'll fare, but he's still fighting."

She let out a breath. "Even if he lives, he'll go to jail."

"I think he'll get some psychiatric help first."

She sat with that for a minute, then finally looked up and met his gaze. "Elsie?"

"She's fine. They want her to stay overnight for observation, but she's recovering nicely. All the men we stopped have been arrested, and the Ross Industries warehouse is being raided by the feds."

Willa stroked the cat with one hand, the dog with the other. A goat stood behind her quietly munching on something. Another cat sat on a pail in the corner, and three dogs lay as one in some hay right next to her. This was where she was meant to be. Not off chasing bad guys. Here. Living a real life. A normal life. Well, sort of normal.

Why did he suddenly want one of those?

"There's more, isn't there?" she asked on a sigh.

Holden didn't see how he could keep it from her. "There are still two hit men out there. Sabrina's already made progress on the name your mother gave us, and she had information about the second name. So we're doing everything we can to save both men."

"Why would the hit men still kill them if there's no one to pay them?"

"We don't think Ross Industries is the only group involved. Just another arm. But we cut off this one. That's something."

"Ah." She nodded, stroking the animals. "So you have more work to do," she said softly.

He supposed he did. And for the first time in his life…
"I've never not wanted to go back and get a new assign-

ment. I've never…wondered what a different life might look like."

This time when she smiled it was bigger, gentle, but still so sad. "That's because you didn't care if you were alive."

It was true. He hadn't realized it, but it was the simple truth since the day the state took away his sisters and brothers. Since the foster homes kept them apart. His parents were gone, and his siblings taken away from him, and it hadn't really mattered if he'd survive. He'd decided he wanted to put that to good use, and he had.

He'd done good things not caring if he survived them. But today had been different. She'd made it all different. He moved forward. He didn't know what to say or what to do. He didn't know how to be this person she'd made him into.

But he understood, because he knew her, that no matter what he offered, she would find some way to make it…make sense. So, he found a way to scoot his body in between her and her menagerie of animals. Jim wiggled over to him, resting his head in Holden's lap.

Willa leaned over and rested her head on his shoulder, so he wrapped his arm around her. "I care now."

She flung her arms around him then, the cat meowing irritably between them. It was bizarre and somehow… exactly right.

# *Chapter Twenty-Two*

There was no more talking after that. Not of her father, this group that was after her, or the future. Shock and adrenaline seemed to wear off, and everyone staggered off to beds to sleep.

Holden slept with her that night, or rather, morning by the time they'd gotten there. Willa had woken up once and turned into him, and he'd simply held her. They'd held on to each other. She hadn't cried again. She'd simply relaxed back into sleep, tangled up in him.

There'd been no talk of the future then either. Back in the barn he'd said he cared if he lived, but that didn't mean he was going to…what? Stay?

Willa told herself not to wish for it. Just because the danger was over didn't mean Holden's job was over. Dad wasn't out of the woods. Cutting off an arm certainly didn't end any danger.

This time when she rolled over, the spot next to her was empty. She poked her head over the other side of the bed to where Jim had been, but like Holden, he was gone. Jim hadn't left Holden's side since last night. Or this morning.

She squinted at her clock. Seven thirty. And based on the fading light outside her window, seven thirty at night. Oh, her poor animals. What had they been through these past few days? And now she was back and not even taking care of them.

Willa swung out of bed, ignoring the throbbing pain in her head and Pam's irritable meowing. She pulled on a sweatshirt and some thick socks and headed downstairs. She'd tend her animals, try to get her thoughts around what to do about Holden and then maybe have an actual talk with her mother about…everything.

Her heart pinched at that. Truth be told, she didn't want to have that conversation. She didn't want…

Well, this. But she had to face it. A lot sooner than she'd like, because when she got to the kitchen, her mother and Shay were sitting at a table, Holden standing behind them with Jim at his feet.

"Hi," Willa said, wishing she'd stayed in bed.

Mom smiled. "Have a seat, sweetheart. We need to talk about some things."

*Great.* But Willa didn't have a choice, so she slid into a seat across from Shay. She looked up at Holden, but his expression was blank. Unreadable. Oh, to have that superpower.

But she had emotions, and she'd never wanted to learn how to school them that much.

"First, your mom called the hospital, and your father's prognosis is pretty good. He came out of surgery, and the doctors believe he'll make a good recovery."

When Holden delivered that news, there was some spark of…him. Warmth. But then Shay began to talk.

"Willa, your mother, Holden and I have had some conversations about what the future looks like."

"Without me," Willa noted.

"You were asleep," Holden pointed out.

Willa glared at him. "You could have waited."

"We could have," Shay agreed, with a conciliatory note

to her voice. "But there were some time-sensitive things North Star needed to take care of, and it led us to have some conversations about what North Star could do to protect your family."

Mom reached across the table and took her hand. "Yes, we came up with some ideas, but we're not going to force you into anything, Willa. We just…" She trailed off, looking over at Shay.

"North Star came up with a plan," Shay said calmly. "It's been approved by the feds. Holden's agreed. Your mother has agreed. You don't have to. You have an equal say in this, but before being angry about how we came up with the plan without you, why don't you let us tell you what it is."

Willa didn't know what to say or feel, but Shay's calm helped some. "All right."

"In this plan, the North Star tech team would pull the necessary strings to have William, Vera and Willa Zimmerman die in a car accident tomorrow. This will keep those that have your name from coming after you. We *think* we have most of the men with your name currently being processed by the feds, but this is an extra precaution."

Willa looked at Mom. "So, we just wouldn't exist?"

"You'd be dead," Shay said. She was so calm, so straightforward it didn't feel quite as crazy as it should. "Which means your farm would go up for auction. A nice young couple named Holden and Harley Parker would purchase the farm, to live in with Holden's mother, Reeva Parker." Shay nodded at Willa's own mother. "There'd be no connection to who you were, and you wouldn't have to leave. We can create whatever kind of cover we need for Holden so he wouldn't have to be here 24/7."

24/7. Because Holden was still an operative. Not…hers.

"What about…" Willa didn't know how to bring up Dad. She didn't know how not to.

"A man by the name of Josh Parker, Holden's father and Reeva's estranged husband, will be placed in a psychiatric hospital. Should he recover, it's very possible he could join you here," Shay continued in her very bland tone.

Willa felt like her mind was whirling in circles. They were going to fake kill her off. Like a soap opera. Except this wasn't some brand-new identity she was being given. Not exactly.

"But it's your name," Willa said, staring at Holden. He was giving her family his *name*.

"Holden Parker doesn't exist and hasn't since I joined North Star." He shrugged. "It's a good enough name to give."

Willa pushed out a breath. "I don't know what to say."

Mom cleared her throat, and Shay pushed back from the table. She nodded at Holden, and without a word, they left the room so that it was just her and her mother.

"Mom…"

"I know this is a lot. But I'd hoped… You'd still have this place. You'd still get to be you. It would give your father and I a chance to quit in a way we've never been able to." Mom's eyes were shiny with tears, but they didn't fall. She squeezed Willa's hand fiercely. "I want you to be safe, and I want you to have what we couldn't give you before. This does that. But if you don't want it…"

"I want it. I do." They were giving her the life she'd always wanted. Separate from what her parents were. "Would you quit?"

Mom nodded. "I told Shay that I could help her group as a kind of consultant if North Star ever needed it, but I don't want to be in the field anymore. Not after…" She swallowed. "Your father has been unraveling for a while now. I didn't know how to stop it. I didn't know how to get us out. So I just kept pressing forward, hoping something would…get better. I'm sorry it took…this. But this is what he needs. To be out."

"He tried to kill us."

This time a tear did fall over Mom's cheek. "I know. And I know he would have done it. He was…so lost. So broken. The stress of what we'd done… He couldn't handle it, and I can't… Oh, Willa, I know it's awful. I wish I could be angry, but I'm only sad."

Willa swallowed at her own lump and nodded. "Me too. He wasn't…him. Even when he was fighting me, it was like I was fighting someone else."

Mom nodded. "So, with this plan, he gets help. And maybe he comes home. Maybe he doesn't. I can't think that far ahead. I just know…when you love someone, you figure it out. I love your father. I… I know he would have killed us. I don't know how to reconcile that. His brain let him down. It couldn't bear the weight of the stress any longer. I saw it coming, but I just kept hoping…" She shook her head. "We'll get him the help he needs. One step at a time."

One step at a time. Willa took a deep breath. "Okay. I'll do it."

"I don't want you to do it just for us. Just for him. I want—"

"Mom, I love you. And Dad. And this place. And in this scenario, I get everything I love, everything I want." She thought of having Holden's name. But would she have him?

One step at a time.

"We'll do it. We'll become new people and have new lives." Willa smiled and squeezed her mother's hand. "And we'll be together. There's nothing I want more than to have that."

HOLDEN FELT LIKE Willa had been inside forever. Shay had gone to her room to check in on Sabrina's progress. Holden had needed fresh air. The stars.

He paced the porch, Jim at his heels. Waited forever and ever. When Willa finally came outside, Holden felt like his nerves were strung so tight they'd snap. But he'd made his choices, hadn't he?

She looked down at Jim, watching Holden's every move. "You have a devotee."

"Yeah, he's all right."

She smiled at that.

Ever since Shay had brought to him her plan to give Willa and her family new identities, he'd had a plan. She could have what he'd lost. A family with his name. He'd give it to her willingly. He'd protect her with everything he was, even if it was simply a name.

But it was bigger than that, and he didn't know how to tell her. Didn't know how to…explain anything. Which was why he ended up sounding like an idiot.

"We, uh, have to get legally married. I mean, the tech team is going to forge it, but it'll be…a legal thing even though we didn't…"

She cocked her head and studied him. "I've never seen you quite so nervous."

He straightened. "I'm not nervous."

"You seem very nervous about legally marrying me via forged document."

He sighed. "Well, you're back to your normal self." *Thank God.*

She smiled up at him. "I'm getting there."

She stood there in the evening dark, haloed by the lights on inside the house. Her house. *Our house.* She was…like no one he'd ever known. She'd chained him to a bed. She'd fought him. She'd survived all this and could still...smile. Even after she'd cried.

There were things in front of them that wouldn't be easy, but that didn't change what he felt. What he wanted. "I love you."

"That sounded less nervous."

"Damn it, Willa."

"I think I'm Harley now."

He pulled her to him, because she was toying with him and he probably deserved it. "You're still Willa. You'll always be Willa. You're safe now." He let out a long breath, framing her face with his hands, careful of the bandage. "I want to make us work, I do. But I have to go. Sabrina's trying to stop a hit man from taking out the name your mother gave us. She's like...my sister. If I can help, I have to."

Willa nodded, wrapping her arms around his neck. "But you'll come back."

"If you want me back."

"We're going to be married, as far as I can tell, so you kind of have to."

"It's not real. I mean, it's real, but... You can have that life you wanted. Where you talk to the lady at the post office and have friends and... You might find there's someone better suited to—"

"I won't find you out there, and you're who I want. Maybe it's soon and fast, and maybe we'll find out something that can't be overcome. But I doubt it. Because I love you, and when you love someone, you choose... You choose to figure it out."

*Choose.* That was a word that hit him hard. "I didn't get to choose when I was a kid. Losing my parents. My siblings. I didn't have a choice in any of that. I think I went through life without making any real...choices. Not the kind you build your life on. Because you're right, I didn't care if I was alive. At best, I cared about doing a little good in the world, but that was only at best."

"Your best is pretty good, Holden Parker."

He didn't realize he'd needed to hear that. Needed someone to say, out loud and to his face, that he'd done okay.

"Go. Help your sister. Then come back to me, and Jim. In one piece."

He lifted her hand to his mouth and pressed a kiss to her palm. "I promise."

That was a promise Holden kept.

* * * * *

# COLTON 911: GUARDIAN IN THE STORM

**CARLA CASSIDY**

For my father, who taught me everything
I needed to know about laughter and love.
I will love you forever, Daddy!

# *Chapter One*

Simone Colton walked out of the large brick building that housed the psychology department on the University of Chicago campus. As she stepped into the sunshine, she drew a deep breath of the fresh early June air.

She should be feeling a big sense of relief. Today had been the last of the psychology classes she taught during the day. She had only a couple of night lectures left and then she'd be completely finished with the semester.

She had decided not to teach summer school and so she had two months of free time. Under normal circumstances she would have been looking forward to lunches with good friends, long naps and reading for pleasure and not research.

However, these were not normal circumstances. Nothing had been anywhere near normal since her father and her uncle had been brutally murdered, gunned down in the parking lot outside Colton Connections, their very successful family business.

The murder had occurred six months ago, and since that time, not only had Simone dealt with a mountain

of grief, but also with the burning need to create a profile for the killer.

Right now, she was on her way home to change
clothes and then she was meeting her sister Tatum
at her restaurant. She needed to hash over the family
meeting they'd had the night before with FBI agents
Brad Howard and Russ Dodd, a meeting that had only
renewed her burning need to catch a killer.

It was a short walk from the college campus to her
condo in Hyde Park. She'd loved the condo the first
time she'd looked at it and had considered it a lucky
score in an area that was highly desirable.

However, since the murder, there had been no solace
within the walls she called home. All she thought about
was that her father would never be able to walk through
the door again. He would never stop by to share a cup
of coffee again. He would never, ever again be able to
give her the big bear hugs that she'd loved, that she'd
always counted on from him.

She now walked through the front door and tossed
her briefcase on the overstuffed beige sofa that was
bedecked with throw pillows in the color of soft pink
magnolia. The same colored blinds hung at her floor-
to-ceiling windows. The colors had once created a
warm and soothing ambience, but nothing soothed
her since her father's death.

The kitchen was updated with granite countertops
and stainless-steel appliances, although she wasn't
much into cooking.

The condo had two bedrooms and she now walked
into the smaller of the two. This was her home office,
where she graded students' papers and made up her les-

son plans. Right now, the whiteboard that hung on the wall held notes that had nothing to do with her classes.

All the notes were on deviant personalities and behaviors, five months of her work in an effort to come up with a profile of her father and uncle's killer.

Despite her best efforts, she couldn't have been more wrong about things. It was time...past time for her to clear the whiteboard. She grabbed her eraser and slowly erased the notes she'd worked on so feverishly since the night of the murder up until a couple of weeks ago.

When she was finished, her heart clenched as she stared at the board of nothing that was left. It had been that easy for two thrill-seeking kids to erase her father from her life forever. Her grief was still like a clawing, vicious animal inside her that refused to relinquish its hold on her.

She whirled out of the office and went into her bedroom before the tears that were always close to the surface broke loose. It took her only minutes to change from the casual clothes she'd worn for class that day into black slacks and a dressier blouse. She always dressed up when she went to her sister's restaurant.

Minutes later she was on the train and headed downtown. As the train moved down the tracks, she leaned her head back and released a weary sigh. Since the murder, she'd been suffering from nightmares, haunting and horrible dreams where her father begged her to find the killers and seek justice for him and his brother. The nightmares didn't occur every night, but they did happen often enough that she sometimes felt like she was moving through life in a bit of a fog.

Seventeen minutes later the train halted at the stop closest to her sister's acclaimed restaurant. The restaurant, True, had opened two years ago to critical acclaim and commercial success.

Tatum had her dream come true with the restaurant and now she had the love of her life in the handsome Cruz Medina. Cruz was a Chicago cop who had gone undercover in the restaurant to investigate a potential drug ring working out of True. By the time the case wrapped up, the two had fallen in love.

Simone now walked through the front door of True. Wonderful scents immediately assailed her nose. Even though it was late for lunch and early for dinner, the place was still packed with diners.

Before the hostess could greet Simone, Tatum approached with a smile on her face. Simone could always tell what her sister was doing in the restaurant that day by her hairstyle. If her blond hair was down and wavy, then Tatum was working front of the house. If it was a day when she was cooking, her hair was pulled back and up. Today it was down and she was clad in navy blue slacks and a blue floral blouse that emphasized her bright blue eyes.

"Come on, sis, I've got a two-top table in the back just waiting for us."

"Sounds perfect," Simone replied. She followed her sister through the stylish main dining room, where there was a large marble bar with tons of seating. Located in a warehouse, the restaurant boasted high ceilings painted green and huge windows that provided lots of natural light.

The space was decorated with a touch of a European bent, and the food was fresh farm to table. They went to the back and into a more private and quiet area. The minute the two were seated, a waitress with the name tag Annabelle appeared.

"Why don't you start us off with two glasses of white wine," Tatum said. "Thank you, Annabelle."

Minutes later the two had their wine and had ordered their lunch. "How are you doing?" Tatum asked.

Simone shrugged. "Still working through the grief."

Tatum nodded. "Aren't we all."

"It's somehow more difficult to get past knowing that there was absolutely no motive, that they were killed by two teenagers because they were in the wrong place at the wrong time," Simone said. "And then the killers went on to kill two more men, also with no motive whatsoever." A new wave of grief swept over Simone.

"I know, but thanks to Allie Chandler at least now they have one of the teenagers behind bars and they know who the other one is," Tatum replied.

Allie Chandler was a private investigator hired by their cousin Jones Colton. She was the one who had found social media posts from both of the boys. Jared Garner and Leo Styler had each written "score" on the nights of the murders.

"Thank goodness Allie wasn't hurt when they basically kidnapped her." Tatum took a sip of her wine.

Allie had gone undercover as a college student in an effort to get hard evidence that the two were responsible. She'd gotten herself invited to a party, but then the two boys had taken off with her in their car and ended up in Leo's parents' basement. When they'd discovered she was wired, the two teens had gone wild. Thankfully the FBI had broken in. Jared was arrested, but Leo had gotten away.

"I can't believe right now the only charge Jared is facing is kidnapping when we're all certain he killed Dad and Uncle Ernest," Simone said, her frustration evident in her tone.

"Unfortunately, Jared's and Leo's parents alibied them for the time of the murder."

"Yeah, their very wealthy, privileged parents and we have some proof that they were probably lying. Let's just hope the FBI can find Leo before his mommy and daddy can get him a ticket out of the country," Simone said.

The conversation was interrupted by the return of Annabelle with their meals. Everything that came out of the True kitchen not only had tremendous flavors but also beautiful presentations. Even the house salads that both of them had ordered looked like colorful works of art.

"Did you get the text from Heath about the family meeting tonight?" Tatum asked as soon as Annabelle had left their table.

"Yes, do you know what it's about?" Simone speared a cherry tomato with her fork.

"I don't have a clue."

Simone frowned thoughtfully. Heath was their eldest cousin and had temporarily stepped into the position of president of Colton Connections after the murder had occurred. "I just can't imagine what he would have to discuss with us. I'm assuming everything is going well at the business."

"I guess we'll find out tonight," Tatum replied.

For the next few minutes, the two ate and talked about their work and how other family members were doing. There were six cousins all around the same age and they were a very close-knit group.

"So, what are your plans for the summer?" Tatum asked when they were almost finished with their meals.

"I want to find Leo Styler and prove that those two little creeps are cold-blooded killers," Simone said fervently.

"Oh, Simone, please leave it all up to the FBI now," Tatum said, a troubled look on her face. "The last thing any of us would want is to lose somebody else."

"Don't worry. I'm not going to get myself into any kind of trouble," Simone replied. "However, I do intend to talk to Agent Howard and see if I can sit in on one of their interviews with Jared."

"He's not going to allow that. He seems to be a by-the-books kind of agent."

"His by-the-books style didn't catch the bad guys. A private investigator did." Simone shoved her plate aside and reached for her wineglass.

"That's not fair," Tatum said softly.

Simone released a deep sigh. "I know. I'm just sick of all the red tape and regulations. Besides, you know I'm always interested in what drives deviant behavior. I just want to learn more about Jared Garner and what drove him and his friend to commit such a terrible crime."

"You seem very intense whenever Agent Howard is around." Tatum arched an eyebrow and smiled. "I thought maybe something else was going on."

Simone looked at her sister blankly. "Like what?"

"Like maybe a little bit of attraction?"

"Don't be ridiculous," Simone scoffed even as she felt a rise of heat fill her cheeks. She wouldn't want anyone to know just how hot she found FBI agent Brad Howard.

His dark brown hair was worn short and neat and his hazel eyes appeared to change colors depending on what color of shirt he wore. He was tall with broad shoulders and an athletic build. She definitely found him more than a little bit attractive.

"I don't even like him very much," she told her sister. "I feel like I've dated versions of him in the past. He strikes me as being very stubborn and far too confident in himself. He probably finds it difficult to listen to anyone's advice and would never consider a woman his equal," Simone finished.

Tatum stared at Simone as if her head had just dropped off her shoulders and rolled across the floor. "That certainly hasn't been my impression of Agent Howard. I think maybe you're projecting shades of Dr. Wayne Jamison on him."

"Ugh, don't remind me of him." Wayne was a history professor at the college. She had dated him for a little over six months and had made herself believe she was madly in love with him. But the longer they had dated, the more controlling and superior he'd become. She'd finally realized he wasn't the man for her and so a year ago she'd broken things off with him. She hadn't dated anyone since then.

And the last thing she wanted from Brad Howard was any kind of a personal relationship. All she wanted was for him to alow her access to sit in on Jared Garner's interview. She might be able to help him put away two teenage serial killers.

FBI AGENT BRAD Howard was frustrated. He'd been frustrated for the past two months, ever since he'd been called to Chicago from his Washington, DC, office to investigate the potential of two serial killers in the early stages of their "careers."

He now sat in the small office he'd been moved to a week ago. It was little more than a closet, but the Chicago PD had needed back the space he'd originally been assigned.

It didn't matter to him what kind of room he worked from. All he really needed was a desk, his phone and his work computer. Finally, they'd gotten the break they'd needed to identify two potential suspects. One was in jail and the other one wasn't, which created a lot of Brad's frustration.

He had spent much of his first month here assuming they were looking for a single killer. Serial killers working in duos certainly weren't unheard of, but they were relatively rare. One of the most famous killing duos was probably cousins Kenneth Bianchi and Angelo Buono Jr.

Together they had kidnapped and strangled ten women and girls, earning them the name of the Hillside Strangler in the press.

However, it was almost unheard of to have a couple of teenagers on a path of death. Jared Garner and Leo Styler were only nineteen years old. They both came from affluent backgrounds and right now Brad's biggest enemies were their parents, who were not being cooperative in the investigation. Rather, they were overbearing and overly protective people who used their money and their power to try to intimidate.

He now powered down his computer with thoughts of dinner on his mind. He'd been eating so much fast food and sandwiches in the past two months he'd decided that this evening he'd treat himself and go to a restaurant and have a real, good sit-down meal. However, before he could get away, an officer stepped into the room.

"Simone Colton is here to speak to you. Do you have a minute for her before you head out?" he asked.

"Of course. Send her on back," Brad replied. He braced himself for seeing her one-on-one. There was something about Simone that somehow unsettled him. More than any of the other family members, her grief haunted him and her intelligence challenged him.

He hadn't realized just how small his new office was until she was seated in a chair in front of his desk. Instantly he was engulfed by the smell of her perfume... an appealing scent of fresh flowers and a hint of fresh citrus.

"What can I do for you this afternoon, Miss Colton?" he asked.

"I've told you before you can call me Simone," she replied. Her eyes appeared a startling blue today. Her medium brown hair curved around her chin, emphasizing her delicate features. She was clad in black slacks and a tailored black-and-white blouse that showcased her slender shapeliness. "I was wondering if it would be possible for me to sit in the next time you interview Jared Garner."

He stared at her in disbelief as he shook his head. "You know I can't allow you to do that."

"Why not? I promise you I would be completely professional." She sat up straighter in the chair.

"That's not the issue. You're the victim's daughter, and in any case, it's against regulations." He could tell his words irritated her.

"I've spent all of my adult life studying the human

mind and deviant behavior. I feel like I could help. Maybe I can see things in Jared that nobody else has seen…something that could help to get him to confess to the murders and give up Leo Styler's location." She leaned forward, her eyes burning with intensity. "I can help, Agent Howard. Please let me help."

He understood her desire…her absolute need to see that her father's killers were arrested and went to prison. He'd worked with enough victims in his career to know where she was coming from, but there was no way in hell he could or would allow her into an interview room with a suspect. It would certainly give a defense lawyer plenty of ammunition to use and there was no way Brad would risk the case they were building against the teens.

"I'm sorry, Simone. It just isn't allowed," he finally said. He watched as the flame in her eyes dimmed and instead a bleak despair darkened them. His chest tightened with sympathy.

"I still believe I might be able to pick up on things that everyone else has missed. I've been studying people and their behaviors for years," she repeated and then stood.

"Wait," he replied and frowned thoughtfully. An idea blossomed in his head, an idea that might give Simone what she wanted and still keep the integrity of the investigation.

She sank back down in the chair and looked at him hopefully. God, she was so attractive. There was something about her that drew him in a very unprofessional way and that was the last thing he needed or wanted.

"I suppose if you want to come in tomorrow morning around ten, I could share with you the interviews we've already done with Garner," he offered.

Immediately her eyes brightened. "Oh, thank you. That would be wonderful. Then I'll see you at ten tomorrow." She jumped out of her chair, murmured a goodbye and then practically ran from the room as if afraid he might change his mind.

Even though he could think of all kinds of reasons why what he'd just offered her was probably a bad idea, he only hoped it helped in some way to ease her grief and come to terms with her uncle and father's murders.

Yes, for some inexplicable reason Simone's grief hit him much harder than any of the other Colton family members'. It was her sad eyes that haunted his dreams, her tears that had pushed him to try harder.

If he was perfectly honest with himself, he'd admit that the reason he'd just made the concession to allow her to see some of the interview recordings was because he'd pretty much failed her. He'd failed them all.

He'd worked dozens of serial killer cases in the past. In each case he had successfully worked up accurate profiles that had led to arrests in almost all of them.

In the past two months he'd done what he'd always done...tried to profile the kind of person the killer might be. Then two weeks before, a private investigator had shone a light on two nineteen-year-old college kids, proving that all of Brad's theories about the killer had been wrong.

He was now even more determined to prove that Jared Garner and Leo Styler had not only murdered Ernest and Alfred Colton in cold blood, but two other older businessmen as well. More than anything, he wanted to prove himself to all the Coltons, but particularly to Simone.

And that worried him. The last thing he wanted was any kind of tangled relationship with a member of the victims' family. Besides, hopefully it was now just a matter of days before they got Leo Styler behind bars and the case would be closed.

And it was probably just a matter of days before he would be back home in DC. After two months of living in a hotel and being immersed in murder, he should be looking forward to getting back to his life in DC. It worried him just a little bit that he wasn't.

When the case was over, he wouldn't mind hanging out here in Chicago for a little while longer. When he tried to identify why he would want to remain, it worried him that Simone Colton's beautiful face filled his mind.

There was no way he was going there. He was thirty-six years old and married to his work. Besides, no matter how attractive he found Simone Colton, he knew he would probably always remind her of one of the very worst times in her life.

# Chapter Two

Heath had gathered the family together in Simone's mother and father's home. Her uncle Ernest and aunt Fallon's and Simone's parents' homes shared a common backyard with a large pool, pool house and tennis courts.

Although her aunt and uncle's place was exquisitely decorated in a French provincial style, it was somehow colder…less inviting than Alfred and Farrah's warm, Tuscan-feel home. Therefore, this was the place always chosen for family gatherings. Besides, with a mother-in-law suite attached, it made it easy for Grandma Colton, who lived in the suite, to be included in all the gatherings.

They were all seated on the overstuffed sofas and on chairs brought in so everyone had a place to sit. Simone was grateful to sit on the sofa next to her mother.

Her aunt Fallon and her mother were twins. The main way people told them apart was that Farrah's dark brown hair was worn short and curly and Fallon's hair was longer. Simone's mother had always been the louder of the two. She was wonderfully loving and was the creative force in Gemini Designs, an interior design company she had started and now operated with her twin sister.

Since the murder, the spark in her mother was gone and her beautiful green eyes often held the same sadness, the same grief that Simone felt. It hurt Simone to see both her mother and her aunt trying to deal with the unexpected deaths of their husbands.

"I'm sure you're all wondering why I got you together this evening," Heath said and stood from his chair. Her cousin's dark blond hair was shaggier than usual and it was obvious he'd forgotten about shaving again.

Heath had stepped in as the president of Colton Connections, the company started by Ernest and Alfred and that was now valued at over sixty million dollars. The two men had created a series of innovative inventions and owned numerous patents.

"I'm sure wondering why we're all here," Grandma Colton replied.

Everyone looked at Heath expectantly. He drew in a deep breath. "Uh, something unexpected has come up concerning Colton Connections."

What now? Simone reached out and took her mother's hand in hers. Her mother squeezed her hand tightly, as if expecting bad news.

"My office has received a letter saying that half of Colton Connections's holdings rightfully belong to two other men. They are twins Erik and Axel Colton and they are claiming to be the illegitimate children of Dean Colton."

Gasps of surprise filled the room, along with exclamations of disbelief. Simone's stomach sank. Illegitimate children of her grandfather? Was this somehow true? Or were these two men simply vultures who were trying to capitalize on a double murder? As if they all didn't have enough to deal with already, and now this?

Heath raised his hands to quiet everyone. "They claim to be rightful heirs because of a special codicil Grandpa Dean drew up and they are therefore due the same amount of money that went to my dad and Uncle Alfred."

"I certainly never heard Alfred talk about having two illegitimate brothers," Simone's mother said.

"Same with me," Aunt Fallon added. "Ernest never mentioned having other brothers and I can't imagine Dean having an affair. But then before six months ago I wouldn't have imagined that my husband and his twin brother would be murdered."

There was a long moment of silence. "So, how serious are we taking this?" Simone's youngest sister, January, asked, breaking the hushed quiet that had momentarily overtaken everyone. January was a social worker for the county and volunteered for multiple organizations.

"Serious enough that I've gotten our lawyers involved. I just wanted to let you all know what was going on," Heath said. "And I'll continue to keep you all up to date as this whole thing unfolds."

A half an hour later Simone and her sisters left the house. "Oh, by the way, tomorrow I'm going to watch the files of the interviews of Jared Garner with Agent Howard," she told Tatum.

"You actually got him to agree with that?" Tatum asked in surprise.

"Wait…what's going on?" January asked. At twenty-seven years old, she was five years younger than Simone. January looked even younger than her age and was model pretty, so she was often not taken seriously, but Simone knew her baby sister was smart as a whip.

She quickly explained to January what she was doing the next day, and when she was finished, concern shone from January's green eyes. "Oh, Simone, I wish you would leave this all alone and let law enforcement do their jobs."

"That's exactly what I told her earlier today when we had lunch," Tatum said.

"I am letting them do their jobs," Simone protested. "I'm just hoping to help a little bit. I need to do this."

"I know how badly you're hurting, Simone. We're all hurting, but I don't want you anywhere near Jared Garner. Have you forgotten that Leo Styler is still on the loose? I don't want you getting any attention that might put you at risk," January exclaimed.

"My feelings exactly," Tatum chimed in.

"Don't worry. I'm just going to be in a little office with Brad Howard and nobody will even know I'm there. Trust me, I'll be fine." Simone hugged January and then Tatum.

"What do you think about what we just heard from Heath?" Tatum asked.

"I find it darned suspicious that after all these years and only after Dad and Uncle Ernest are gone, these twins magically appear out of the blue," January said.

"I agree, but I also trust Heath and the attorneys to sort it all out," Simone replied. "And on that note, I'm heading home." She hugged each of her sisters once again and then got into her car and headed back to her condo.

Once there she found it impossible to think about

what had just happened when her head was so full of what she hoped would happen the next day. She desperately hoped she'd see something on the file that could be used to break Jared into confessing to the murders.

She changed out of her clothes and into a sleeveless summer nightgown. After washing her face and brushing her teeth, she finally climbed into her king-size bed. She'd bought the bed when she'd thought she was going to have a future with Dr. Wayne. He'd lived in a cramped apartment and so they had spent most of their time together here in her place.

But she had refused to let him move in with her and she also didn't like him spending the night with her. In her mind that was something engaged or married couples did.

She'd finally kicked out the doctor but had kept the bed. There were times she felt very lonely. At thirty-two years old she had the career of her dreams, but she was missing the dream man in her life.

Eventually she wanted a big family and she'd begun to hear the faint tick of her biological clock. Still, she wanted to be married only once and so it was important she get it right the first time.

She fell asleep almost immediately and into the dream that far too often haunted her nightscapes. She was in a graveyard and walking along a dark path between the headstones. The moonlight was full and cast down a haunting silvery light. Her heart clenched as she came to the headstone where her father's name was written.

In her dream she sank down to her knees before it, tears half blinding her. "Daddy, I miss you so much.

You've always been my hero and now I'm absolutely lost without you."

A mist began to form across the front of the headstone, a mist that came together and became her father's beloved face. "Help me, Simone. I need your help, baby girl. I'm stuck and I can't move on unless you help me."

"Anything, Dad. Just tell me what you need me to do," she said fervently.

"Get the killers, Simone. See that they spend the rest of their lives in jail. If you don't, I'll never be at peace. Do you hear me? I'll never be at peace." His voice became a roar and his face twisted with rage.

"Save me, Simone." Skeletal hands reached out toward her. She gasped and scooted back away from the headstone, but the hands kept coming and wrapped around her neck. Cold ghostly fingers squeezed tight, making it difficult for her to scream out her terror.

She awoke and jerked up with a deep gasp. Her breathing came in rapid pants and the horror of the dream still raced through her. Tears burned at her eyes as she thought of the beginning of the dream, when her father's pleas to her had been so heartbreaking. She didn't want to even think about the end of the dream. That man, that angry monster who had tried to strangle her, wasn't her loving father.

Still, the nightmare reminded her that she needed to do whatever she could to help find Leo Styler and she believed the answers to so many things were in Jared Garner.

And today she would get access to his interviews. At that thought a burst of adrenaline raced through her and she jumped out of bed.

An hour later she had showered and dressed in a pair of jeans and a coral-colored sleeveless blouse. She sat at the table with a cup of coffee and a toasted bagel in front of her, counting down the minutes to the meeting with Brad Howard.

As she ate, she thought about what her sister had said the day before about sensing some kind of attraction between her and Brad. Of course, the idea was utterly ridiculous.

He was just a very hot-looking FBI agent in town to do a job. All she really wanted from Agent Howard was answers that would lead to both of the teenagers in jail and eventually convicted for their crimes. It was the only way her father would find peace. It was the only way she would find some semblance of peace. And hopefully when that all happened, the nightmares would stop.

At nine thirty she left her condo. She carried with her a legal pad so she could take notes and her purse. At precisely ten she walked into the police station and asked for Brad.

When he came out to greet her and lead her back to his office, she couldn't help but notice how his black pants fit his slim waist and long legs and how his gray dress shirt emphasized his broad shoulders.

He carried himself with the confidence of a man sure of himself. She'd always found a confident man attractive, but only if that self-assurance didn't border on arrogance. In Agent Howard's case, she didn't know enough about him to know if he was an arrogant man or not. In any case, she shouldn't care. He was simply the man in charge of a criminal case, a case where her father and uncle had been murdered.

When they reached the small space he worked from, there were two chairs on one side of the desk and the computer screen was turned toward the chairs.

Simone took the chair closer to the wall. Brad closed the office door and then sat next to her. Simone was instantly aware of his nearness, not as the FBI agent who might help her, but as a handsome man whose cologne tantalized her. It was a scent of something spicy and slightly mysterious.

"I have to confess I wrestled with myself all night long about having you here today," he said. His eyes were a golden green today and he held her gaze steadily.

She leaned forward and placed the legal pad on the desk in front of her. "Why would you have any doubts? I'm hoping I'll be able to give you some insight that will further the investigation."

"Ultimately that's why I didn't call you to cancel this viewing," he replied. "However, I want you to understand that this access to these files is highly unusual and I need to have your promise that you won't take what you see or hear on them outside of this room."

"I can promise that," she replied. He held her gaze for several long moments, as if gauging if he could trust her or not. He must have been satisfied with what he saw in her for he turned to the computer.

"I figured I'd start with the first interview with Jared and his parents." He pushed several buttons on the computer and then an image of Jared, his parents and Brad in a large interview room came into view. Jared's lawyer sat in the background.

Simone leaned forward once again and grabbed her legal pad. She then withdrew a pen from her purse as she waited for the video to begin.

And then it was playing. Simone intently watched the interplay between all the people. She wrote down her impressions and thoughts as it played.

Simone had a good understanding of the human mind. She was also good at picking up cues and tells in behavior, behavior that often occurred in people in an effort to hide real emotions.

She knew that Jared's parents, Rob and Marilyn, owned a furniture store and that Jared had a grandmother who lived overseas. She also knew Jared's parents had been desperately making arrangements to send him overseas to escape the charges against him. Fortunately, he had been arrested before that could actually happen.

The interview lasted about an hour. "Thoughts?" Brad immediately asked when it was finished. "Opinions?"

She frowned. It had been a bit difficult to stay completely focused on the tape as she had found Brad's closeness to her a bit distracting. His body heat had radiated toward her and a couple of times his arm had brushed against hers, shocking her as pleasant tingles had rushed through her.

"I'd like to see more before I tell you what I'm thinking. Do you have additional video of Jared and his parents being interviewed?" she asked.

He nodded and pulled up a new file and opened a new video of the same five people. Once again, she did her best to focus on not only what was being said, but what was not said, which could be equally as revealing.

The video was a little over an hour and a half long, and by the time they were finished, it was nearing one thirty. "You want to take a break and let me treat you to lunch?" he surprised her by asking. "There's a little deli around the corner that serves great sandwiches, and to be perfectly honest, I skipped dinner last night and so I'm starving."

"You don't have to take me to lunch," she protested.

"Really, Simone, I'd like to."

It was the first time he'd called her by her first name and she was surprised by how much she liked her name on his lips. "I only had a bagel for breakfast, so lunch sounds good."

"Then let's get out of here." They didn't speak again until they stepped outside of the building.

"Ah, fresh air," he said. "I love spring and early summer. What about you?" They fell into step side by side in a leisurely pace down the sidewalk.

"I prefer summer and winter," she replied.

"Ah, a woman of extremes," he said.

"Not really. There are just so many storms in the spring and fall, and I'm definitely a bit of a scaredy-cat when it comes to thunder and lightning."

A touch of emotion rose up in her chest. "I can't tell you how many times when I was little that my dad would hold me and rock me in a rocking chair I had next to my bed until the storm outside passed."

To her surprise, Brad reached out and touched the back of her hand. It was brief, but she knew his intent was to comfort. "I'm so sorry, Simone. I'm so damned sorry about what happened to your father and your uncle."

"Thanks. I'm just hoping we can get these two killers in prison where they belong. Just imagine how many more people they would have killed if they hadn't been found out. Just imagine if Leo is still out there killing people."

"Now, that's the stuff of my nightmares," he said ruefully.

Their talk stopped as he led the way into the little restaurant. It was a typical deli with a long counter and different kinds of meats and cheeses in a refrigerated display case. Small tables were scattered around the space and a huge handwritten menu blackboard offered a variety of sandwiches and a special of the day. Today the special was a cup of tomato basil soup and a turkey-avocado sandwich. Since it was late for lunch and too early for dinner, only a few of the tables were occupied.

"I'm sure this isn't exactly the kind of place you usually eat at," Brad said. "But over the last couple of months I've tried pretty much everything on the menu here and I can tell you it's all good."

She looked at him curiously. "What makes you think this kind of place is out of my wheelhouse? There are many days when I eat in the college cafeteria or I grab a sandwich at a deli near the campus."

"I just figured with your family background you were accustomed to a finer dining experience," he replied.

She laughed. "It's obvious you don't know me at all. I'm really just a nerdy professor."

He smiled. "Then maybe I'll get to know you better over lunch."

For some reason his words caused a pleasant rivulet of warmth to rush through her. She quickly broke eye contact with him and instead looked up at the menu.

Minutes later they were seated at a table in the back

with their lunch before them. Simone had ordered a turkey-and-cheese sandwich and Brad had ordered a ham and swiss. They both had chips and sodas.

"You want to talk about what you've seen so far on the videos?" he asked.

She frowned thoughtfully. "Not yet. You said you have more video of Jared being interviewed with his parents?"

"I have two more, but unfortunately I'm not going to be able to show them to you today. I have some meetings later this afternoon that I need to attend."

"Would I be able to view those tomorrow?" she asked.

"I can set you up to see them tomorrow at the same time as today. Does that work for you?"

"That definitely works for me," she agreed. This close to him, she noticed that his eyelashes were sinfully long. He had an intense way of gazing at her, as if he were trying to delve into her very soul. If she was a criminal with something to hide, she would find his gaze quite daunting. "Thankfully I finished the last of my daytime classes and I'm not working through the summer," she added.

"Do you enjoy teaching psychology classes?" he asked.

"I love it, although for the last couple of years my schedule has become pretty heavy. Everyone likes to take classes in psychology and then three years ago I added courses in deviant behaviors and the criminal mind. What I didn't expect was for those classes to become so popular. I'm just grateful I only have a couple of night classes left to finish up and then I have two months free."

When she got nervous, she tended to talk too much and she flushed as she realized that was what she was doing. "I'm sorry. I'm doing all the talking here. So, what about you? Do you like what you do?"

"I feel like I was destined to hunt down killers." He looked at her for a moment and then stared at someplace just over her head. "When I was twelve, my mother was killed by a serial killer."

Simone gasped. "Oh my God, I'm so sorry."

He smiled at her. "Thank you, but it was a long time ago. But it set me on the course of what I wanted to do with my life."

"Did the authorities catch the person who killed your mother?" The fact that at one time in his life he'd probably felt the same emotions, the same pain that she felt somehow made her feel a strange connection with him.

"No, they didn't. He raped and killed six women in six days and then stopped the killing spree. He left few clues behind and the authorities were unable to arrest anyone for the crimes. It has remained a cold case. I'm just glad we were able to give you some answers about who killed your father, although it was no thanks to the profile I worked on."

"What do you mean?" She picked up a chip and popped it into her mouth.

"I spent so much time trying to tie your father and your uncle to the other two victims. I was convinced there had to be some connection between them and I spun my wheels trying to find it."

She smiled at him. "Don't beat yourself up. I did the same thing. I worked for hours trying to profile the killer but never guessed that it was two teenagers killing random victims."

She didn't want to talk murder anymore. She'd been immersed in it for the past six months. Now she found herself interested in the man seated across from her.

"So, tell me more about you. I know you live in Washington, DC. Do you have a family there? A wife and children?"

"No, it's just me."

"So, you aren't married?" She wasn't sure how old he was, but he appeared to be in his midthirties or so.

"No. Got close once, but it fell apart before we could get to the altar. She thought I was already married to my job and she refused to marry a man she didn't believe would make her a priority. What about you? Have you ever been married?" Once again, his eyes held an intensity that threatened to half steal her breath away.

"No. My last relationship broke up a little over a year ago and I haven't really dated anyone since then." She smiled at him. "I, too, have been accused of being married to my job."

For the next few minutes, they ate and small talked about the weather and life in Chicago. She told him about the sudden appearance of two mystery heirs attempting to claim part of the family business and he asked questions about Colton Connections.

She was surprised by how easy he was to talk to. He'd always appeared stiff and professional when he'd met with the family about the murder. But today he was a bit softer and far more approachable than she would have thought. She could have sat and talked to him forever, but she was also aware that he needed to get back to his very important work.

When the meal was finished, they stepped outside into the bright sunshine. "Thank you, Agent Howard, for allowing me the opportunity to view the tapes, and thank you so much for lunch," she replied.

"No problem, and please call me Brad."

Once again, he'd surprised her. "How about I call you Brad only when the two of us are alone?"

He smiled at her, a wide smile that slightly crinkled the outward corners of his eyes and filled his features with a heart-stopping warmth. "That works. And I'll see you again tomorrow morning at ten."

"You can count on it," she said with a smile of her own.

A few minutes later Simone was heading home with thoughts of the attractive FBI man in her mind. She should be thinking about the taped evidence she'd seen, but thoughts of Brad intruded.

Today she'd seen pieces of the man and not the agent in charge of her father's murder. And she'd liked what she'd seen. She tried to tell herself she was eager to go into the station the next day to see more video, and she was. But the truth of the matter was she was also eager to spend more time with Brad.

She needed to get her head in a better space and focus on the fact that it didn't matter how attracted she was to him. Ultimately he was doing a job, and when the job was finished, he'd go back to his life in Washington, DC. Besides, what would a very hot FBI agent find attractive about a nerdy professor who was scared of storms?

BRAD LEFT THE deli and Simone, and then headed back to headquarters. He shouldn't have had lunch with her, and he definitely shouldn't have gone into any details about his personal life. The fact that he'd been reluctant for the lunch to end was definitely problematic.

In all his years of working as a homicide detective, he'd always managed to keep professional and personal very separate. There was just something about Simone Colton...

Maybe it was because her bright blue eyes emanated not only strength and intelligence, but also a soft vulnerability that somehow drew him in. Or perhaps it was because her hair looked so shiny and soft and touchable and her lips had a small pout that looked extremely kissable.

Jeez, what was wrong with him? It was definitely time he wound up this case and got back to his life in DC—his very lonely life in DC.

He shoved this thought away. He knew part of the flaw he suffered from was most of the time he preferred to spend time in the minds of killers rather than in the minds of ordinary people.

At thirty-six years old he'd pretty much written off love and marriage for himself. It had also become more difficult to have a group of buddies to hang out with.

Most of his friends were now married with families of their own and Brad no longer felt comfortable being a third wheel in their lives. The exception to that was his partner, Russ, and his wife, Janie, who always invited him to dinner or to spend special occasions with them.

The single men who worked with him tended to be bitter, burned-out cops who drank too much and talked about their ex-wives and taking early retirement.

He had no idea what he found so appealing about

Simone, but it was an attraction he certainly didn't intend to explore. In fact, as he settled back down in his office, he consciously shoved all thoughts of her out of his mind.

As soon as he settled back in, he made a series of phone calls to check with the men who were out on the streets looking for Leo Styler. The kid had to be somewhere, but so far they hadn't been able to find his location.

He pulled up a photo from a social media profile. Styler looked like a punk wannabe. He was fond of camo pants and black T-shirts. A heavy gold chain and lock that could be used as a weapon hung around his neck, but Brad sensed they were used just to intimidate others.

In talking to some of Leo's peers, Brad had gotten a picture of a kid who wanted to connect with members of the opposite sex, but his antisocial behavior was a big turnoff.

Neither of the boys were big in academics, which was why they were attending a community college rather than the kind of colleges their parents could afford. However, the two boys were into the sport of mag-fed paintball gaming.

Brad had needed to educate himself in the sport when he heard about it. He'd learned that *mag-fed* meant magazine-fed paint guns, giving the player the experience of loading and shooting guns that were similar to the real thing. There were two such clubs in Chicago and Brad had men undercover and hanging around them in the hopes that Leo might show up at one of them. But so far the kid had been a no-show.

Brad didn't believe that Leo's parents had managed

to get Leo out of the states and now his name was flagged, so it would be difficult for him to even get a bus ticket out of town. James and Miranda Styler professed they didn't know where their son was, but Brad was betting they were somehow keeping him funded so he had a motel or someplace to crash in and food to eat.

He had men sitting on the Styler home to see if the kid tried to sneak back home. Brad felt as if he had covered all the bases and it was just a matter of time before they got Leo behind bars.

The day was long with the task force meeting to update each other. Brad was the liaison between the two FBI agents who had come with him from DC and the three Chicago detectives who had been lent to him during the investigation.

Unfortunately, there was no news. He had another interview scheduled with Jared and his parents the next day. He was hoping to get a confession out of Jared so that when they found Leo they could book him on murder charges.

It was almost dark when he left the police station and headed back to the hotel that he'd called home for the past two months. He stopped in the deli and grabbed a sandwich to take with him and then walked on.

Minutes later he was in his hotel room. The room was nothing fancy, but it had a good king-size bed, a small round table with chairs, a television with cable and a mini fridge.

He made himself a cup of coffee in the one-cup coffee maker and then sank down at the table and opened the sack containing his sandwich.

As he ate, all the events of the murders rushed

through his head. For months the officials had worked the case believing that the killer was perhaps a family member, a disgruntled worker at the family business or a business enemy.

With Colton Connections having fifty full-time employees, it had been a time-consuming process for the Chicago PD to interview each and every one of them.

Then Larry Kidwell and Jonathon Paxton had been shot, using the same MO as in the Colton case. The two businessmen had been killed in the parking lot outside their business warehouse, just like the Colton men. At that point the FBI had been called in. Nobody had anticipated that the killers were a couple of kids.

Brad had just finished with his sandwich when a knock fell on his door. Even though he suspected who it was, he still grabbed his gun before opening the door.

FBI agent Russ Dodd grinned at him and held up a six-pack of beer. "Feel like a cold brew before bedtime?"

"Sounds good to me." He ushered Russ in and to the table. Russ was also from DC and had worked with Brad for the last six years. The two men had both a good professional relationship and a strong friendship. Russ now slid one of the cold brews across the table to Brad. They both opened their beers and then settled back in their chairs.

Russ took a deep drink and then released a deep sigh. "Well, another night ends without that little punk Leo in jail," he said.

"Yeah, and no confession from Jared."

Russ snorted. "You'll never get a confession from him as long as his parents are hovering around, answering questions for him and telling him to keep his mouth shut."

"Don't remind me," Brad replied. "How's your family doing?"

Russ grinned, causing the freckles on his face to dance with the gesture. "They're doing okay. They miss me, but I FaceTime once a day with the two kids and then I FaceTime Janie right before I go to bed."

"You're a damned lucky man that you found a woman who supports your work," Brad replied.

"Trust me, I know how lucky I am." He released a small laugh. "And if I threaten to forget it, Janie reminds me just how lucky I am." Russ took another drink, and when he finished, he eyed Brad curiously. "Speaking of women, I couldn't help but notice you had Simone Colton in your office for a long time today. What's up with that?"

"You know she's a psychologist and she's studied extensively in the area of deviant human behavior."

"And?" Russ raised one of his light red eyebrows.

"And I'm allowing her to view the taped interviews we've conducted with Jared so far. What I'm hoping is that she'll pick up on something that I've missed, something that might help me crack Jared."

"Interesting," Russ replied with a grin. "And it doesn't hurt that she's very attractive."

Brad felt himself flush with a sudden heat that fired through him. "That has absolutely nothing to do with my decision to allow her to watch the interviews. I'm just looking for a way to break this case. If we could get Jared to talk, then he might be able to lead us to where Leo is hiding out."

"Right now, his parents are alibiing Jared for the

night of the murder," Russ replied. "There's no way you're going to get through them to get Jared to confess to anything. Hell, he's now saying that he won't even talk to you at all without them in the interrogation room. You're never going to break that kid."

"Thanks for the vote of confidence," Brad replied drily.

"Hey, I hope Simone Colton can see something we've missed. Jared and Leo definitely need to be taken off the streets for a very long time. Even though they're both young, they are also cold-blooded murderers."

For the next few minutes, the two kicked around theories of where Leo might be hiding out. When their beer cans were empty, Russ stood. "I'll get out of here so you can get some sleep. Besides, I need to call Janie before it gets too late."

Russ grabbed the four remaining beers and then Brad walked him to the door. "I'll see you tomorrow, Russ."

"Yeah, and maybe it will be a good day and we'll get Styler under arrest."

"That would definitely be a stellar day," Brad replied.

An hour later Brad had showered and gotten into bed. The lights from outside the hotel room drifted in through a crack in his curtains and he stared up at the ceiling where shadows formed an intricate pattern.

His mind suddenly formed a picture of Simone. Surely his interest in her was only because he hoped she might be able to move the investigation forward and nothing more.

He'd been far too open with her today. It was just that she'd been so easy to talk to. He'd definitely felt a spark with her, a spark he hadn't felt for a very long time and one he needed to douse as soon as possible.

Tomorrow he'd make sure he was more professional when he was with her. He wouldn't invite conversation unless it had something to do with the case. He needed to keep clear boundaries where she was concerned.

As beautiful as he found Simone, as drawn to her as he found himself, ultimately he was here to catch a killer and nothing more.

# Chapter Three

Simone walked briskly toward the police station, eager to have another opportunity to view more video of Jared Garner and his parents as Jared was being interrogated. She'd come to several conclusions about what she believed the dynamics were between the three, dynamics that had formed Jared's character. However, before she shared her conclusions with Brad, she wanted to see the rest of the videos he had to confirm her findings.

When she arrived, Brad greeted her and led her back to his office. Today he again wore a pair of black pants, but this time a dark green button-down shirt stretched across his broad shoulders. He also wore his shoulder holster with his gun.

When she'd dressed that morning, she'd pulled on a summer dress in shades of pink, a dress that had earned her many compliments whenever she'd worn it. She'd also applied a little more mascara than usual. It was only when she was putting on a pink shiny lip gloss that she wondered what in the heck she was doing.

She was dressed more for a date than for a professional consultation. She was conscious of Brad's gaze sweeping the length of her as she sat in the same chair as she had the day before. His gaze felt like a caress and warmed her in a delicious and slightly disturbing kind of way. Definitely not the way to keep things professional between them.

"Shall we get started?" he asked as he cued up a video.

"Ready when you are," she replied. She tried not to notice the attractive scent of Brad as she focused on the computer screen, where the video had begun.

In the first interview she had seen of Jared, he'd been dressed in a pair of khaki slacks and a kelly green designer shirt. He'd had a wholesome appeal with his blond hair styled in a short preppy style and his smile full of straight white teeth.

In this video he was clad in an ill-fitting jailhouse-orange jumpsuit. His hair had grown out a bit, but the one thing that remained the same was the soulless look in his blue eyes. They were eyes that said the person behind them was badly broken.

There was no question that even though she tried to focus solely on the interview, she found Brad a distraction. She didn't understand why she seemed to be so hyperaware of him.

There was a decided difference about him today. Where he had shown some warmth and friendliness the day before, he was strictly professional today. He didn't invite any idle conversation and that was fine with her. That was the way it should be.

They watched two more taped videos and then Brad looked at her curiously. "That's all I have to show you. Now I'm very interested in what you can tell me about what you've seen."

She flipped to the beginning of the notes she'd taken

on her legal pad and scanned the things she'd written down both that day and the day before.

"You do realize these are just my own impressions?" she began.

"Yes, but I consider them expert impressions," he replied, and a hint of warmth filled his gaze.

She smiled. "Let's see if you feel the same way after you hear them." She cleared her throat and once again looked at her notes. "It's obvious to me that Jared holds a tremendous amount of anger directed toward his parents. He appears calm in their presence, but his anger bubbles just beneath the surface."

She had written down the time stamps on each video where she had seen the tells of Jared's underlying rage. "I suspect either one or both of his parents are physically and mentally abusive to him." She shared the times she had seen the indications and body language to support that and Brad wrote down the times on his own legal pad.

He then leaned back in his chair and looked at her with obvious curiosity. "Tell me more."

She didn't know if he was simply indulging her or if he was really taking in her thoughts and theories and actually considering them. He was difficult to read. "I also don't believe Jared is the mastermind of these murders. I think probably Leo offered Jared the friendship and compassion that was lacking in Jared's life. Jared strikes me as a follower, and I think if approached correctly, he could be reasoned with."

"It's difficult to get much of anything out of him with him insisting that his parents be there in the interrogation room. His father is very overbearing and his mother is just as bad. Jared seems afraid to answer any questions without their approval," Brad replied.

"You need to try to appeal to Jared not just with questions about the crimes, but also show an interest in his life…his likes and dislikes. Show him friendship and compassion. I believe that's what might break him despite his parents' influence."

Brad tapped the end of his pen on his notepad, checked his watch and then gazed at her thoughtfully. "Simone, I need to wrap this up for now, but I'd like to take you to dinner this evening and discuss all this further."

"Oh…" She looked at him in complete surprise. Of all the things he might have said to her, an invitation to dinner was the very last thing she'd expected from him.

"I'd definitely like to pick your brain a little bit more about things," he added. "So, would you let me take you to dinner this evening?"

Of course, he wasn't asking her out for a real date. It was more of a professional consultation over a meal. "How about we meet at my sister's restaurant, True?"

"That sounds good to me. A couple of the Chicago PD officers took me there to eat when I first got to town and the food was fantastic. Shall we say around six?"

"Six sounds perfect," she agreed. She didn't even try to analyze why her heart fluttered just a little bit at the thoughts of the night to come.

"Great, then I look forward to it." He stood and she did as well. He walked her out and then they said their goodbyes. He disappeared back into the police station and she headed back home.

He had given her no clues to indicate that dinner would be anything but a professional collaboration, but that didn't stop her from feeling just a little bit giddy at thoughts of sharing dinner with him.

What was wrong with her? Why was Brad Howard affecting her in a way she hadn't felt for a very long time? Surely it was only because he was treating her like an intelligent woman whose opinions mattered.

That was what had been lacking in her relationship with Wayne Jamison. Wayne had often dismissed her thoughts and opinions. It had been vitally important to him that he be the smarter, the funnier and the more respected of the couple.

Eventually she had just grown tired of being dismissed by him. She was a strong, independent and smart woman and she deserved a man who respected her on all those levels. However, at this time in her life, she wasn't even sure a man like that existed.

At quarter till five she showered and got ready for her date. No, not a date, she corrected herself firmly. It was nothing more than two professionals sharing a business dinner.

So, why then did nerves twist her stomach so tight? Why did she feel so excited about the night to come? She pulled on a pair of black slacks and a forest green blouse that somehow made her think of Brad's eyes.

There was no question she felt a physical attraction toward Brad. What living, breathing woman wouldn't? It was just a reminder that she'd been alone for too long. There were several men at the college who had invited her out over the past year, but she'd declined all of them. Maybe it was time she began dating again.

She missed being in a relationship. She was tired of eating alone each night. She wanted somebody to share special moments with, to do something as simple as share a beautiful sunset or talk about the ordinary events that made up a day. She wanted a snuggle bunny at night, somebody who could take her breath away with a single kiss.

Maybe that was why she felt a bit vulnerable to Brad Howard. She was just lonely and he was giving her a little bit of attention. He seemed to be actually interested in hearing her opinions and it felt good.

Even though it wasn't a date, she took extra care with her makeup and made sure she looked nice. She needed to take special care if they were meeting at True. She certainly wanted Tatum to be proud of her whenever she visited the restaurant.

She arrived at there at exactly six o'clock. She stepped inside and immediately saw Brad seated at the bar. For several moments he didn't see her and she took the opportunity to watch him.

He looked bigger…stronger than the other men at the bar. It wasn't in his physique, but it was the way he wore his confidence. He appeared to command the space around him more than any of the other men seated there.

While she found that appealing in theory, she wondered if that confidence could be arrogant. If it could be demeaning and hurtful.

At that moment he turned and saw her. A wide smile curved his lips and her heart fluttered way more than it should. He stood from the stool, threw a few dollars on the bar and then hurried over to her.

"Have you been waiting long?" she asked.

"No, not at all," he assured her. "Our table is ready if you are."

"I'm ready," she replied.

He took her by the elbow and led her through the main dining room. As they walked, she looked around for her sister but didn't see her anywhere.

Their table was a two-top in a corner in the back of the restaurant. It was semi-secluded, the perfect place for a romantic interlude, or in this case, the perfect place to talk about all things murder.

The minute they settled in, a waitress arrived to take their drink orders. She ordered a glass of white wine and he ordered a scotch and soda. Once the drinks had been delivered and dinner orders had been taken, he offered her that smile that warmed her from head to toe. "So, how was the rest of your afternoon today?"

"It was fine. I have a lecture tomorrow evening at the college, so I spent some time going over my notes," she replied. "What about you?"

"We had a little bit of excitement. An anonymous phone call came in telling us Leo had been spotted at a McDonald's restaurant. Several squad cars descended on the place, but there was no Leo. The officers showed his picture around and none of the staff or customers had seen him."

"Do you get a lot of false alarms like that?" she asked, disappointed that yet another day was drawing to an end without one of her father's murderers in custody.

"Unfortunately, we do. Anytime we have a case where we've set up a TIPS line and have shown the suspect's picture all over the news and on social media, we get a lot of calls. We check out each and every single one, but unfortunately, they are mostly crank calls."

"It just seems like it's been forever since the murders occurred and there's still no justice for my uncle and my father. I still can't believe they're really gone. I always dreamed of my father walking me down the aisle on my wedding day and being a terrific and loving grandpa to my children."

To her horror, tears suddenly burned in her eyes and her ever-present grief closed up the back of her throat. She quickly looked down at the tablecloth in an effort to gain back her control.

To her stunned surprise, Brad reached out and grabbed one of her hands in his. She looked up at him and instantly wanted to fall into the soft pools of compassion his eyes offered her.

"We're going to get him, Simone." He gave her hand a gentle squeeze. "I swear we're going to get him, and both Leo and Jared are going to spend the rest of their lives in prison for the murder of your father and uncle." He gave her hand another squeeze and then released it.

She quickly managed to get her emotions back under control and took a sip of her wine. "Sorry, I didn't mean to get all emotional on you."

"Please, don't apologize. Even getting the two of them in jail won't take your grief away, Simone. I wish there was something magical I could do that would accomplish that. I'd love to see your beautiful eyes without the grief that shines so sadly from them. Unfortunately, it's my experience that only time will help."

He'd called her eyes beautiful and had made her heart flutter once again. She tried to ignore that and looked at him curiously. "Do you still grieve for your mother?"

"To me, grief has been a funny kind of animal. When the crime first happened, my grief for my mother was like a hard rock concert. It was all bass and cymbals crashing in my head. Now it's more like a nighttime lullaby that isn't sung every night, but occasionally it whispers through my head on a wave of soft notes."

"That's nice," she said. "But I'm still in the rock concert stage."

"I know, and I hate that for you."

She took a sip of her wine and then set the wineglass back down. "I just feel like I can't even start the healing process until the murderers are put away where they can never hurt anyone again."

She would do anything she could to help Brad get the two teenagers in jail. She needed to think about what exactly she could do to hurry this case along. She definitely would do anything to stop the horrifying nightmares that tortured her at night.

BY THE TIME dinner arrived, all talk of grief was gone. Instead, the conversation revolved around more pleasant topics. They talked about favorite sports—he was a baseball fan and she loved football. They spoke about favorite music and what they enjoyed watching on television—she liked jazz and he liked old rock and roll, and they both enjoyed watching crime dramas.

Someplace in the back of Brad's mind, he knew they should discuss the case and her insights more, but right now he was just enjoying watching her relax.

She looked beautiful in her slacks and the forest green blouse, a color that only seemed to emphasize the bright blue of her eyes. He was grateful that as their conversation had continued her eyes had lost some of their sadness.

"This is the best steak I've ever eaten," he said as they continued with the meal.

"They get great reviews on their steaks, but I've never eaten one."

"You're not into steak?" he asked curiously.

"It's okay. I just like chicken better," she replied.

"I'm assuming your sister is an amazing cook. Do you enjoy cooking as well?"

"Absolutely not," she replied and then laughed.

It was the first time he'd heard her laughter and he loved the low, slightly throaty sound of it. "That was pretty definite," he said with a laugh of his own.

"Tatum always enjoyed puttering in the kitchen. I've never particularly enjoyed being there. Normally my schedule stays fairly busy, so it's easy for me to grab lunch out and order in for dinner," she explained.

"Why psychology?" he asked.

She set her fork down and took a drink of her wine. "When I was in high school, I was stalked by a boy. His name was Bill Jacobs. I was in my junior year and he had already graduated. I dated him for a month and then broke up with him because he was too controlling. After that, whenever I went out with somebody else, Bill was always there. Even when I went out with my girlfriends, we'd spy his car following several car lengths behind us. It was creepy and it went on for a couple of months."

"Did he ever get violent with you?" Brad asked. The idea of anyone ever hurting her certainly didn't sit well with him.

She took another drink of her wine and then shook her head. "No, it never escalated into anything like that, although I was afraid it might. Eventually it just stopped and I never saw him again, but I was always intrigued by what drove him. Then when I got to college, I took a course in psychology and realized that was my true passion…to try to understand the human mind."

"It always amazes me how events in our childhoods form the people we become," he replied.

"And that's definitely what drew me to psychology," she replied.

"Did you ever think about going into private practice?"

"I considered it, but I really enjoy teaching. It's very rewarding to think I'm educating young minds and maybe some of my students will go on to become good therapists or whatever."

He smiled at her. "I have the utmost respect for teachers."

"And I have the utmost respect for law enforcement," she replied.

For a long moment their gazes remained locked and Brad felt a surge of emotions fill him. It wasn't just physical attraction. It was more than that. It was a desire to get to know her better, a need to protect her and do everything in his power to make her happy.

It scared the hell out of him. It had been a very long time since he'd felt this kind of interest in a woman. And she was definitely the wrong woman for him to feel this way about.

She broke the eye contact and he cleared his throat. "So, what dessert do you recommend?" he asked.

"It depends on what you like. My favorite is the raspberry torte, but honestly you can't go wrong with any of the desserts here," she said.

When the waitress arrived to clear their dinner

dishes, he ordered two of the tortes and two cups of coffee. Once their desserts arrived, he felt the need to distance himself by taking the conversation back to the interview videos he'd played for her.

"Have you had any more thoughts about Jared?" he asked.

"I spent part of the afternoon going over my notes, and I stand by what I told you," she replied.

He hated that her eyes darkened. "So, maybe it's time I take a different approach in the interview room. Be more friendly with the kid and try to build a relationship with him despite his parents' presence. I've been playing bad cop and what you're suggesting is that I need to play good cop."

She smiled. "Maybe honey is better than vinegar in this particular case. I have a feeling he's been fairly lonely for most of his life. He had to have been to hook up with a friend like Leo." She placed her napkin on top of the table. "Could you please excuse me for a minute?"

"Of course." He stood as she did and watched as she wove her way through the tables to disappear into a side alcove where the restrooms were located.

He frowned thoughtfully and picked up his coffee cup. Maybe she was right. He was definitely not getting anywhere with Jared playing the tough cop. Still, he had to admit it hurt his ego just a little bit to realize it took an outsider to see things he and his team might have missed.

He'd been the one conducting all the interviews with Jared and his parents, and there was no question that so far he'd felt as if he were spinning his wheels.

Funny, it was much easier to think about a serial

killer than to examine all the inappropriate emotions that Simone stirred inside him.

Maybe the real problem was that he was just a lonely man and he would have reacted positively to any attractive woman he spent a little bit of time with. Once he finally got back home, maybe he needed to make more of an effort to have a little social time, to maybe pursue a dating life once again.

He was about to take another drink of coffee when a commotion near the restrooms drew his attention. He was surprised to see Rob and Marilyn Garner, who had apparently just been seated at a table, and Simone.

Simone looked like a deer in the headlights as Rob rose from his chair and pointed his finger in her face. "My son is innocent and you need to mind your business, you Colton bitch," he yelled.

Brad jumped out of his chair and hurried toward them. He didn't hear what Simone said in return, but Rob took a step closer to her and his finger became a fist.

"You've just stirred up a lot of trouble for yourself, missy," Rob raged. "You'd better watch your back, you hear me?"

Simone stumbled backward. Brad grabbed her by the arm and pulled her away. "You need to sit down right now, Mr. Garner," he yelled at the obviously angry man, and then he quickly led Simone back to their table.

She was visibly upset. Her face was ashen and her entire body trembled. "I… I came out of the restroom and saw them. I just asked them if they would sit down with me sometime and let me ask them a few questions. He…he just exploded."

Dammit, how had this happened and why in hell had she approached them in the first place? "Simone, you shouldn't have talked to them."

"I… I just wanted to…" Her voice trailed off.

"Simone, you need to stay away from those people. Rob Garner is a loose cannon and there's no telling what he might do if he sees you as a potential threat to his son," Brad said.

Her cheeks finally began to refill with a touch of color. "I'm so embarrassed. I was just so…so shocked by his reaction." She reached up and tucked a strand of hair behind her ear and he couldn't help but notice that her hand still trembled.

"I almost feel sorry for Jared growing up with that man," she finally said.

"Still, you shouldn't have talked to them."

Before he could say anything else, Tatum Colton appeared beside their table. She placed a hand on Simone's shoulder. "Simone, are you okay?" she asked worriedly.

"I'm fine," Simone replied, although her voice still held a slight tremor.

Tatum frowned. "Some of the staff told me what just happened. I'm going to get security to ask the Garners to leave."

"Oh, please don't do that, Tatum. It will just make another scene, and besides, Brad and I are finished, so we'll be leaving," Simone replied.

"I didn't even realize you were here. Why didn't you tell me you were going to be here this evening?" Tatum asked. Her gaze shot to Brad and then back to Simone.

"We were just having a…uh…consultation together." Simone's cheeks dusted with a blush. "But we're ready to leave now. Right, Brad?"

"Definitely," he agreed. They had pretty much finished up with their dessert and coffee, and there was really no reason to linger any longer. Even if Simone had wanted to linger for another cup of coffee, which he was sure she didn't, he would have wanted to get her out of here as soon as possible anyway.

He wanted to get her as far away as possible from Rob Garner. He wanted to yell at her for speaking to them at all, for insinuating herself into a place where she didn't belong. But she looked so shocked, so utterly vulnerable at the moment, the last thing he wanted to do was come down too hard on her.

He paid their tab and then together they left the restaurant. They stepped out into the evening air and simply stood on the sidewalk away from the crowd waiting to get into the restaurant.

She still appeared traumatized. Once again, she tucked a strand of her hair behind her ear and he noticed that her hand still trembled. "Are you sure you're okay?" he finally asked. He put his arm around her shoulders and pulled her closer to his side.

She stayed there for a long moment and then stepped away from him. She nodded. "I'm all right, just still a little bit shaken up and shocked."

"Simone, you can't try to talk to them again. It should be apparent to you now that Rob Garner is not the kind of man to mess with," he replied. "I don't want you to go anywhere near him again."

"I was very civil when I approached them. All I asked was if they'd be willing to sit down with me and have a short chat."

"I'm sure you were civil, but Rob Garner is not," he replied. "And I know you want to help, but you need to step back now and leave it all up to us."

She released a deep sigh. "Oh, well, aside from that, it was a lovely evening and I really enjoyed having dinner with you."

"I enjoyed it, too," he replied. "Can I take you home?"

"No, I'm fine to get home on my own," she replied and offered him a beautiful smile. "Thank you again, Brad, and I hope you'll keep me updated on the case."

"Of course I will." He already wanted to see her again. Not as professionals meeting to discuss Jared Garner, but rather as a man and a woman getting to know each other better.

And that was why he shouldn't see her again. The timing and circumstances were all wrong for him to be distracted in a romance that ultimately would go nowhere.

They said their goodbyes, and as he watched her walk away from him, he thought about how Rob Garner had yelled at her, basically threatening her life.

It made Brad worry for her. He hoped she stayed as far away from Rob as possible. He wanted Rob to forget all about Simone. But the truth of the matter was he had no idea what Garner might do now that Simone was on his radar. And that scared the hell out of him.

# Chapter Four

"I'm not sure my client is going to agree to this." Roger Albright, Jared Garner's lawyer, frowned at Brad. The two were seated in an interview room.

Albright was a tall, dark-haired man who looked like big money in a three-piece suit that Brad knew cost more than Brad's monthly salary. The man even smelled expensive. However, Brad found him incredibly arrogant and condescending.

"Legally his parents don't have to be in the room when I question your client. At nineteen years old, Jared is an adult," Brad reminded the man. "I've been quite accommodating to your client by allowing them to sit in."

"I'm aware of that," Albright said with cool disdain. "However, my client has told you he doesn't intend to speak to you without them present in the room."

"As you know, we have another interview scheduled with Jared in an hour and I'm not going to allow his parents in the room. I'm not accommodating that request anymore going forward."

Albright raised one of his dark brows. "You do realize it's possible Jared won't cooperate without them there."

"He hasn't cooperated with them in the room. I certainly hope you encourage your client to start to fully cooperate with us. At the very least he's on the hook for kidnapping charges and he's also going to be charged with four murders," Brad said.

Albright waved his hand dismissively. "All false charges. Jared has a solid alibi for the nights of the murders."

Brad nearly snorted in derision. Jared's "alibi" was that he had been at a family function on the night the Colton men had been murdered, an alibi provided strictly by Rob and a handful of other family members, and one that was on very shaky grounds.

"I just wanted to inform you that today his parents are not welcome when I speak to Jared," Brad said.

"I'll let him know." Albright rose from his chair. "And I'll see you in an hour."

Brad remained seated at the table where he would soon be interrogating Jared. With Simone's observations fresh in his mind, he hoped to break through to Jared in a way he hadn't before.

It had been three days since he'd seen Simone, three days since they'd had dinner and she had been threatened by Rob Garner. Brad had called her yesterday just to check in with her. The conversation had been brief, but he had been glad just to hear her voice and to know she was doing okay.

He had a niggling worry about her. He had no idea if he should take the threats Rob had made to her in the restaurant seriously or not.

When he'd spoken to her on the phone, he'd reminded her to stay as far away from the Garners as possible, but he wasn't sure if she was taking his advice to heart or not. She was so desperate to get Jared and Leo sent to prison that he feared she wouldn't take her personal safety seriously.

However, he couldn't entertain thoughts of Simone right now. He needed to study the notes he'd written for this particular interrogation with Jared. He hoped like hell the kid would cooperate without his parents present.

There had been no more sightings of Leo. Brad had no idea how Leo was managing to exist off the grid. They had officers sitting on his parents' home and they'd interviewed the few friends the kid had. Nobody had seen him or appeared to be helping him in any way.

Somehow, someway, either his parents or Jared's parents had to be funneling Leo money, but the police had yet to figure out how. The kid was considered armed and dangerous, and his photo was still being flashed on the news and on all the social media platforms.

Forty minutes later Albright returned to the interview room. He greeted Brad once again and then sat in a chair just behind the one Jared would sit in.

Five minutes later Jared was led into the room by an officer. Clad in a jailhouse-orange jumpsuit and with shackles on his ankles and wrists, he looked especially young and vulnerable. But four men were dead due to this kid and his friend. That was the bottom line.

Once Jared was seated at the table, the officer unlocked Jared's wrist shackles and then stepped out of the room.

"Hi, Jared," Brad said.

"Why can't my parents be here? You've pretty much

always let them be in here before." Jared's gaze skittered around the room nervously.

"We've been very good about granting your wish that they can occasionally be here when we talk to you, but today I just want to talk to you without them here," Brad explained.

Jared finally met his gaze. "I've already talked to you, like, a hundred times. I got nothing else to say."

"I just wanted to get to know you a little better, Jared," Brad replied. "I've spoken to you a number of times, but I don't feel like I've gotten to know the real Jared. For the most part, you seem like a good kid. How are you finding life in jail?"

"The food sucks," Jared said. "And the bed sucks," he continued. "It's totally boring. The time goes really slow. They won't let me have my cell phone in here or anything."

"What do you like to do on your cell? Are you into any kinds of games on your phone?" Brad asked.

"I like Zombie Island and House of Thunder."

Brad frowned. "I'm not familiar with those. Tell me what they're about."

As Jared explained each of the games, Brad could tell he was starting to relax a bit. Brad was vaguely surprised to learn that in each of the games Jared identified with the "good" guys and tried to rid the environment of the bad people. So, what had happened that in real life he'd decided to be a bad guy? A murderer?

"I know you also enjoyed playing mag-fed paintball," Brad said when Jared had finished explaining the cell phone games he liked to play.

"Yeah, Leo got me into that. It's cool and we played

whenever we got the chance." Jared frowned. "My dad thought it was a stupid waste of time and money."

"I've noticed in our interviews that your father is pretty hard on you."

Jared's nostrils thinned and his eyes narrowed. "Yeah, so what?"

"I think maybe he's hard on you sometimes when you don't deserve it."

"My dad can be a real son of a bitch." The words exploded out of him as if forced out by a tremendous pressure. He then clamped his mouth shut as if sorry he had said that much. He looked at the wall just over Brad's head.

"It's okay, Jared. I get it. My dad was a real son of a bitch, too. Nothing I ever did pleased him. No matter how hard I tried, I couldn't do anything to make him happy with me. I felt like he didn't want me and he definitely didn't love me."

Jared stared at Brad for several long moments. "For real?"

"For real," Brad replied and held Jared's gaze. However, nothing could be further from the truth. Brad's father had been a loving, supportive man until he had passed away five years ago. But Brad would gladly lie in this moment if it was a lie that moved them closer to the truth in the case.

"Did your dad ever hit you?" Jared asked.

"He punched me a few times when he thought I needed it. It was nothing for him to smack me upside the head or slam my back with his fist. Does your dad hit you?"

Jared's eyes turned an icy blue. "Yeah."

Albright cleared his throat as if to warn Jared. Jared

turned around and glared at the man. "I can say what I want here. You're my lawyer, not my father's," he said angrily.

Jared then turned back to Brad. "Yeah, my old man hits me. He punches me whenever he feels like it and my mother calls me a loser and a poor excuse for a son. She tells me she should have aborted me."

Brad was shocked by what the kid was sharing about his parents, but he didn't show it. "So, your friends must be really important to you as an escape from your home life," Brad said.

"I'm not stupid. I know you want me to talk about Leo."

Brad leaned forward. "I'm trying to understand your relationship with Leo. He's not like you, Jared. I sense that you have a good heart and I'm not sure if Leo does."

Jared shrugged. "He's been a good friend to me. He listens to me when I talk about my parents. He gets it and he gets me like nobody else ever has. He's my best friend."

"That's good that you found a friend like that. Where were the two of you planning on going?"

"What do you mean?"

Albright leaned forward. "Agent Howard, you're traveling in dangerous territory."

Brad looked at Jared innocently. "I don't know what's dangerous about what I just asked. We all know you and Leo had bug-out bags ready to go when you were arrested, so we know the two of you were planning on taking off somewhere."

When the FBI had burst into Leo's parents' basement, where the two boys had their "hangout," space, two bags were found. The bags had extra clothes, some cash and other items that the two boys might have needed for a life on the run.

"We were just planning on leaving home. We were ready to get away, but we never really talked about where we were going. If you want me to tell you where Leo is right now, I can't. You can beat me and everything, and I wouldn't be able to tell you. I don't know where he is or what he's doing." Jared frowned thoughtfully. "Sometimes he was kinda secretive, even with me."

"You know, it's possible I could get the authorities to allow you a little access to your phone for playing your games if you could think of anything that might help us find Leo," Brad said.

"Agent Howard, don't try to make deals with my client," Albright said.

"I just want to do something to help you, Jared," Brad continued, pointedly ignoring Albright. "Eventually Leo will be caught and I truly believe he's going to try to pin everything on you, Jared. He's going to throw you under the bus and I'd hate to see that happen to you. You've had enough people in your life who have let you down. I want to do right by you, Jared. I like you and I think you deserve a break. I just want you to think about things, and no matter if it's day or night, if you think of something that might help us and help yourself, let me know."

Jared's eyes were troubled. "I'm not a snitch."

"I don't think about it as you being a snitch. I think about it as you being smart," Brad replied. "And I know you're an intelligent guy, Jared."

Jared snorted. "Yeah, go tell my old man that."

Brad pushed back from the table. "I think we're done for now. Remember, if you think of anything that might be important, or you decide you want to come clean about everything, don't hesitate to contact your lawyer and I'll be available to you." There really wasn't much more he could say without coming off as a big phony, and that was the last thing he wanted Jared to think of him. Hopefully he'd built something with the kid, something that would pay off.

Minutes later Jared was led away by the jailer and Albright left the room. Brad could only wait and see if this short interview yielded anything.

There was no way Brad believed that the two teenagers hadn't talked about where they would go to hide out after the police were onto them for the murders. He believed Jared knew much more than he was telling.

Along with Leo, Jared had killed four men and Brad wished he would just confess to the murders. He could only hope the chat today had convinced Jared to come clean. Only time would tell.

It was possible Jared could be rehabilitated and eventually, at some point after serving years, he could get out of prison. Brad knew once Leo was captured, Jared's chances for that happening diminished. A judge might look more favorably on Jared if he confessed now and was truly remorseful for his actions.

Brad returned to his office, where he fielded some phone calls, coordinated with the officers working the case, and then when a lull occurred, he found himself thinking about his own father.

Certainly while Brad had never doubted his father's love for him, after the murder of Brad's mother, Brad had found himself having to take on the role of parent to his grieving father.

Before Brad's mother's death, Hank Howard had always appeared to be the strong one in the marriage, but Brad realized soon after his mother's death that Hank had depended on his wife a lot.

He'd had no idea about finances or how to shop or cook. He appeared helpless in the little things that held a family together. Brad had to step up and become the one who held his father together, who made sure things got done so they could function.

He hadn't minded, and not a day went by when his father didn't thank Brad for his strength. Not a day went by that his father didn't tell Brad that he was his hero.

Hank had never dated or thought about another relationship. He had loved his wife and had mourned for her all the rest of the days of his life. When he finally passed, Brad was happy only in the thought that his parents were united once again.

A knock fell on his door and Russ stuck his head into the office. "Simone Colton is here to see you," he said.

Brad frowned. What was she doing here? "Send her in," Brad said and ignored the googly eyes Russ made just before he closed the door.

A moment later the door opened and Simone stepped inside. She looked like a hot little firecracker in a red skirt and a red, white and blue blouse.

"Hey, I didn't expect to see you here today," he said as he got to his feet.

She smiled. "I stayed up last night and worked on a new profile for both Jared and Leo." She held out a sheath of papers, fastened together with a large blue paper clip. Her cheeks were dusted a charming shade of pink. "I hope you don't mind, but this was something I wanted to do and I hope you find it all useful."

"Thanks, Simone." He took the paperwork from her and laid it on his desk. "I'll be sure to read through it. How are you doing?"

"I'm good...just anxious for this all to come to an end," she replied.

"That makes two of us."

An awkward silence ensued, and then they both began speaking at the same time. They laughed and she took a step backward. "I know you're busy, so I'll get out of your hair now," she said. "I just wanted to drop off that paperwork. I don't know, but maybe it will help."

"Thank you. I appreciate it." He would have liked it if she lingered for a few minutes. But there was no reason for that to happen, and he needed to gain some distance from her.

He opened the door and she stepped out into the hallway. At the same time somebody yelled from the opposite end of the hall.

"Hey, stop. You have no right to barge in here," Russ's voice yelled.

"I'll barge in whenever I damned want to." At that moment Rob Garner appeared, barreling forward with Russ close behind him.

Garner's eyes widened and then narrowed at the sight of Simone. Oh, no, this was the last thing Brad wanted...another confrontation that put Simone in Rob's head.

"You," he snarled and pointed a finger at Simone.

His hands balled into fists at his sides. "What in the hell are you doing here?" He didn't wait for an answer. "Was it your idea for my boy to be questioned without my presence? I warned you, lady. I warned you to keep your nose out of this. You're going to be damned sorry."

"I'm not going to stand here and listen to you threaten somebody," Brad said with a rising anger of his own. "If you want to speak with me, then have a seat in my office."

He turned to Simone. "Agent Dodd will see you out."

"This way, Miss Colton." Russ put himself between Simone and Garner. Garner stepped into Brad's office at the same time Russ disappeared down the hallway with Simone.

Brad remained in the hallway for several moments, tamping down the anger that threatened to consume him. Dammit, this was the very last thing he had needed. He'd seen the rage that had blackened Rob Garner's eyes as he'd confronted Simone. It was a rage that definitely concerned Brad for Simone's safety.

What was Garner really capable of? If he truly believed that Simone was somehow helping to put his son away, then how dangerous might he be to Simone?

Unfortunately, Brad didn't have the answer to that. Drawing a deep breath, he turned to go into his office to face Rob's wrath.

SIMONE ADDED THE finishing touches to her dining room table and then sank down to wait for her sisters and one of her cousins to arrive. It was rare that all three of them had a day off at the same time, but today they did and so she'd invited them all to lunch.

She'd ordered in chef salads and a light pasta salad as well. The food had already arrived, the table was set and she was eager to check in with Tatum and January. She'd also invited their cousin Carly and Simone was pleased that she was able to make it, too. The four girls had grown up together and Simone considered Carly like another sister.

It had been two days since she'd encountered Rob Garner at the police station. The more she saw of the man, the more she thought about what it must have been like for Jared to grow up with such a brutal man as a father.

She could feel sorry for the kid, but that certainly didn't excuse the choices he'd made, horrible choices that had resulted in four men being brutally murdered. When she thought about never seeing her father again, whatever Jared might have suffered as a kid didn't matter to her. He had still chosen to become a killer.

There was no question in her mind that Leo had been the dominant one in their friendship, that Leo had been the mastermind behind the murders. Leo was definitely a sociopath and he'd found the perfect partner in a boy who wanted to please and feel accepted by him.

A knock on the door pulled her out of her seat and out of her thoughts about Rob and Jared Garner. When she opened the door, Carly greeted her with a big hug.

"Come on in," Simone said. "You're the first to get here." She led Carly to the sofa, where they both sat. "How's work?" Simone asked.

"Good, but busy as usual." Carly was a pediatric nurse at Chicago University Hospital. "What about you?" Her bright blue eyes sparkled with interest.

"I've got a lecture tonight and then I'm finally all

finished for the semester," Simone replied. "And how is Micha?"

Carly's eyes sparkled even brighter. "He's great."

Carly reached up and twirled a strand of her light blond hair. "Things are finally going really well and I couldn't be happier."

Carly had been engaged to Micha Harrison, a special forces army lieutenant. On his last mission he had been taken prisoner by a terrorist group out of Baghdad and Carly had gotten word that he was dead.

She had mourned long and deep for him and then a couple of months ago he'd walked back into her life. Scarred and having suffered a broken back, he'd decided it was better for him to let go of Carly so she could find another man to love, but he hadn't been able to stay away from her.

"I'm just glad Micha and I got a second chance together," Carly said.

Simone smiled. "And I'm so happy for both of you." Before she could say anything else, another knock sounded. It was Tatum and January.

Greetings and hugs were exchanged all around and then they all got seated at the table and began to catch up with each other. "I have a little confession to make," Tatum said. "I've started working on a cookbook."

"That's awesome," January exclaimed. "Are you going to publish it yourself? You know you could sell a lot of copies just by having it available in the restaurant."

"That's true, but I'd really like to find a publisher who could get me better distribution than just selling it out of the restaurant. So, keep your fingers crossed for me because I've been sending out some queries," Tatum replied.

She turned and looked at Simone. "What I really want to know from you is when Special Agent Howard became Brad." She raised an eyebrow and both January and Carly looked at Simone quizzically.

"Oh, please, do tell," January said.

Simone's cheeks warmed. "Look, she's blushing," Carly exclaimed. "Simone, I swear, I have never seen you blush like that before."

"I'm not really blushing and there's nothing much to tell," Simone replied. "I... We... I've just been working with him a little bit."

"According to my staff, you looked pretty cozy at the restaurant before all hell broke loose," Tatum said.

"What happened? What hell broke loose?" January asked, looking first at Tatum and then at Simone.

Simone explained about approaching the Garners that night in the restaurant and how Rob had come at her. "He's a horrid man and he should have never become a father."

"Simone, you have to stay away from this," Tatum said. "I know you're just trying to help, but you just said yourself that Rob Garner is a horrid man. Who knows what he might be capable of?"

January reached out and took one of Simone's hands in hers. "The last thing we want is for anything to happen to you, Simone. In fact, we've been a little worried about you."

"Worried about me? Why?" Simone asked in surprise.

"You don't seem to be moving on," Tatum said softly. "It's been almost seven months now and you just seem completely obsessed."

"We don't want you anywhere near anything that might put you in danger."

"I know." Simone gave her sister's hand a squeeze and then released it. "In any case, that man would be a fool to come after me, especially now that he's threatened me in public twice."

"Twice?" Carly stared at her. "When did he threaten you the second time?"

Simone sighed. She hadn't intended to tell them about running into Rob at the police station, but inadvertently she had just busted herself. She told them about what had happened two days ago and listened to all three of them voice their concerns for her all over again.

"Don't worry. I don't expect to run into him again, and in any case, I think he's just a blowhard bully." What she didn't tell them was for the past two days as she'd run errands around town and in the neighborhood, she'd felt as if somehow somebody was following her...watching her, but she'd chalked it up to her own silly paranoia.

From that the conversation turned to how their mothers were doing and grilling Carly about what was happening with her two brothers.

The lunch lasted about an hour and a half. There was plenty of laughter, and by the time the others left, Simone was in a much better mood than she had been before they arrived.

Thank God she had her family. She wasn't sure how she would have survived this ordeal of loss without them. As she cleaned up the kitchen, thoughts of her father once again played through her mind.

She had definitely been a daddy's girl. Not only

had he soothed her through stormy weather, he'd also been the one who had told her that the boy she'd liked in eighth grade was a jerk for not liking her back. He had taught her how to dance and how to drive a car. He'd also told her when her dress was too short and how to respect herself as a woman.

He had been the one man who had encouraged her drive and her thirst for knowledge. He'd been proud of who she had become and she'd loved to sit and talk to him for hours on end.

And now he was gone forever. The rock concert of grief suddenly screamed in her head. She hoped Brad was right and in time her grief would only be a whisper of a lullaby that occasionally played in her head.

Brad. The man was spending far too much time in her head. Of all the men in Chicago, why did it have to be a handsome FBI agent from Washington, DC, who drew her in?

She enjoyed watching the ever-changing colors of his hazel eyes…from green to gold to goldish brown. Why did his broad shoulders and strong arms beckon her to fall into them and just be for a moment? Why did she enjoy talking to him more than she had to any other man?

It was wrong…all wrong, and she knew it. He had a job to do here, and once that job was over, he'd return to whatever life he had in DC. Besides, he was probably just being kind to her because she was the daughter of a victim and because she'd pretty much been in his face for the last week or two.

Or maybe she was just thinking about him so much because he was a distraction from her grief. Certainly it was easier for her to think about the handsome FBI agent than to think about her father's forever absence from her life.

She just had to stop thinking about him altogether now. He would contact her and the rest of her family if anything changed with the case. She'd done what she could to help and now there was no reason for her to spend any time alone again with Brad.

After the kitchen was once again clean, she sat down at the table with her notes for the night's lecture before her and read through them. She'd been there for only about a half an hour when rain began to patter against the window.

She got up and turned on her television in an effort to catch the weather report for the evening. The forecast wasn't great. It was supposed to rain all night and through tomorrow. There was no way she'd be walking to the college tonight. She definitely wasn't into walking in the rain no matter how big the umbrella she carried.

By six thirty she was in her car and headed to the campus. The rain had continued to come down steadily throughout the afternoon and it had turned unusually cool.

As much as she loved the students she would be teaching tonight, she was eager to get back to her condo, change into her nightgown and cuddle down beneath a soft, warm blanket.

She parked in the staff parking lot, opened her umbrella and grabbed her computer case and then hurried toward the lecture hall for the last time until next fall. Once again, she had that odd feeling of somebody watching her. She threw a glance over her shoulder but saw nobody anywhere near her.

Still, she breathed a small sigh of relief as she entered the building. She closed the umbrella and smiled at the security guard who stood just inside the door. "It's a wet one out there tonight, Eddie," she said.

Eddie Judd had worked security for as long as she could remember. He was a really nice older guy who had retired from the police department and then had picked up the job working security.

"Supposed to be wet for the next week or so," Eddie replied. "Have a good evening, Professor Colton."

"Thanks, Eddie. You do the same." She hurried down the carpeted hallway toward the lecture room that held two hundred students, although the class tonight wasn't that big.

Once inside, she went to the lectern, prepared her notes, connected her computer to the audio/video system and then greeted the students as they began to trickle in. Once seven o'clock came, the hall was three-quarters of the way full and she began her lecture, complete with an elaborate PowerPoint presentation.

As always, the students were quiet and attentive until around eight o'clock when she asked for questions. They were a lively bunch and for the next half an hour they not only asked questions of her, but also challenged each other with opinions and theories.

At just after eight thirty she closed by telling them all goodbye for the summer. It took another fifteen minutes or so for the hall to empty and for her to pack away her notes and computer and then prepare to leave the building.

"Good night, Eddie. I hope you have a great summer," she said as she approached the door.

"Back at you, Professor Colton," the older man replied. "Try to stay dry."

"You do the same," she replied.

It was still raining when she stepped back outside with her keys and umbrella in one hand and her computer case in the other. She hurried toward her car parked in the staff parking area as the rain thrummed a tune on the umbrella material over her head.

She was almost to her car when she heard a slapping of footsteps on the pavement behind her. Her heartbeat accelerated and she half turned but was suddenly struck hard in the back by somebody.

She cried out and stumbled, but before she could regain her balance, she was pulled backward by a viscous yank on her hair. She pressed the alarm button on her car and heard it begin to shrilly beep and then she was falling…falling backward.

She gasped in excruciating pain as the back of her head crashed into the concrete. For a brief moment myriad stars danced in her head and then the stars dissolved and there was nothing but darkness.

LEO CURLED UP beneath the tent under the highway overpass and watched the rain pour down. There was a little tent city in this spot. Homeless people and drug addicts were his neighbors, although he certainly hadn't interacted with them.

He was good for now. He'd found enough to eat in a garbage dumpster behind a food store. His phone was fully charged thanks to a charging station at a truck stop and he'd managed to dye his dark brown hair a funky red that he hoped would keep the feds off his back.

He'd ditched his signature chain and lock that he was known for wearing as well as the camo clothing that might help somebody identify him. He'd also stolen a kid's skateboard. Now he looked like just one more of the skateboard kids who ran the streets. He hated it. He deserved so much better than this.

If only Jared hadn't gotten caught. The stupid jerk hadn't even been able to get out of his own way the night the FBI crashed in. Now Jared was in jail and it probably wouldn't be long before he'd not only confess to the four murders, but he'd also try to throw Leo under the bus.

Rob Garner had convinced Leo that he was keeping his son strong and not talking, but for how long? Unfortunately, when Leo had jumped out of the window to escape that night, he'd had to leave his bug-out bag with all his cash behind. And now his own parents weren't helping him at all. They had basically disowned him. It would serve them right if he broke into the house in the middle of the night and slashed their throats.

All he needed was enough money to get out of town until things cooled down and then eventually he might be able to get out of the country. All he needed was somebody to give him a freakin' break.

At that moment his phone rang. It was a burner phone and he knew exactly who was on the other end. "Yeah," he answered.

"Something has to be done about that Colton bitch. She's going to somehow burn you both."

"So, what do you want me to do about it?" Leo asked. Bingo. This was definitely his freakin' break.

"She needs to disappear…permanently. I tried to

take care of the situation tonight, but I'm not sure it worked."

"Again, what do you want me to do about it?" Leo repeated. Rob Garner wasn't a stupid man. He knew it was in Jared's best interest if Leo was never brought in.

Although Leo wasn't sure if Rob truly knew how bad it would be for his son. Leo wouldn't have a problem throwing Jared under the bus. He would get all choked up while he told a jury how Jared had manipulated him into shooting the gun and killing those men. He'd sob nearly uncontrollably as he told them he had feared for his own life with Jared and his father's threats.

"She's tight with that FBI agent, Howard. It wouldn't hurt if something bad happened to both of them. It would probably slow down the case and give us more of a chance at a really good defense," Rob continued.

For the first time since he'd shot those old men outside their businesses, a fresh, sweet adrenaline rushed through Leo. "So, tell me exactly what you have in mind."

## Chapter Five

It was a few minutes after ten and Brad was ready to call it another failure of a day. Styler was still out there. Rob Garner was still bitching and moaning about Jared now being questioned without him present and about everything else concerning the case against his son. And Brad hadn't seen or spoken to Simone in two days.

As it should be, he reminded himself. He'd read over the notes she'd given to him and marveled at her insights. If the notes were any indication of how she taught, then he could understand why her classes were so popular. She had a way of laying out information that made it easy to understand, yet her intelligence in the subject matter shone through.

However, at this point there was nothing more she could do to help and the two of them had absolutely no reason to get together again. In fact, as far as he was concerned, it would be utter foolishness for him to pursue anything with Simone Colton.

He had just undressed and crawled into bed when a knock sounded at his door. He jumped up, hoping it was somebody telling him they'd finally caught Leo.

He yanked on a pair of jeans, grabbed his gun and then answered the door. It was Russ. "Hey, I just got word from a Chicago PD friend of mine that your girl has been taken by ambulance to Chicago University Hospital."

His girl? Simone? "What? Did he know why?" Every muscle in Brad's body tensed as his mind went wild with worry.

"He didn't have any real details, but he thought it was something about a carjacking." Russ frowned. "I figured you'd want to know. Do you want me to go with you?"

"No... I'm fine to go." Brad grabbed the shirt that he'd worn that day and pulled it on. "You get some sleep and I'll be in touch tomorrow."

When Russ left the room, Brad quickly got on his socks and shoes. A carjacking? She had to have been hurt to be taken to the hospital. Oh God, had she been badly hurt? All kinds of crazy thoughts rushed through his head, only making him more anxious and eager to get to her as soon as possible.

A few minutes later he left the hotel room and headed for the police-issued unmarked car that had been at his disposal since he had arrived in Chicago. Rain fell at a moderate pace, as it had all evening long.

As he drove to the hospital, his brain continued to go wild with suppositions. Had a gun been involved? Had she been shot? Or had this been something much more dangerous...much more insidious than a carjacking?

Rob Garner. A vision of the man angrily threatening Simone filled his head. Did he have something to do with Simone being in the hospital? Or was Brad overthinking things? There was plenty of crime on the Chicago streets without Rob Garner being in the mix.

Right now he didn't care so much about answering these questions. All he really cared about was her condition. It seemed like it took him forever to reach the hospital. Traffic was slow and people drove like they had never driven in the rain before. He found a parking space in the hospital lot and then raced for the emergency room.

The waiting area was half filled with people. A little boy fussed and cried in his mother's arms and an old man had one hand wrapped in a makeshift bandage. A young couple sat side by side, her head resting on his shoulder. Two young women paced the floor, looking sick and strung out.

A hospital was definitely not Brad's favorite place to be. His mother had lingered three long days before succumbing to the wounds from her killer. Brad's father had brought him to visit every day.

He'd been convinced that Brad's mother would rally, that she would somehow be okay, but Brad had smelled the death in the room, had seen the shadow of death on his mother's face and had known even at twelve years old that she wasn't going to have a miraculous healing.

He now went to the desk, where a harried-looking nurse sat behind a glass partition. He flashed his credentials and she opened the window. "Can I help you?"

"A woman named Simone Colton was brought in here by ambulance about an hour ago. I need to speak to the doctor in charge of her case."

"Please, have a seat and I'll see what I can do," she replied.

With a sigh of frustration, he sank down in a chair near the window. He waited ten minutes and then finally the nurse waved at him and opened the door

that separated the waiting room from the curtained-
off emergency beds.

Brad hurried through the door and was met by a
young doctor who wore the name tag of Dr. McCoy.
Once again, Brad showed his credentials and then en-
quired about Simone.

"Miss Colton was brought in after having suffered
a head trauma that rendered her unconscious. She regained consciousness soon after arriving. We've now
run the appropriate tests to make sure she didn't have
a fracture or any brain bleed. Both tests came back
negative, but I've had her transferred to a bed upstairs
for a night of observation."

"What room has she been transferred to and can I
see her?" Brad asked, his emotions flying all over the
place. He needed to know how she had ended up here
with head trauma.

"She's in room 605. I'll tell you what I told the officers that came in with her. I don't want her stressed
by too many questions. The main thing she needs right
now is rest."

"Got it," Brad replied and hurried back to the exit
of the waiting room. Once there he went down a long
hallway and came to the elevators that would take him
up to the sixth floor.

His heart thundered in his chest. She'd suffered a
head trauma... What did that even mean? Had somebody tried to jack her car and hit her over the head
with the butt of a gun? With a crowbar? Where had
this happened? He didn't even know what kind of a
car she drove.

Once the elevator doors whooshed open, he quickly
stepped out, checked the sign on the wall and then

raced in the direction of her room. The halls were quiet and the lights were dimmed at this time of the night.

He was vaguely surprised when he reached her room to find nobody else there with her. She lay in the bed, a lamp just above her head casting light on her pale face. Her eyes were closed and she looked small and achingly vulnerable in the big hospital bed.

He needed to contact somebody. He needed answers as to what had happened to her, but at the moment he just needed to stand in the doorway and watch the steady rise and fall of her chest beneath her blue-flowered hospital gown. He needed to gaze at her beautiful face and assure himself that, at least for now, she seemed to be safe and resting peacefully.

Suddenly he was gazing into her bright blue eyes. "Simone," he whispered softly.

Her eyes widened. She looked around the room and then back at him and then a deep sob escaped her and she raised her hands to hide her face.

"Simone..." In four long strides he was at her bedside. "Please don't cry," he said.

"I... I can't h-help it, Brad. I was so...so scared and m-my head is k-killing me."

He sank down next to her in a chair. "Simone, crying is only going to make your head hurt more. You're safe now." He reached out and pulled one of her hands away from her face. He held on tight and slowly she lowered her other hand and gazed at him through tear-filled eyes.

He continued to hold her hand as she drew in a few deep breaths in an obvious effort to calm herself. For several moments they were silent. Although there were a hundred questions he wanted to ask her, he also wanted to give her enough time to gather herself together.

Finally, her tears stopped and her eyes were more clear. "Simone, I don't want to upset you, but I need to know what happened tonight."

She reached for a water cup on a small tray on the opposite side of the bed. She took a swallow, then set down the foam cup. "I... I had my last lecture tonight. It all went great and afterward I headed for my car in the staff parking lot." She paused and a whisper of fear darkened her eyes.

"It was raining and I... I was almost to my car," she continued, "when I heard a couple of footsteps behind me. I started to turn and then I was shoved hard and my hair was yanked. Somehow, I managed to push my car alarm before I fell backward and hit the concrete with my head. I woke up here. The doctor told me the two police officers who followed the ambulance believed it was a carjacking gone awry."

She winced slightly and then pulled the thin hospital blanket up closer around her neck. "To be honest, I don't know what to believe. It all happened so fast. I suppose it might have been a carjacking. I can't imagine what else it would have been."

"Were there other cars in that parking lot?" he asked.

She nodded and then winced again, her headache obviously causing her pain. "There were a few."

He asked her several more questions and he could tell she grew more and more weary.

She drew in a deep, heavy sigh. "Brad, I don't want any of my family knowing about this. I'll be out of the hospital tomorrow and there's no need to worry any of them."

"I will do my best not to tell anyone," he replied. "Now, the best thing you can do is get a good night's sleep." He rose from the chair.

The instinct...the need to lean down and kiss her on the forehead or on her cheek shocked him. Instead, he quickly stepped back from the bed. "I'll be back in the morning, Simone."

"Thank you, Brad." Her eyes slowly drifted closed and he stepped outside of the room. He hurried down the hallway a little ways and then pulled his cell phone from his pocket. He was far enough away that she wouldn't be able to hear his conversation, but close enough that he still had his eye on her room.

He needed to speak to the officers who had responded to the scene, but first he needed to call the lieutenant who was the liaison between the FBI agents and the Chicago PD. He wanted to arrange for a guard on Simone's door.

Even though the police had believed it was a carjacking, Brad's gut instincts told him that there was a real possibility it might be something different. It was just too coincidental that Rob had threatened her and then she was attacked in a staff parking lot.

There was no way to be sure his instincts were right or wrong, but he wasn't taking any chances with Simone's safety. It took forty-five minutes for a police officer to show up for the guard duty. He settled into a chair in the doorway of her room and told Brad he would be there until Brad returned the next morning.

The next place Brad went was to the police station to see if he could hunt down the two officers who had responded to the 911 call made by a security guard at the college. He got lucky and found both of them together at their desks.

They agreed to meet with him in one of the interrogation rooms that currently wasn't in use. "I just want to get the rundown on what happened when you arrived at the call on the campus earlier."

Mike Walker was a young patrolman. He frowned. "When my partner and I arrived on scene, Miss Colton was unconscious on the ground. Her car alarm was going off, which had alerted the security guard who called it in."

"I immediately checked the area for a perp, but I didn't see anyone around." Paul Winthrop appeared to be the older, the more seasoned of the two.

"Where were her car keys?" Brad asked.

"In her hand," Mike replied. "Although her computer case and an umbrella were on the ground near her. It looked like an open-and-shut case to me."

"If she was unconscious with her keys in her hand, then why wasn't her car stolen?" Brad asked.

"It would be my speculation that the alarm scared the carjacker off," Paul said.

"Do you know how long the alarm rang before the security guard responded?" Brad asked.

"He wasn't sure. He only heard it when he stepped outside to have a smoke. Do you know how she's doing? She was still unconscious when we were with her earlier," Mike said.

"I just left the hospital and she's going to be okay. She's being held overnight for observation, but she should be out of the hospital sometime tomorrow," Brad explained.

"That's good to hear," Paul replied.

"Can you email me your reports when you get them written up?" Brad asked.

"I've already written mine up," Paul replied. "Just give me your email and it will be done."

Brad gave the two men his email address and then thanked them. When they parted ways, Brad's impulse was to rush back to the hospital, but he knew he had other things to do in order to assure Simone's safety going forward.

He went back to his office and read Paul's report and then just sat for several minutes trying to clear his mind. He needed to think rationally and not emotionally.

It was evident that everyone he had spoken to believed it had been a carjacking gone awry, but all his instincts screamed it had been Rob or somebody close to Rob who had attacked her.

He'd seen the hatred in the man's eyes both times he'd encountered Simone. Worse than the hatred had been the whisper of fear he'd seen in Rob's eyes.

Brad believed Rob saw Simone as a viable threat to Jared's freedom, and if that was the case, then he was a clear and present danger to her. If what Brad believed was true, then tonight Rob had attacked her. The car alarm very well might have saved her life.

If Rob's intention had been to take her out permanently, then tonight he had failed. What scared Brad was that meant another attack was possible, and the next time Rob just might succeed.

SIMONE AWAKENED WITH the morning light drifting in through the blinds at the window. For a moment she was disoriented. Then the memories of the night before slammed into her.

Her headache had finally abated, but she now felt more aches and pains in her back from hitting the concrete. As she thought of the sudden, violent attack, a chill swept through her. Everything had happened so fast and she desperately wished she had seen her attacker so that the police would have a physical description of whoever it had been.

Unfortunately, because it had all happened so fast and she'd been attacked from behind, she hadn't seen the person. The police had been certain that it had been a carjacking. For as long as she had worked at the college, she'd never heard of any carjackings occurring there. But she supposed it was possible that was what it had been. There was really no other scenario that made any sense.

A vision of an enraged Rob Garner filled her head. She still didn't believe she needed to take his threats seriously, and she didn't think he had anything to do with what had happened to her the night before. But what if she was wrong? She didn't want to believe that it was anything other than a random act of violence. To believe that Rob Garner had been behind the attack was just too frightening to consider.

Her thoughts turned to Brad. Thoughts of him always made her heart flutter just a bit. There was no question that she felt a strong physical attraction toward him, but what woman wouldn't? He was definitely easy on the eyes. While she had found him easy to talk to, there was no way there would be anything between them except the murder that had temporarily brought them together.

Her thoughts were interrupted by the appearance of a nurse, who took her vitals and pronounced all of them good. "The doctor will be in soon," she said and then left the room.

It wasn't the doctor who came in next, though. It was breakfast. She ate the toast and drank both the orange juice and coffee but didn't have the appetite for the scrambled eggs or the limp bacon. She pushed the tray away and then settled back into her pillow.

She didn't realize she'd fallen back asleep, but when she opened her eyes, Brad was seated in the chair next to her bed. "Oh my gosh, how long have you been there?" she asked and raised up the head of her bed.

"Not too long. How are you feeling?"

He looked great in a pair of jeans and a navy polo shirt. As usual, a shoulder holster with his gun was his only accessory. Her hand self-consciously went up to her hair and then dropped back to her lap. She had no idea what she looked like at the moment, but in the end it really didn't matter.

"My headache is better, but I've definitely discovered some new body aches and pains today," she replied.

"I'm not surprised. You took a hard fall last night." His gaze was warm and intense as it lingered on her. "When I got the call that you'd been taken to the hospital, it scared the hell out of me."

"I have to confess, when I woke up in the hospital, I was pretty scared myself. I just wish I could have given the police officers a description of the person or persons so they could get him…or them off the streets."

"There's no question things would be different if

you had seen who attacked you. However, I'm not convinced what happened to you was a carjacking."

She stared at him. "You think it was Rob Garner?"

"I do." A muscle throbbed in his lower jaw. "I warned you to stay away from him."

She picked up on a bit of frustrated anger in his voice and it stirred a touch of defensive anger in her. "I'll admit I made a mistake when I approached him in the restaurant, but it wasn't my fault that we ran into each other in the police station when I brought you my notes."

For a long moment their gazes remained locked. Finally, he raked a hand through his short hair and released a deep sigh. "Sorry, I'm not angry with you. I'm just angered by this whole situation."

"I'm not exactly happy about it, either," she replied drily.

At that moment a doctor entered the room. He introduced himself as Dr. Matt Jacobs. "How are you feeling this morning, Miss Colton?"

"Make it Simone and I'm feeling much better. Please tell me I can go home."

"Only if you promise that if your headache returns or if you suffer any dizziness or unusual drowsiness, you'll either follow up with your doctor or return to the emergency room," he replied.

"I promise," she said.

"Then I'll have the nurse work up your discharge papers."

"Thank you, Dr. Jacobs."

"Would you please step out so I can get dressed?" Simone asked Brad once the doctor left the room.

"Of course," Brad replied. He immediately stood and headed for the doorway.

Simone got up and checked the closet, where she found the clothes she'd had on the night before hanging there. Her purse and her computer case were also there. She assumed one of the officers had sent them along with her in the ambulance. She dressed quickly and then went to the door to let Brad know he could come back in.

She was surprised to see him speaking to a police officer who was seated in a chair just outside her room. She stepped back before either man saw her and instead she sat on the edge of her bed to wait for Brad and her discharge papers.

He knocked on the door and she told him to come in. When he entered the room again, she looked at him curiously. "Who is the officer in the chair?"

"His name is Officer Eric Mendez. I had him sit on guard duty outside your room all night long."

"Did you really think that was necessary?" she asked. Her heart began to beat a little bit faster. She suddenly felt as if her orderly life was spinning out of control and she didn't like the feeling at all.

"I would prefer to err on the side of safety," he replied. "And with that in mind, I hope you don't mind but I've called your sisters to meet me and you at your place at two o'clock this afternoon." He once again sat in the chair next to the bed.

She stared at him for a long moment. "Did you tell them what happened to me?"

He hesitated a moment and then looked away. "Yeah, I did."

Another edge of anger rose up inside her. "I asked you not to tell them."

He looked back at her and there was a hard glint in his eyes. "Simone, I am first and foremost an FBI agent, and I thought it was in everyone's best interest to know what happened to you last night."

"But why? It could only have been one of two things. Either it was a random act or it was Rob Garner. In either case, why did they have to know anything?"

"I'll explain more about it when we're all together with your sisters," he replied. "I'll take you home and we'll wait for them there."

"Where is my car? Is it still at the college?" She was trying not to be upset, but once again she felt as if her carefully structured world was turning upside down.

"I arranged for your car to be taken back to your condo parking spot." He stood and reached into his pocket. He pulled out her key fob and held it out to her. She took it from him and dropped it into her purse.

An awkward silence ensued. She knew Brad wasn't telling her something and that worried her. What was going on that he felt the need to involve her family at all? She refused to beg him for the answers right now, but she couldn't help the nerves that jangled inside her.

Thankfully the nurse walked in at that moment with her discharge paperwork, breaking the sudden tension that had risen up between them.

Once Simone was free to go, she and Brad left the hospital and he led her to his car. Since he'd flown into Chicago, she knew the car wasn't his personal one, but rather one the Chicago PD had loaned him for the duration of his time here.

The brief sunshine of the morning was gone and

rain had moved in again. Unfortunately, her umbrella hadn't been with her clothes and purse, so they raced to get to the car. Once there, Brad quickly opened the car door for her and she slid inside.

The car interior smelled like Brad's cologne, and even with everything that was going on, her stomach tightened with what only could be described as a faint hint of sexual tension. Or was it simply anxiety? Because she knew something was about to happen and she had no idea if that something was going to be good or very, very bad.

*Chapter Six*

Brad knew instinctively that Simone wasn't going to be happy with his plans for her, but he would do anything he needed to do to keep her safe from harm.

Still, he could already feel her tension radiating toward him in the car. It felt very negative and as if she'd closed herself off.

"Headache still gone?" he asked in an effort to break the uncomfortable silence that had grown between them.

"Yes, thank goodness," she replied. "Last night I could scarcely think it pounded so hard."

"I'm glad you're feeling better today." He flashed her a smile, hoping to break the tension.

"I'm just glad I'm finished up with all my classes. I'll also just be glad to get home and relax for the next few days."

Brad didn't reply because that wasn't at all what he had in mind for her. Again silence fell between them until he pulled up in a parking space across from her condo. Thankfully the rain had stopped, but the skies were still dark gray.

She released what sounded like a sigh of relief. "Oh, it's good to be here instead of the hospital," she said as they got out of the car. "The first thing I want to do is take a nice, long hot shower."

Instantly a vision of her naked and beneath the shower spray filled his head. He could imagine the soap sliding down her body... The scent of her filled his head and a rush of heat took over his body.

Jeez, what was wrong with him? Where was his professionalism when he needed it? How could he be thinking of her in that way when it was possible her life was in danger? He gave himself a hard mental shake.

As she unlocked the door to the condo, he was interested in what her home looked like. You could tell a lot about a person by the things they chose to have around them.

She opened the door and ushered him into an attractive living room. The floor plan was open and airy. Pictures of her siblings and parents covered one wall. It was proof that the person who lived here had strong family ties.

The color combinations were relaxing and the overstuffed sofa looked inviting. The whole space felt warm. He could also tell there was a place for everything and everything was in its place, whispering of a bit of a control issue? Or just a person who was well organized?

"It's after noon. Do you want me to make you something for lunch?" she offered.

"No, thanks, I'm good. Why don't you go ahead and take that shower you wanted," he replied.

She gave him a grateful smile. "Thanks. I'll be back in a few minutes."

"Take your time." As she disappeared from the room, he stepped over to the wall of photos. He couldn't help the way his heart responded to the pictures of Alfred with his wife and three daughters. His murder had been so senseless and now there would never be a family photo with all of them present in it again.

As he heard the water turn on in the bathroom, he sat down on the sofa and went over the plans he had made the night before. He'd been up all night making sure his plans were in place and everything was taken care of.

It was really perfect, but he had a feeling Simone was going to kick and buck, which was why he'd invited her sisters to be here for backup and support.

He hadn't gone into much detail when he'd spoken to each of them, but his instinct in this matter was that they were definitely going to be on his side. He hoped Simone would be reasonable and realize she needed to do what was necessary.

Twenty minutes later Simone walked back out. She looked amazing in a pair of jeans that hugged the slender length of her long legs and a blue-and-white sleeveless blouse that emphasized the thrust of her breasts and her small waist.

She smelled like clean female with a hint of the perfume that made him think of snuggling and hot sex. Criminy, this was going to be the most difficult thing he had ever done in his entire career.

"Are you sure you aren't hungry?" she asked. "I'd be glad to make you a sandwich or something while we wait for my sisters to get here."

"Yes, I'm sure, but feel free to make yourself something if you're hungry."

"I'm not," she replied and sank down in the chair facing him. "Brad, I'm sorry you've had to deal with all this. I'm sure there are far more important things you should be doing with your time right now."

"Actually, there isn't. I've got a good team and they all know what we need to do. Of course, the main goal is to get Leo behind bars."

She frowned. "Do you think he's somehow managed to get out of the country?"

"No. I don't even think he's made it out of Chicago. My guess is that he's hunkered down someplace and is waiting for the heat to ease off him before he'll make a move."

"But how is he existing? His parents have to somehow be getting money to him," she said.

"If they are, we can't figure out how. We have eyes on all their financials and nothing suspicious has shown up. We also have tails on them, but again they haven't done anything to indicate they have aided Leo. They've told us they've washed their hands of him and have no desire to help their son given the crimes he will be charged with."

She released a deep sigh and then leaned back in the chair. "So, you want to tell me now why you've invited my sisters to meet us here?"

"I'll wait until we're all here together. It won't be long before they'll be here," he replied.

"You're driving me crazy with your mysteriousness."

He smiled at her. "Normally I'm not mysterious at all. I'm pretty much an open book kind of guy."

She returned his smile. "Brad, I just want to thank you for everything you've done. Not just for me, but for my entire family."

"I'm just doing my job," he replied.

"Being at the hospital to take me home was certainly going above and beyond your job," she replied.

"Simone, you're a party of interest in an ongoing investigation. What happens with you *is* part of my job," he replied. And he needed to keep reminding himself that he was just doing his job and it had nothing to do with his intense, inexplicable attraction to Simone.

For the next few minutes, they talked about the case and threw out speculations on where Leo might be hiding. At precisely two o'clock, their conversation was interrupted by a knock at the door.

"I'll get it," Brad said and quickly jumped up from the sofa. With his hand on the butt of his gun, he opened the door. He relaxed at the sight of Tatum. She greeted him and then quickly beelined to Simone.

She grabbed Simone's hand and pulled her up off the chair and into a big hug. "Oh my God, Simone. Are you okay? I couldn't believe it when Agent Howard told me what happened to you last night."

"I'm fine," Simone assured her. "I've just got a little bump on the back of my head." She returned to her seat and gestured for Tatum to sit on the sofa.

"I've got a million questions to ask you about exactly what happened, but I'll wait until January gets here because I know she'll have the same questions I have." The words had barely left Tatum's mouth when another knock sounded at the door.

January flew through the door and more hugs were given. Finally, everyone was settled in. The two sisters and Brad on the sofa and Simone in the chair.

After a fifteen-minute session of asking Simone for all the details concerning exactly what had happened to her the night before and Simone answering all the questions, they then looked expectantly to Brad.

He cleared his throat and stood. "I'm sure you all are wondering why I've brought you together. Now that you know what happened to Simone last night, I have to tell you I don't believe it was a carjacking or a random attack."

"Then who do you think attacked her?" Tatum asked.

"All my instincts tell me it was Rob Garner, or somebody working with him," Brad replied.

"Why would Jared Garner's father be after Simone? What would he have to gain by attacking her?" Tatum stared at Simone and then looked back to Brad. "We know about the two encounters she had with the man, but do you really believe he'd follow through with physical violence?"

"This is what I think," Brad said. "I believe Rob now believes that Simone is actively working to see his son put away in prison forever. I believe he sees her as a danger to his family, and because of that, he's a real danger to Simone. I think he tried to kill her last night and was unsuccessful. I think he'll try again. My plan is to get Simone out of town and hidden away until either Jared confesses or Leo is captured."

"Oh, no," Simone instantly said. She halfway rose from the chair and then sat back down again. "I'm not leaving my home because of this bigmouthed bully."

"Simone, he's more than a bully. Even you know that he beats his son. He's a brutal man and I believe he'll come after you again," Brad said firmly.

"Then you have to go, Simone," Tatum said firmly.

"Simone, there's no question about it. You must go,"

January added. "We can't take any risks with your safety. I refuse to lose another family member. Mom would want you to go, too."

"I think you're all overreacting," Simone said, her slightly narrowed eyes telling Brad she was irritated with him.

"But what if I'm not?" Brad replied. The whole situation had burned in his gut all night long. He'd tried to make himself believe that the attack on her had been random and had nothing to do with Rob Garner, but he'd been unsuccessful.

He truly believed he needed to get her away from Chicago and he'd made the perfect arrangements. The only thing he needed to do now was convince her to go with him.

"Simone, you have no work to worry about right now. You have nothing on your plate that is more important than your very life," Tatum said.

Simone looked at both her sisters and then released an audible deep sigh. She looked back at Brad. "Okay. What do you have in mind?"

"My buddy has a small fishing cabin about five hours from here. Nobody will know we're there and I can keep you safe ."

She frowned. "Do we really need to do this?"

"Yes," both of her sisters exclaimed at the same time.

Simone looked at Brad once again. "When would we have to leave?"

"Immediately. I already have my bags packed and in the car. All you need to do is pack whatever you need for a week or two and then we'll get on the road," he replied.

Tatum got up from the sofa and grabbed Simone's hand. "Come on, I'll help you pack."

"You'll keep her safe?" January asked him as the other two left the room.

"I'll die before I let anything happen to her," he replied with all the determination in his heart, in his very soul.

January held his gaze for a long moment and then nodded, as if satisfied. It was true. He would protect Simone with his life, not just because it was his job, but also because it was his desire. He couldn't imagine anyone hurting her and it wouldn't happen on his watch. The Colton families had already endured enough.

"Let me go see how they're doing," January said and then disappeared into the room where the other two had gone.

Brad walked over to the window that looked out onto the street. He was eager to get on the road, but before they left town, they needed to stop by a grocery store and get food and anything else they might need for the next couple of weeks.

If he remembered right, Glen's cabin was fairly isolated and there was just a very small general store a few miles away. The store sold only the very basics but had a large supply of alcohol.

Rain had begun to fall again from the gray clouds above. He hadn't heard any weather reports in the last couple of days, but he was definitely hoping the clouds would break up and the rain would stop once they got underway.

He'd received permission from his superior to get Simone out of town. There were only a few people at the police station who knew where he was taking Simone. He definitely hoped there would be no leaks that might let the Garners, or anyone else nefarious, know where they had gone.

He turned around from the window when the three women returned to the room. Simone carried one medium-sized suitcase and Tatum had a smaller one.

"All set?" Brad asked.

"Not really," Simone replied. "I'm not happy about any of this."

"Simone, I'd rather have you unhappy and safe than happy and dead," Tatum said. "Go with Agent Howard and don't be stubborn about things."

"You need to listen to him and do everything he tells you to do," January added. "We'll explain all of this to Mom."

"Let's get on the road," Brad said.

He took her bags and they left the condo. The sisters all hugged and said their goodbyes and then it was just him and Simone in the car and he pulled away from her condo.

"Well, that was certainly quite manipulative of you, Agent Howard," she said coolly.

He shot her a look of surprise. "What are you talking about?" he asked.

"Planning ahead to have my sisters there to coerce me into coming with you. It was a really sneaky thing to do."

"Okay, I'll admit it was a little manipulative, but I just wanted to make sure you came with me. As far as I'm concerned, this is a matter of life or death and I would do it all over again for this intended result."

"I much would have preferred if you had approached me on an intellectual level rather than on an emotional one," she said, her voice still decidedly cool. "If I were a man, would you have had my two brothers waiting to talk me into coming with you?"

"It would depend on how stubborn you were as a man," he said in an attempt at levity. It didn't work. Without even looking at her, he felt the weight of her baleful stare.

He released a deep sigh. They were about to be alone for a week or two in an isolated cabin by a river in the woods. He hoped she managed to forgive him soon. Otherwise, rather than being a hideaway of protection, it would wind up being the hideaway from hell.

THE FOUL MOOD had Simone around the throat and she was having trouble climbing out of it. There was no question that she was irritated with Brad for involving her family members in her drama, but she could admit to herself that she probably wouldn't have agreed to come without her sisters' insistence.

However, her real irritation was at the whole situation, at the fact that she was now in a car heading to a cabin in the woods because some psychopath decided she was a danger to him and his family. Her well-structured life was now no longer in her control and she felt as if her world had been tossed on its head.

"There's a grocery store a couple of blocks from here," he said. "We'll stop there to shop for food to take with us. I've got a cooler in the trunk full of ice for the trip."

"Sounds like you've thought of everything," she replied. Good grief, even to herself she sounded cranky.

"I've tried to," he replied, as if oblivious of her current mood.

Minutes later they entered the grocery store and she walked beside him as he pushed the cart. As they shopped, she felt her bad mood slowly lifting.

Even though she didn't want to be here, she needed to make the best of things. Just as it really wasn't her fault that Rob Garner had a problem with her, it wasn't Brad's fault, either. He was just trying to keep her safe and that was what she needed to remember.

They passed an aisle with candy bars and she grabbed a chocolate bar and tossed it into the cart. "Chocolate makes me less witchy," she said and then laughed when Brad grabbed a handful and added them to the cart.

Forty-five minutes later they were back in the car. "I think we bought enough groceries to last a month," she said as he pulled out of the grocery store parking lot.

"I'm sure we won't be gone that long, but I like to be prepared," he replied.

"Could you please do something about this rain?" she asked as the wipers worked overtime to keep the car window clean.

"Ha, wish I could. Hopefully it will stop soon or we'll eventually drive out of it."

"So, tell me about this cabin we're going to."

"Glen Tankersley works as a police officer in a small town in Wisconsin. I met him while investigating a serial killer that was working there and we became good friends. He's a fishing freak and years ago bought a cabin that's on the bank of a small river. He did tell me it's been a while since he'd been there."

"You still haven't told me about the cabin itself," she replied. She looked at him, unable to ignore his handsome profile.

"It's been years since I've been there, but it's a one-bedroom with pretty much everything you need. It has a stove and fridge, a wood-burning fireplace and a bathroom. Unfortunately, there's no tub, just a shower. I remember it as a cozy little getaway."

"Sounds like the perfect hideaway," she agreed and then looked back out her passenger window. A one-bedroom cabin. Did he assume that they would sleep together in the bed?

And why did the very idea shoot a tiny whisper of a thrill through her? It was going to be difficult to share a small space with him and stay as completely distant from him as she knew she should.

Still, she couldn't remember ever feeling the kind of physical attraction that she felt toward Brad for any other man. She had to keep reminding herself that he was just doing his job, and when his job was finished, he'd go back to his life in Washington, DC.

The windshield wipers beat in a rhythmic manner that, along with the grayness of the day, slowly relaxed her. Oddly enough she hadn't felt any danger, but right now in this moment with Brad taking control, she felt completely safe and protected. She closed her eyes and let the movement of the car and the patter of the rain against the window lull her to sleep.

She awakened to the darkness of night and the windshield wipers still working overtime. "Wow, how long have I been asleep?"

"About four and a half hours. We're pretty close to the cabin now," he replied.

"I'm so sorry. I certainly didn't intend to fall asleep or to sleep so long," she said. She hadn't realized how bone-weary she'd been since her father's murder. Between the grief and the nightmares, she'd apparently gone without any real, good sleep for too long.

He flashed her a smile, his perfect white teeth visible in the illumination from the dashboard. "Don't apologize. You must have needed the sleep."

"Are you doing okay? Do you want me to drive for a little while?" she offered. "You can tell me the way if you're tired of being behind the wheel."

"No, I'm fine."

"I see the rain is still falling," she said. She sat up straighter in her seat.

"Yeah, although it's lighter than it was. I'm still hoping it stops altogether by the time we get to the cabin."

"At least there's been no thunder or lightning with the rain we've had." She wrapped her arms around herself and tried not to think of her irrational fear of storms.

"I'm definitely ready for some sunshine. Have you ever been fishing?"

"Never," she replied. "I like my fish perfectly cooked on a plate and served with maybe some rice pilaf on the side."

He laughed. "And I'll bet you've never been camping before, either."

"You would win that bet. But please don't tell me there isn't really a cabin and we're going to be living in a tent and catching our own fish to eat," she said.

He laughed again. "I promise you there really is a cabin and I believe you were with me when we bought all the meat at the store to bring with us."

She really liked the sound of his laughter. It was a deep and smooth rumble, and it warmed her insides like a jigger of good whiskey. "So, are you a camper and a fisherman in your spare time?" she asked curiously.

"Not really. I visited the cabin with Glen a couple of times and we did some fishing, but I'm not really the type to sit around and commune with nature."

"Too high-strung?" she asked, half-teasingly.

He flashed a grin at her. "Probably, and I've been called a lot worse."

"Oh, interesting. So, what else have you been called?" she asked.

"Arrogant, demanding and a control freak, just to name a few."

"People have called you those things to your face?" she asked incredulously.

He laughed again. "Rarely to my face, but I eventually hear about them anyway."

"And are you all those things?" She hoped he said yes. She hoped he was actually an arrogant jerk. That would certainly cool her attraction to him.

"I hope I'm not really those things. Yes, I expect a lot from the people I work with, but I expect the same things of myself. I can be demanding when it comes to hunting down a killer. I never lose sight of the victims and the need to get a murderer behind bars." He shot her a glance. "What about you? What do your students say about you behind your back?"

"Probably that I'm arrogant, demanding and a control freak," she replied with a small laugh.

"Then I think you and I might have issues," he replied lightly. "But I'm sure we'll work together just fine for the duration that we're in the cabin. And speaking of the cabin, it's just up ahead."

She looked out the front window. The headlights

shone on a small, rustic-looking cabin tucked inside a stand of tall trees. It looked like a pretty picture post-card, a serene little place in the woods.

Maybe this short getaway would be good for her soul. For the last six months she'd been totally immersed in grief and thoughts of murder. Maybe she could find a little peace here in the charming cabin and then go back to her life with a new perspective. She knew her sisters were right, that she hadn't even begun to move on from her grief. And it was time.

Brad pulled up and parked, and then together they got out of the car. Thank goodness it had stopped raining again. She could immediately hear the sound of the nearby river running in its bank, a sound that, along with the wind rustling through the tops of the trees, was oddly soothing.

"Why don't we go inside and check out everything before we unload," he suggested.

"Sounds like a plan to me," she agreed. They both got out of the car and approached the cabin.

He turned on the flashlight on his phone and stepped to the right of the small porch. He moved aside some of the tall grass and then picked up a rock and grabbed a key that was hidden beneath. He turned and flashed her a grin. "I think this key has been hidden under that rock for the last fifteen years or so."

With the key in hand, he grabbed the handle of the screen door and opened it. It screeched like a cat in heat. "We'll definitely have to find some oil for that," he murmured.

He unlocked and opened the front door. He flipped on a light just inside and then ushered her in. The air smelled nasty, like layers of dust and old wood with a hint of mildew.

The sofa was a horrendous lime-green color and appeared to be lumpy and half-broken-down. A beige-and-green-striped chair looked to be in the same poor condition.

Large cobwebs hung from every corner of the room, looking like creepy, dirty lace. It was obvious that nobody had been inside for a very long time. A large supply of split logs was stacked next to a blackened stone fireplace and the nearby oven and refrigerator looked like they belonged in another century. She was scared to even look in the bedroom and bathroom.

Was this some kind of a joke? Did he really think she would be comfortable here? She wasn't a snob, but this place was absolutely filthy.

She turned to stare at him. He offered her a weak smile. "Maybe everything will look better in the morning," he said.

"I don't think so," she replied. "Are we really going to stay here?"

"We are," he said firmly. "We're completely off the grid here and my number one priority is keeping you safe. Now, you just relax and I'm going to unload the car."

The moment he left the cabin, she gingerly sat on the edge of the sofa. She might be safe here, but she was pretty sure there wouldn't be any peace. In fact, she'd be lucky if she got out of this experience without completely losing her mind.

## Chapter Seven

Brad awakened early the next morning, his body aching and burning from sleeping on the lumpy sofa all night long. He got up and quickly pulled on a pair of jeans and then walked over to the window, where no sun shone and instead the skies looked dark and angry. He stretched in an effort to alleviate the kinks in his back, and once he felt a little better, he turned and headed for the kitchen area.

Thankfully there was a coffee maker on the small countertop by the stove. He found the dishwashing liquid they'd brought with them and immediately cleaned the machine. He then started a pot and returned to the sofa to wait for it to brew.

He could definitely use a cup of strong coffee. The cabin was definitely not in the same shape he had remembered it to be. But it had been years since Brad had been here. Glen had said it'd been several years since he'd been here, too, but something hadn't connected in Brad's mind when he'd thought of bringing Simone here.

He hadn't thought of the mustiness, of the cobwebs and the overall neglect of the place. Seeing it through the eyes of a wealthy Colton woman had been particularly disheartening. He was vaguely surprised that Simone hadn't jumped back in the car and demanded he take her someplace else.

It had helped that he had brought along clean sheets and towels. The bedroom had been as depressing as the rest of the place. The queen-size bed had been bare and thankfully stain-free, but cobwebs hung in every corner and the mustiness smelled worse in the small room.

She'd been quiet when he'd helped make up the bed and then she'd gone to bed right after that. The bedroom door was still closed when he poured himself a cup of coffee and sat at the small table for two.

He'd charged his cell phone overnight and he now checked it for messages concerning the case. He was disappointed that there was no breaking news from anyone.

Checking the local weather was equally as disappointing and a tad bit concerning. Rain, rain and more rain. Flood watches were beginning to show up in areas and he could only hope the rain would stop before any flooding could occur.

The cabin was located on a six-mile area on high ground, but it was between two winding rivers that, if the waters rose a lot, would cut them off and isolate them from any outside resources. There was one road in and that was it. Still, they would have to get a ton of rain for the road to flood and cut them off.

He finished his cup of coffee and then, in hopes of putting Simone in a good mood for the morning, he pulled on a T-shirt and grabbed an iron skillet and a pound of bacon. He hoped it was hard for her to be in a bad mood when a man cooked breakfast for her.

He was just taking the crispy fried bacon out of the

skillet when the bedroom door opened and she stepped out. She was once again dressed in jeans but had a different blue blouse on than the day before. Her hair was slightly and charmingly mussed and she appeared to still be half-asleep. "Ah, just in time to tell me how you like your eggs," he said brightly.

"Any way is fine," she said and shot directly toward the coffeepot.

"Then I guess this morning I'll make them scrambled." As he grabbed a few eggs out of the fridge, she poured her coffee and then sank down at the table.

He shot her a glance as he poured his egg mixture into the awaiting skillet. She appeared to be staring blankly down into her coffee cup. He decided the next conversation needed to come from her and he just had to wait for it.

Within minutes he had plates on the table for the two of them along with a bowl of scrambled eggs, a platter of strips of bacon and a smaller plate of several pieces of buttered toast.

"Thank you, Brad. This all looks wonderful." She curled her fingers around the coffee cup. "In case you hadn't already noticed, I'm really not much of a morning person."

He smiled at her. "By using my great powers of deduction, I kind of figured that when you stared into your coffee cup like you expected the brew to reach up and shake you awake."

She returned his smile. She looked so pretty with the color of her blouse making her eyes appear even more blue. It was then he realized she wore no makeup and still looked gorgeous. Her skin was clear and beautiful and her eyelashes were long and thick.

"I'm usually not ready to engage with anyone until I've had two cups of coffee."

"Then I feel very privileged. You've only had one cup and yet you're being nice to me."

She laughed. "It's hard to be mad at a man who knows how to do crispy bacon right."

"There's nothing I hate more than limp, under-cooked bacon," he replied.

"That makes two of us," she agreed.

They each filled their plates and began eating. "Unfortunately, it's supposed to rain all day, so I thought we'd just kind of relax today. Maybe it will clear up tomorrow and we can go out and do a little walking."

"I hate that it's going to rain again, but there's no way I intend to just hang out and relax," she replied.

"Then what do you want to do?"

"Are you kidding? Look around us. I'm going to clean. I intend to attack every single one of the horrifying cobwebs in this place just for starters."

He laughed and looked around the room. "That could be an all-day job for us."

"I'm definitely ready to get to work...as soon as I have my second cup of coffee."

He placed two more strips of bacon on his plate and then gazed at her. "Thanks for being a good sport about this place. I had no idea it had fallen into such disrepair. I'm sure when you stepped in here last night you wanted to turn around and run away and I would have been tempted to run with you."

"I'm not going to lie, that thought did cross my mind, but then I realized you have me out here in the middle of nowhere and I wouldn't know where to run to." She got up from the table and poured herself another cup of coffee and then returned to the chair. "Besides, at least the bed mattress is good and we can clean dirty and make the best of things."

"Then you slept well?" he asked and tried not to think about how miserable his night had been on the uncomfortable sofa.

"Despite my long nap in the car, I slept like a baby. What about you?"

"I slept okay." There was no way he'd admit to her that the sofa was an instrument of torture and he'd much rather be sharing the bed with her.

Criminy, even thinking about being next to her under the sheets filled him with a heat that was difficult to ignore. He had to remember that he wasn't here to romance Simone. He was here to protect her from any and all harm.

When they were finished with breakfast, she insisted she'd do the cleanup. While she did that, Brad stepped outside to check things out before the dark clouds unleashed their fury.

The outside air felt heavy with the scent of wet earth and impending rain. The nearby river roared with swollen waters from the rain that had already fallen.

He walked around the cabin, checking windows and making sure there was no way for anyone to easily break in. Even though only a couple of law enforcement officials knew he'd brought Simone here, he was very aware that leaks could happen and there was no guarantee that Rob Garner had no idea where they were.

He was satisfied that the cabin windows were in relatively good shape and he saw no indication of anyone lurking nearby. He knew there were other cabins in the area. From the back of Glen's cabin, he could see another one tucked away in the woods, but he didn't think anyone was staying there.

As he headed back inside, the rain began to fall. He was surprised to see that Simone had changed into a pair of sweatpants and a T-shirt. On the table, she'd gathered cleaning supplies that she'd obviously found somewhere.

"Wow, bleach...furniture polish...glass cleaner and a bag full of cleaning rags, you found the mother lode. But it doesn't look like you found any cobweb cleaner," he said teasingly.

She gestured to a broom leaning again the wall. "That is the ultimate cobweb cleaner."

"Then let's get started."

For the next hour and a half, he attacked the cobwebs that clung in the corners while she cleaned the wooden walls with the lemon furniture cleaner. The rain pitter-pattered at the windows, creating a cozy feeling inside the cabin. As they worked, they talked about their childhoods. She shared some of the funny stories about growing up with her sisters, and he shared a little bit about life with his father. They took a break for a quick lunch of sandwiches and then returned to their cleaning.

Despite the odor of the lemon polish and the faint mustiness of the cabin, the scent of her perfume permeated the air. He wondered if he'd find the source of it behind her ears or down the side of her throat. Or maybe she had dabbed it on between her breasts, where it drifted up and out to torment him.

"I'm going into the bedroom to tackle the cobwebs in there," he said, feeling as if he just needed to get away, to gain a little distance from her for just a few minutes.

"Knock yourself out," she replied.

The minute he stepped into the bedroom, he realized it was a mistake. The scent of her was even stronger in here, and as he stared at the neatly made bed, all he could think of was the two of them beneath the sheets making love to the steady beat of the rain against the window.

He attacked the cobwebs more forcefully than necessary. He jabbed the broom into one of the corners, inwardly cursing himself. He was a professional, not some horny teenager. Yet something about Simone shot his testosterone skyrocketing. He felt like a horny teenager whenever he was around her.

In short order he had all the corners of the ceilings clean. He left the bedroom to find her seated at the kitchen table. "Ah, has the cleaning warrior pooped out?"

"No, actually I think we got everything," she said. "I'm not sure how we're going to clean all the rags I went through. They're all pretty dirty."

"At least the dirt is now on the rags and not on the walls anymore. There's a little general store not far from here with a couple of washers and dryers inside. At least they were there the last time I was here with Glen. We can plan a day to go there and do the laundry," he replied.

"Sounds like a plan." She got up from the table. "And now I need a shower." She grabbed the bottle of bleach. "I'll be back," she said and then disappeared into the bathroom.

He remained at the table and tried not to think when

minutes later he heard the sound of the shower water running. If he were to let his mind wander, then he would imagine her naked and that was exactly what he shouldn't think about.

Instead, he got up and headed to the refrigerator. Before he'd cooked breakfast, he'd pulled out of the freezer a couple of nice pork chops for dinner that evening.

After she'd gone to bed the night before, he had unloaded more of the supplies and put them away. He'd left a lot of the canned goods in the car, knowing there wasn't room for everything in the few cabinets.

He knew by her own admission that she didn't cook. So, he knew he'd probably be in charge of cooking the meals, and that was okay with him as long as she wasn't expecting anything gourmet.

Once he had in his mind what he was making for supper, he turned and headed for the coffee table. It had a drawer in it and at one time Glen had kept a deck of cards and a chess set there. Brad hoped they were still there. With no television and with the rain still falling, they needed something to do to pass the time. He breathed a sigh of relief when he discovered the items were still there. Now hopefully she'd be up to passing the time by playing cards and chess.

A half an hour later she walked out of the bathroom clad in a pair of navy jogging pants and a light blue T-shirt. She looked pretty, relaxed and refreshed.

"How was the shower?" he asked.

"Surprisingly good," she replied and sank down on the sofa. "I was expecting a cool drizzle, but it was nice and warm and had a good spray."

"That's good because in just a few minutes I need

to take a shower." Although he probably needed to make it a very cold one to douse the fire of desire she stirred in him. "I just wanted to talk to you about dinner. I figured I'd make us pork chops with baked potatoes and a salad."

"That sounds perfect to me," she agreed.

"And I found a deck of cards and a chess set in the coffee table drawer. Do you play chess?"

"I know how to, but it's been years since I've played." She looked toward the window, where the rain was still coming down at a steady pace, and then she gazed back at him. "Do you play?"

"I'm the same. It's been a long time since I played, but hopefully playing will help us pass the time here," he replied.

"Have you checked in with anyone? Has there been any news at all?"

She looked at him hopefully and he knew she was talking about her father's case and not wanting to know about world news. He wished he had something good to tell her, but he didn't.

"Unfortunately, there is none. I hope you know that you can't contact anyone in your family while we're here."

"I figured that out all by myself," she replied. "There's no need for you to tell me what to do or not do when it's obvious."

He looked at her in surprise. Why was she suddenly having attitude with him right now? "I apologize. I didn't mean to come off as condescending. And I think now is a good time for me to go take my shower."

She was silent as he got what he needed from his opened suitcase in the corner of the room and then went into the bathroom. He hoped she wasn't going to be a moody type of woman. The last thing he wanted to do was spend his time trying to figure out what he'd done to offend her. That would definitely make their time together here miserable.

A STAB OF guilt shot through Simone as she stared at the closed bathroom door. She'd been rude to him, and he hadn't deserved it. But she was so attracted to him she felt like she needed to put a little distance between them.

Watching his muscles work beneath his T-shirt as he'd held the broom overhead and stretched to reach the cobwebs had heated her in a way she hadn't been heated for a long time. Working next to him, she had smelled the faint scent of his cologne and even that had stirred her.

He seemed to be a nice guy, but he could never be *her* guy and being a little bitchy with him was the only way she knew how to deal with her emotions where he was concerned.

This whole setup felt far too intimate and too cozy and domestic and she didn't want her crazy desire for him to make her make a mistake where Brad was concerned. And hooking up with him would be a big mistake. She had a feeling it would be a hot, delicious memory…something she'd never forget, but a mistake nevertheless.

She was ready for love in her life, not an affair with a man who couldn't be available for her in the future. Therefore, Brad was off-limits…not that he'd made any kind of an advance toward her.

Once he got out of the shower and was dressed in

jeans and a brown polo shirt, the tension between them was definitely awkward. He went directly to the refrigerator and began to gather the items to cook for dinner.

Neither of them spoke and the silence weighed heavy as it lingered. This wasn't what she wanted, either. This time together was going to be absolutely miserable if the tension lingered for too long.

"I'm sorry I kind of snapped at you," she said, finally breaking the long silence.

He flashed her an easy smile. "That's okay. We're in close quarters and I'm sure there's going to be times when we'll get on each other's nerves."

She moved from the sofa to the kitchen table. She almost wished he would hold a grudge against her, but she was also grateful he hadn't.

She watched as he placed the pork chops in a baking pan and then seasoned them on either side. "You look very relaxed in the kitchen," she observed.

"When I was growing up, I spent a lot of time in the kitchen cooking for my father," he replied. "I took over the job after my mother's death."

"Then you were very young to take on that kind of responsibility." She remembered him telling her that his mother had passed away when he was twelve. At that age she was still playing with fashion dolls and just being a kid.

"Necessity is the mother of invention," he replied. "I cooked all the meals because not only did I need to eat, but I knew my dad needed to eat, too, and he wasn't capable of taking care of me or himself. I cooked and cleaned, and I took over paying the bills, something my mother had done."

"That must have been really tough," she replied.

"I didn't think it was tough at the time when I was doing it. I considered it a way to show my father how much I loved him."

She couldn't imagine being a young boy whose mother had been murdered and who had taken over all the responsibilities of running a household. He must have been a very strong boy to step into the role of parent.

"So, now that you're older, are you looking for a woman to cook and clean for you?" she asked lightly.

He laughed. "I'm not really looking for a woman at all. If one happens to find me and she can deal with my crazy work hours, then she wouldn't even need to cook." He scrubbed down two potatoes, wrapped them in foil and then popped them into the oven.

"I've pretty much given up on marriage at this point in my life," he added. "If it happens…fine, but I'll be okay if it doesn't happen."

"Don't you want children?" she asked.

"Sure, if one day I found that woman, then I wouldn't mind having a couple of kids."

"I want it all," she said. "I'd like to find a wonderful man who respects me as his equal, a man who loves me to distraction. I want the white picket fence and a couple of babies that will play with my sisters' children and keep the family strong. I want what my mother and father had."

She was shocked to feel a sudden rise of emotion as thoughts of her father and mother's marriage filled her head. They had loved each other deeply and it had been obvious to everyone around them.

She swallowed hard against the grief, not wanting it to grip hold of her. "I know my mother envisioned growing old with my father. It stinks that some punk kids stole that away from her."

"It definitely stinks," he agreed. "Whenever there's a murder, there are far more victims than just the person who is killed. It's a ripple effect that affects so many people."

He slid the pork chops into the oven and then leaned against the counter, his gaze appearing a bit reflective. "That's the part of my job that's so difficult, seeing so many people as they grieve."

"I imagine that can be a bit depressing over time." She couldn't imagine having the job that he did, especially speaking to the family members of victims of horrendous crimes.

"It can be, but getting murderers off the streets is what I love doing. I can't imagine doing anything else. By the way, do you know anything about guns?"

She blinked at the sudden change of subject. "It's been a while, but I used to date somebody who enjoyed them and I went to a shooting range with him and shot at targets a few times… Why?"

"I brought an extra gun with me and I'd like you to keep it with you at all times. Could you shoot somebody who was threatening you?"

She frowned thoughtfully. "If I feared for my life, I could absolutely shoot somebody," she replied.

"Good answer," he said with a smile. "So, after we eat, I'll give you the gun so you can familiarize yourself with it."

They continued to talk about his job throughout dinner. He told her about some of the strangest cases he'd worked and they talked about the psychology of some of the most famous serial killers.

The meal was delicious and she found the conversation both fascinating and stimulating. Rain still pattered against the windows, and with the coming of night, a cold chill had filled the air.

"Is it possible to turn on the heat?" she asked after she'd washed the dishes and they had settled in side by side on the sofa.

"There is no heat to turn on, but I can certainly build a fire to take away the chill," he said. He got up and moved to the stack of wood next to the fireplace. "Thank goodness we have plenty of wood, kindling and old newspapers here."

"I hope there's a lighter there, too, unless you're going to impress me by rubbing two sticks together to make a fire," she said lightly.

He turned and showed her the torch lighter in his hand. "I could rub sticks together and totally impress you, but I think just for tonight I'll use this."

She laughed and then froze as a rumble of thunder shook the cabin. She immediately wrapped her arms around herself and closed her eyes. She was already anxious about the fact that a man wanted to kill her, that she was forced to be in this little cabin with a man she hardly knew. It didn't seem fair that she had to deal with a thunderstorm, too.

When she opened her eyes, she watched as Brad fed slender pieces of kindling to a small flame. Within minutes a real fire began to dance in the fireplace and he rejoined her on the sofa.

"Hmm, that heat feels good," she murmured.

"It does, doesn't it? I've always liked a fire, although I rarely have to build one in June."

Lightning lit up the room and within seconds another loud boom of thunder sounded. "Storms aren't supposed to happen in June," she replied as ridiculous tears filled her eyes.

"Simone, is there anything I can do?" he asked softly.

"Make it stop." She released a small, anxious laugh.

He smiled at her with a gentleness that touched her. "I wish I could make it stop just for you." He scooted over close to her and put his arm around her shoulders. "Does this help?" he murmured.

"It does. I don't know why I'm this way about storms. It's just so silly, but I can't help it." Thunder once again sounded and she snuggled deeper into his side. The warmth of him helped. The very scent of him calmed her just a little bit more than it should.

As the storm raged outside, Brad began to talk about the pets he'd had as a child. There had been a goldfish called Rudy and a frog named Sam. He'd had a hamster named Harry and a dog named Bo.

"One morning I woke up and Rudy was floating belly-up. My mom explained to me that Rudy's soul had gone to Heaven and so we had a little funeral and then flushed him down the toilet."

His voice was so deep and soothing as she listened to him and focused on watching the flames dance in the fireplace. Eventually the thunder and lightning stopped, but still she lingered in his half embrace.

"You do realize I've just been talking nonsense. There really was no hamster named Harry or a dog named Bo. However, there was a goldfish and a frog," he said.

"What happened to the frog?" she asked.

"I'd caught him in our backyard. I kept him in a

box for about two weeks and then my mother told me the frog had told her he was very sad living in a box and that I needed to release him back into the wild."

"So Mr. Frog had a happy ending," she murmured softly.

"Definitely," he replied just as softly.

Everything about Brad at the moment was stirring something inside her. The warmth of his breath in her hair, the perfect way she fit against him...everything about him combined and created a storm of desire for him inside her.

She knew she should move away from him. It was dangerous to linger in his warm body heat and in the heady scent of him. She just needed to stand up, call it a day and go straight to bed.

"Brad..." She raised her face and gazed up at him. She wasn't even sure what she intended to say. But his face was intimately close to hers and his eyes held a flame that half stole her breath away.

"Simone," he whispered softly.

She knew if she leaned into him, he would kiss her...and she would kiss him back. And then she would want more...and more from him. Instead of leaning into him, she jumped up from the sofa. "I... I think it's time for me to head to bed. I'm completely exhausted."

He cleared his throat and stood as well. "The storm seems to have passed, so you should sleep well."

"Then I'll just say thank you and good-night." She went into the bedroom, sank down on the edge of the bed and drew a couple of deep breaths. The storm outside might be over, but a storm inside her continued to rage on.

All day long she had been far too conscious of him.

Even when she'd gotten an attitude with him, he hadn't held it against her. He was appealing on so many levels and her desire for him was off the charts.

However, she didn't want just a quick tumble in the sheets with a man she knew was all wrong for her. He wasn't her happily-ever-after and she didn't want her heart to get hurt by her making a foolish mistake.

She had a man who wanted to kill her, but right now she felt the real danger to her was from FBI agent Brad Howard.

Leo cursed at the rain as he rode the motorcycle that Rob Garner had provided for him. Well, in truth it wasn't Rob himself who had made it possible. Rather, it had been one of Rob's cousins who apparently wasn't on the authorities' watch list.

The bike had been waiting for him, all tagged and legal, and the GPS system Leo had picked up now told him exactly where Simone Colton and her "bodyguard" had gone. It had been so easy to put a tracker on his car when it had been parked in front of Simone's house.

A rifle was fastened to the side of the bike and the saddlebags held not only Leo's clothes, but also a tiny tent and a revolver. Oh, yes, good old Rob had made it easy for Leo.

Rob Garner was rabid about the psychology college professor. He wanted her dead and he had made sure Leo had all the tools he needed to accomplish that goal.

Leo's payoff would be enough money so he could hire a private plane to get him out of the country. What Rob didn't know was Leo would have happily killed her for free.

He was about two hours out from where the FBI

agent's car had been stopped for the past night and day. Leo would find a place to hole up, wait for the rain to stop, and then he'd fulfill Rob's wish.

Despite the rain that drenched him and the possibility of eating bugs, Leo threw back his head and laughed with the anticipation of taking another life. Hell, if he was lucky, he'd not only kill her but also the FBI agent who was with her.

# *Chapter Eight*

For the next three days it rained continuously. Brad now stood at the window and peered outside. It was going to be another gloomy day, but at least it wasn't raining at the moment. He turned from the window and sat down on the sofa. It was early and Simone wasn't up yet.

Simone. She'd become a sizzle in his blood, a flame that burned hotter and hotter with each minute he spent with her. The night of the thunderstorm, he'd almost kissed her. God, he'd wanted to take her lips with his and kiss her until they were both completely breathless.

He'd thought he'd seen a moment in her eyes where she would have welcomed his kiss, but then she'd jumped up and run to bed. Still, he wanted her more than he'd ever wanted a woman before.

During the last three rainy days, they'd each played games on their phones and then had spent the time playing endless games of chess and cards.

He'd found her a worthy adversary. She was as competitive as him, and both a gracious winner and loser. She was quick-witted and their senses of humor were alike. She challenged him intellectually and he found that totally hot. In fact, he found everything about her totally hot.

In another lifetime he would have vigorously pursued her. But they were stuck in this lifetime, where having a sexual relationship, where having any kind of a relationship other than a professional one, would be all wrong.

His role was to be her protector, and through this ordeal of staying together in such an intimate environment, he hoped they would walk away from this cabin as friends and she would be safe to pursue the life she wanted.

He had given her the spare revolver he'd brought with him and they had gone over everything she needed to know to use it. He felt confident in her ability.

There had still been no breakthroughs on the case. Leo remained on the loose and Jared still wasn't talking. The entire case was basically at a standstill. Brad had no idea how long it would be before he thought it was safe for Simone to go back home, but he knew they couldn't stay holed up here forever.

However, it was far too early in the game to be thinking about heading back to Chicago. He roused himself from the sofa, poured himself a cup of the freshly brewed coffee and then pulled some breakfast sausage links out of the freezer to cook. Breakfast today would be the sausage and pancakes.

He and Simone had fallen into an easy routine. He cooked breakfast and she took care of lunch, usually sandwiches, and then he made dinner. He cleaned up after breakfast, she cleaned up after lunch and then after dinner they took care of washing and drying the dishes together.

Maybe today if it remained dry, they could get out of the cabin for a little while and go for a short walk. Maybe the fresh air would cool his simmer of desire for her, but he seriously doubted it.

By the time the sausage was finished cooking, her bedroom door opened and she stepped out. Clad in a pair of yellow-and-white-striped capris and a yellow blouse, she looked bright and beautiful. But he didn't say a word to her as she beelined to the coffee-pot, poured herself a cup and then sat at the table. He had definitely come to respect the time it took for her to fully wake up in the mornings and be ready to socialize.

He placed the bottle of pancake syrup, the butter and a platter of the sausage links in the center of the table and then began to make the pancakes. When he had a stack of five made, he carried them to the table and sat across from her.

"Good morning," she finally said and offered him a small smile.

"Back at you," he replied with a smile of his own. "You look as bright as a ray of sunshine this morning."

"Thank you." She served herself two of the sausage links and two pancakes. "Just so you know, pancakes are my most favorite of breakfast foods." She slathered them with butter and then poured a liberal amount of syrup over them.

"Hmm, I'll have to keep that in mind." He served himself. "Looks like the rain has stopped, so maybe later we could take a walk and get some fresh air."

"That would be great. Maybe if we find a dry enough spot, I could put together a little picnic for lunch," she replied. She licked a drop of shiny syrup off her bottom lip and Brad felt the earth tilt as a fiery heat filled him. Oh, he wanted to be that dollop of syrup that lingered on her lip. He wanted to reach across the table and slowly lick it off.

"Brad?" She looked at him expectantly. She must have asked him something, but damned if he knew what it was.

"I'm sorry?"

"I asked if you thought we could actually find any dry ground out there today," she replied.

"To be honest, I doubt it. The ground has to be really saturated after all the rain that has fallen. I checked the news earlier and there is historic flooding happening all over the place."

Her eyes darkened. "But we're okay here, right?"

"Right. Even though the river is practically outside our front door, the riverbed is so deep we don't have to worry about it flooding," he assured her.

"That's good, but I feel sorry for anyone the flooding affects."

"I just hope the rain is finished for good. It's definitely time for some days of sunshine." At least if it stopped raining, he could spend more time outside, where the air didn't smell like her, where her nearness wasn't torturing him every single minute of every single day.

After breakfast they settled in on the sofa. "Do you want to play a game?" he asked.

"Not really," she replied. "I'm kind of gamed out after the last three days. When do you think we can go outside?"

"I'd say we need to give it a couple more hours of drying out. Maybe after lunch?"

"A picnic sounded good, but maybe I'll plan on tomorrow when things are definitely drier," she said.

A silence rose up between them. She stared into the fireplace that now held nothing but ashes, and he gazed at her. He wondered if he would ever tire of looking at her, of admiring the length of her lashes and the soft curve of her jaw, the sparkling blue of her eyes and the shape of her generous mouth.

"I'm sorry things are so boring," he finally said to break the silence.

She turned her head and cast him an impish grin. "I haven't found it too boring beating you at almost every game of gin rummy."

He laughed. "That was low. I'll concede that the cards fell in your favor."

"How dare you blame it on card luck when it was my awesome intelligence that won those games."

He looked at her more seriously. "That's important to you, isn't it? For people to know you're smart," he observed.

She immediately frowned thoughtfully. "I'm certainly sorry if I come off as arrogant or some kind of way."

"You don't," he assured her. "I've just noticed you get a bit defensive when it comes to you being a smart woman."

She released a deep sigh. "Maybe you're right. I'm in a male-dominated college world where woman professors are sometimes undermined and overlooked, and in my last relationship my partner often went out of his way to make me feel dumb. So, maybe I've been overcompensating since then."

"That was definitely uncool of him. So, how long were you with him?"

"A little over six months," she replied.

"Why were you with him as long as you were?"

She stared at him as if he'd just asked her what life was like on Mars. "I don't know. I guess I was hoping somehow that he would change but, in the end, that didn't happen and the whole relationship was just a waste of my time and his."

"So, if you could build yourself the perfect man, what would he be like?" He wasn't sure why, but her answer seemed incredibly important to him.

"My perfect man would appreciate my intelligence and not try to demean it. He would want the same things as me…a monogamous marriage and a couple of children. I just want a man who loves me and who wants to build a healthy, happy marriage that lasts a lifetime."

"That doesn't sound like too much to ask," he replied.

"What about you? What is the perfect woman for you?" She looked at him curiously.

"I would want a strong woman who respected my job and that sometimes my hours are crazy. I'd like an intelligent woman who enjoys deep conversations. I, too, would want a monogamous marriage and I'd be open to having children." He wondered if she realized they'd just described each other. "I really hope you find what you're looking for, Simone."

She smiled. "And I hope the same for you. So, tell me about the woman who almost got you to the altar."

"Her name was Patty and I was introduced to her

through a mutual friend. She was a barista at a coffee shop and we hit it off right from the very beginning."

"What was she like?" Simone asked.

He frowned. "She was pretty...but kind of loud and brassy. Initially I kind of overlooked those qualities about her because she could also be quite charming and kindhearted."

"How long were you with her?"

"A little over a year. We fought a lot, mostly about my job. She was pressuring me to quit and find another career."

"And yet you asked her to marry you," Simone said with a quizzical gaze.

"I did. I didn't believe she was really serious about me quitting my job and she was pressuring me to put a ring on it. But once we got engaged, our fighting grew worse. She was angry with me all the time. If I missed a dinner or a social night out because of my work, she'd punish me for days."

"Were you in love with her?" Simone asked softly.

He smiled. "I was, but like you with your professor, I kept hoping she would change. I wanted out, but I didn't want to hurt her. Ultimately she broke up with me because I refused to quit my job and we both got on with our separate lives."

"I would never ask a man to quit his job, just like I wouldn't be with a man who asked me to quit mine," she said.

Just looking at Simone right now, any thought of Patty was nothing more than a distant memory. He wanted to pull Simone into his arms and feel her body close to his. He wanted to kiss her over and over again.

He wanted to make sweet, hot love to her. Instead, he jumped up off the sofa and went to the window.

"I don't think we're going to see any sunshine today," he said, although the weather was the last thing on his mind.

"Maybe tomorrow," she replied.

He drew in several deep breaths and released them slowly in an effort to get all inappropriate thoughts about Simone out of his head. Even though it didn't completely work, he turned around and rejoined her on the sofa.

Thankfully the conversation was much lighter after that. They talked and laughed about childhood antics and humorous workplace events. He loved laughing with her. There were times it was easy for him to forget that they were here for a reason and not just as a couple enjoying time spent together in a cozy cabin.

But he had to remember why they were here. He'd been in contact with Russ every night concerning the case. Everyone was frustrated by the lack of information concerning Leo's whereabouts. There hadn't even been any sightings of him or clues as to where he might be coming in over the TIPS line.

"So, tell me more about your family," he said. "I've met all of them, but I don't know too much about them."

Her features immediately brightened. "You know January is a social worker. She's passionate about trying to protect the children she's assigned to. She's engaged to Sean Stafford."

"Who is a homicide detective with Chicago PD," Brad added. "He seems like a great guy and he's definitely a good cop."

"I'm just glad they're so happy. Then you know Tatum has the restaurant and now is dating Cruz Medina."

He nodded. "Another good detective. And you're really close with your cousins, right?"

"We grew up with them right next door and it was like they were our siblings. Carly has finally gotten together with the man she was meant to be with, a man she thought was dead."

Brad listened with interest as she told him about Micha Harrison, a special forces army lieutenant who had nearly lost his life in service to his country. He'd been Carly's fiancé before he'd been hurt and he'd believed it was in Carly's best interest to believe him dead.

"But he couldn't stay away from her. He started following her and watching her and finally she caught him," Simone continued. "And now they're getting their chance at the happiness they both deserve. I think it's all quite romantic."

"And then you have two male cousins. I've had some conversations with Heath and I know he's temporarily running Colton Connections. He seems like a real stand-up kind of guy," Brad said.

"He is, and the best thing he ever did was realize his love for Kylie. She'd worked as his right-hand woman for years and she was there for him as he grieved."

"Jones has definitely been a high-profile guy around the police department," Brad said.

"I know he was warned to stay out of the investigation. I think Jones has a ton of regret. Right after high school, he left Chicago and kind of drifted around for the next ten years. Then he came back and started his microbrewery, which is fairly successful. But when his dad was murdered, I think Jones had a lot of regret about losing those years and not building a better relationship with his dad."

"All I know is him hiring Allie Chandler to go undercover was the best thing that happened to the investigation. Otherwise we would still be spinning our wheels trying to figure out who the bad guys are."

"I'm happy he hired Allie because they are now in love and hopefully she's helping Jones deal with his grief." She shifted positions on the sofa.

"So, all your sisters and cousins have now found their significant others."

"Yeah, everyone but me. But I'm sure it will happen for me when the time is right." She stood from the sofa.

"Your family is so interesting to me. The fact that your mother and aunt are twins and they married twin brothers is so unusual."

"And then they went on to buy land and build homes right next to each other and had their children at almost the same time," she added. "We all grew up with really strong family ties." She frowned at him. "Do you have any cousins or anyone else in your family that you're close to?"

"No. Both my parents were only children and so there were no aunts or uncles in my life."

She studied him with an expression of sympathy. "I'm sorry you don't have anyone."

"I've never known anything different. Besides, I now have some good friends and coworkers."

"Russ is a good friend?"

He smiled as he thought of his redheaded coworker. Russ had gone with him to several of the meetings he'd had with Simone's family. "Yeah, I consider Russ my very best friend. He and his wife, Janie, invite me to their home a lot and I enjoy spending time with them. They have two kids who call me Uncle Brad."

"Good. Now, I'll bet you're getting hungry. How about some lunch?"

"Sounds good." He got up and moved to the kitchen table while she rummaged in the refrigerator for sandwich fixings.

"You ready to head outside?" he asked her after they had eaten the sandwiches and chips for lunch.

"Thank goodness I decided to throw some tennis shoes into my suitcase. Let me go change into them and then I'm absolutely ready to get out of this cabin for a little while," she said.

She disappeared into the bedroom. He pulled his athletic shoes out of his suitcase and put them on, eager to get outside for a change. He also pulled on his shoulder holster with his gun in the holster.

Minutes later Simone returned clad in a pair of expensive, white shoes. "Oh, those shoes are so going to be ruined," he said.

She laughed. "I know, but when I was packing, I didn't think about having to traipse through mud. I'm willing to sacrifice them to the gods of the muddy earth just to go outside and get some fresh air."

"Then let's go." He opened the door and together they stepped outside. The air was warm and humid, and the wet ground squished beneath his feet.

Brad looked around the area, making sure that nobody was lurking nearby. Even though he was relatively certain nobody knew where they were, he also knew he couldn't ever let his guard down. Simone's very life depended on it.

He saw nobody anywhere around them. He still doubted that the nearest cabin to them was even occupied right now. They first walked through the trees, talking about the wildlife that might live there.

"Maybe this is where Big Foot lives," she said as they continued walking.

"Do you really believe there is a Big Foot?" he asked.

"I'm not sure what I believe, but I do believe that there are things on this earth that we don't know or understand," she replied.

"What about UFOs?"

"I do believe there are things not of this earth that we don't know enough about," she replied. "In other words I'm very open-minded about these kinds of things."

"What about woodland elves? Do you think there are tiny people hiding someplace around here and right now they are watching us?"

She laughed. "Absolutely," she replied. "You have to say that so if they really exist you don't make them mad," she added in a whisper.

He grinned at her. "You definitely don't want to get woodland elves riled up."

"In case you haven't noticed, I'm really kind of a dorky college professor," she said.

"I must be dorky, too, because I don't think you're dorky at all."

They walked and talked for about a half an hour and then returned to the front of the cabin.

"I want to take a look at the river," she said. Once again, he looked around to make sure they were all alone, then he watched as she walked over toward the edge.

"Don't get too close," he warned. He barely got the words out when he heard an ominous rumble and a tremor in the ground, and suddenly Simone was gone.

SHE WAS FALLING...FALLING.

It took only a moment for Simone to realize the earth had given way under her feet and then water and mud completely engulfed her. She was in the river. Her brain screamed the words as she flailed her arms and legs beneath the water's surface.

Which way was up? When she tried to open her eyes, all she saw was water so muddy it was impossible to see anything else. Her feet hit what she thought was the bottom and she thrust herself up, finally managing to get her head above the water. She spat and gagged on the mud as she tried to gasp for breath.

Above the rush of the river, she could vaguely hear Brad yelling her name. But she couldn't concentrate on him as her body was buffeted by fallen tree limbs and other debris and she was sucked under once again.

Beneath the surface it was pure darkness and the cold of the water ached in her legs, throughout her entire body. Once again, she fought to find the surface as her lungs burned painfully from a lack of oxygen.

She finally managed to get her head up and she gasped for air as the river carried her. If she didn't do something, she was going to die. With this thought screaming in her head, she began to try to grab at exposed tree roots or limbs...anything that would halt her horrifying progress downriver.

She felt as if she'd been in the water for hours, even

though she knew it had just been minutes. She finally managed to grab hold of an exposed tree root, and even though her hands ached with the cold, she grabbed on to it and held tight. Her breaths ached in her chest as she gasped for air.

Mud clung to her face. It was in her hair and half blinded her. She desperately needed to swipe her face with her hand, but she was afraid to take one hand off the root that held her in place. The rushing water buffeted her, and limbs and debris smacked into her.

She should have known that a landslide was possible. She'd been a fool to walk so close to the edge knowing the amount of rain that had fallen.

Now she was going to die because she'd been a stupid fool. Her heart banged so hard she could scarcely breathe. She was freezing, and she knew if she lost her grip on the roots, then she would be swept to her death.

"Simone!"

She looked up to see Brad above her. He was lying on his stomach on the bank above her and he had one hand stretched out toward her. "Grab on to my hand, Simone," he yelled.

She cried, terrified to take one hand off the tree root that held her in place, yet knowing he was the only way she'd be able to climb up the steep bank to safety.

But how could he ever pull her up? She was covered in mud and waterlogged. Was he even strong enough to pull her up? If he couldn't, then she would fall back into the river and somebody would eventually find her body floating somewhere.

"Come on, baby…you can trust me," he cried. "Take my hand, Simone." He reached down even farther so his hand was only half a foot or so away from hers.

If she didn't grab hold of it, she would probably tire and lose her grip on the root. She'd be cast down the river, her body pummeled by the weight of the water and the mud and debris. And she would surely die.

Her arms already trembled with her efforts to hang on and the cold now encased her entire body, making her teeth chatter uncontrollably.

"Come on, honey…let me pull you out. Simone… grab my hand," he cried.

She had to trust that he'd catch her. Drawing a deep breath and releasing it on a sob, she let go of the root and reached for his hand.

He grabbed on to her, wrapping his hand tightly around her wrist. As he pulled her up, she tried to find purchase on the side of the riverbank with her feet to help him. Slowly she rose from the water. His arm trembled with the effort, but his grip remained strong.

When she finally reached the top, she rolled on her back, once again gasping for breath as tears choked her. He got to his feet and then scooped her up in his arms and hurried toward the cabin.

She clung to him, her arms tightly wrapped around his neck and her face buried in his broad chest. Her teeth still chattered with the cold and sobs continued to choke through her. Thank God he'd been able to get her up. Thank God she was now safe.

He carried her directly to the bathroom, where he put her down on her feet in the shower stall and he turned on the faucets to start the shower. He quickly took off his gun and holster.

He was covered with almost as much mud as she was, and once the water was hot, he pulled her against him beneath the warm spray. They didn't speak.

He held her tight for several long minutes. He then reached up and began to work his fingers through her hair, obviously trying to get out as much of the mud as possible.

She stood perfectly still, sobbing as she allowed him to minister to her like she was a helpless child. He grabbed the bottle of shampoo she'd left on the floor of the shower and squeezed a liberal amount into her hair. His fingers worked to lather and scrub as she continued to cry from the trauma she'd just endured.

She'd been so scared. She'd been so terrified of drowning...of dying. It was a combination of that fear and the gratitude that he'd saved her that kept the tears coming.

Finally, she began to warm up enough that her teeth had stopped chattering and her tears came to an end, although there was still a deep chill inside her. He grabbed a bar of soap and cleaned the mud off himself. He stood beneath the streaming water for another minute or two and then reached out, grabbed a towel and stepped out.

"I'm going to go build us a fire," he said and then pulled his wet T-shirt over his head. Still clad in his wet jeans, he wrapped the towel around his shoulders and left the room.

Once he was gone, she peeled off her clothes and finished washing herself until there wasn't a single shred of mud left on her. Only then did she shut off the water and grab a towel.

She used the towel to dry off her hair and then wrapped it around her and ran from the bathroom to the bedroom. She dressed in a pair of jogging pants and a T-shirt, and then walked back into the living room, where Brad had built up a roaring fire. He'd also changed into clean, dry clothes.

He spread a blanket out on the floor in front of the flames and she sank down, still trying to warm the chill that lingered deep inside her.

He then sank down next to her and grabbed one of her hands in his. "Are you okay?" His gaze searched her features, as if to assure himself that she really was all right.

She nodded, for a moment not trusting herself to speak as the horror of it all washed over her once again. He squeezed her hand. "God, Simone, I've never been so terrified for somebody and it's all my fault that it happened."

"How on earth was this your fault?" she asked as she finally found her voice.

"I should have known the ground was too saturated, that it was possible that a landslide might happen."

He looked absolutely miserable. "Oh, so now you aren't just an FBI agent, you're a geologist as well?" she replied. "It was my fault, Brad. I was the one who got too close to the edge." Her words were suddenly swallowed by an unexpected sob.

Immediately he pulled her into his arms and held her as she began to cry all over again. She buried her face in his chest and his hands stroked up and down her back in an effort to soothe her.

The terror she'd felt played again and again through her head. Once again, she could feel the water and the mud fighting to drown her. She would never forget the feel of her falling…falling into the deepest darkness.

She cried until she thought there were no more tears left inside her. "I… I was so afraid," she finally managed to say. "I was so sure I was going to drown…from the water and from all the mud. Thank God you were there to pull me up."

"You were so brave, Simone. You were so smart to keep your head and grab on to something and hold on. That allowed me to get to you." His breath was soft and warm against her ear. "You're safe now and I swear I'm not going to let anything else happen to you."

"Thank goodness you were strong enough to get me out."

"Failure wasn't an option," he replied.

She knew she should move out of his arms, but she didn't. Finally, the chill inside her was gone and she was wonderfully warm between the heat of the fire and the warmth of his embrace. He smelled like minty soap and clean male.

She wasn't sure when things changed, but suddenly his caresses up and down her back came slower and grew more languid, and she thought his breathing had quickened just a little bit.

Her body responded. Despite the warmth, her nipples grew hard and she breathed faster as a swift, sweet desire rocked through her. She didn't want to fight it. She had been fighting against that desire since they'd arrived at the cabin. Rather than fight it, she wanted to let it loose to run wild.

With her heart pounding, she raised her head to look at him. His face was mere inches from hers, his eyes dark and holding a touch of the same wildness that whipped through her. She parted her lips and he took the hint.

His lips took hers in a kiss that instantly half stole her breath. A new warmth rushed through her and she wound her arms around his neck and pulled him closer toward her.

His tongue touched her lower lip, as if tentatively seeking entry. She opened her mouth wider to allow him in. Her heart raced as their tongues swirled together in a mad dance.

The longer they kissed, the more she wanted of him...from him. She tasted his desire for her and it stirred her on every level. His hands slid beneath the back of her T-shirt, stroking her bare skin and only making her want him more.

A churning, burning need built up inside her. He kissed her harder and she matched his passion with her own. She couldn't remember ever wanting a man as badly as she wanted Brad right now.

When the kiss finally ended, she moved back from him and pulled her T-shirt over her head. She knew she was taking a chance at being rebuffed. But she'd always been the kind of woman who went after what she wanted...and she desperately wanted Brad.

The minute her T-shirt came off, Brad's eyes flamed as bright as the flickering blaze that danced in the fireplace. He yanked his T-shirt off and then reached for her again.

"Simone." He whispered her name in her hair and that only sent her desire for him higher.

His arms wrapped around her back and his fingers went to her bra fastening. "Tell me to stop and I will," he said, his voice husky and half-breathless.

"Don't stop. I want you, Brad."

He unfastened her bra and she shrugged it off her and tossed it to the side of them. She then stretched out on the blanket and pulled him down beside her.

His lips claimed hers once again as his warm hands covered her breasts.

She was on fire with the scent of him, with the way his back muscles tightened as her palms swept across the wide expanse. She felt as if he'd been quietly seducing her for days with his heated glances when he thought she wasn't paying attention, with the inadvertent touches they shared during the course of the day.

His lips left hers and traveled down her jawline, igniting new fiery flames inside her. She gasped as his mouth moved down to one of her breasts, where he began to lick and nibble on first one sensitized nipple and then the other.

She moaned his name with her pleasure. Hunger clawed at her in a way she'd never felt before. She arched up to encourage him to keep licking and teasing her nipples.

After several minutes she pushed him away to take off her jogging pants, leaving her clad only in a pair of wispy pink panties. His gaze never left hers as he stood and took off his jeans. With him clad in just his black boxers, she could tell that he was fully aroused.

He got back down on the floor and pulled her against him, and their mouths once again found each other in a blazing kiss. She was vaguely aware of their frantic breathing. Her heart pounded so loudly in her head she could think of nothing else but him.

She was out of her mind with need. It had been so long…so achingly long since she'd felt a man's desire for her. Still, she didn't want just any man. She only wanted Brad.

One of his hands slid down her belly and lingered at the top of her panties. She arched up, inwardly screaming with the need for him to touch her. And then he did. His fingers slid beneath her panties and danced against her heated flesh.

She clutched at his shoulders as a tension began to build inside her. He moved faster and faster against her, touching her at the perfect spot, and she climbed higher and higher. The tension pulled tighter and then suddenly sprang loose. She cried his name as wave after wave of intense pleasure rippled through her.

When her climax was over, she kicked off her panties and plucked at his boxers, wanting…needing to touch him, to give him as much pleasure as he had just given her.

He took off his boxers and she took him in her hand. His hard length pulsed as she stroked him and their gazes remained locked. "I want you, Brad. I want you inside me," she said.

His eyes flared with fire and he gently pushed her onto her back and then moved between her open thighs. "Tell me to stop, Simone, and I'll stop," he whispered.

"Please, don't stop," she practically hissed.

He entered her slowly and for a long moment they remained locked together yet not moving.

He raised his hands and tenderly framed her face. He kissed her gently and then began to thrust into her. Slow at first, and then with a moan he increased the speed of his hips against hers.

She moaned along with him, her heartbeat pounding as the tension began to build inside her once again. She met each of his thrusts with her own, wanting him to feel as much pleasure as he'd already given her.

Faster and faster he moved against her until she

was climaxing once again. He stiffened against her and groaned as he found his release at the same time.

They remained locked together for several minutes as each of them waited for their breathing to return to normal. He then collapsed on the blanket next to her.

He was so handsome with the golden light of the fire playing over his beautiful and perfect naked body. She was boneless and utterly sated. She smiled at him. "That was absolutely wonderful, Brad."

He frowned, grabbed his boxers and jeans and then got to his feet. "I'm sorry, Simone. That was totally unprofessional of me and it won't happen again." With those words, he stalked into the bathroom.

# *Chapter Nine*

Brad stared at his reflection in the small mirror above the bathroom sink. He had just been a perfect example of a major jerk to a woman who had not deserved it. He sluiced cold water over his face and then looked at his reflection again. "You're still a jerk," he muttered to himself.

He'd been so shaken up by what they had shared, by the passion he'd had for her, a passion that had stolen all rational thought from his head.

He had never, ever had such a mind-blowing bout of lovemaking in his entire life. The moment he'd tasted her lips, he'd been lost in her. He'd thrown all caution to the wind and had forgotten all about the reasons why they shouldn't make love.

And what bothered him more than anything was that he knew if given the chance , he would make the same mistake and make love with her all over again.

Now she was in his very blood. He wouldn't be able to look at her without remembering the sweet, hot taste of her lips or how her naked body had felt against his. He now would never be able to forget the throaty little moans she had made and how her eyes had glowed like those of a hungry wild animal as he had stroked into her.

He couldn't regret what they had shared, but they definitely needed to have a conversation about it and he owed her an apology for the way he had just acted toward her. He'd diminished what they had shared and that wasn't fair.

He got dressed and then stepped out of the bathroom.

She sat, fully dressed, on the sofa. She stared into the flames in the fireplace and didn't look at him as he sank down next to her.

"Simone," he said softly.

"What?" She still didn't look at him as she wrapped her arms around herself.

"I'm sorry for being a jerk."

"You were a jerk," she replied.

"I know. I was just afraid if I told you how great our lovemaking was, if I stayed there next to you for another minute, I'd want you all over again."

She finally looked at him, her eyes holding a vulnerability…and a touch of hurt. He hated that. He hated that he had put that hurt in her eyes. "I just wanted to linger for a moment in your arms. I just wanted to bask for a moment in the…you know…the afterglow." A blush colored her cheeks.

"And I should have given that to you, but I was afraid that it would lead to another mistake. Simone, it's obvious we share an intense physical attraction to each other. Acting on that attraction was my mistake. While it was an incredible experience for me, it was still a mistake. There's no future for us and it would be irresponsible for us to think otherwise."

"Brad, I wasn't looking for a future," she replied. "I was just acting on what I wanted in the moment. I wanted you and I knew you wanted me. We are two consenting adults and so we acted on it. It was nothing more than that. I'm well aware of our positions and that when this case is over we will never see each other again."

He somehow wanted to protest her words, but he couldn't. The truth of the matter was that they would probably never see each other again once Leo was under arrest and Rob Garner was no longer a threat.

"And it was a mistake that I didn't use any protection," he added. "Unfortunately, I didn't have any."

She stared back into the dying fire. "If you're worried about me getting pregnant, I'm on the pill. And if you're worried about catching something from me, I got tested and was clean after my last breakup and I haven't been with anyone since then."

"I haven't been with anyone in years," he said. He hated the topic of the conversation and for some reason thinking about the idea of never making love to her again depressed him more than he wanted to admit. He stared at her profile for a moment. "Simone, I do care about you."

"You have to care for me. It's your job," she replied, her voice emotionless.

"Beyond that, Simone." It suddenly seemed important that she knew she wasn't just a job. "I care about you as a woman, beyond this job."

Once again, she looked at him and this time a smile curved her lips. "It's okay, Brad. Let's just move on from here. Besides, I'm exhausted. It isn't every day that I almost drown in a river." She stood. "I'll just say good-night and I'll see you in the morning."

He wanted to say something to stop her from leaving, but he didn't know what to say, and in any case, he wasn't sure more conversation wouldn't make things worse.

"Good night, Simone." He watched her until she disappeared into the bedroom and the door closed behind her.

He got up from the sofa, too restless to sit still. The scent of her perfume lingered on his skin, in his head. He walked over to the window and peered out into the darkness of the night.

His mind took him back to that moment when Simone had been standing on the riverbank and then she was suddenly gone. He'd faced down depraved killers before, and had been in life-and-death situations, but nothing…absolutely nothing he'd ever experienced before in his life had prepared him for the sheer terror of knowing Simone was in the river.

Even now, just thinking about it, his heart began to race. He'd watched helplessly as the water had swallowed her up. He thought he'd lost her to the raging river. Horror had gripped him around the throat and then thankfully he'd seen her head bob to the surface.

Thank God she'd grabbed on to that root, and thank God he'd been able to pull her to safety. Standing in the shower with her afterward, all he'd wanted to do was get the dirt and filth off her, warm the chill that had a grip on her and hold her until the fear left her eyes. He'd needed to hold her until the fear for her left him.

He hadn't planned on making love to her. He tried to chalk it up to the fact that they'd just been through a life-and-death experience and had needed a life-affirming action. And of course there was the fact that they had been fighting against their attraction to each other and that attraction had finally exploded. He just hoped they could deal with the aftermath without things getting awkward or weird between them. Still, he knew it couldn't ever happen again.

He turned around, grabbed the blanket he'd been using at night on the sofa, then shucked his jeans and took off his T-shirt. Once he was on the torturous sofa and covered up, he stared into the last dying embers in the fireplace.

He desperately needed Leo to be found and arrested as quickly as possible. Not just to end the case, but to end his time with Simone.

She wasn't just a physical temptation. She was in his head in so many other ways. He loved the sound of her laughter and the way her eyes lit up with her smiles. He loved the serious conversations they had and he even liked the slight edge of defensiveness she displayed when it came to how smart she was.

He loved the little wrinkle that danced across her forehead when she was concentrating on a chess game and her utter loyalty to and love of her family.

The realization struck him like a thunderbolt stabbing through his chest. He was falling in love with Simone Colton. Rather than fill him with happiness, it had heartache written all over it.

Of all the women in the world, why did it have to be a woman he had to protect against a potential killer? And why did it have to be a woman with whom he would never have a future?

If his job and location weren't enough to keep them

apart, the fact that she was a Colton, an esteemed college professor, and he was nothing but a civil servant should be enough to squash any relationship he thought he could have with her.

Somehow, someway, he had to gain some emotional distance from her. He prayed the sun continued to shine tomorrow so he could spend a lot of time outside and away from her.

He finally drifted off to sleep with a deep sadness weighing in his heart. He jerked awake suddenly, his heart beating fast and with fight-or-flight adrenaline rushing through him. He grabbed his gun from the coffee table and shot upright.

What had awakened him? What had pulled him from his sleep? He then realized Simone was half screaming in the bedroom. Had somebody managed to get inside? Had somebody broken in through the bedroom window and was now trying to harm her?

He jumped off the sofa and raced to the bedroom. He yanked open the door and then halted. Enough moonlight drifted through the window for him to see there was nobody in the room except Simone, who thrashed and moaned in the throes of what he assumed was a bad nightmare.

He set his gun on top of the chest of drawers and frowned, unsure what to do. Somebody had once told him it wasn't a good idea to awaken a person in the middle of a nightmare, but he couldn't just stand here and watch her suffer.

And it was obvious she was suffering with whatever was going on in her dreams. "Simone," he whispered her name softly and took a step toward her.

She half screamed again, flailed her arms wildly and

then brought her hands up to her throat as if fighting off an attacker. "Simone," he said a little louder. Still she didn't awake.

He walked the last three steps to her bed and sank down on the edge of the mattress. "Wake up, Simone. You're having a nightmare." He gently took hold of her shoulder and gave her a little shake.

She gasped and shot straight up. Her eyes flipped open. For a moment she stared at him blankly, as if she had no idea who he was, then with a deep sob she flung her arms around his neck and began to weep.

He hesitated only a moment and then gathered her into his arms. "Shhh," he whispered against her ear. "It's all right, Simone. Was it a nightmare?"

She nodded and continued to cry, deep sobs that convulsed her body. He held her tight and continued to croon soothing things. Finally, her sobs stopped, but she didn't attempt to move out of his arms. "It must have been a bad nightmare. Do you want to talk about it?" he asked softly.

She leaned back from him but didn't completely leave his arms. His heart broke for her as the moonlight played on her slightly swollen and red eyes.

"It's always the same thing," she said, her voice trembling slightly. "I'm in a graveyard and standing in front of my father's headstone. Then his face manifests out of a mist. He begs me to get his killers behind bars. He tells me he can't rest until I do."

Her body began to shake and tears once again filled her eyes. "Then he gets angry and starts yelling at me that he can't rest until I get the killers in jail. His skeletal arms come out of the headstone and his hands wrap around my neck and they start strangling…and then… and then I usually wake up."

She leaned back in, pressing her face against his chest as she began to cry once again. "It…it's so terrifying."

"It's just a dream, Simone. You know your father would never try to strangle you," he said softly. "He'd never want to hurt you. He would only want good things for you."

She cried for a minute and then she regained control. "You must think I'm the biggest baby in the world," she finally said. "I cry over thunderstorms and over bad dreams, and I cry because of my father's murder. I really am a strong woman, Brad. I'm really not a crybaby."

He released a small laugh. "Oh, honey, I know that." He rubbed her back until she leaned away from him. She appeared exhausted but still haunted by her nightmare. "Come on, get back beneath the blanket and I'll tuck you in."

She reached out and grabbed hold of his hand. "Brad, will you stay with me…just for a little while? Just until I fall back to sleep?"

A little alarm went off in his head, telling him it wasn't a good idea, but how could he deny the plea in her eyes, the faint fear that still lingered there?

"Okay, I'll stay here for a little while," he replied. "Just until you fall back to sleep."

"Thank you," she whispered softly. She settled back into the mattress and closed her eyes as he began to rub her back.

There was no way he was going to get beneath the blanket with her. He just didn't trust himself. He continued to rub her back and finally felt her relaxing. Thankfully within minutes she was once again asleep.

He waited a few more minutes and then he got off the bed, grabbed his gun from the top of the dresser and then returned to the uncomfortable sofa to finish out the night.

God, he needed to keep his head about him where she was concerned. Unfortunately, he could do nothing about how deep his heart had gotten involved.

SIMONE AWAKENED EARLY. A mere whisper of light lit up the eastern skies. She dressed and quietly left the bedroom and went to the table and sat.

Brad was still asleep on the sofa, and although she'd like a cup of coffee, the last thing she wanted to do was awaken him. She had no idea how long he'd stayed with her the night before after the terrible and familiar nightmare. She was just grateful that he'd been there to soothe her back to sleep.

He was such a good man. He was exactly the kind of man she wanted in her life forever. He was funny and smart and incredibly sexy. He was caring and brave and she was in love with him.

She nearly fell off her chair as the realization hit her hard. When had it happened? When had her physical attraction transformed into something deeper, into something far more meaningful?

Was it when they'd laughed together or had it happened when they were having one of their serious talks? Was it when they had trash-talked each other while playing cards or when she'd thought about the lengths he had gone to in an effort to assure her safety?

Had it happened when he'd pulled her from the river and then made sweet, hot love to her?

It didn't really matter when she'd fallen in love with Brad. What mattered was that she was in love with him and there was no future between them. What mattered was that she was headed for a deep and painful heartache where he was concerned and there was nothing she could do about it.

At that moment Brad moaned and he sat up. His hands immediately went to his back and he moaned once again. He stood and walked over to the window. He stretched with his arms overhead and continued to groan.

It was obvious he was having some back pain. The sofa was uncomfortable just sitting on it. She hadn't even considered how terrible it would be to sleep on. And he'd been sleeping on it every night without complaints.

Even thinking about how hard it had been for him, she couldn't help but admire his physique. He was clad only in a pair of black boxers and the muscles in his broad back were well-defined and perfectly toned.

He turned away from the window and jumped at the sight of her. "Jeez, Simone. You scared me half to death. How long have you been sitting there in the dark?"

"Just a few minutes and it's not completely dark," she replied.

"I don't smell the coffee, so I can't believe you're actually talking to me." He reached for his jeans at the foot of the sofa and quickly pulled them on. He then turned on the light overhead.

"I was going to start the coffee, but I didn't want

to wake you. But since I was up before you, I'll take care of the coffee this morning." She got up, and as she made the coffee, he sat at the kitchen table.

"Thank you, Brad." She turned around and leaned against the counter as she waited for the coffee to drip through the carafe.

"Thanks for what?" He looked at her curiously.

"For last night, for making me feel safe after my nightmare," she replied. That was exactly what he'd done for her… He'd made her feel safe and protected after the horror of the dream.

"I'm glad I could be there for you. I'm just sorry you have that nightmare at all."

"I'm hoping it will go away forever once Leo is behind bars," she replied.

"I hope so," he said. "I would never wish that kind of nightmare on anyone."

She turned back around and poured two cups of coffee and then carried them to the table. "Brad, I didn't realize how much you've been suffering by sleeping on the sofa every night."

"What are you talking about? It's been fine," he protested.

"No, it hasn't been fine. I heard you moaning and groaning when you first got off it this morning. I know it's hurting your back."

He shrugged his shoulders. "It's okay. I'm dealing with it."

"You shouldn't have to deal with it," she replied. She took a sip of her coffee and eyed him over the rim. She put her cup down. "Starting tonight, you're welcome to share the bed with me."

His golden-green eyes stared into hers. "I'm not sure that's a good idea."

"We're both adults, Brad. Surely we can share a bed and not go where we shouldn't. I know you'd sleep better in the bed and that's what's important." She offered him a teasing smile. "Besides, how can you protect me from a morning threat if you can barely crawl from the sofa?"

He studied her for another long moment. "We'll see how we're both feeling when night comes," he finally replied.

For a few minutes they drank their coffee and enjoyed some casual conversation as the early morning sunlight slowly filled the room. "It's so nice to see the sun," she said.

"Enjoy it while it lasts. When I checked the weather last night, the weatherman said more rain could be moving back in this afternoon."

She shook her head. "I can't remember a time when it rained so hard and for so many days in a row."

"According to what the news is saying, it's a historic year for the amount of rain we've received."

"I'm sure we'll both remember these rainy days and this time here for a very long time to come," she said thoughtfully.

His gaze held hers intently. "I know I will."

"Someday I'll tell my children about the handsome FBI agent who saved me from a raging river."

He released a small laugh. "And I'll tell my buddies about the time I plucked a beautiful mermaid out of the water."

She laughed with him. "Right, a mermaid who was

covered in mud and muck and crying her fool head off. I'm sure that's every fisherman's fantasy."

He opened his mouth as if to say something but instead raised his cup and took a drink and then stood. "So, what do you feel like for breakfast this morning?"

"Could you make some more of those pancakes we had before?"

"Pancakes coming right up."

"Can I help?" she asked and was unsurprised when his answer was no.

She watched as he worked, admiring his efficiency, his complete ease in the kitchen. It was far too easy for her to imagine him in her condo, whipping up breakfast for the two of them after a night of lovemaking.

It was a fantasy that caused her heart to squeeze tight with pain because she knew it would never happen. She would never tell him the depths of her love for him. She wouldn't burden him with her love.

He could never be hers, so there was no point. He had his life in DC and she had hers in Chicago. When this ended, he would go his way and she would go hers. Maybe she'd eventually meet a man just like Brad, but right now welcoming another man into her life felt too painful.

She got up to pour herself another cup of coffee as a wave of depression tried to settle over her head. It didn't take long for the pancakes to be ready and they sat down to eat.

Already clouds were moving in and stealing the sunshine that had briefly shone through the windows. The clouds only made her bout of depression harder to fight off.

"You're very quiet," he said when they were halfway through the meal.

She released a deep sigh. "I'm a little tired of the clouds and I'm just wishing this was all over." The latter part wasn't exactly true. She wanted to spend as much time as possible with him, but she also was aware of the fact that spending more time with him would only make it more difficult to tell him goodbye.

"How long do you really think we'll be here?" she asked.

He frowned. "To be honest, I'm not sure. I definitely don't want to take you back if I still think you'll be in danger."

"But, realistically, we can't stay here forever," she replied. "What if Leo is never arrested? Then what? Sooner or later I have to go back to my life."

"I know and realistically I can't give you a definitive answer as to how much longer we'll be here. Right now I'm just taking it day by day and hoping Leo will be caught."

"And you believe when that happens Rob will no longer be a threat to me?"

"I believe once we get Leo in jail, then that will be the final catalyst for Jared to talk and I think he will confess to everything and that'll mean the end of any threats against you." He reached across the table and lightly touched the back of her hand. "Are you sick of me already?" he asked with a touch of humor in his voice.

"Of course not," she replied with a smile. "Come on, I'll dry if you wash." She stood up, grabbed her plate and carried it to the sink.

As they washed the dishes, rain began to pelt against

the windows. "So, want to play some cards?" he asked when the last dish had been dried and put away.

"I guess I could take another day of beating the pants off you," she said with a grin even though she was a little sick of playing cards.

They played for the rest of the morning as the rain continued to beat against the windows. When they decided to break for lunch, she had an idea to break up the monotony.

"Can I help with lunch?" he asked.

"Yes, you can go sit on the sofa and let me take care of it," she replied. Even though it was raining outside, that didn't mean they couldn't have a picnic inside.

For the next half an hour, she boiled eggs and deviled them, then she made a quick macaroni salad and sandwiches and packaged them all in separate storage containers. She then added two of her chocolate bars, some potato chips, and placed it all in one of the grocery bags.

She then went into the bedroom and grabbed the lamp on the nightside table. She took off the shade and carried it into the living room, where she plugged it in and turned it on.

"Now, that really brightens things up in here," he said.

She smiled and then spread a blanket out on the floor. "Consider it artificial sunshine. If we can't have a picnic outside, then we can have one inside." She waved her hands over the blanket. "Welcome to my picnic."

He slid from the sofa to the blanket and sat cross-legged while she grabbed the grocery bag off the table.

She joined him on the blanket and then began pulling out the food containers. "Wow, how did you know that I love a good picnic with macaroni salad?" he said with a goofy smile.

She laughed and threw a potato chip at him. "You're a dork."

"I thought you were the dork," he replied teasingly. "Besides, on the hundredth day of rain you have to get a little dorky to stay sane."

"So, do you like picnics?" she asked.

"To be honest, I've never been on a real picnic before."

She looked at him in surprise. "For real?"

"For real. If I ever had a picnic with my mother and father, I don't remember it. And after my mother's death, the last thing on my or my father's mind was a picnic in a park."

"Do you have a lot of memories of your mother?" she asked. She saw the splash of grief that crossed his features. "I'm sorry... I shouldn't have asked that," she said quickly.

"No, it's okay. Unfortunately, I don't have a lot. When you're a kid, you just assume your parents are going to be there forever and so you don't gather memories. I have more impressions than any single memories. I do remember she smelled like spring flowers and she loved to laugh."

A warmth leaped into his eyes. "She worked part-time as a waitress, but she was always home when I got in from school. She was soft-spoken and I didn't know until after her death that she was the gears that kept everything running smoothly. Whenever I'd screw up, she'd have a teachable moment with me."

"And what did a teachable moment look like?" Simone asked curiously. The rain that had beat against the windows seemed to have stopped for now. However, the room was semi-dark other than the halo of light the little bedroom lamp provided.

"A calm discussion where we talked about what I did and why I did it." He released a sudden laugh. "And then it looked a lot like extra chores and groundings."

"That's the way it was for me and my sisters. Mom knew exactly what to say to make me feel so guilty and sorry for whatever I'd done." She froze as the sound of a vehicle pulling up sounded from outside.

Brad jumped up from the floor and grabbed his gun off the coffee table. She also got up and stood just behind Brad as he approached the door. He opened the door, his gun pointed in front of him.

Standing on the stoop was a man with a grizzly gray beard and a chubby face. He was clad in a bright yellow rain slicker. "Whoa!" he exclaimed when he saw Brad's gun. His arms shot up in the air. "I'm Nico from Nico's Grocery just down the way."

Brad held the gun pointed at him for another long minute and then lowered it. "Sorry about that," he said without any other explanation. "What can we do for you, Nico?"

"I'm just driving around and letting everyone in the area know the road coming in has flooded and it doesn't look like it's going down anytime soon. So if you need anything, I'm all you have for now."

"We haven't seen anyone anywhere around here, so I'm not sure who all will be affected by the flooding," Brad replied.

"There's the Ingram family's cabin beyond those trees."

"I didn't think anyone was in that cabin," Brad replied.

"They're there. They're a nice couple with two children. I'm sure they're really sick of this rain."

"Aren't we all," Brad said.

"And believe it or not, there's some people camping here and there. How would you like to be in a small tent through all this?" He laughed. "Shoot me now, right?" His laughter stopped and his eyes widened. "I mean, don't shoot me."

Brad laughed. "Don't worry. I'm not going to shoot you and we appreciate you stopping by to let us know where things stand."

"No problem, and just remember I have some supplies if you need anything. And now I'll just leave you alone."

The two men said goodbye to each other and then Brad closed and locked the door. He turned and looked at Simone, his eyes dark and troubled.

"So, what exactly does this mean?" she asked, not liking the look in his eyes.

"It means two things. If there's somebody hiding around here who wants to harm you, we can't get out. And if we find ourselves in a tough situation, nobody can get in to help us."

Simone stared at him and her heart beat a little faster. "Surely if anyone is out there wanting to hurt me, they would have already tried something."

"I hope you're right. Right now it's like we're on an island and we only have each other to depend on." He offered her a smile. "We'll be fine."

"Of course we will," she replied, but an unsettling disquiet swept through her. Brad's smile had curved his lips, but it hadn't lightened the darkness in his eyes. He was worried, and that worried her.

Was there really somebody out there watching and just waiting for the perfect opportunity to take her out? Was it possible they were trapped on this "island" with a killer? A cold chill grabbed hold of her knowing they were now cut off from any backup if a killer suddenly showed up.

LEO FELT AS if he'd been wet for months. He'd been hunkered down in his little tent, trapped by the torrential rain that had fallen, a tent that had collapsed on top of him more times than he could count.

Dammit, he deserved so much better than this. Once this was over, he'd make Rob pay him enough money to not only get out of the country but also enough so he could live the kind of life he deserved no matter where he landed.

He was wet, cold and hungry. And he was majorly ticked off. The only thing that drove him now was the fact that he was going to kill Simone Colton. He couldn't wait to pull the trigger and watch the blossom of blood explode out of her chest. Or maybe he'd take a head shot and watch her brains blow out.

It was just like mag-fed paintball. Load the gun, pull the trigger and watch the paint explode on your target. Only in this case it was load the gun, pull the trigger, and instead of paint, it would be blood exploding from the target.

He'd killed four men before and now he looked forward to killing a man and a woman. The freakin' weather had kept him hunkered down, but now it was just a matter of time before FBI agent Brad Howard and Simone Colton would be dead. His blood sang through his veins as he waited for the perfect opportunity to play a little mag-fed paintball with a real rifle.

*Chapter Ten*

They returned to their indoor picnic, but Brad could tell Simone wasn't feeling it anymore. She was quiet as they finished eating, and when she offered him one of her chocolate bars, he declined.

They cleared the mess and then she settled on the sofa with her chocolate bar and he grabbed his cell phone to text Russ for an update in the case.

Nothing. Still nothing to report. Where the hell was that kid? Where on earth had Leo disappeared to? He tossed his phone on the table and then went to the front window and peered outside.

Was there any kind of danger lurking outside? Or had he overreacted to the whole Rob Garner thing? Had he torn Simone from her home and her family because of his gut instincts…instincts that had been all wrong?

Now even if he wanted to take her back home, he couldn't. Suddenly his head was filled with so many doubts. Had he overestimated Rob's wrath? Was he really just a bully who beat kids and mouthed off to women and wasn't a physical threat at all? Had the carjacking really been a random act?

He glanced over to where Simone had fallen asleep curved into the arm of the sofa. Love for her buoyed up inside him. He had no idea exactly what she thought about him. Granted they shared an off-the-charts mutual physical attraction for each other, but when they'd had sex, love had had nothing to do with it. It had just been raw, wild sex.

Still, he knew he was in love with her. In any case, it didn't matter…it couldn't matter.

It was just a strange twist of fate, or his own paranoia that had them here spending this time together in such close quarters. In reality, even if she told him she loved him, what could he offer her?

A long-distance relationship that would only fail because no matter how hard he tried to maintain it their work schedules would work against them. He'd really never believed much in long-distance relationships. That wasn't what he wanted for himself and it wasn't what he wanted for her.

She deserved a man who was present in all the hours of her life. She needed a man who cheered her on in her work at the college, one who would hold her through the nights.

It was a lose-lose situation no matter how he looked at it. Somehow, he needed to gain back his professionalism where she was concerned.

Even knowing that, when bedtime rolled around and she insisted he share the bed with her, he didn't put up much of a fight in favor of sleeping on the sofa.

She went into the bathroom, took a shower and then changed into a cotton nightgown with a sleeping moon on the front. He then took a quick shower and pulled on a pair of navy boxers, then went into the bedroom.

She was curled up under the covers on one side of the bed and he placed his gun on the nightstand, then slid beneath the covers on the other side. "Ready for the light to go out?" he asked.

"Ready," she replied.

He reached out and turned off the lamp on the night-stand and the room went dark save for a small sliver of moonlight that danced through the window. The bed felt wonderful after so many nights of the lumpy, uncomfortable sofa. In fact, he felt as if he hadn't gotten a good night's sleep since they'd arrived here.

He lay on his side of the bed, careful not to encroach on hers. It was enough that he could feel her body heat and smell the heady scent of her.

Every muscle in his body remained tensed, waiting for her to go to sleep before he did. The minutes ticked by and he could feel her tension.

She released a deep sigh. "I guess I shouldn't have taken that nap this afternoon."

"Not sleepy?" He raised up on one elbow and gazed down at her. She looked positively beautiful with the silvery moonlight painting her face. He fought against his instant arousal.

"Not very. What about you?"

"I'm tired," he admitted. "This bed feels amazing."

"You should have told me how miserable you were on the sofa after the first night you slept there," she replied.

"I was afraid to mention it. I was afraid you might see it as a ploy to move in here and jump your bones."

She laughed. "I probably would have thought that."

He frowned thoughtfully. "Simone, all day long I've wondered if I was wrong to take you away from your home and family. I've wondered if I overreacted to Rob's threats against you."

She eyed him soberly. "But what if you didn't? I'd rather be safe than sorry." She grinned at him. "I think we're on the same side, Brad. In fact, I think that, no matter what, the time here has been good for me. I've had some peace and quiet and I finally feel like my grief over my father isn't screaming so loud in my head anymore."

"I'm glad, Simone. Let's just hope your nightmares go away soon, too," he murmured.

"Let's hope so," she agreed. "In any case, thank you for keeping my safety first in your mind."

"No problem," he replied.

She closed her eyes and within minutes her breathing slowed and she fell asleep. Brad released a deep, exhausted breath and then closed his eyes. He thought it would be difficult to share the bed with her and not be overwhelmed with desire. However, the lack of any real good sleep for the past week swept over him and within minutes he was asleep.

He awoke the next morning to find that in the night they had spooned together. His arm was thrown around her waist and she was snuggled up against him.

He closed his eyes again and reveled in the feel of her closeness. She was so warm with her shapely bottom curved into him. He was surrounded by the scent of her, a scent that always stirred him to his very soul.

Needing to get away from her for his own good as well as hers, he gently pulled his arm from her and then quietly slid off the bed. He grabbed his jeans and then left the bedroom.

When he was in the living room, he grabbed a clean pair of jeans and a clean navy polo shirt, then went to the coffee machine. He pushed the button to turn it on, but nothing happened. No little green light appeared.

What the heck? He unplugged the machine from the wall and then plugged it in again. Still the power light didn't come on. Great, he thought, did this mean they were going to have to do without coffee? Maybe one of the items Nico carried in his little shop was a new coffee maker.

He glared at the machine in frustration and then grabbed his phone off the charger. Once again, he frowned. The phone was dead. It should have been fully charged.

The electricity. He tried the light switch. Nothing. What in the hell was going on? What had happened to the electricity? Had a storm blown through in the middle of the night? He immediately dismissed that idea. If there had been a storm strong enough to knock out the electricity, surely Simone would have awakened and she would have awakened him.

So, if it hadn't been a storm, then what the hell had happened ? Hopefully this was just some sort of weird glitch and the power would be back on before long. He thought about all the supplies they had in their refrigerator and freezer. Hopefully it would come back on before all of that was at risk.

He walked over to the window and peered out, where the sky appeared cloudless and the sun was rising, promising a clear, bright day ahead.

He returned to the table and sat to wait for Simone to get out of bed. She was not going to be happy with this new situation.

It was about a half an hour later when Simone came out of the bedroom. She was clad in a pair of jeans and a lavender sleeveless blouse that showcased her slender but lovely figure. As usual, she beelined to the coffeepot and then turned and frowned at him. "Are we out of coffee?"

"No, we're out of electricity."

She joined him at the table, her frown still cutting into her forehead. "What happened to it?"

"I don't know. Apparently, it has been off for a while because my cell phone is dead."

"My phone was dead this morning, too. But I thought maybe I didn't get it plugged into the charger good last night."

"I was waiting for you to get up and I figured I'd go outside and see if I can find what the problem is."

"Do you know anything about electricity? I don't want you to tinker with things and wind up somehow frying yourself on a loose wire," she replied with a frown.

He released a small laugh. "Trust me, I have a healthy respect for electricity. I'm not going to do anything stupid. I just want to walk around and see if I can tell what might be the problem."

"Just don't try to be a hero," she said.

He grinned at her. "I want to be a hero, but I don't want to be a foolish hero." He rose from the table. "At least it looks like the sun is going to shine today."

"Well, that's one positive."

"How do you feel about hot dogs for breakfast?" he asked.

"Hot dogs?" She raised one of her perfectly arched brows.

"When I get back in from outside, I'll build a fire in

the fireplace and we can roast some hot dogs. At least it will be a hot meal to kick off the day."

She shrugged easily. "Sounds good to me."

"Good, then while I'm outside, I'll look for a couple of good sticks to use," he replied.

She got up and walked with him to the front door. "I'm really hoping the problem is just a fluke and it will right itself before too much more time passes," he said.

"Let's hope so," she replied.

He opened the door and gazed back at her. For a crazy moment he wanted to pull her into his arms and kiss her. He just wanted to lean forward and capture her lush lips with his own.

But any more intimacy between them would only complicate things further. Instead, he headed outside. The early morning air smelled fresh and clean and the sun warmed his shoulders as he began a walk around the cabin.

It was probably going to take several days for the floodwaters to go down. But he needed to figure out if it was safe for her to go home or not. Once the water did go down and they could drive out, he definitely didn't want to make a mistake in his assessment of the situation.

When he reached the back of the cabin, he instantly saw where the electrical wires went into the back of the house. He walked closer to them. He stared at the wires in shocked disbelief as he realized in an instant that they had been cut.

He grabbed his gun from his holster and looked around. Who was out here? Who would want to intentionally cut off their electricity?

He narrowed his gaze and scanned the area. He

looked in the trees and in the underbrush, but he saw nobody. He left the cut wires, knowing there was nothing he could do about the situation. He continued around the cabin until he reached the front once again.

He kept his gaze shooting first left and then right in an effort to see somebody and then he noticed the flat tires on the vehicle they had arrived in. Four flat tires. On further inspection he realized they had all been slit. What the hell?

His heart began to beat an accelerated, irregular rhythm. They had no way to drive out of here, and with the electricity not working, their cell phones were useless.

Trouble. It certainly didn't take a rocket scientist for him to know they were in trouble. Somebody was definitely out there. He could smell the danger in the air. It sizzled through his veins.

Once again, he looked around, wondering who was out there. It had to be somebody who had managed to follow them from Chicago to this small cabin, but who? Was it Rob himself? Or was it somebody else… somebody Brad didn't know? How in the hell had this happened?

A boom sounded, sending birds flying from the treetops. A bullet whizzed by his head. He hit the ground. His heart nearly exploded out of his chest.

Oh, yeah. They were definitely in trouble.

SIMONE HEARD THE gunshot and ran to the front door. Brad was on the ground and crawling toward the cabin. "Stay inside," he yelled. "Simone, get back and stay inside."

She backed up, her heart crashing in her chest as a

swift terror shot through her. Oh God, what was happening? Why was Brad crawling toward the door on his hands and knees? Had somebody shot at him?

He got through the door, slammed it shut and then moved to the window to peer outside. "Brad, what's going on?" Her question was a mere whisper as abject fear half closed up the back of her throat.

He pointed his gun toward the window, his entire body visibly tensed. "The electricity wires have been cut, the car has four flat tires and somebody just shot at me."

She stared at his broad back in disbelief. Terror clawed at her insides, a screaming terror she'd never felt before in her life. "D-do you think it's Rob Garner?"

"It's got to be him or maybe somebody he hired, but right now I don't know who in the hell it is. Dammit, if my cell phone worked, I could call and see if anyone in Chicago could get eyes on Garner."

"Does it matter whether it's Rob himself or somebody he hired?" she asked.

"No, it doesn't matter. All that matters is whoever is out there has made sure we can't call anyone for backup, and no matter what the conditions of the roads, we can't drive out of here on four flat tires."

Simone's heart beat so hard in her chest that for several long moments she felt as if she couldn't draw a breath. She sank down on the edge of the sofa, trembling as her mind worked to process everything that had happened.

"I think he's hiding in that stand of trees a couple hundred feet ahead. It was definitely a rifle that shot at me. I might have thought it was some crazy hunter if not for the cut wires and the flat tires," he said.

"So, what do we do now?" Her voice trembled as much as her body did, and her mouth was unaccountably dry. This was all her fault. She had started this cascading waterfall of terror by speaking to Rob and Marilyn Garner that night in True. If only she had walked past them without saying a word.

He turned to flash her a dark glance. "For now we sit tight. I need to figure out if there's more than one of them out there."

More than one? The words screamed through her brain. "How did they even find out we were here?"

"I don't have a clue." He remained at the window looking outside. "There were only a couple of people who knew my plans in the Chicago PD. And Russ knew, but he would never betray my confidence and he needed to know."

"My sisters knew we were going away, but they didn't know exactly where we were going, so they certainly didn't tell anyone," she said.

"At this point it really doesn't matter who leaked the information or how it got out. Right now all that matters is there's a man in those trees with a rifle who took a shot at me."

"So, what can I do to help?"

Once again, he turned and frowned at her. "You could get the gun and go to the bedroom and look outside the window to see if anyone is coming at us from that direction."

She got up from the sofa, and with fingers that trembled, she picked up the spare gun from the coffee table and then went into the bedroom and peered out the window.

Dear God, what had happened to her neat and orderly life? She was an esteemed college professor, for crying out loud, and now she felt like a gunslinger waiting for high noon. She'd laugh if she wasn't so damned afraid.

Minutes ticked by and she kept her gaze focused on the trees in the back. She nearly screamed as she saw sudden movement. She pointed the gun in that direction and then released a gasp of relief as a squirrel ran down the trunk of a tree and raced to another tree.

Was this how her life was going to end? Trapped in an isolated cabin by a gunman? Had she survived the rage of the river only to die now? Surely fate wouldn't be so cruel. But then she hadn't thought fate would be cruel enough to take away her father, still it had.

Tears momentarily blurred her vision. She wasn't ready to die right now. She needed to say goodbye to her family before she left this earth. She wanted to find her perfect love and know the joy of carrying a baby and then giving birth. She wanted her happily-ever-after.

She angrily swiped her tears away. Now wasn't the time to allow her fear to make her weak. Dammit, she was a strong woman and she had to stay strong now, no matter what happened next.

She had no idea how long she stood at the window with the gun in her hand before Brad called to her. "See anyone?"

"Nobody," she yelled back.

"Come on back in here," he said.

She left the window and the bedroom. Brad was still at the front window. "It's been almost thirty minutes since the first bullet flew and I haven't seen anyone move any closer to the cabin. The shooter is still hunkered down in that stand of trees. Unfortunately, he's too far away for my bullets to reach him, but his rifle can reach us."

"Then we're safe as long as we don't go outside," she said, trying to find something positive to hang on to.

"For now," he replied.

She stared at his broad back. "For now? What does that mean?"

He turned around to look at her. She'd never seen his eyes so dark and so focused. That alone made her bone-chilling fear rear up all over again. "I think we'll be okay until darkness falls. My gut instinct tells me that's when he'll move in to try to take us out."

He leaned on the wall next to the window and stared at her. "I'm sorry, Simone. I'm so damned sorry I got you into this mess. I... I thought I was doing the right thing. I really thought you'd be safe here. I don't know how anyone found out we were here, but it's obvious somebody did. Somehow, I bungled this whole thing."

His facial features twisted with what appeared to be a guilt so deep she felt it in her own heart. "Oh, Brad, you didn't bungle anything." Being careful not to walk in front of the window, she approached him.

She stopped when she stood mere inches from him. He appeared positively tortured and she couldn't stand to see him this way.

She reached up and gently placed her hand on his lower jaw, where dark whiskers shot a tactile pleasure through her despite the dire circumstances.

"None of this is your fault, Brad. If Rob went to all the trouble to find us here, he would have already killed me if I'd stayed at home. No matter what happens now, I don't want you to blame yourself for anything because I certainly don't blame you."

His gaze held hers for a long moment and then he grabbed her to him and crashed his mouth down to hers. His lips were hot...frantic as they plied hers with a hunger...a need that she answered to.

She wrapped her arms around his neck and leaned into him and opened her mouth to encourage him to deepen the kiss. Someplace in the back of her mind she realized this might possibly be her very last kiss on this earth. And she was so glad it was with Brad.

Everything seemed so much more intense than it had the last time they'd kissed. She was acutely aware of the familiar scent of him, the thrill of how their bodies fit together so perfectly. Her love for him trembled on her lips, begging to be spoken aloud, but she didn't allow herself to speak it. Now was certainly not the place or time to burden him with the depth of her emotions where he was concerned.

He finally tore his mouth from hers and then he placed his hand against her jaw and rubbed his thumb across her cheek. "It's not over yet," he said. He released his hold on her and turned back to the window.

"Do you have a plan?" she asked tentatively.

"I'm working on one," he replied. "I just need a little more time to get it all straight in my head."

For the first time since he'd crawled through the front door after the gunshot, a tiny ray of hope filled her heart...until she saw that his eyes were even darker than they'd been and his features were taut with tension.

No matter what his plan was, there was always room for error and in this case that error could mean the death of both of them.

## Chapter Eleven

Brad remained at the window for an hour…then two hours. His eyes looked for places of cover and his brain worked to make a plan that would save her…possibly save them both. However, no matter what, he needed to make sure Simone got out of this alive.

Simone sat on the sofa behind him. Even though she didn't speak, as always he was acutely aware of her presence. She was depending on him. Her very life depended on him doing something…anything to take out the shooter.

He'd already failed her. Instead of snuggling into the bed with her last night he should have been out here on the sofa. Maybe then he would have heard the perp approach the car. Maybe then he could have neutralized the threat last night instead of being utterly helpless against it today.

There was no way in hell he just intended to wait for night to come. He'd much rather be on the offensive than on the defensive. He knew there was really only one thing to do.

It was approaching noon now. Within the next hour he'd make his move. His hand tightened on his gun as he contemplated the risk he'd be taking.

He moved away from the window and turned to gaze at Simone. "I need to know one thing from you, Simone," he said.

She gazed intently at him. In the depths of her amazing blue eyes he saw her fear, a fear he knew he couldn't take away and he hated that. "What do you need?" she asked.

"I need to know that you're strong enough to shoot a man, and you need to shoot to kill."

Her face paled. She'd told him when they'd first arrived that she could shoot to save her own life, but the conversation had been theoretical. Now everything had changed and this was for real…very real.

She sat up straighter and threw her shoulders back. Her eyes suddenly blazed with strength. "I can do whatever you need for me to do in this situation. If I need to shoot somebody who is trying to kill you and me, then I will do it."

"Even if something happens to me? You'd still be able to defend yourself?"

She frowned. "Nothing is going to happen to you, Brad. I don't even want to think about something like that happening. Whatever your plan is, it better include you and me walking out of here alive and together."

"That's definitely what I want to have happen," he replied. As he continued to hold her gaze, his love for her swelled in his chest. It tightened and physically ached inside him.

Although he desperately wanted to tell her how he felt about her, it would be the most selfish thing he could ever do. He couldn't burden her with his love when there was no hope for a future between them. He definitely shouldn't burden her with his feelings at this point in time. It would be enough for him if she walked away from him...from this safe and sound. That was the only thing he wanted to happen.

With his love for her still resonating inside him, he turned back to peer out the window. He caught movement in the trees and knew the shooter was still out there waiting and watching.

It was time to make a move. He turned back around to Simone. "The only way to get out of this is for me to go out there and try to take him out."

"No, Brad." She jumped up from the sofa. "It's too dangerous." She walked over to him, wrapped her fingers around his wrist and stared up at him. "Please, Brad, don't do that. He has a rifle and you only have a revolver. He has the upper hand and it's just too dangerous for you to go out there."

"There's enough cover between the cabin and the trees where he is. I can use the cover to get close enough to him where my revolver will be able to reach him." He gently pulled his wrist away from her grip. "It's the only way for us to get out of this. I need to neutralize the threat."

Tears welled up in her eyes. "There's got to be another way."

"There isn't," he replied firmly.

"Then at least let me provide you backup."

"No way. You need to stay inside and stay away from the windows and doors," he replied fervently. "Don't forget that you're the number one target."

"But I could help," she protested.

"I don't want your help, Simone," he said. "I want you to stay here, and if somehow this creep manages to get around me, if he comes for you, I want you to kill him."

He held her gaze for a long moment. "Now, go sit and wait for me. Hopefully I'll be back soon."

He waited until she was again seated on the sofa. He then drew a deep breath and opened the door. He raced to the back of the car and a gunshot boomed. The bullet whizzed by him and pierced the passenger's side door.

Using the car as cover, he crouched low and moved to the front of the driver's side door. From here he surveyed the area just ahead of him. There were a couple of lone trees about halfway between him and the shooter. If he could just reach them, then his revolver would be in play.

Tightening his grip on his gun, drawing several slow, deep breaths to focus him, he finally took off. He ran a zigzag pattern as bullets kicked up the ground all around him.

He reached one of the trees and slammed his back against it, his heartbeat racing so fast he had to catch his breath. This was it. He'd either succeed or fail and the idea of failure was absolutely abhorrent.

He peered around the tree trunk. From this vantage point he could see the person in the woods, but he was still too far away to identify him. He needed to get closer.

He fired his gun and then raced to another tree. When he looked again, he realized the shooter had retreated deeper into the trees. Apparently he now realized Brad was a good shot and the bullets could reach him.

Brad moved again, edging closer to the stand of trees where the perp had been. The rifle boomed once more and the bullet seared through Brad's belly. He gasped in pain and clutched his stomach, where blood immediately began to seep through his shirt.

Dammit. This wasn't supposed to happen. And dammit, he should have taken the time to put on his bulletproof vest. It had been stupid, a rookie mistake, for him to forget it, but it had been locked in the trunk of his car.

The excruciating pain doubled him over. He sucked in a deep breath, trying to get on top of the pain. He couldn't stop now. No matter how much pain he was in, he had to take out the perp for Simone's sake.

He raced to the next tree despite the weakness, the dizziness that threatened him. Blood dripped from his wound to the ground. He felt his heartbeat slowing and he knew he was in trouble, a lot of trouble. Still he raced forward, going from tree to tree as the two men exchanged more gunfire.

He was cold yet sweat beaded on his forehead. His vision blurred to the point he had trouble seeing. The gunshot wound ached with an intensity that half stole his breath away. He took another step forward in an effort to shoot the man who threatened them, but he suddenly realized he was on the ground.

*Get up*, a voice screamed in his head. *You have to get back on your feet.* He tried to push himself to get up, but he couldn't. His body wasn't responding to his desire.

He managed to roll over on his back and stared up at the blue sky…blue like Simone's eyes.

Simone.

His heart wept with the knowledge that she was all alone now. A darkness edged into his vision. He'd wanted to save Simone, but he couldn't. He could only pray she could save herself. He tried to fight against the darkness, but it consumed him and he knew no more.

DESPITE BRAD'S INSTRUCTIONS for her to sit tight on the sofa, the minute he disappeared out the door she jumped up and went to the window.

She watched breathlessly as Brad raced from the front of the car to a tree trunk, where he remained for several long moments. Her heart had never beat as fast as it did as she saw him moving from tree to tree.

Then he went out of her sight and several more shots rang out. She waited for him to reappear again. Seconds ticked by… Minutes passed and she had no idea what was happening.

Time continued to pass and there were no more gunshots. Where was Brad? What had happened? What was happening?

She left the window and grabbed the gun on the coffee table. She wasn't willing just to sit this one out. The fact that Brad hadn't walked out of the woods yet scared the hell out of her and spurred her into action.

With the gun clutched tightly in her hand, she left the cabin and raced to the side of the car. There was no responding gunfire.

From the car she raced to the same tree that he had hidden behind. Again there was no responding gunfire. Had Brad managed to take the killer out? Hope buoyed up in her heart as she raced to another tree. If he'd been successful, then where was he?

That was when she saw it…a splatter of blood on the ground. She stared at the bright red blood dotting the dirt and fallen leaves and her heart stopped.

Had Brad been hurt? Had he been shot? Why was there blood? Why on earth was there so much blood? Oh God, she needed to find him. How badly had he been hurt? She followed the blood trail, her heart now beating so fast she felt as if it might explode right out of her chest.

Where was he? And where was the shooter? The trail of blood took her deeper into the woods. Her gaze shot frantically from side to side. She held the gun in front of her, ready to fire if she needed to.

Dear God, there was so much blood…too much blood, and the sight of it scared the hell out of her. Brad had to be okay. He just had to be. She couldn't face the guilt she'd feel…the grief she would feel if he wasn't all right.

She broke into a small clearing and then she saw him. He was on his back and not moving and Leo Styler stood over him with his rifle to Brad's head. Everything that happened next seemed to happen in a slow-motion dream.

"Leo." She called his name loud and clear.

He looked up. His rifle began to move upward and she fired her gun. Her hand kicked up from the velocity of the bullet shooting outward. The blast nearly deafened her. She gasped in stunned shock as blood exploded from his chest. She'd done it! He stared at her in surprise as the rifle fell from his hands. Then he tumbled to the ground.

She'd shot him! Not because she'd feared for her own life, but because she'd feared for Brad's. She ran to Leo's side and kicked the rifle away from him, but it was obvious he was badly wounded and unconscious.

She raced to Brad, tears chasing down her cheeks,

half choking her as she fell to her knees beside him. Blood covered his shirt and he was unconscious as well. "Brad," she cried. "Brad, please wake up."

He didn't respond. As she stared at the bleeding wound in his stomach, she knew he needed medical help immediately. But how was she going to get it for him? They were cut off from the outside world by the flooding. Her cell phone was dead and he needed help now.

She did the only thing she knew to do. She screamed... and screamed. "Please, somebody help me," she cried. "We need help here."

There had to be somebody around, somebody who would have a working phone and could call for help. Nico from the grocery store had mentioned that there were other people in cabins and camping out. It seemed like she screamed forever when a voice finally sounded from the other side of the trees.

"We heard the gunshots. Is everyone okay?" a male voice asked.

"No, no...we're not okay. We need medical help." She got to her feet. "My cell phone is dead and I need somebody to call the Chicago Police Department and tell them FBI agent Brad Howard has been shot. Somehow, they need to get him to a hospital immediately. Tell them that Leo Styler is here and has been shot as well."

A tall, dark-haired man stepped into sight. He looked at her and then eyed the two men on the ground. "I'm Kyle Ingram, we're staying in a cabin nearby. Are you all right?" he asked.

"I'm fine. Just please make the call for me."

"I'm calling right now," he replied.

She fell back to the ground next to Brad. She grabbed his unresponsive, cold hand. Why was he so cold? "Please, hang on, Brad. Help is coming." Even as she said that, she had no idea how help would get to them. She had no idea how long it would take.

"You have to hang on, Brad." Tears fell from her eyes and onto his chest. "Please, you have to live, Brad. I... I love you. I... I'm in love with you. You have to survive, do you hear me?"

"I made the call," Kyle said. "Is there anything else I can do?"

"Are you a doctor? Do you have any medical training?" she asked.

"I'm sorry, I don't," he replied.

"Then you can just pray for me...for us," she said, and then tears choked her all over again. Blood continued to ooze from his wound. She'd never felt so helpless in her life.

She glanced over to Leo. He appeared to still be breathing, but it sounded labored. They'd thought it might be Rob Garner in the woods, but it had been the nineteen-year-old creep who had killed her father. And he'd shot Brad.

How had he known they were here? How had he gotten here? As far as she knew, he was a kid without a car, without any transportation or money. The questions flew through her head, a race of questions that, at the moment, had no answers.

Minutes ticked by and her hope of some sort of rescue happening began to wane. Even if law enforcement had been notified, how were they going to get an ambulance into an area where the road was flooded?

Ignoring Kyle, who hovered nearby, she grabbed

hold of Brad's hand once again. "Please, Brad. Open your eyes and look at me," she begged. She leaned over and kissed his cheek. "I love you, Brad. Please wake up."

She continued to sit next to him and talk to him as she waited for something to happen, even though she had no idea what that something might be. She couldn't imagine just sitting here beside him and watching him die, but she feared that was what was happening.

Then she heard it, the whop-whop-whop of an approaching helicopter. Were they here for Brad? Was this finally the rescue she'd been praying for? She jumped to her feet and waved her arms over her head to get their attention.

The helicopter hovered overhead, whipping the leaves on the trees into a loud cacophony of sound. Then a basket with a man inside it dropped out of the aircraft. Joy filled her heart as the basket slowly descended.

She looked back at Brad and the burst of joy dissipated. Was it too late for him? Had he lost too much blood? Were his wounds bad enough that he might succumb to death before he could be taken to a hospital?

The basket reached the ground and a blond-haired man who looked to be about thirty years old jumped out of the basket. "Here, take him first." She yelled to be heard above the noise as she guided the man to Brad.

"You'll have to help me get him into the basket," the man said.

She nodded. With his instructions, together the two of them managed to get Brad into the bottom of the basket. The man rode with Brad as the basket ascended into the bowels of the helicopter.

The man rode down a second time and they loaded Leo. "I'll be back for you," the man yelled, and then once again the basket went up.

As Simone waited, she wrapped her arms around herself, saying prayer after prayer for Brad. Even though she knew they would never be together, even though she knew she was just a job to him, she needed to know he was alive and living his best life.

Her father had already been stolen from her by Jared and Leo. She didn't want to believe that Brad would be stolen from her...from this life as well.

As she waited for the basket to return one final time for her, a thousand thoughts once again whirled around in her head. How had Leo found them here? How had he gotten here? Who was financing the teenage killer?

Still, the number one question in her mind was if Brad was going to survive this ordeal. She grabbed the rifle and then Brad's gun, not wanting to leave them behind for some unsuspecting kid or anyone else to stumble upon.

Within minutes she was being loaded into the helicopter, where Brad and Leo were on pallets on the floor and a doctor was administering fluids. She sat buckled into a seat and watched, praying that Brad would finally open his eyes.

"Where are we going?" she asked the pilot once they were underway.

"Chicago. We have trauma teams standing by at Chicago University Hospital," he replied.

She leaned back and closed her eyes. At least she knew he would get top-notch care at that hospital. While she took comfort from that, it scared her to death that he hadn't regained consciousness. There was only so much a doctor could do in a helicopter in midair.

Before she knew it, they were landing on the pad connected to the hospital. Gurneys awaited them and both of the patients were loaded up and whisked away.

She was directed to the waiting room, where she sank down among a group of patients waiting to be seen. She hoped somebody came out to tell her something about Brad's condition.

It wasn't long before FBI agent Russ Dodd walked into the room. She knew him from the many family briefings he'd attended with Brad. She also knew Brad considered the redhaired agent his best friend.

He immediately spied her and sank down in the chair next to her. "Simone, how are you holding up?" he asked.

"I'm here, I'm okay, but I'm terrified for Brad."

"A doctor is supposed to come out and speak with me as soon as they know his condition," Russ replied. "Can you tell me what happened out there?"

For a brief moment, memories cascaded through her brain. They weren't memories of gunshots and fear, but rather ones of laughter and fun games, of stolen kisses and sweet lovemaking.

But she knew that wasn't what Russ wanted to talk about. It seemed unreal that it had only been that morning that she and Brad had awakened without any electricity. This single day had lasted forever and it wasn't over yet.

She went through all the events that had happened from the time Brad had left the cabin to when she had shot Leo. "I couldn't believe my eyes when I saw him standing over Brad. He was the last person I expected to be there," she said.

"There will be a full investigation into how Leo found you guys and who made it easy for him to get there," Russ said. "And now do you want to hear a little good news?"

"What?" she asked. The only good news she wanted to hear right now was that Brad was going to be all right.

"As soon as I heard Leo was down and in custody, I had a brief interview with Jared. He confessed to everything, the kidnapping and the four murders. With the confession, we can now put them both away."

"That is great news," she replied, and yet her heart squeezed tight. "But it's not worth Brad's life."

He studied her for a long moment. "You care about him."

"More than you know," she replied, her heart aching with the need for Brad to pull through. "Is the doctor even allowed to talk to you about his condition? Aren't there privacy regulations against that?"

"Right now Brad is a victim and I'm a member of law enforcement following up on his case. The doctor will speak with me," Russ assured her.

They settled back to wait. One hour turned into two. Several times Russ got up to make or take a phone call. Simone didn't contact anyone in her family. She wasn't ready to talk to anyone. She felt as if she needed to process everything that had happened before she spoke to anyone. More than anything, she just wanted to know if Brad was dead or alive.

Finally, a doctor stepped out and called Russ's name. She jumped up with Russ and followed behind him as the doctor took them to a small office. The doctor was a small man with a name tag that read Dr. Anthony Montello.

She sat in a chair next to Russ's as if she had a right to belong there. However, the doctor looked at her, then looked at Russ with a raised eyebrow. "Is it all right for me to speak freely to you in front of her?"

"Absolutely," Russ said without hesitation, and she wanted to lean over and kiss him on the cheek in gratitude.

"So, the bullet that your agent received struck around his appendix area and exited his back. Unfortunately, the appendix ruptured. Thank goodness he was brought in when he was. We performed an emergency appendectomy and cleaned up a few other areas and we're hitting him with plenty of antibiotics. The surgery went well and he's now out of danger and resting peacefully in a room."

Simone gasped in relief. Thank goodness the helicopter had come when it had. Brad was going to be okay and that was all that mattered. "Can I see him?" she asked.

"He's still asleep from the anesthesia, but he's in room 1045. If he does wake up, I don't want him stressed. His body has been through a lot."

"I promise I won't stress him," she replied.

"As far as the other patient who was brought in with Agent Howard, I spoke briefly to the other surgeon that attended to him before I came out here to speak to you," the doctor said. "He's been touch and go and they are performing surgery on him as we speak. The bullet ripped through his stomach wall and bounced around in there doing some damage before exiting out his back. I'll have more information for you once the surgery is finished."

"Thank you, Dr. Montello." Russ stood as did the doctor. The two men shook hands, Simone got out of her chair and a moment later she and Russ were in a hospital hallway.

"Well, I guess I know where you're headed," Russ said to her.

"I just need to see him. I… I need to assure myself that he's really okay. He almost died protecting me, Russ. He was a real hero out there."

Russ smiled at her. "He was just doing his job, Simone. Could you please call me when you're ready to leave the hospital? I want to provide you an armed escort to take you home."

She looked at him in surprise. "Why? Leo isn't exactly going to jump off the operating table to come after me."

"He won't, but we can't lose track of the fact that Brad was worried about Rob Garner coming after you," Russ replied. "What I suggest is we get you home safely and then you stay put for the next several days until the investigation has a little more information for all of us."

She eyed him soberly. "I'll call you when I'm ready to leave." It would be an insult to Brad if after all he'd gone through she didn't take Russ's assessment and advice seriously.

He nodded and the two said their goodbyes. She wasn't sure where he was headed off to, but she was headed straight to Brad's room.

*He was just doing his job.* Russ's words played and replayed in her head as she rode the elevator up to the tenth floor. Of course that was what Brad had been doing. Just because the two of them succumbed to their sexual yearnings didn't mean he loved her. It was just something that had happened while he was doing his job.

When she reached the doorway of room 1045, she stood in the threshold and her heart constricted tight in her chest. Brad was in the bed, an IV attached to his arm and his face as pale as the pillowcase behind him. The room was in semidarkness and his eyes were closed.

Quietly she made her way to the chair next to his bed and sank down. She just wanted to gaze at him, to memorize his features and keep them forever in her brain…in the very depths of her heart.

As she sat there, all their time together rushed through her brain, from the moment she had first met him to this moment in time.

He was the man of her dreams, the man she wished she could spend the rest of her life with. And it broke her heart because she knew that wasn't going to happen. Still, it was going to be difficult for any other man to find a place in her heart for a very long time to come.

She must have been exhausted by the day's events for she fell into a deep sleep in the chair. When she finally awoke, it was to faint morning light spilling through the hospital window.

She looked at Brad and was shocked to discover him gazing at her. "Brad," she said softly. She got up out of the chair and moved to stand at his bedside.

"Simone," he replied, his voice sounding slightly hoarse and dry.

There was a cup of water with a straw on a metal

table and she picked it up and offered him a drink. He drew on the straw for a moment and then she placed the cup back on the tray.

"When I got to the hospital last night, I regained consciousness long enough to learn what occurred after I passed out. I know now what happened to me and I was told about what you did," he said.

His brows knit together and he frowned at her. "Dammit, Simone, you could have been killed." His voice had a ring of anger. "You should have never come out to find me."

She stared at him in stunned surprise. "If I hadn't, then you would be dead and Leo wouldn't be in this hospital under police custody right now. I did what I had to do." She held his gaze with a touch of anger of her own.

He finally looked away and drew in a deep breath. "I'm sorry," he said and gazed at her once again. "I didn't mean to jump at you. I'm glad things have turned out the way they have. A full investigation is going on and I need to know you'll still be safe from Rob Garner."

"I'm supposed to call Russ when I'm ready to leave here and he's providing an officer to take me home."

"Good. I need to know you're still staying safe until the investigation is over and we know all the pieces. In the meantime, I imagine I'll be in here for a couple of days and then I'll be heading back to DC."

Oh, the words broke her heart even though she had known this was what was going to happen. "Would you stop by my place to tell me goodbye before you leave town?"

"Absolutely, and I'll make sure Russ keeps you informed about the ongoing investigation." His voice was completely professional and sounded weary and she knew he'd distanced himself from her.

She forced a smile to her lips. "Thank you, Brad, for everything."

"No need to thank me. I was just doing my job," he replied.

*Just doing his job.* She'd grown to hate those words. At that moment a nurse entered the room. Simone murmured a goodbye and then stepped out. She held it together when she called Russ and then waited for an officer to arrive. She kept her emotions in check as the officer drove her home.

When she finally stepped into her condo and was all alone, she collapsed on her sofa and began to cry. She cried for the wounds Brad had suffered in trying to protect her. Her heart wept with the love she had for him. Her feelings for him had been so unexpected, so achingly real, and now she had no idea where to put those emotions.

Somehow, someway, she had to get over him. But right now with everything, with him so fresh in her mind, she felt like she'd never be able to put her love for him behind her and move on.

# Chapter Twelve

"Hey, man," Brad greeted Russ as he came into the hospital room. He'd been in the hospital for five long days and he was going stir-crazy. He'd been spending most of his time sleeping. The antibiotics were doing their job and he'd been weaned off his pain meds.

"How you feeling?" Russ asked as he sank into the chair next to Brad's hospital bed.

"Physically I'm feeling pretty good. Mentally I'm going nuts. I need to get out of here and get back to work."

"You need to follow your doctor's orders and stay put as long as he thinks you need to," Russ replied. "But the good news is I've come with updates from the investigation."

"Good. Tell me all," Brad said eagerly. He needed something, anything to think about other than Simone.

"Rob Garner has been arrested," Russ said.

Brad looked at him in surprise. "For what?"

"He's being charged with conspiracy to commit murder, aiding and abetting, and a number of other crimes."

"So he was helping Leo." Brad raised the head of his bed a couple of inches.

"Leo told us everything. It was Rob, through a cousin of his, who got Leo the motorcycle that he drove to follow you to the cabin. The cousin swears that he had no idea what Rob was up to. Anyway, Leo managed to put a tracker on your car before you left Chicago."

"Damn, I should have checked for something like that before we headed to the cabin. But it never entered my mind." Inwardly he cursed himself. It had been his mistake that had brought Leo to them. He was an FBI agent and a nineteen-year-old kid had gotten one over on him.

"According to Leo, Rob was crazed with the need to kill you and Simone," Russ continued. "So, Leo rode the motorcycle to the woods near the cabin, where he camped out in a tent during the rain and waited for an opportunity to take you both out."

"What did he hope to gain?" Brad asked.

"Rob really believed that if the two of you were killed, then it would complicate things and slow down the case against Jared. It would give them more time to build a defense case."

Brad shook his head. "I was pretty sure that was the motive, but if we'd both died, that wouldn't have slowed the case against Jared and Leo at all."

"All I can tell you is that's what Leo said Rob believed."

"I swear, the longer I'm in this business, the crazier I think people are," Brad replied.

For the next twenty minutes or so, the two men continued to talk about the case. Leo was recovering from his surgery but was still listed on the critical list. Brad hoped the kid lived so he could spend the rest of his life in prison for the four men he'd killed and for almost killing Brad and Simone. Death at this point was far too easy for the psychopath.

"Have you spoken with Simone?" Brad finally asked the question that he'd wanted to ask since the moment Russ had appeared. When Brad hadn't been sleeping, thoughts of her had consumed him.

"Yeah, I called her to let her know that Rob had been arrested and she was no longer in any danger."

"I'm sure that made her happy." Instantly Brad's mind pulled up a vision of Simone laughing and her beautiful eyes sparkling.

"I don't know about it making her happy, but I'm sure she was relieved to hear the news," Russ replied. Russ looked at him for a long moment. "You're really into her, aren't you?"

"I'm crazy about her." Brad's love for Simone pressed against his chest, momentarily making it difficult for him to draw a breath.

"So, what are you going to do about it?" Russ asked.

Brad released another heavy sigh. "Nothing. I'm going to go back to DC and put this all behind me."

"She seems pretty crazy about you, too."

Brad's heart hurt just a little bit more. "I'll admit that we got really close in that cabin, but I'm sure now that she's had a few days to process everything, she's back to reality. I'm sure she now realizes that any feelings she might have had for me were due to our circumstances and nothing more."

"Whatever, dude," Russ replied. "I've just never seen the look on your face that I've seen when you just speak her name." He gazed at Brad for another long moment and then stood. "In any case, it's time for me to get back to work. I'll stop in tomorrow."

"Thanks, Russ." He watched as his colleague and friend left the room.

Brad lowered the head of his bed. He closed his eyes as his thoughts were consumed with Simone. Under different circumstances she would have been the woman he wanted to marry, the woman he'd want to have his children.

He knew she'd make an awesome wife and an incredible mother. She was the woman who would fill all his needs and all his wants and it completely broke his heart that it wasn't going to happen with her.

Whatever they'd shared in that cabin had been fantasy. Now that she was back in her condo, back with her family and friends, he was sure she'd already moved on from their experience.

He would just have to figure out a way to return to his life and forget about her. But right now that seemed impossible.

It was five days later that he was finally released and Russ picked him up from the hospital to take him to his hotel room.

"We're done here," Russ said. "Chicago PD is now in charge of the case and we have airline tickets waiting for us to head back home tomorrow. I have keys to a vehicle you can use today and then tomorrow we have a car picking us up at ten to take us to the airport."

"Sounds good," Brad said, but he was already thinking about his promise to tell Simone goodbye before he left.

Once they were back at the hotel, Brad took a long shower and changed into a pair of clean jeans and a green polo shirt. Although he was healing up nicely, he hadn't quite regained all his energy, but the doctor had assured him he'd return to normal with a little more time.

The one thing he wanted to do right now was head over to Simone's condo to tell her goodbye. It was going to be one of the most difficult moments in his life, but he needed to get it done. He needed to get it over with as soon as possible.

As he drove, he steeled himself for seeing her again. He tried to shut off all his emotions. He knew it was going to hurt to tell her goodbye. He knew it was going to hurt badly, but it was time for him to move on. His work here in Chicago was done, and that meant it was time for him to move on and prepare for his next case.

He pulled up and parked in front of her condo. He didn't even know if she was home or not. He hadn't called beforehand. He got out of his car and drew in several deep breaths and released them slowly.

When he felt centered enough, when he felt strong enough, he walked to her front door and knocked. His heart fluttered as he heard somebody approaching the door from the other side.

Then it opened and she stood before him. In an instant he took in the sight of her. She was clad in jeans and a bright pink T-shirt that emphasized the blue of her eyes. They were eyes that widened at the sight of him.

"Brad," she said softly, and one of her hands reached up to smooth her hair. "Please...come in." She opened the door wider to allow him entry.

He stepped inside and instantly her scent surrounded him, that evocative, wonderful scent that would always remind him of her. She gestured him toward the sofa. He sank down on one end and she sat right next to him. "How are you doing?" she asked as her gaze searched his features.

"I'm doing well. I just got out of the hospital a little while ago and I leave to head back to DC tomorrow," he replied.

"Oh." She looked surprised. "So soon? What about the case?"

"It's pretty well wound up with the boys both confessing to the murders. Chicago PD and the prosecutor will take things from here. I hope you and your family have found some closure knowing those two young men will go to prison for a very long time." He looked at some point just over her head because it was just too painful to gaze directly at her.

"There will never be complete closure. There will always be a hole where my father once was, but I think we're all coming to a kind of peace now," she replied.

He finally met her gaze with his. "I'm glad, Simone. That's all I've really wanted for you since the beginning of this case."

The depth of her blue eyes filled with emotion, although he couldn't discern exactly what emotion it was. "Brad," she said softly. "I don't want you to go, but before you do, I just want you to know that I'm in love with you."

The unexpected words hung in the air between them. He stared at her in stunned surprise. This was the last thing he'd expected from her. And as much as the words torched through his heart, he didn't really believe them.

"Simone, we went through a very intense time together. It was a crazy time with some life-and-death situations. It's only natural that you might think you have some feelings for me because of everything we went through together," he said. "Once you get some time and distance from everything, you'll realize you don't really love me, that what you feel is probably gratitude."

She frowned at him. "Brad, I know what my feelings are for you. It wasn't in the life-and-death situations that I fell in love with you. It was in the quiet moments we shared. I fell in love with you when we had our long talks and when we laughed together." Tears filled her eyes. "Please don't try to minimize my love for you."

"Simone," he replied softly...painfully. "We both have lives to get back to. We're from totally different worlds. You have your life here and I have mine in DC." He got up from the sofa. He couldn't sit next to her another moment. He wanted her so badly, but he didn't see a life together for them beyond this moment in time. "Simone, I've got to go." He took several steps toward the front door.

She got up from the sofa and followed him. Before he could open the door, she stopped him by placing her hand on his arm. "Brad, I know you have to go. I know you don't believe that I love you with all my heart and soul, but could you please kiss me one last time before you leave?"

Her eyes were filled with such yearning it nearly stole his breath away. Even though he knew it was all wrong, he wanted to kiss her. He wanted one last taste of her to take with him.

Before he realized what he was doing, he gathered her into his arms. She leaned into him and raised her face. He took her mouth with his, and with all the love and all the passion that was in his heart, he kissed her.

She opened her mouth to him and he deepened the kiss, swirling his tongue with hers and building a sharp desire inside him. She wrapped her arms around his neck and pulled him even more intimately close to her.

He wanted to pick her up in his arms and carry her into her bedroom. He wanted to crawl into her bed and make love with her. But someplace in the back of his mind was a voice of reason that told him that would be a huge mistake. It was time to say goodbye for the last time.

He finally pulled away from her and took a step back. A wealth of emotions tightened his chest as he gazed at her. "It's time for me to say goodbye, Simone. I care about you more than you'll ever know, but I do think this is gratitude."

He didn't wait for her response. If he stayed another minute and looked at her, he would crumble and tell her just how much he loved her, and that would only complicate things for both of them moving forward.

He walked back to his car and got inside. He dropped his head back and closed his eyes. His heart ached like it never had before. No woman had ever gotten so deeply into his heart like Simone had. He couldn't imagine loving another woman like he loved her.

He finally put the car into gear and drove away. He wondered how long it would take for him to feel whole again. How long would it take for him to forget how much he loved Simone Colton?

Forever, his heart whispered. It would take him forever to get over this heartache.

IT HAD BEEN just a little over a week since Brad had left town and still Simone found herself bursting into tears at unexpected moments during the days and nights. She tried to fight against the depression that challenged her. She kicked herself for losing it so much over a man.

But he hadn't just been any man. He'd been *her* man...the one she'd wanted to build a life with. He'd been the man she'd been waiting her whole life for. She'd somehow believed that when she'd confessed her love for him that he would have taken her in his arms and professed his love for her and they would have figured out some kind of a happily-ever-after. But that hadn't happened.

He'd easily walked away from her when she'd believed he truly cared for her. Had she been wrong when she'd thought she'd seen love shining from his eyes? Had she mistaken the caring in his eyes when he thought she wasn't looking?

It didn't matter today. It was the Fourth of July and within minutes she was going to head to her family home for a big barbecue with the whole family.

It was a day for celebration...for freedom and the love of family and country. After the barbecue there would be a display of fireworks to finish out the night.

She dressed in a pair of white jeans and a red, white and blue blouse and at four o'clock she left her condo to head to her mother's home.

As she drove, she anticipated spending time not only with her sisters, but also with her cousins. It was time they all had some fun together. They were all beginning to heal from the deep wounds the murders had created. After almost seven months, it was time to heal.

It was amazing to her that once she found out Jared

had confessed and Leo was in custody, her nightmares had stopped. Finally, she felt as if her father had gotten the justice he deserved, the justice he'd needed to move on. And she truly believed he was now resting in peace.

By the time she arrived at the house, things were already in full swing. Three picnic tables covered in red tablecloths had been set up in the common area between the two homes. On top of each picnic table were red, white and blue floral arrangements.

The air was redolent with the scent of baked beans and potato salad, of deviled eggs and a warm barbecue grill awaiting burgers and other meats.

January and her fiancé, Sean Stafford, were playing cornhole against Micha and Carly. All of them were laughing as trash talk went back and forth and Jones and Allie provided comic relief from the sidelines.

Tatum and Cruz stood at the barbecue grill next to Heath and Kylie, the two men arguing about the best barbecue sauce for ribs.

Meanwhile Simone's mother and her aunt sat side by side in lawn chairs. Simone walked over and kissed her mother on the cheek and then kissed her aunt Fallon on her forehead.

"Sit down, honey," her mother said and gestured to the lawn chair that was still vacant next to her.

It wasn't lost on Simone that out of her sisters and her cousins and of course, aside from her mother and aunt, she was the only one here without a significant other. Her heart ached with the absence of Brad, as it had since the moment he'd walked out of her door.

"Did you make your famous potato salad?" she asked her mother.

"I did, and your aunt Fallon made the baked beans," Simone's mother replied.

"And Tatum bought several other side dishes from True," her aunt Fallon said. "Along with dessert."

Simone continued to visit with the two older women, grateful to see that a lot of the sorrow that had clung to them had eased away. While she knew the twin sisters would never get over the loss of their husbands, Simone was just grateful to see them moving on.

She left her chair only when Heath asked her to be his partner in the cornhole game. After several games, she sat at one of the picnic tables as the men began to cook the meats.

As dinner commenced, there was a lot of laughter. When the meal was almost finished, somebody suggested that they go around the table and tell what they were thankful for.

"Aunt Fallon, you start," Simone said, and they all fell silent and looked at Fallon expectantly.

"I'm happy to announce that I'm looking forward to getting back to our interior design business and Farrah and I are planning a trip to Europe together."

All the children clapped and hooted at the news. Simone smiled at her mother proudly. She was so happy that the two sisters could finally breathe again after the tragedy and a trip to Europe was a great way to help the two sisters leave the bad times behind and kickstart their design business.

"I'll go next," Heath said and stood from his seat. "First of all, I want to thank you all for your support in allowing me to be the new, permanent president of Colton Connections. And today I filed for the first patent of my own."

Once again, cheers rang out. "Apparently, the apple didn't fall far from the genetic tree," Simone said, thinking of her father and uncle's genius when it came to patents that were often bought for huge chunks of cash, or sent off for developmental application.

"Me next, me next," January exclaimed and jumped to her feet. She pulled Sean to stand next to her. "I just want to let you all know that our wedding is going to be moving up…because we're expecting…twins!"

Simone and Tatum got up and hugged their sister with excitement. "And so the next generation begins," Farrah said as she dabbed at happy tears with her napkin.

"Next," January said, and she and Sean sat back down.

Jones stood and cleared his throat. "I've named a new manager at the microbrewery. As much as I love you all, I've decided to do some traveling with this woman." He grabbed Allie's hand and kissed the back of it. "While she's investigating stories around the country, I'll be sharing in the adventures with her."

It was great to see Jones happy. He'd taken the death of his father very hard, but Simone had a feeling he and Allie had a wonderful future together.

Then it was Carly's turn to tell everyone that she and Micha had decided to sell her little bungalow and purchase a home closer to everyone so they could start on building a family.

Tatum then jumped up from her chair, her eyes sparkling brightly. "Yesterday I signed a fairly lucrative contract with a publisher for my cookbook. And that's not the only thing that happened yesterday." She held up her left hand, and on the ring finger was a beautiful diamond ring. "I got a cookbook deal and a fiancé," she said joyfully.

Once again, congratulations rang in the air and then everyone turned and looked at Simone expectantly. She smiled and stood, and then to her horror, she promptly burst into tears.

Much to her embarrassment everyone rallied around her while she insisted she was fine. She tried to convince everyone they were just happy tears because she was so thrilled that everyone had found their special person and had great plans for their futures.

The porch lights came on against the fall of dusk as they all settled back in for dessert. Farrah and Fallon went inside and came out a few minutes later with strawberry shortcake from True and the housekeeper followed behind them with a huge red, white and blue cake complete with lit baby sparklers.

They were in the middle of dessert when the housekeeper returned and bent down next to Simone. "There's somebody here to see you, Miss Simone. He's waiting in the foyer."

Simone excused herself and left the table. Who would be here to see her? Was it possible Wayne, the history professor, was coming to see her in an effort to convince her to go round two with him? He'd called her several times since he'd learned about her ordeal at the cabin. But she definitely had no interest in going there again.

Or was it possible…? She was afraid to hope. She was afraid to even wish in case she was bitterly disappointed. She stepped into the foyer and saw him. He was turned away from her and staring out the window, but she would have recognized that broad back anywhere.

Brad. His name fluttered in her head...in her heart. What was he doing here? Did he have something new to discuss with her concerning the case? Something that couldn't be settled by a phone call?

"Brad," she half whispered his name.

He whirled around at the sound of her voice. "Simone."

"What are you doing here? Has something come up with the case?" she asked. The very sight of him caused her love for him to slam into her all over again. She crossed her arms in front of her as if that would defend her against her own emotions where he was concerned.

"No, I'm not here about the case," he said. His eyes were dark and unfathomable. "Simone, I'm sorry to interrupt what I'm sure is a family gathering, but it's important that I speak with you."

"About what?" Her heart began to beat an irregular rhythm in her chest.

"To start with, I want to talk about me."

She frowned. "Okay...what about you?" This whole thing seemed odd and surreal. He came here to talk about himself?

He gazed at some point over her head. "I was sure when I left here that I was doing the right thing. I was sure that the best thing I could do for you was to walk away and let you get on with your life. In my head it was the noble thing to do."

He released a small, humorless laugh. "I realized quickly that being noble wasn't going to work for me. Even though I threw myself back into my work, I couldn't get you out of my head."

His gaze finally met hers. They were a beautiful golden green today, and she wanted nothing more than to fall into their depths, but still she was afraid.

"Simone, all I can think about is you. I miss laughing with you. I miss talking to you. I know I'm taking a chance on coming here. I'm taking the chance that your mind hasn't changed about me. And even if it has, I have to speak my truth to you."

Her heartbeat quickened, making her feel half-breathless with anticipation. "So, speak your truth," she said softly. "Tell me why you're here, Brad."

"I'm here because I love you, Simone. I love you more than I've ever loved a woman in my life. I can't imagine my life without you." The words rushed out of him as he took a step closer to her.

"I want to marry you, Simone. I want you to have my babies and I want to build a future with you. I want us to grow old together and…"

He paused as she stepped closer to him and placed her finger over his lips. "Yes," she said, a tremendous joy filling her heart. "Yes, yes," she repeated. "Oh, Brad, I want that, too. I love you, Brad, and I can't imagine wanting a future with any other man but you."

"Speaking of our future, I have a few cases I need to finish up in DC, but I'm putting in for a transfer to the Chicago department. I'm hoping to be here full-time in the fall. Will that work for you?"

"Of course it will. In fact, I'm going to lighten my fall schedule so I'm not teaching as many classes. I want to have plenty of time to spend with my man. Are you really ready to be in a relationship with a nerdy professor?" she asked.

He laughed. "The sexiest professor I've ever known."

"If that's the case, then kiss me, Brad."

He pulled her into his arms and crashed his lips to hers in a kiss that stole her breath away, shot tingles through her and tasted of the laughter, the mutual respect and support, and the love they would share for the rest of their lives together.

She was vaguely aware of fireworks going off outside, but the fireworks going off in her heart, knowing her future was with Brad, were all she needed to be happy.

\* \* \* \* \*

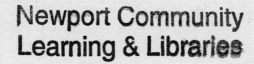

# COMING SOON!

We really hope you enjoyed reading this book.
If you're looking for more romance, be sure to
head to the shops when new books are
available on

# Thursday 10<sup>th</sup> June

To see which titles are coming soon, please visit

## millsandboon.co.uk/nextmonth

# LET'S TALK
## Romance

For exclusive extracts, competitions and special offers, find us online:

- facebook.com/millsandboon
- @MillsandBoon
- @MillsandBoonUK

**Get in touch on 01413 063232**

For all the latest titles coming soon, visit
## millsandboon.co.uk/nextmonth

# MILLS & BOON

## THE HEART OF ROMANCE

---

## A ROMANCE FOR EVERY READER

---

### MODERN

Prepare to be swept off your feet by sophisticated, sexy and seductive heroes, in some of the world's most glamourous and romantic locations, where power and passion collide.

### HISTORICAL

Escape with historical heroes from time gone by. Whether your passion is for wicked Regency Rakes, muscled Vikings or rugged Highlanders, awaken the romance of the past.

### MEDICAL

Set your pulse racing with dedicated, delectable doctors in the high-pressure world of medicine, where emotions run high and passion, comfort and love are the best medicine.

### True Love

Celebrate true love with tender stories of heartfelt romance, from the rush of falling in love to the joy a new baby can bring, and a focus on the emotional heart of a relationship.

### Desire

Indulge in secrets and scandal, intense drama and plenty of sizzling hot action with powerful and passionate heroes who have it all: wealth, status, good looks…everything but the right woman.

### HEROES

Experience all the excitement of a gripping thriller, with an intense romance at its heart. Resourceful, true-to-life women and strong, fearless men face danger and desire - a killer combination!

---

To see which titles are coming soon, please visit

## millsandboon.co.uk/nextmonth

# MILLS & BOON
## *Desire*

Indulge in secrets and scandal, intense drama and plenty of sizzling hot action with powerful and passionate heroes who have it all: wealth, status, good looks... everything but the right woman.

# MILLS & BOON
## MEDICAL
### *Pulse-Racing Passion*

Set your pulse racing with dedicated, delectable doctors in the high-pressure world of medicine, where emotions run high and passion, comfort and love are the best medicine.